The Sur

Joanna Dodd is fascinated by toxic friendship and family groups and the long shadows cast by old secrets. She lives in London and enjoys acting in plays, running very slowly, and spending time with her (lovely and not at all toxic) family and friends.

THE
SUMMER
DARE

JOANNA DODD

hera

First published in the United Kingdom in 2024 by

Hera Books
Unit 9 (Canelo), 5th Floor
Cargo Works, 1-2 Hatfields
London SE1 9PG
United Kingdom

A CIP catalogue record for this book is available from the British Library.

Print ISBN 978 1 80436 842 8
Ebook ISBN 978 1 80436 841 1

Look for more great books at www.herabooks.com

Printed and bound in Great Britain by Clays Ltd, Elcograf S.p.A.

1

For my parents

Prologue

1999

Four seconds in. Eight seconds out. Deep breaths are calming. Four seconds in. Eight seconds out. But the small room she's in smells of damp and, humiliatingly, of her own urine. Suddenly she's coughing and gulping at the air. How long does it take to suffocate? Or perhaps she will starve to death before she suffocates.

She wraps her arms tightly around her knees and tries not to think about how hungry she is. At least she still has half a bottle of Coke that she's been eking out. She should have put something to eat in the rucksack, but it only contains the stupid costume. She remembers how excited she'd felt as she picked it out; she can barely recognise that person now. The glittery cardigan and the white slip dress, so she'd look like the ghost from the story. It seemed like such a good plan at the time. Now it just seems childish. If she gets out of here, she'll be different, she promises herself. More grown up – not that grown-ups are particularly grown up in her experience. She'll stop running away and face up to things. When she gets out. Because of course they'll come back: they're her friends. Her best friends in the whole world. Lucy will tell them the plan and they'll work out something must have gone wrong, and they'll come back to find her.

She's been repeating this like a mantra for hours, but, with each repetition, it loses a little of its power, and now there's a part of her that doesn't believe it at all. A part of her thinks she's going to die here. The room is so small that when she stands in the middle and spreads out her arms, she can almost touch the door and the back wall at the same time. It's a little longer than it is wide, and she's explored every cobwebbed centimetre of it now. She's tried and tried to lift the trapdoor in the corner of the floor, in the hope that it offers another way out, but it won't budge and all she's succeeded in doing is making her fingers bleed.

Maybe she should shout again. She's lost track of how long she's been here – more than twenty-four hours she thinks. She wonders why the summer camp leaders haven't got worried and come looking for her. It must be daytime again because she can see light in the crack between the hinge side of the door and the wall. There might be somebody out walking. The fields aren't that far away and, okay, it's private land, but maybe there's a footpath she hasn't noticed or maybe someone from the hostel will be passing. She stands up and places the palms of her hands against the rough wood of the door, readying herself for another attempt to attract attention.

After a few minutes, she pauses. Then she hears it. The squeak. Was that… could that be a door opening? The empty house has tricked her before with its noises. But, then, yes, definitely, there are footsteps. She feels her stomach lurch; tastes the relief, metallic on her tongue. Somebody must have heard her shouting after all. She's going to get out, she's going to see her parents again, tell them how frightened she was – now that she's safe, she allows herself to acknowledge it – to feel their arms around her. There are tears spilling down her cheeks.

She's about to cry out, but something about the purposefulness of her silent rescuer makes her hesitate. They've made straight for the little room as if they know she's there, but if so, why haven't they called out to her? Instead, they've stopped outside. Standing there. Saying nothing. She can feel them close by. And she can feel something else too. A word she's heard her dad use. *Malevolence*. Now she's holding her breath.

Because for the first time it occurs to her that suffocation and starvation aren't the worst ways to die.

Chapter One

Lucy, Present

It's the woman in the coffee shop who makes me think about our friendship. This is one of our regular Saturday morning catch-ups and the Wandsworth branch of Gail's is its normal weekend scene of fraught middle-class leisure time. Dads with buggies the size of small SUVs are manoeuvring past huddles of women in lululemon leggings, clutching water bottles and flat whites, and a harassed waitress is trying to find someone willing to claim a smoked salmon and scrambled egg brioche. We've got one of the big wooden tables and are quizzing a reluctant Jenna about her new man.

'Is it somebody we know?'

'Look, I wish I'd never mentioned it.' Jenna drops her gaze to fiddle with her Garmin running watch. 'It's not what I thought, okay. But it's no big deal. It was all a bit messy.'

'But you said you'd liked him for ages.'

A woman approaches the table.

'Excuse me, are you using the highchair?'

'We will be in a minute,' Hayley says, tucking a strand of expertly highlighted blonde hair behind her ear, barely glancing at the woman.

'Oh okay, no worries.' But she sounds stressed, and I turn to study her properly. Her little girl is about one – not much older than Ruby. The woman herself looks as if her face is somehow too small for her skull, the skin pulled tight. I know what that sort of tiredness feels like. It's only recently that Ruby has started sleeping through and too often I still feel as if my entire waking life is taking place under a layer of cotton wool, with my thought processes and movements muffled.

'You can use it if you like,' I say.

A smile flickers across her face, and briefly transforms it. It makes her look familiar and I wonder if I've met her before at a baby class. Ruby and I have tried most of them over the past eight months.

'Are you sure? Thanks. I won't be long,' she says. I think how lucky I am. I have good friends – people I can relax with. This pale, pinched woman looks like she longs to have that.

'You realise we'll never get that back now,' Claire says, her usual frown more pronounced.

'It doesn't matter. Ruby can sit on my knee.'

'She's still sound asleep,' Hayley says, peering into the pushchair, a curtain of hair falling over her face. 'She's such a cutie.' I've already had to stop her Instagramming Ruby sleeping to all 42,479 of her followers. @heyhayley is going to have to do without photos of my daughter, at least until she's old enough to have a say in the matter.

'He's not married is he?' Claire asks, with characteristic abruptness.

'Why would you say that?' Jenna's voice is defensive.

'Because you're being so mysterious about him,' Claire says.

She's actually more than mysterious; for Jenna, she's almost twitchy.

'Look, can we just change the subject.' Jenna pushes her coffee cup away and pulls her long dark hair into a ponytail. 'Lucy, how's work going?'

'Oh, all right I suppose.'

'Is Bitch Lady still harassing you?' Hayley says.

'Who's Bitch Lady?' Jenna says.

'See!' Hayley waves her coffee cup in triumph. 'That shows how distracted you've been, Jenna.'

'She's Lucy's latest project,' Claire says. 'The ghostwriting client who climbed up from hell to haunt her.' There's a sudden uneasy silence.

'She's not so bad,' I say, breaking it quickly. Bitch Lady is my best job for some time and I feel guilty that I bad-mouthed her to the others. 'I think I'm just finding writing for someone else all the time frustrating. You know, it's about time I managed to get something published with my own name on the cover.'

'You will, babe,' Hayley says.

'Not any time soon,' I say through a mouthful of chocolate croissant. 'It's so hard finding the time to work on my own stuff.'

'I hope Joe is pulling his weight.'

'He's just been kind of distracted recently.' Joe and I have been having a difficult few weeks. I think it's mainly that we're both trying to function with eight months' worth of lost sleep. 'It's coming up to exam time again and he had that big conference thing last week for heads of year so he's been out a lot preparing for that.'

'When Tallulah was little,' Hayley says, 'I had to make Frank take her out of the house every morning so that I could get on with stuff.'

6

'Oh come on Hailz,' Jenna says, 'you didn't have to make him do anything. Frank loves spending time with Tallulah and Benji.'

We glance over at Hayley's kids. Tallulah, aged six, is ladling jam onto her three-year-old brother's head as he bends over a colouring book, seemingly oblivious. Suddenly we're all laughing.

'Yeah, yeah, okay, it's a wonder anyone loves spending time with them,' Hayley says when she's recovered sufficiently. She removes the jammy teaspoon from her daughter's grip and Tallulah says very politely: 'I was using that, Mummy.' Which sets us all off again.

See, this is us. See how normal we are. How much fun we're having. I glance over at the next table, where the woman is feeding her little girl from a packet of those organic baby crisps that Ruby is addicted to. She has a single cup of coffee in front of her; none of our cosy jumble of plates, with bits of pastry, condiments and earlier drinks spread around. I wonder why her solitariness makes me feel so much better about myself. *Hey, I haven't done all that badly. Look at my mates. Look how cool they are.* I still have that thirteen-year-old-girl thing of wanting to belong, which is ridiculous in a thirty-seven-year-old woman.

So what if, underneath, this is not what it seems? It must be all right because it looks like it's all right – better than all right, in fact: it looks good, something you'd envy. And we never talk about what's underneath. Well hardly ever. We never talk about the thing we did and, most of all, the thing we didn't do. Our silence about that summer is the thing that binds us together. The reason the four of us are still friends twenty-five years later. Close friends, or so we tell ourselves. Because it's not the good times that

7

really tie you to people; it's the worst times of all. Those are the people you can never truly escape.

'Yes, all right Benji, I know,' Hayley says, 'but it's actually stuck in your hair, so you're going to have to hold still for a bit longer.'

'So what's the book about, Lucy?' Jenna asks, glancing at her phone as it pings and then turning it face down.

I hesitate fractionally too long.

'It's actually about the stars of early Hollywood,' I say brightly. A perfectly good subject for a book, but one that holds a particular meaning for the four of us. I watch as the awkwardness of this apparently innocuous statement hits my friends.

'Okay, that's…' Jenna trails off.

'That's so weird,' says Hayley. 'Or is it weird? I mean, you know. Are you writing about *him*? Did you—'

I definitely don't want to talk about *him*, let alone write about him. I cut Hayley off quickly.

'It's just a job. I'm not in a position where I can turn jobs down. Bitch Lady – I mean Harriet – Harriet's great-grandmother was a silent movie star, so it's mainly about her.'

'And Bitch Lady herself is…?'

'This really successful film producer. But not much of a writer. She's sold the idea to a publisher – British actors who went to Hollywood in the 1920s – using her great-grandmother's diaries, and so on. Anyway, how's your new job going?' I ask Claire.

'Like my old job, but with even more work.'

'Yeah well now you're a partner you've signed away your soul,' Hayley says. 'And any hopes of having a life.'

Claire flushes, but as she starts to defend herself, Ruby wakes up and starts crying. It takes me a while to untangle her from her blankets and lift her out. I'm holding her on my knee, bouncing her gently to distract her, and the sobs are dying away, although her cheeks are still heartbreakingly wet. A tuft of chestnut hair is standing up on end and her big brown eyes lock onto the pendant round my neck, which she loves playing with. She's perfect and I feel a rush of love. Look what I did. I created new life. When I look up Hayley is standing beside me with the highchair. I glance sideways at the table where the woman was sitting and I realise she's left and I didn't even see her go. And there is something about her disappearance that makes me think of that other disappearance so long ago and everything I've tried so hard to forget.

Chapter Two

1999

Fears grow for missing teen
Hampshire Chronicle, 29 July 1999

Fears are growing for popular local schoolgirl Maddie Blake, who has been missing
since Tuesday. Maddie, 15, was attending a
summer camp in the village of Poison Cross
in the New Forest. She was last seen by
her friends on the morning of her disappearance in the bedroom she shared with
them at the youth hostel. They said that
Maddie was feeling unwell and when they
later returned to her bedroom to check on
her, she had gone. There have been a number
of unconfirmed sightings since, but Maddie
has failed to make contact with family or
friends. Police are increasingly concerned for
her safety and have appealed for the public's
help. Maddie's father and mother, Robin
and Naomi Blake, and brother, Joseph, 17,
issued the following statement: 'We just want
Maddie to come home. She's not in any
trouble. If anyone knows where she is or

believes they may have seen her, we beg them to contact the police as a matter of urgency. We just want this nightmare to end.'

Chapter Three

Lucy, Present

'Lucy! What are you doing down there? Ruby's going to need the milk as soon as she comes out of the bath.'

My husband, Joe. He's right. But I can't move from the kitchen chair on which I've sunk. I can hear splashing and Ruby's cries of happiness, which will turn to wails of dismay if there's no bottle to greet her when Joe lifts her out, but all of it seems to be happening at a tremendous distance. None of it matters. The world has changed in a moment, and I can't focus on anything else.

'I can't find my phone!' I shout back in what I hope passes for my normal voice. It's not as if Joe will be surprised: my habit of fiddling with things and then forgetting where I put them is legendary. I am in fact holding my iPhone tight, the case digging into my hand.

'Why do you need it?' He sounds annoyed. 'We just need the milk. There's some in the Sainsbury's bag if it's not in the usual place.'

I ignore him. The message comes from a number that isn't in my contacts.

Why didn't you tell them where I was?

My heart is beating so fast I think it might explode out of my chest. I try to take a deep breath. And another. I tell myself it could be a mistake. I've had my share of random messages. *Tell Dora I can't make bridge on Thursday. Don't forget your appointment with Dr Taylor.* But I don't think this is a mistake. How could it be?

I think the message is from Maddie. Maddie who's been dead for a quarter of a century. And I feel as though it's all about to start again.

I don't know how long I sit there before Joe comes downstairs, dark, lean and impossibly handsome, even when wearing a sick-stained t-shirt. He's carrying a screaming Ruby, wrapped in her dolphin blanket. I can't tell him about the message, because if I do, I'll have to tell him why I think it's from Maddie, and I can't tell him that. I've never told him, and it's far, far too late now.

'Lucy? What's going on? Look at her. It's going to take me ages to get her off now.'

Then he sees my face, and the lines of frustration on his forehead soften and his eyes sharpen with anxiety.

'Luce? What's the matter? What's wrong?'

His eyes move to the phone I'm clutching. I have to think of something fast. I hate lying to Joe. I suppose in a way I've been lying to him for years. But by omission – not a deliberate, outright lie.

'Nothing.' My voice wobbles. 'I've just had some bad news. I'm really sorry.'

'What is it? Tell me, please. You're scaring me.'

Now his voice is shaking too. Because Joe is all too familiar with bad news. The worst news. I feel terrible that I've done this to him. I say quickly:

'It's a friend I met at baby massage – Sarah – she's got to have a mastectomy.'

Even as the words leave my mouth, I feel a wave of revulsion that I am capable of saying them. Joe sinks into the chair opposite me, a beam of early evening sunlight catching the side of his face, so that I can see dark stubble against tanned skin. Ruby's screaming has changed to a high-pitched, serious wail. I get up to take her from Joe and hug her as close as I can. Joe stares at me, his eyes brimming with tears, and then he buries his head in his hands.

'Jesus, Luce, I thought—' He doesn't finish. For a long minute, he just sits there, his head in his hands, and then he looks up. 'I'm sorry. It's terrible news. Your poor friend. Sarah? Have I met her?'

Ruby is giving small weepy gulps now, as if she's actually comforted by my presence. The woman who just made up a story about a friend with cancer.

'I'm sorry, I didn't mean to do that to you.' I'm jiggling Ruby up and down as if both our lives depend on it. 'It's just a shock. That's all. She's so upset.'

Then I remember my phone. I dropped it on the table when I went to pick up Ruby. The first time it's been out of my grip since the message arrived. I panic that I might have left the screen on. Can Joe see the text? I whip round, but the screen is dark. When I look up Joe is watching me. The tears have been wiped away, but his face is troubled, eyelids swollen. For a moment, we look at each other.

'Come here, both of you,' he says suddenly, getting to his feet, and he folds me and Ruby into a hug. I try to relax. I try to feel safe. But what I really feel is guilty. Guilty about what I've just done to Joe, and guilty – except that's not a strong enough word for it – about what happened to Maddie all those years ago. Over Joe's shoulder I can see all the usual detritus of our lives scattered on the kitchen surfaces. The bottle of formula I came down to fetch, a folder of essays that Joe needs to mark, the sterilising machine for Ruby's bottles, a jar of pesto sauce that Joe got out for dinner, a half-full bottle of Sauvignon. And it seems to me incredible that all this stuff can still be there, unaltered.

Can the message really be from Maddie? I've long resigned myself to the idea that she's dead. If she was alive now, she'd be the same age as the others. She'd be thirty-nine. Two years older than me. And it's strange that I find this so hard to imagine because, after all, I have a living connection right in front of me. I married her older brother. I didn't see Joe for ten years after Maddie disappeared, but then we met again at a wedding and although at first it was just as difficult as you could imagine, very quickly it felt right.

We went for a walk the next day, while the other wedding guests nursed their hangovers, and it was like talking to someone I'd known all my life. I think we both knew then that we would be together. My daughter is Maddie's niece. Sometimes I search for Maddie in Ruby's face. Ruby has Maddie's chestnut hair, but she has my features: a round face and hamster cheeks. Joe and I never talk about Ruby's connection to Maddie and the one time my mother-in-law brought it up, it led to a Blake family row. Soon after we brought Ruby home from hospital, Naomi – I've never managed to call her Mum, she's far too grand, and over the years she's stopped asking – said it was lovely to see Maddie living on in Ruby, and Robin, my father-in-law, flipped. He went puce and said that Naomi was being ridiculous, that 'Ruby is Ruby' and Naomi was forbidden to make her feel like her purpose on earth was to be an antidote to tragedy. Joe, the peacemaker as always, calmed them both down and in the end I think Robin realised he'd overreacted. But that's what mentioning Maddie's name does to the Blakes: it wakens grief that is still raw after all these years.

Somehow, I get through dinner, although mainly I push the pesto-covered pieces of chicken and pasta around my plate. The smell of basil and pine nuts is making me want to vomit, but I manage to put a few pieces in my mouth and swallow them. I barely touch the wine. My head is fuzzy enough already without alcohol. Joe, who's watching me anxiously, asks me questions about Sarah. Is she the one who grew up on a farm? Has she got a family history of cancer? Is she married? How many children do they have? I field these questions about my non-existent friend as best I can, trying to encourage Joe onto a different subject — every time I tell him another lie, however trivial, something inside me physically twists tighter — and all the time, just under the surface, I'm thinking about what I'm going to do.

My phone beeps with an incoming message. What if it's her again? I long to look at it but Joe has finally found another topic of conversation and is telling me something about his dad not turning up when they were supposed to be playing golf together.

'It's not like him to forget.'

There's one very simple thing I could do. Phone the number. That would clear it up. Speak to the person who picked up the phone and say 'Hello, are you my long-dead friend Maddie Blake from twenty-five years ago? No? Oh, sorry to have bothered you.' But I can't do this. I just can't. I'm a coward. If I wasn't a coward, I wouldn't be in this situation at all. Situation. What an inadequate word for the anguish and deceit of the past quarter of a century.

Another beep from the phone. I reach for it, but Joe says: 'What do you think Luce?'

'What?'

'Is it okay if I rearrange for next Saturday?'

'What? I don't know. Yes, probably.'

'I'm sorry. You're still thinking about your friend. I shouldn't be bothering you with this.'

'No, it's fine. Sorry. What were you saying?'

'Here, give me your plate. I'll clear up. Why don't you go and have a bath? Finish off that wine and have a good long soak.'

Oh god, yes. Solitude. The bathroom. Time to think. I garble my thanks, snatch my phone off the table like a teenager, and practically run up the stairs, shutting the bathroom door behind me, sinking onto the floor with my back against it.

The two new messages are both from my hairdresser, double reminders about a fifty per cent off colour sale. Nothing more from the number that texted me earlier. I risk another look at the message, as if there might be something about it that I missed: a name or an explanation that I didn't take in. But of course there isn't. Just those plain, unforgiving words. There are only four people in the world I can tell about this – the only people who will understand exactly why the message terrifies me. We have a WhatsApp group together – the Fab Four, Hayley's name – and I click on it. The last message is something from Hayley early this morning about running late to meet us in Gail's. My fingers seem to be locked in grip mode, and it's really difficult to type at all, but eventually I write:

> Has anyone else been sent a weird text?

It's a bit blunt, but I can't manage anything else and straight away I can see Claire is typing back. I wait, eyes fixed on the screen. I'm vaguely conscious I'm sitting in a pool of water from Ruby's bath time earlier. I should start running a bath anyway, otherwise Joe will wonder what I'm doing up here.

I stand up and turn on the taps. When I glance back at the screen, Claire's message has appeared:

> Nope. What kind of weird? You all right?

And then a few seconds later Hayley:

> Me neither babe – whats up?? Is Joe with you? Xxxx

I can't decide whether it makes me feel better or worse that the others haven't received a message. Maybe the fact that they haven't makes it less likely that it really is something to do with Maddie. I type back:

> I can't explain now. I need to talk to you all

Typing is easier this time, as if the act of telling other people has already made this slightly less terrifying. Hayley quickly replies:

> Come round an hour earlier tomorrow and
> I'll get rid of Frank and the kids. Hope your
> ok xxxxxx

I'd forgotten we were all going round to Hayley and Frank's for Sunday lunch tomorrow. It's Frank's birthday and, as she does most years, Hayley has decided that what he would like best is to hang out with her friends and their partners. I reply:

> Thanks see you at 12. Just the four of us

The water is still thundering into the bath and I reach over to turn the taps off. I undress and sink into the water: it's too hot and stings my skin, and I notice absently I've forgotten to add any Radox. I reach over the edge of the bath and pick up my phone again. There are now more concerned messages from Claire and one from Jenna as well, hoping I'm okay and agreeing to meet early tomorrow. I type:

> It's probably nothing. Thanks guys xxx

And then I sit in the scalding water, knees up to my chest, teeth chattering.

Chapter Four

Lucy, Present

'You hadn't forgotten I was coming, had you?'

Harriet Holland – also known as Bitch Lady – is standing on my doorstep, in the hazy Sunday morning sunshine, looking as groomed as it's possible for a successful film producer to look. My head is still so full of the strange message that it's almost impossible to think of anything coherent to say and, for a few moments, I just stare at her.

'Of course not,' I manage eventually. One of those small white lies we tell all the time – not the kind of lying I did to my husband last night. 'It's just that we had a bad night with Ruby.' Back onto the firm territory of truth. Ruby, perhaps picking up on the tension in the kitchen just before she went to bed, woke four times last night, the final time at five a.m., when she didn't go back to sleep. 'We're catching up with ourselves a bit I'm afraid.'

'May I come in?'

She's wearing sunglasses, a cream silk shirt and a pale blue blazer. I'm worried she'll get stains on her if I let her over the threshold. My Sunday morning outfit of pyjama bottoms and an old Gap hoodie looks a little unprofessional by comparison. I can see why she might think I've forgotten she's coming. I open the door wider and Harriet steps inside. She's carrying an A4 folder full of documents. I wish I could remember what we agreed to discuss this morning. I try to avoid holding meetings at the weekends, but one of the disadvantages of being a freelancer is that you have to work around your clients' availability – especially when the client is as important as Harriet.

'Come into the living room,' I say, mainly because the only other room downstairs is the kitchen and that currently resembles a battlefield after the food fight to end all food fights – I'd been about to start the clean-up operation when the doorbell rang. The living room is at least vaguely tidy, but it also contains Joe and Ruby.

'Joe, this is Harriet. You remember? My client.'

Joe scrambles to his feet.

'Great to meet you,' he says, as if his Sunday morning has been made by this poised stranger invading his living room. His eyes are sending me 'why didn't you warn me?' signals and I'm trying to mime my apologies without Harriet seeing.

'Likewise,' she says crisply, studying Joe intently. Probably she's wondering how somebody as good looking as that ended up married to me. This happens a lot. On a good day, when I haven't got Ready Brek in my hair and I've had a chance to put some make-up on, I think I look okay. But Joe is something else. Even now, dressed in tracksuit bottoms and an old t-shirt that he wears to bed, he looks handsome and rumpled, rather than sordid and sleep-deprived.

'And this is Ruby!'

'Yes, we met before,' Harriet says, as if Ruby is an employee she's previously been introduced to at a networking event.

'Tell you what,' Joe says, 'why don't I take Ruby out for her morning walk and give you two a bit of space.'

'If you don't mind, that would be perfect,' I say, gratefully. 'Do you want me to watch her while you get dressed?'

'No, I'll put her in her bouncer.' Joe scoops our daughter up off the floor and I ruffle her hair, which is already standing on end. She smells of sour milk and wet wipes, a reassuring smell. Harriet's complete indifference has made me feel oddly protective of Ruby. It's not like I was a baby person before I had her – I'm not even sure I'm a baby person now – but I think I managed to show some vague interest in other people's when I was presented with them. Ruby's face breaks into a smile and briefly the weight that's settled on me since I opened the message last night lifts.

'Well, good to meet you, Harriet. Hope the book's going well.'

Joe pads out of the room, holding Ruby on one hip. Harriet stares after both of them. 'Baa, Baa Black Sheep' is playing softly somewhere in the room from one of Ruby's toys. I pray that it will stop soon.

'Please – have a seat,' I say and, after a moment, she does. Harriet's too socially trained to brush the sofa down before she sits on it, but I can see by the glance she gives it that she wants to. I go to my little desk, which features a framed photo of Ruby as a newborn and perilous piles of books. I open my Mac, trying desperately to remember anything at all about *Brits Who Shaped Hollywood*, which is the working title of the book I'm writing for Harriet, but the events of the past twelve hours or so seem to have wiped everything from my mind. Nothing matters except the message. And what the others will say when I show them later.

I click on my latest draft and scroll down to the end of the document. I last worked on this on Friday, but it seems like two years rather than two days ago. As I read over what I wrote, though, I start to feel a bit less muddle-headed.

'I'm making good progress,' I say, as 'Baa, Baa Black Sheep' gives way to a jangly version of 'Jack and Jill Went Up the Hill'. 'I've just finished the chapter on Elizabeth Allan. I can email you what I've got if you like?'

I just need to get through this meeting with Harriet and then I can go and talk to Hayley and the others and show them the message.

'I want to talk to you about Edward Duval,' Harriet says.

I nearly tip backwards and in righting myself I send a pile of books from the corner of my desk tumbling onto the floor. Why this morning, of all mornings, has Edward Duval come back into my life?

'I thought we agreed not to include him.' It comes out much sharper than I intended. But when Harriet replies she doesn't sound annoyed; she sounds excited.

'I've made a discovery.'

'A discovery?' I echo. I don't like the sound of this at all.

'Yes. An important one, I think.'

'It's just that Duval didn't make that many films,' I say, refusing to engage with the discovery, and speaking so fast that my words come out in a jumble, 'and no one now has even heard of him. I'm not sure there's that much to say.'

'Surely there's a great deal to say, Lucy.'

'Yes, but not about the films,' I say desperately, 'and that's what this book is about, isn't it? It's not a true crime book. You have to be careful you don't mix the genres too much – publishers hate that.'

'I don't think that's a risk here.'

'Well, you're the boss,' I say brightly. Far too brightly. I sound deranged.

In the hall, I can hear Joe grappling with the pushchair and then the thump of the front door as he leaves. I wish I could escape with him.

'You know I don't see it like that,' she says. 'It's a collaboration. I trust your judgement, Lucy, that's why I asked you to be my ghostwriter.'

As if to prove how nice she is after all, she even helps me to pick up the books from the carpet. All secondary sources about Hollywood in the first half of the twentieth century – there to supplement her great-grandmother's diary. Not many of them do more than mention Duval in passing. But I don't need a book to write about Edward Duval. I learnt all there is to know about him nearly twenty-five years ago: Edward Duval, silent movie star, suspected murderer and the reason Maddie took us all to a haunted house in the dead of night to carry out the dare. I suddenly can't deal with this anymore.

'Would you like a coffee? Let me get you a coffee,' I say and, without waiting for an answer, I dart out of the room, leaving her reaching down to retrieve a paperback that's gone under the sofa.

When I come back, I've managed to pull myself together. There's a cafetiere of coffee and even a little jug of milk, and my hands holding the tray are almost steady. Harriet's still standing over by my desk, and maybe I'm so twitchy myself that I'm projecting it onto other people, but it's almost like she jumps when she sees me. Has she been reading my laptop? But when I glance at it, the screen saver is on.

'So, tell me about this discovery,' I say, managing to sound reasonably normal again.

She sounds so calm when she replies that I think I must have imagined that guilty start when I came back into the room just now.

'I found some letters.'

'From your great-grandmother?'

'From Edward Duval *to* my great-grandmother. Written in the 1920s, after the murder.'

'No one knows for certain it *was* a murder.' Like Maddie, but more than seven decades earlier, Duval's alleged victim was never found. It's one of many similarities between the two cases. My voice has become all bright again and I wonder if Harriet can tell there's something wrong. Her expression gives nothing away.

'Disappearance then.'

She holds out the manila folder that she'd placed next to her on the sofa, but I make no move to take it.

'They're quite lengthy. Mostly complaints about various other people in the industry who've dropped him or haven't replied to his correspondence. But there's some bits in there about what happened and how he feels about it.' When I don't reply she says: 'I wonder if he might actually have been innocent from the way he writes about it.'

'I think that what you might have here,' I say carefully, 'is a different book. There is a market for this kind of thing – forgotten crimes. But it's not the kind of thing I've had any experience writing.'

'No. That's not my kind of book either. Look, Lucy, I don't want to push you into writing something you're not comfortable with. Let me leave them with you, will you, and see what you think. If you really don't think they fit, then fine, I'll go with your judgement.'

I finally take the folder she's offering me and this time there is no disguising the fact that my hand is shaking.

'Lucy? Is everything all right?'

'Sorry,' I say, avoiding her cool gaze. 'I'm not really firing on all cylinders this morning. I'll be fine when I've had some sleep. I'll take a look at the letters and get back to you, and I'll email you that last chapter I finished.'

She gets to her feet.

'Look, I'll leave you to it. I'm going to be out of the country for a few weeks – we're filming in Guadalajara – but I'll have WiFi and let's catch up properly when I'm back.'

On the doorstep, she pauses.

'I drove down there the other day.'

'Where?'

But I already both know and dread the answer.

'Poison Cross.' The place where Duval lived and Maddie disappeared. 'Duval describes the house in one of his letters to my great-grandmother and I'd heard it was still there. I was curious to see it.'

'It must be little more than a ruin now,' I manage. I am trying so hard not to think about the last time I went to the house at Poison Cross. About the dare. About Maddie.

'There are hoardings going up so it's hard to see much of the old house but I took some pictures if you'd like to see them?'

I'm now physically backing away from her. But then, miracle of miracles, Joe and Ruby turn into the drive and

I greet them as if it's my first sight of them after a year of enforced separation.

'Anyway, we'll talk again soon,' she says, politely acknowledging Joe again and climbing into her red Audi convertible that looks so out of place in our street full of Fiats and Fiestas.

As I help Joe manoeuvre the pushchair over the door-step and into our cramped hallway without waking Ruby, I'm not seeing him at all. I'm seeing the Grecian good looks of Edward Duval, long-dead Hollywood icon, and the sleek beauty and promise of my friend Maddie. In my head, they are dancing together, round and round an empty ballroom.

The two of them – Maddie and Duval – have always been inextricably linked in my mind. Duval was, legend has it, a murderer as well as a silver-screen star, and Maddie's disappearance has disturbing echoes of the disappearance of the girl he was accused of killing. But the murder he's alleged to have committed took place in the 1920s and Duval killed himself in 1935. Whatever else he may or may not have done, he cannot have murdered Maddie in 1999.

But although Duval was dead decades before Maddie was even born, I've always held him partly responsible for what happened to her. Maddie would never have wanted to visit the house at Poison Cross if it hadn't belonged to the celluloid legend that was Edward Duval, and if she hadn't wanted to visit the house, none of the other terrible things that followed might ever have taken place. So it's not surprising that the idea of ghostwriting a book about 1920s Hollywood makes me feel on edge. I took the job because I needed the work and I thought at the time I'd be able to get away without referring to Duval, but now Harriet's turned up with a folder of letters written by the man himself. And all of this just one day after I got the strange message. I'm trying to get my head around what this could mean and whether there could possibly be some link between the two things.

I know this can't be what is really happening, but as my fingers fumble to unbutton a sleeping Ruby's cardigan, I feel like Duval is cursed and, in agreeing to write the book at all, I've unleashed a whole new nightmare for us all.

Chapter Five

Extract from Brits Who Shaped Hollywood *by Harriet Holland*

Edward Duval is perhaps the most tragic figure among the British actors whose talent lit up the screens of the early movie theatres. Duval, who was born Edward Farmer in 1895, in a village just outside Brighton, showed an aptitude for the stage from an early age. Unlike many of the stars in this book, though, Duval didn't come from a theatrical background. The child of a Church of England clergyman, in later years, Duval was to recall that his first foray into the world of acting — playing the part of one of the mechanicals in a village charity performance of A Midsummer Night's Dream *— earned him a harsh beating from his father.*

There was, however, no holding the young Duval back. In an interview with Screen Idols *in 1923, Duval recalled buying a copy of* The Complete Works of Shakespeare *at a village bring-and-buy sale, and hiding it from his father. Duval described how he would go up the hill behind the village and practise speeches to hone his craft. The reality was probably less romantic. In later years, Duval's sister was to describe their father as a violent brute who rarely let his children out of his sight. The taint of violence was to stay with Duval always.*

Duval left home as soon as he could, aged fifteen, and joined the Southampton Repertory Theatre, then under the management of Sebastian Cane, who had in his time been an actor-manager to rival Henry Irving. Working with one of the greats of the Victorian stage undoubtedly helped Duval, as it did so many of the other young British actors who thrived in the bright lights of the nascent Hollywood studio scene. We would probably consider his style of acting melodramatic by twenty-first-century standards. Even a contemporary review of Mrs Warren's Profession, in which he played the young lead, noted that his performance was 'overly emotional and verging on overwrought'. But it was precisely these qualities that were to attract the attention of Cecil B. DeMille when Duval starred in a revival of Trelawny of the Wells, at Irving's old haunt, the Lyceum, in 1920. DeMille was particularly struck by the actor's emphatic, almost mannered, delivery and thought it would translate well on celluloid. It helped that Duval had the looks of a young Greek god.

Duval's rise was a meteoric one – just as his fall was one of the most dramatic plunges from grace that Hollywood has ever seen. Within a week of arriving in Los Angeles in 1921, he was signed up to Paramount Pictures on a salary of $5,000 a year. His first film, an adaptation of Thomas Hardy's novel Tess of the d'Urbervilles, was a huge success. Duval's career was brief, but he warrants a mention in this book because he was to create the mould for male Hollywood movie stars for a generation. Errol Flynn could never have existed without Edward Duval. His chiselled features and smouldering manner contained more than a hint of danger and it was this quality more than any other that drew hundreds of fans to write to him every week. Duval was the original celebrity and if few people have heard of him now, it is because ultimately the flame of publicity that lit up his name was to consume him in a blaze of revulsion and horror less than four years later.

Chapter Six

Lucy, Present

'Doogie, no! Sorry, Luce.'

Doogie is Hayley and Frank's labradoodle, and the star of Hayley's Instagram account @heyhayley. Doogie the doggie. Named by Tallulah, Hayley's eldest, whom he, literally doggedly, adores. Right now, as if sensing that I need comfort, he's attempting to clamber up onto my lap, dirty paws and all. I momentarily bury my face in his pale gold curls and take in the pungent canine smell of him.

'It's all right, I don't mind.'

'He'll get mud on your pretty dress.'

Hayley pushes him off and he grunts and settles himself under the large round patio table, in the shade. The four of us are sitting at the end of Hayley's garden and I feel safer having this chat outside, even though Hayley has been as good as her word and got rid of Frank and the kids. Somehow she's persuaded him to take them to Tooting Bec Lido and not come back until one o'clock. Happy birthday, Frank.

'I told him that it was part of his birthday surprise,' she says airily.

'What about when he comes back and discovers there isn't one?' Claire asks, reaching for the sunglasses that are nestling in her curly brown bob and putting them on.

'Oh, you know Frank,' Hayley says. And we all do. The world's most amenable man – and god knows he needs to be living with Hayley – right up until the point he's pushed too far, when he loses his temper in a spectacular fashion.

Jenna pours herself a glass of water from the bottle of San Pellegrino that glistens with condensation, and cuts to the subject that we've all been carefully treading around for the past few minutes: 'So, why don't you tell us what's been going on Lucy?'

It's a strange thing, because although I've been longing for this moment ever since I sent my WhatsApp message last night, now that I'm here, I almost want to put it off. To carry on talking about Doogie and Frank. To take in the scent of honeysuckle. To pretend that everything's normal. I sense the others all stiffen slightly at Jenna's words – a mixture of anticipation and dread. Wondering if I really am going to mention the thing we hardly ever mention. And I realise that this was never normal, and I might as well get on and say it.

Lowering my voice, even though Hayley and Frank's next-door neighbour is in her eighties and never goes into her overgrown garden, and fixing my gaze on Doogie's dozing form under the table, I tell them quickly about the text. Their instant reaction is, strangely, relief. I realise that they've been expecting something worse.

'Honestly lovely, it's just a wrong number or something,' Hayley says.

'I can see why it would spook you though,' Jenna says.

'It's a fairly normal kind of message,' Claire adds.

They ask to see it. And then they become more worried. I can almost see it creeping over them. Somehow seeing the words written down has brought it home to them. There's a silence broken only by the roar of a motorbike on a neighbouring street.

'Supposing…' I say, 'supposing, it really is from Maddie.'

There. I've done it. I've said her name.

'How could it be?' Hayley says. But she doesn't sound like Hayley at all. She sounds like a frightened child.

'Let's just dial the number,' Claire says, ever-practical.

'I thought of that, but I can't.'

'Give it here,' she says gently. She takes my phone and, for a moment, her finger hovers over the screen. Then she taps dial and raises the phone to her ear, turning away from us as she does so. I watch her, thinking Claire is the nearest thing I have to a big sister. She used to look out for me when we were younger, and she still does it now. Seconds later, she's putting the phone back on the table.

'It's switched off.'

We all breathe again. Somehow we knew it wasn't going to be that easy.

Claire is in lawyer mode. 'What, logically, are the possibilities?'

The rest of us seem incapable of speech.

'Okay,' she continues when it becomes clear that no one else is going to speak. 'I think there are three. One, it's a wrong number. Still the most likely possibility.'

'Why does no one answer?' Hayley asks.

'Not all of us are glued to our phones twenty-four-seven, Hayley.' Claire removes her sunglasses and puts them down on the table. 'Two, like Lucy says, it's from Maddie.'

Even though I said it first, hearing the same words from Claire makes me feel winded.

'I know,' Claire says, looking round at our shocked faces. 'I don't really believe it either, but it has to be a possibility, doesn't it? If the message isn't a wrong number and it was deliberately sent to you, there aren't many people who could have sent it. Maddie is one of them. We've all assumed she's dead. Everyone has. But they've never found her body, we all know that.'

So much of the colour has drained from Hayley's face that her skin seems almost translucent.

'There was that boy who said he saw her getting on the train,' Jenna says.

'Sam,' I whisper. Toned muscles, blond hair, biking leathers.

'He was the one who first told us the ghost story,' Hayley says. 'About Edward Duval.'

I haven't told the others about the letters Harriet brought over earlier and my ridiculous fear that in agreeing to write the book for her, I've somehow opened a door to the past and triggered the message. I have an almost superstitious dread of talking about Duval. As soon as Harriet left, I buried the folder containing the letters at the bottom of one of my desk drawers, in the age-old hope that hiding something will make it go away.

'But if Maddie has been alive all along, where has she been and why would she suddenly get in touch now?' Jenna asks. 'After nearly twenty-five years?'

'Maybe something happened that we don't know about. Something that caused her to make contact. Or maybe she suddenly came across Lucy.'

In spite of the heat, a shiver passes over me. A few months ago, I finally got around to setting up a website for my ghostwriting business. Could that be it?

'Sorry, Goose,' Claire says, unconsciously using my long-ago nickname. 'I really don't think it *is* her. I'm just trying to talk through what this could be.'

'But why would she get in touch in such a weird way?' Jenna asks.

'I don't know, Jenna,' Claire says. 'Maybe she's not ready to confront us directly yet.'

There's a moment while we all absorb this.

'What's the other one?' Jenna asks. 'You said three possibilities. What's the third?'

'The third possibility, I suppose, is that the message was sent by someone who saw what we did that night. Someone who knew that we went to the house.'

'Oh fuck.'

Doogie, picking up on the sheer panic in Hayley's voice, uncurls himself from under the table and starts barking. Hayley doesn't even try to stop him. It's Claire who hushes him, and he looks at her warily, pink tongue lolling out of his mouth, unsure why everyone in his world is suddenly so agitated. We are also all staring at Claire, appalled at what she has already said, terrified about what she is going to say next – yet unable to stop listening.

'Again, I'm not saying it's likely,' Claire says. She still sounds unemotional – like this is a knotty legal problem that we're trying to unravel.

'Jenna, you thought someone was there,' Hayley says. 'Do you remember?'

Jenna shakes her head, but I'm not sure whether she means she doesn't remember, or she just can't engage with this question.

'That person could just be a witness,' Claire says. 'Or I suppose—'

'They could also be the person who killed Maddie,' I say, burying one of my hands in Doogie's warm fur. The urge to get the worst out of the way – to state it openly – has become overwhelming.

'We should call the police,' Jenna says instantly.

'No,' Claire says just as quickly. And, with a curious sense of detachment, I notice that now she too sounds panicked. 'There's no way the police are going to take us seriously. Like we all said, it's probably just a wrong number.'

'And if we called the police, we'd have to explain, wouldn't we?' Hayley says. 'We'd have to explain what we did. The lies we told. And that wouldn't look good for a newly promoted partner in a law firm.'

There's real venom in her voice. I suddenly wonder whether any of us like each other at all.

'It wouldn't look good for someone who runs their own life-coaching business either,' Claire says crisply.

'It was twenty-five years ago,' Jenna says. 'We were children. Surely no one would hold it against us now.'

There's a birdsong-filled silence while we all wonder. Would they? Would Joe? Would Maddie's parents? Does Maddie, if she really is still alive?

'Oh god, I want a cigarette,' Hayley says, burying her head in her hands. 'So, no police, then.'

'It's not like we have anything to show them,' Claire says. 'Just Lucy's text. Believe me, they'd laugh at us.'

'Okay, but we should do something,' I say. 'I need to know what this is. I can't deal with not knowing.' In my head, I sound reasonable, rational even. But out loud I must sound something else entirely because Jenna grabs my hand and says: 'Don't worry, Luce. Please don't get so upset.'

'I'm not saying we do nothing,' Claire says. 'Let's dig around a bit, by all means.'

'Dig around?'

'Well, for a start, Lucy could you ask your in-laws whether they've heard anything?'

'What are you talking about? I can hardly pick up the phone and say, "Oh hi Naomi, has Maddie been in touch recently?"'

'Look, I think we're all losing it a bit,' Claire says. It's as if, now she's worked us up into a frenzy, she's reining us back in. 'My fault. Let's just try and focus on what's most likely.'

Jenna takes a deep breath.

'Okay. Claire's right. It's almost certainly a simple wrong number, but it might just be worth seeing whether Naomi and Robin have had any strange messages too. You don't have to mention Maddie.'

'I suppose it's a good place to start,' Hayley says.

'Hailz!' Frank is standing on the far side of the lawn, glimmering in a white shirt. Beside him is a tall slender woman with dark hair pulled into a bun. 'Didn't you hear the door? We have a guest.'

We all stare, transfixed, and I wonder if the others are thinking what I'm thinking. Then the woman morphs into Nic, Claire's new girlfriend. Claire gets up and starts moving towards her across the lawn.

'Oh shit!' Our hostess scrambles to her feet. 'Nic, I'm so sorry.'

We follow Claire across the grass, and Frank and Nic come to meet us.

'I'm a bit earlier than you said,' Nic says, 'but my class finished early so I thought I'd head over.'

'Hey,' Claire says, giving her a quick hug and a kiss. 'Not a problem. Like I said, the four of us were just—' I never get to find out what excuse she has given Nic for coming to Hayley's early, because she breaks off to chastise Doogie, whose enthusiasm for humans he has never met before knows no bounds.

'Doogie, no!' Frank says, pulling Doogie's wriggly brown form away, to Nic's evident relief.

'Nic, let me get you a drink,' Hayley says. 'We've got bubbles in the fridge.'

'Do you have any coconut water?'

'I think we do,' Frank says. 'Champagne for everyone else? Lucy, I think I just saw Joe pull into the drive. Hailz, I can smell something burning.'

'Shit. Sorry everyone.'

Hayley sets off towards the house as fast as her Zara wedges will carry her. Doogie bounds after her, tail rotating in delight. He's already forgotten the tension of the past half hour, and now the rest of us need to do the same, because what passes for normal life is about to resume. Although thanks to that long-ago summer dare, it's a very long time since any of our lives have been normal.

Chapter Seven

Lucy, 1999

'Naomi Blake says she'll ask her daughter to look out for you at school tomorrow. Lucy, are you listening to me?'

Lucy, who was in fact listening to Celine Dion singing 'My Heart Will Go On', pressed stop on her Walkman and removed her headphones. She hoped she'd misheard.

'Her name's Maddie. She's a couple of years older than you, I think.'

'Mum, you didn't.'

'What have I done wrong now?'

'Oh my god, Mum, why do you have to interfere?'

'Oh my god, Luce,' imitated her mum, pitch-perfect. 'I wasn't interfering. It just came up in the course of conversation. Naomi asked how you were settling in at St Peter's and I said that it's taking you a while to meet new people.'

'I don't want to meet new people.' Lucy got up from the sofa, sending her Walkman, *The Murder of Roger Ackroyd* and a pile of pick-n-mix wrappers tumbling onto the living room carpet. 'I've got friends already.'

'And that's great sweetheart, but they all live two hundred miles away.'

'Whose fault is that?'

'Luce, we can't keep having the same argument. You know why it was better for us to move. It's a fresh start.'

'You didn't tell her, did you?'

'No, of course I didn't.'

To her horror, Lucy felt her eyes start to fill with tears. She'd already ruined the fresh start; her mum just didn't know it.

'Maddie Blake is the coolest girl in the whole school,' she said huffily. 'There's no way she's going to waste her time on me. It's embarrassing that you'd even suggest it. She's like this Queen Bee, ruling over everyone.'

'Well, I thought she seemed lovely and she lives right next door to us. Why wouldn't she want to be friends with you, Luce?'

Her mum reached out and wrapped her in a hug and, after a few seconds, Lucy felt herself relax.

'It would be like hanging out with the Heathers,' she mumbled, and then remembered it was a film that she definitely wasn't supposed to have seen.

But Maddie surprised Lucy. The next day, in the school canteen, as Lucy was carrying a tray of fish fingers and chips to the furthest end of the furthest table, a slim figure with a swishy ponytail of long chestnut hair sashayed up to her. She was even smiling.

'Your mum's Sonia Keeble, right?'

Lucy opened her mouth but no sound came out. For some reason, she had become fascinated by the plate of fish fingers: three of them, luminous orange and burnt around the edges. Slowly, she made herself raise her gaze to meet Maddie's.

'The actress?' Maddie said, a hint of impatience in her voice now.

'Um yeah.'

'I want to be an actress too.'

'Great. That's great. Really great. Great.'

There was a snigger from one of the three girls standing behind Maddie. Lucy knew them as Sun-In, Sporty and Frowny: Maddie's clique. It was Frowny laughing at her, but she still managed to look cross as she did it.

'Have you ever been to the Oscars?' asked Sun-In.

Lucy shook her head, worried that if she started talking again, she'd say something idiotic.

'It's on my list of life goals,' said Sun-In. 'I'm going to be the Anna Scott of my generation.'

'Seriously Hayley? You do realise she's not even a real person? You mean Julia Roberts.' This from Sporty, whose real name Lucy knew because she'd recently given a talk to Lucy's class: Jenna, captain of the netball team. She'd ignored Lucy then, but now she was smiling at her and Lucy had a sudden flash of hope that these golden people might actually want to be her friends. That she might finally fit in here.

'Hayley probably thinks *Notting Hill* is a documentary,' Frowny said.

'That film was wicked,' Hayley said, unfazed.

'Let's go,' Maddie said. And now her voice wasn't even impatient – it was just bored. 'We're going to be late.'

She turned away and the others followed, a tight group of four, and Lucy knew she'd blown it. She should have said something. Anything. Even 'great'.

But just as she was thinking this, Maddie turned back.

'Hey?'

'Yes?'

'I'm having a sleepover on Friday. We're watching some films. Come along if you want.'

'Great,' Lucy heard herself say.

And then it was all over and Maddie really had gone and Lucy was alone again with her fish fingers and the prospect of another miserable lunch at the weird kids' table. But perhaps her conversation with Maddie had been noticed because, for once, no one threw chips at her and when she walked past Ricky Hooper and his mates, he didn't try to trip her up. He just mumbled: 'All right, Feeble,' with what might even have been grudging respect. For the first time since they'd moved, she wondered whether it might all be okay after all. Perhaps she was finally going to make some good friends.

Chapter Eight

Lucy, 1999

The talk of the sleepover was the thefts at school.

'I tell you, it's Alison Andrews,' insisted Frowny, who turned out to be called Claire. 'She's seriously weird.'

Lucy could attest to this. She'd sat next to Alison Andrews at lunch for her entire first week at St Peter's.

'She's a Christian,' Hayley said, through a mouthful of Monster Munch. Whether this made it more or less likely in Hayley's eyes that she was the thief Lucy wasn't sure. Mainly, she was just happy to be there, wrapped in her sleeping bag, secretly trying to memorise all the posters Maddie had up on her bedroom wall. That afternoon, she'd been so nervous she'd actually thrown up, hunched over the avocado-coloured toilet bowl in the bathroom her mum hadn't yet got round to replacing. But, despite her pleas, her mum refused to phone Maddie's mum and tell her Lucy was unwell, and now here she was, if not part of the gang, then at least in the same room as them.

The choice of films had been unexpected. Back in Nottingham, her friend Sarah had been obsessed with horror, and had an older sister who smuggled videos into the house for them to watch when Sarah's parents were out. As a result, Lucy knew more than she ever wanted to about Freddy Krueger. Maddie, it turned out, loved old black and white films. So far they'd watched *It Happened One Night* and *The Philadelphia Story*, and Lucy had enjoyed them both, or at least enjoyed them more than she had *A Nightmare on Elm Street 4*.

'Maddie wants to be Katharine Hepburn,' Hayley said, helping herself to a drink.

'Better than wanting to be Anna Scott. At least Katharine Hepburn was real – and she won four Oscars. Does your mum get to go to any awards ceremonies, Lucy?'

Lucy, who'd been relieved to be in the background, listening but not contributing, felt all the eyes in the room swivel in her direction. She knew she was going red.

'I think she's been to a few. Not the Oscars,' she added quickly, not wanting to overplay her hand.

'Cool,' Maddie said, apparently satisfied. 'I'd like to ask her about it some time. You know, like how she got started and everything.' Lucy hastily committed her mum to a conversation with Maddie. After all, she started this – it was the least she could do. Maddie's attention had switched to Hayley: 'Do you swear that's just lemonade, Hayley?'

'I already said.'

The alcohol ban was another surprising thing, although Lucy was privately relieved about it. She didn't want the others to realise she was a total lightweight. She wondered if Maddie's parents were strict about it. She hadn't met Maddie's dad yet, but her mum seemed really nice, although she had a bit of a scary way of focusing her attention on you when she was talking to you, like she was testing you for an exam you hadn't been told about. She was very thin with a sleek black bob and a pale, perfectly made-up face, like a model in a magazine.

There was a knock at the door and almost at the same time it started to open. The head of Joe, Maddie's older brother, appeared.

'All right in here, you lot? I'm heading out. Will you be okay? Mum said she'll be back by half nine.'

'Where's Dad?'

'Still at his work thing.'

'Can I bum a cigarette, Joe?' Hayley said.

Lucy wondered whether Hayley had asked just to get Joe's attention. She could see why you might. Maddie's brother was gorgeous. The whole family was gorgeous. Joe was in year twelve, and she'd only ever seen him from a distance before. Up close, he was even more dazzling. Dark, with tanned skin, and a smile that encompassed everyone in the room, including Lucy herself. And now that he'd put not only his head, but his whole body into the room, she could appreciate that too; slender but muscled.

'Don't smoke them in here.' Joe handed round a packet of Marlboro. 'Mum'll go mental and you know how she can sniff them out a mile off.' Maddie took one too, which surprised Lucy given she'd been so strict about not drinking. When it was Lucy's turn, she shook her head. There was no way she was going to smoke her first cigarette in front of Maddie and her best friends – they were the ultimate intimidating audience. Hayley, wearing her nose stud and all five earrings, her beach-blonde hair in a side ponytail, was effortlessly cool. Jenna, sporty, taller than the others, and wearing a spaghetti strap tank top, looked like she was in a girl band. And Claire, brooding and intense, with her velvet choker and dark curly hair held back from her face by a row of butterfly clips, was like an elegant French girl in a film.

'*Can I bum a cigarette, Joe?*' mocked Maddie as soon as Joe had gone.

'I wanted a smoke.'

'You have a packet in your bag. If you're going to hit on my brother you could at least be a bit more subtle about it.'

'I wasn't hitting on him. Besides, Joe still has a girl-friend, doesn't he?'

'You know he does,' Maddie said. 'Anyway, I thought you were into Mark Rossiter. That's what you told me last week. He sent you that note in assembly, didn't he?'

Hayley, scrabbling through her bag for a lighter, scowled and from the way Claire and Jenna were staring at her, Lucy guessed that Mark Rossiter was news to them too.

'No need to broadcast everything I tell you to the world. And it's not like I'm the only one who fancies Joe. Jenna likes him too.'

'Not me,' Jenna said coolly. 'I'm holding out for Christian Slater.' Lucy, though, had caught Jenna looking at Joe just now and thought Hayley was right: she liked him; she was just less obvious about it than Hayley. Jenna twisted round to look at Maddie: 'How are things going with Amari?'

Lucy knew that Maddie was dating Amari Otedola, who was in the same year as Maddie's brother, and captain of the school football team. The whole school knew it: they were the golden couple. Lucy had seen them a few weeks ago, hanging out in the playground just down from the railway station. They were standing by the swings. Amari had his arm around Maddie's waist and she had her hair down, fanned out over her denim shirt. Lucy thought they looked like an Athena poster.

'Amari's all right.'

'Are you two… you know?' Jenna asked.

'What?'

'Fucking,' Hayley said, turning back from the window, where she was leaning out, expertly smoking her cigarette.

'We've been going out for four months, what do you think?'

'Is that where you were last Friday night when your mum phoned my mum to see if you were at mine?' Jenna said.

'I already told you it was.'

'My mum said she sounded really weird.'

'Yeah well, my mum doesn't have to know everything about my life.'

'And Amari's family were in the restaurant that night, you know. My dad said.'

Jenna's dad ran the most successful of the three Indian restaurants on the high street.

'So what?'

'Only he said Amari was there.'

Lucy held her breath. She had the feeling that they'd forgotten she was there, and if she said anything at all, or even moved, they would all turn on her. But as if Jenna hadn't spoken, Maddie said: 'Becky Rogers had a silver bracelet stolen, you know. That must actually be worth quite a lot. It belonged to her grandmother. It has a little silver bird on it – I remember she showed it to me. It was taken from her locker when she was playing netball.'

Lucy was almost grateful for the change of subject. She wanted to know where Maddie had really been on Friday night and she also wanted to know more about Maddie's relationship with Amari, but she was worried that if the chat about boys continued, at some point it was going to come round to her. She'd read most of Judy Blume's books and part of a copy of Jilly Cooper's *Riders* she'd found in the holiday cottage at Morpeth last year, but her actual, practical knowledge was precisely nil.

Claire, who also seemed relieved to be talking about something else, said: 'They should call the police in for stuff like that.'

From downstairs there was a loud bang.

'What was that?' Hayley demanded, eyes wide.

'How should I know?' Maddie scrambled to her feet. 'Maybe it was Joe slamming the door. Let me—'

The bang was repeated. They all froze.

'It sounds like someone's trying to get in, not out,' Claire said.

Lucy felt her stomach muscles tighten, even though she was with the others, and they were in Maddie's house, and her own mum was next door. Next door suddenly seemed a very long way away.

'It sounds like they're trying to smash their way in,' Jenna said, with a laugh in her voice that rose and ended on a note of panic.

'Stay here,' Maddie said, 'I'll go and look.' Her eyes were darting from them to the bedroom door.

'No don't!' Jenna said.

'You can't go by yourself,' Claire said. 'I'll come too.'

Downstairs, there was the crash of broken glass.

'Stay here, all right?' Maddie said, so fiercely that Lucy felt a fresh cramp of fear in her stomach.

Chapter Nine

Lucy, Present

By the end of Frank's birthday lunch, I'm starting to feel a bit better. It probably helps that I've drunk a couple of glasses of Frank's finest Merlot, which is certainly a lot finer than anything Joe and I ever have in the house. The roasties were irretrievable, but Hayley did a good job of saving the rest of the meal from incineration. Perhaps because I hadn't eaten anything much at all since lunchtime yesterday, I suddenly got my appetite back and finished all of the lamb and most of the vegetables on my plate. Tallulah and Benji were mercifully subdued – worn out by a morning of terrorising other children at the lido – and asked to leave the table as soon as they'd finished eating. Frank, ever the optimist, suggested that Tallulah could read a story to her brother. It's almost certainly not what they're actually doing.

Ruby is sleeping in her travel cot in the corner of the room, so peaceful that every now and then I have to go and check that she's still breathing – a paranoia that feels like it will never leave me. The conversation has been flowing almost as well as the Merlot, thanks mainly to Frank and Joe it has to be said, but the rest of us have gradually grown more voluble as the meal has gone on, the fear induced by our conversation in the garden gradually dissipating in the presence of other people.

Nic is also a surprise. It's the longest I've spent in her company since Claire started going out with her. She doesn't know any of us that well, but she comes across as very confident: a confidence that must come from within rather than from the wine, as she's stuck resolutely to coconut water. Over the roast lamb, she told us all about the course she's doing on angel healing: a form of spiritual therapy that she says helps her to ensure her life is harmonised. I wonder what it would feel like to have a harmonised life.

'So how come you all ended up living in the same part of London?' she asks now, putting down her spoon and pushing away her bowl. 'Claire says you all went to school together down in Winchester, and now you're all living in Wandsworth.'

'Well, who wouldn't want to live here?' Hayley says brightly, eyeing the half-eaten lemon mousse in Nic's bowl.

'Absolutely,' agrees Frank, who was living in Kensal Green when Hayley first met him and who still occasionally hankers after the cool of north London. 'It has an incomparable one-way system.'

Hayley glares at him.

'Wandsworth is a big place,' Jenna says. 'It's not like we all live right next to each other.'

'Joe and I actually live a bit further out.'

'Still, though,' Nic persists. 'It's a bit of a coincidence.'

'I don't think it's a coincidence exactly,' Jenna says. 'Hayley moved here first, way back, to this tiny flat on East Hill. And then when the rest of us moved to London, we looked in the same area. You want to be where your friends are, right?'

It makes sense when she says it like that. And how else can we possibly explain the ties that have kept us all close to each other for more than two decades.

'It's interesting though,' Nic says, filling the silence as the four of us contemplate what those ties are. 'Because most people tend to make new friends when they grow up. They don't necessarily stick with their childhood friendship group.'

'When you find the right friends, you don't need to make new ones,' Hayley says. The atmosphere has got a bit strained. Being forced to confront our geographical proximity to each other, and the reasons for our co-dependency – particularly the unspoken ones – has reignited the tension from our conversation earlier.

'Oh yes, I get that,' Nic says quickly. 'I'm not saying it's a bad thing. I think it's brilliant.'

Frank, perhaps sensing the need for a change of mood, pushes his chair back.

'Shall I clear these bowls away? And who's for coffee?'

'Coffee would be great,' Joe says. He's wearing the blue Ralph Lauren t-shirt I bought him for his birthday a few months ago and it shows off his tanned skin perfectly. I feel a rush of love for him that's as primitive and protective as the love I feel for Ruby.

'Before you clear up,' Hayley says, 'let's get a photo.' Usually, we have to take pictures of the meal before we are allowed to eat it, but today she must have been too preoccupied by our earlier discussion to remember. 'Frank – can you move the roses slightly closer to the water jug, they're just out of shot. Everyone squeeze in.'

There's an awkward moment when Jenna steps on Joe's foot or something and he leaps about a mile backwards and knocks the water jug over. This involves Frank in lots of mopping up, but before long we're all in place again and Hayley extends her arm at just the right angle to get the selfie. 'Come on Nic, I can't see you. Get beside Claire. Don't worry Luce, I promise Ruby's not in it.'

A few more clicks and mercifully she's done and already scrolling through filters on Instagram.

'Sit down, Frank,' I say, as he starts to put soaking wet napkins in piles of bowls. 'You can't clear up on your birthday.'

'Oh god yes,' Hayley says, tapping away at her phone, 'I'd forgotten. Don't worry, Lucy and I will clear away.'

Once we're in the kitchen and I have Hayley by herself I'm tempted to ask her about the message again. What's her reaction now she's had a bit more time to think? As I stack the dishwasher, I try to analyse my own feelings. For the first time since the message arrived, I think I'm starting to feel a bit calmer about the whole thing. Like Claire said, it was almost certainly a wrong number. A wrong number nearly a day earlier, and nothing since. Uneasily, I remember Harriet bringing up Edward Duval. I think of the letters, buried deep in my desk drawer, taunting me to read them. Perhaps I should overcome my superstitious dread of talking about Duval and tell Hayley about them.

But Hayley gets in first. 'Babe, do you think it's weird that we all live near each other?' Doogie is scrabbling at the door into the main house and she reaches out to open it for him. 'Surely that's just normal?'

I force my mind back to the discussion we just had.

'Nic didn't actually say it was weird. She was just interested.'

'It would be weirder not to live near your friends, wouldn't it?'

'I guess maybe living near a group of your childhood friends is quite unusual – unless you're still living in the place where you grew up of course.' I see her face. 'But unusual doesn't make it bad.' Necessarily. 'Hayley—'

Suddenly there's a commotion from the main house. A scream, followed by Doogie's deep barks. Frank is shouting. My instant thought is Ruby and I bolt in the direction of the dining room, Hayley just behind me. We find Nic, white-faced, being comforted by Claire. Frank is holding Doogie's collar. The air is still being punctuated by short high-pitched screams, but these are coming from Tallulah, who has magically reappeared. Ruby is in Joe's arms, grinning broadly and clearly enjoying the whole thing.

'Tallulah, stop it please!' her mother says. There's a fraction of a pause while Tallulah contemplates her options. Then she shrugs her sequin-covered shoulders with all the disdain of a six-year-old, pivots on her bare feet, and leaves the adults to it.

'Nic got startled by Doogie jumping up at her chair,' Joe says in answer to my unspoken question, 'and as she went to get up, she kind of fell over.'

'Oh no!' Hayley addresses her dog: 'Bad Doogie! Nic, I'm so sorry, I should have kept him shut up.'

Jenna takes a chastened Doogie's collar from Frank and leads him back in the direction of the kitchen. Frank moves to Nic's side.

'Are you all right?' he asks. 'Nothing broken?'

'I'm fine. Sorry. It – he, the dog – took me by surprise, that's all.'

'It's a good thing you didn't break anything,' says Claire, who has her arm round Nic. 'Imagine a gardener with a broken arm.'

'Oh, I didn't know you were a gardener Nic!' Hayley says. Claire rolls her eyes. 'Frank used to be a gardener before he went to veterinary college.'

'I mowed some lawns. I'm imagining Nic does a bit more than that.'

'I design gardens for people.'

'I did tell you about it, Hailz,' Claire says, not entirely succeeding in keeping the annoyance out of her voice. 'They're amazing. You should see her Instagram account.'

'Oh wow. Let me find you.' Hayley whips out her phone again. 'You should have a look at ours. I'm sure there's more that we could do with it. I could do before and after pictures. What do you think Frank?'

Frank holds out his hands, indicating that what he thinks is likely to be irrelevant.

'I'd love to.' Nic is adjusting her headband, which has slipped back in the fall. She's one of those people who can pull off a headband. This one is bright red with polka dots on it. I'd look like a very large ten-year-old wearing it, but Nic looks sophisticated. With her hair in a bun as well, she resembles a beautiful ballet dancer. And that's not all she resembles; it wasn't just that moment we saw her across the lawn earlier. Now I've noticed it, I can't unsee it: she does look a bit like Maddie, or how I imagine Maddie might look now.

The talk about gardens continues in a desultory way for a while longer, but the drama with Nic and Doogie seems to have galvanised everyone into realising lunch is over and after a while people start collecting their scattered possessions and preparing to leave. Claire and

I help Hayley finish stacking the dishwasher, while Joe collects up Ruby's things.

Once semi-order has been restored to the kitchen, I retrieve my bag from where I dumped it on the marble work surface of Hayley and Frank's breakfast bar three hours earlier. I'm still slightly fuzzy-headed from the wine that I've drunk because Joe is driving, and I dip into the bag for my phone almost automatically. I haven't looked at it all afternoon. It has the usual mix of WhatsApps, news alerts, and Instagram notifications. But I don't care that my mum's messaged me three times, that a record temperature was recorded at Heathrow, or that @heyhayley has tagged me in a photo. Because mixed up in all the notifications there's another text. This one is unambiguous.

> You must pay for what you did.

Chapter Ten

Maddie, 1999

Shame was a physical thing. She hadn't realised that before Friday night. Usually climbing up here, onto the roof of the kitchen extension and then onto the dormer window, distracted her – it was pretty high up and she had to focus on not slipping – but today it wasn't working for some reason. She could hear the others out in the back garden and wondered how long it would take them to realise she wasn't there and come to find her. She was a bit insulted that they hadn't noticed already, actually. It had been at least fifteen minutes since she'd gone inside to get a Coke.

She imagined their faces when they saw her up here. The mixture of admiration and envy; she needed that hit after what had happened on Friday. She wasn't sure whether they'd believed her explanation: that some mates of Joe's had thought it would be funny to try to break in. But she had at least managed to keep them out of the way long enough to prevent them seeing what really happened. She'd told them her parents were back and dealing with it and wanted them to stay in her bedroom, which was true enough.

Later, her mum had stuck her head round the door as they lay in their sleeping bags, tensely watching *Casablanca*, and they'd taken her visit as reassurance that everything was in fact okay and that the grown-ups had it in hand, but Maddie sensed a lingering doubt about the events of that night, particularly from Jenna and Claire. The glass had been repaired the next day and now, just over a week later, it was as if the whole horrible thing had never happened at all – except that the others wouldn't let it go. Claire had tried to bring it up again earlier by asking whether Maddie's parents had reported it to the police. Maddie had shut her down straight away. 'No way. I told you. They were just messing around.'

'It was pretty extreme messing around,' Jenna said. 'My parents would freak if something like that happened.'

'Jenna, your parents freak if you're out after eight p.m.'

Her response had got a laugh from the others, but it didn't help the ache of fear and embarrassment she'd felt deep in her guts for the past week. She supposed she was lucky her friends hadn't been here any of the previous times. Last time it had happened, about a month ago, she'd just walked out of the house and stayed out. She hadn't come back until gone ten o'clock, even though they were supposed to be going out for a family dinner. She'd spent most of the time down by the river, listening to Radiohead on her new CD Walkman. Her mum had been frantic with worry when she'd finally shown up.

But it hadn't made any difference. In fact, it felt like things were getting worse – more out of control – to the point where it was a bit of a risk having friends over to hers at all, but they all went on about how they loved coming round and no way was she going to stop inviting them.

It actually wasn't that difficult to get up on this bit of the roof. You climbed up onto the roof of the porch using the dustbin, and then it was pretty easy to step across onto the flat roof of the kitchen extension and the only hard bit was pulling yourself up onto the dormer window. When you were up there you could sit down although you had to concentrate and keep your balance because it would be easy to slide off. Usually, she liked it here precisely because it was down the side of the house and nobody could see you, but right now she wanted to be seen. She needed to redeem herself. To be the one they all envied again: the brave one who didn't give a shit. Maddie the fearless. Definitely not the one with a humiliating secret. She'd got some credit for going downstairs to see what was happening, but since then she'd sensed more curiosity than admiration, and admiration was what she needed right now.

'Jesus!'

The cry came not from the end of the garden path, but immediately opposite, over the fence, in Lucy's garden. She recognised Lucy's mum, Sonia Keeble, from their brief meeting at her parents' boring drinks thing for the neighbours the other week. Ever since, she'd been thinking about how cool it would be to have a mum who was an actress. Maddie was surprised to see her now though: she'd got used to the Dooleys – the elderly couple who used to live at number twenty-three. Sonia was laden down with Sainsbury's bags, which she'd dropped on seeing her next-door neighbours' daughter balanced twenty feet above the ground on the ledge above the dormer window.

'Jesus,' repeated Sonia, slightly more quietly. 'What do you think you're doing?'

The others had appeared round the corner of the house from the garden now, drawn by the cries. Maddie saw exactly the looks on their faces that she'd been hoping to see – even more so now there was an adult to disapprove of her.

'Wow!' Lucy said.

'That's *insane*,' Hayley said, as though this was the highest praise she could bestow. Sonia was unimpressed, though.

'You need to get down now.'

High on her friends' approval, Maddie briefly forgot that she wanted to impress Sonia Keeble too – at that moment she was just there in her role as Lucy's mum rather than professional actress and possible route into a world Maddie was determined to join.

'It's no big deal,' she said, her voice off-hand, almost rude. 'I climb up here all the time. I'm fine.'

'Yeah, well, I'm not. I'm shitting myself. Get down, Maddie, please.'

'Oh my god, Mum.' Lucy sounded mortified.

'Lucy, not now. Maddie, wait a moment.' In less than thirty seconds, Sonia was on the other side of the fence, guiding her down, and something about the matter-of-fact way she went about this meant that Maddie, for once, did as she was told.

'Slowly please.'

'Okay, okay. I've done this like a million times.'

'Carefully. That's it.'

'Go Spidey!' Hayley shouted.

'Don't distract her.'

Coming down was slightly more difficult than getting up, particularly the moment where you had to slide off the window and onto the kitchen roof, because you couldn't see exactly where the roof was, and you had to push back a bit as you slid down and feel for it with your feet. Today, perhaps because everyone was watching, it felt harder than usual, and her foot briefly connected with the guttering rather than the roof and she heard the others gasp. 'Further back Maddie!' Sonia shouted, and then Maddie felt her foot make contact with the roof and it was okay again. As she lowered herself down from the porch roof, Sonia was there to help her.

'Thank god. Are your parents in?'

'No. They're shopping in Winchester. Anyway, you don't need to tell them.'

'Maddie, of course I need to tell them. You could have killed yourself doing that.' She rounded on her daughter. 'Lucy, how could you let her do something so stupid?'

Lucy went pink but said nothing. The idea that she had any control over what Maddie did was so comical that Maddie felt almost sorry for her.

'I do what I like, okay?' she said.

This was meant to sound grown-up and independent, but it must have come out slightly wrong, because Sonia suddenly gave her a hug.

'Hey. Look, you're still a bit shaky. Why don't you all come over and watch some TV at our house? I'll make you a tea with sugar in it, Maddie – it's good for shock.'

Maddie could feel the others hanging on her response. She knew that if she said something dismissive they'd follow her lead and head back to the garden with her to pick over the whole event, leaving Lucy to trail home, embarrassed, with her mum. Another Maddie victory, raising two fingers at the stupid, adult world. The adulation would make her feel better, for a while at least.

But another part of her could see the value in doing exactly what Lucy's mum had just suggested. Maddie had made the effort – and it had been one; Lucy was a total baby – to be friends with Lucy in the first place only because she knew that her mum could be useful to her. Being a successful actress was partly about who you knew, she realised that, and Sonia was the first person she'd met who might be able to get her a foothold in that world. It would be stupid to throw that away for a temporary popularity hit.

'Okay,' she said, and for the first time she gave Sonia a smile – the one that adults seemed to like when she bothered to use it on them. 'Thanks.' She could practically hear Lucy exhale with relief.

Once inside, Maddie took the mug of sugary tea and a Penguin biscuit from Sonia. She had no intention of eating the biscuit, because her own mother had told her she needed to lose weight, and she didn't really like tea, but she needed Sonia Keeble to like her and was aware she'd got off to a bad start. Maddie had told Sonia that she wanted to be an actress and Sonia hadn't made fun of her or dismissed the idea. Instead, she'd talked about how she got her break and what it was really like acting for a living.

'Is that why you moved down here? Because it's easier to find work?'

The others had drifted off and were sitting with Lucy in the living room, watching an episode of *Dawson's Creek* that Lucy had on video. Maddie could hear the theme music, but wasn't tempted to join them. She was determined not to waste this opportunity. If she could impress Sonia, she might even take her on set one day, or help her prepare for drama school.

'Partly.' Sonia was perched on a stool across the breakfast bar from Maddie. She looked a bit like an older version of Lucy: round face and the same fair hair, although Sonia's was piled up in a messy bun on top of her head. Maddie thought she would practise doing hers like that when she got home. 'It's definitely easier to find theatre work down here, because it's so much quicker to get to London. Once I split up with Lucy's father, I stopped being able to do plays for a while, but now Luce is a bit older and I can commute to London, I can start auditioning again.'

Maddie wondered why Lucy's parents had split up. It might be useful to find out – it was always good to know things about other people, especially if they were ultimately in a position to do you a favour – and she almost felt like she could ask Sonia: she was easy to talk to, not like Maddie's own mother, who always seemed to be judging her and finding her wanting. With Sonia, it was like they were two grown-ups, having a proper conversation. But she stuck to acting for the time being because she didn't want to seem too nosy about Sonia's personal life.

'What are you working on at the moment?'

Sonia pulled a face.

'I'm about to start shooting the pilot for a new sitcom. Not a very good one. Set in an employment agency. I play the secretary who's mistaken for a masseuse, or maybe it's the other way round – I need to look at the script again. Either way, hilarious consequences ensue.'

Maddie laughed. The kitchen felt safe and comforting. The radio was on low in the background – some news story about the millennium bug and how all computers were going to stop working on 1 January – and there was a huge ginger cat asleep underneath the radiator and Sainsbury's purchases spread out across the worktop, where Sonia had started unpacking them. Maddie felt at home here.

'Feeling better?' asked Sonia over the rim of her mug.

Maddie nodded.

'Much better.'

And she actually was; the shame had receded to manageable proportions again. She thought it might have more to do with Sonia herself than with climbing on the roof and the adulation of her friends. The smile she gave Sonia now was less a conscious decision and more a natural response to her warmth. 'Thanks.'

'You know,' Sonia said, 'when I was kid, a little bit younger than you, and my brother was sick, I used to run across this big six-lane A-road near my parents' house. The terror of it was the only thing that distracted me for a few minutes.'

'What was wrong with him?'

'He had leukaemia.'

There was silence apart from the radio. Maddie was so tempted to tell her – she thought about what a relief it would be to share her secret with someone else. She thought, she almost believed, Sonia might know what to do; that she would understand.

'I'm sorry about your brother,' she said, cautiously. 'Did he get better?'

Sonia shook her head.

'That's awful. I'm sorry.' She took a breath. If she was going to do it, now was the moment. She could feel Sonia's gaze on her.

There was a shriek from the other room.

'There is no way I fancy him!'

Hayley's voice, full of outrage. If she told Sonia her secret, would Sonia tell Lucy? She thought about the others knowing; she thought about what her parents would say if she told. She met Sonia's eyes for a moment, then looked away.

'I guess I'm just bored. There's not much to do in Winchester.'

Sonia was still looking at her.

'Okay, as long as that's all it is. But you have to promise me you won't do it again. It's really dangerous. If you're bored, join a drama group or something.'

'I promise,' Maddie said, wondering if she meant it. She was frightened by how close she'd got to telling Sonia what no one must ever find out.

'Oh Maddie!' Sonia said, putting down her tea and spilling some of it over the work surface. 'I've just had a great idea. My friend Tom is running a drama summer camp at the start of the holidays. I was trying to persuade Lucy to go. You'd love it. Tom's great – I was at drama school with him many moons ago. He runs this camp thing every year, but usually we're too far away for Lucy to go. Anyway, apparently the whole thing lasts five days and at the end of it you all put on a play.'

'That sounds brilliant.' Maddie was instantly hooked. This was exactly what she'd been hoping for, a chance to prove she had what it took to make it as an actress – not to mention a way to escape from home for a while.

'It's usually Shakespeare or something – something where they don't have to pay for a licence and there are loads of parts. It's mainly for fun, but the point is Tom has a contact at the National Youth Theatre so if he does see anyone he thinks is good, well, he can put in a word for them.' Maddie felt her excitement building. The National Youth Theatre was a way into professional acting, but it was famously hard to get into. 'You should all go together. You build a set and make the costumes, and do the lights – it's fun. The others would enjoy it even if they're not that into acting.'

Hayley wanted to be an actress too, but there was no way Maddie was going to tell Sonia that. Hayley could make her own contacts if she was really serious about acting, which Maddie doubted. She was pretty sure Hayley was just copying her. Sometimes it seemed like Hayley just wanted to do the things she wanted to do – like she didn't have an existence of her own.

'I gave Lucy a leaflet – I think it's in her room. Lucy!' Sonia shouted in the direction of the living room. 'Lucy! Can you go and get that thing about Tom's summer camp?'

'I will later!' came back Lucy's reply. Sonia rolled her eyes and smiled.

'Why don't you go and find it, Maddie? It'll be on her desk somewhere. Her bedroom door's just in front of you as you go up the stairs. Don't fall over anything on your way in. It's a bit of a tip I'm afraid.'

Maddie quickly jumped down from the stool and headed out into the hall. The Keebles' house was laid out exactly like her own and Lucy had the room that belonged to Maddie's brother Joe in their house. The house was still decorated in the style of the Dooleys, the old couple who used to live there, but as Maddie went up the stairs, she noticed Sonia had painted test patches of bright colours over the faded flowery wallpaper.

When Maddie returned to the kitchen after five minutes, Sonia was reaching up into the top cupboard to put away a packet of Coco Pops and Maddie was in possession of a leaflet for summer camp, and a piece of knowledge that she intended to use later if she needed it.

Chapter Eleven

Lucy scrambled out of the Volvo and thanked Maddie's dad for the lift. 'Have a great time, girls,' he said. 'Make sure you get all the star roles!'

Lucy thought Mr Blake – 'Robin to you lot' – was the perfect dad. When she'd told Maddie this the other day, Maddie had looked suddenly suspicious, as if she thought Lucy might be laughing at her, but Lucy meant every word of it. Her own dad was so uptight, whereas Maddie's was easy going and told corny jokes that were also somehow endearing – like a dad in an American TV show.

'A proper charmer, that man,' was how she'd heard Claire's mum describe him. And he was clearly proud of Maddie, whereas Lucy's own dad seemed to regard her as an inconvenience – when he remembered her at all – which was mainly just at Christmas and birthdays now he'd moved out. When her parents had first told her they were breaking up, she'd been almost relieved. Of course, they hadn't said 'breaking up' – they'd talked about 'spending a bit of time apart' – but she'd known what that meant and it didn't seem like such a bad thing. Finally, an end to the bickering that increasingly frequently ended up in a full-on shouting match. But she'd believed them when they'd said it wouldn't make any difference to how much they loved her or how often she'd see them, and that bit hadn't turned out to be true at all. Her dad still existed in the background and surfaced in an occasional phone call, but it felt like he'd vanished almost entirely from her everyday life. And although he'd not been particularly easy to live with when he was around, she missed him a lot more than she was willing to admit and felt hurt by his absence. Maddie didn't know how lucky she was with her dad – with everything really – which was true of most lucky people, she supposed. She'd once heard her mum talk about people with charmed lives, and now she'd met Maddie she felt like she knew what this meant.

She carried her rucksack over to where Maddie and Hayley were standing in the middle of the gravel drive, studying the youth hostel that was to be their home for the next week. The main building was a long red-brick farmhouse, which looked really old – it had a dip in the middle of the roof and four huge chimneys – with a large barn attached. To one side were two smaller cottages, built from grey stone. All the doors and windows on both buildings were painted the same bright turquoise, which looked a bit weird in the middle of the countryside.

'Come on, what's keeping you, Griffiths?' Maddie shouted to Claire, who was still fiddling round with her stuff in the boot of the car. Claire didn't reply; didn't even look over. She'd been quiet the whole journey down to the New Forest, and Lucy worried that it was a sign that Claire didn't want to come to summer camp at all. Maddie and Hayley both wanted to be actresses, so of course they were up for it, but Claire didn't even do drama at school. She'd been the least enthusiastic when Maddie had shown them all the flyer, but Lucy's mum had talked her round by emphasising that acting was only part of it.

If Claire didn't really want to be here, it could spoil the whole week and Lucy badly wanted this holiday to be a success. Her whole existence at school would be so much more bearable if she had friends. Especially these friends. As Claire trudged over the gravel towards them, Maddie – who looked like a model, in old red Converse high-tops, Levi's, and a dark green flowery shirt she'd bought in River Island last week – dropped her rucksack and went over to give Claire a hug.

'This is going to be so cool,' she said.

'Yeah,' Claire said, as she emerged from the hug. 'It's going to be the best.' Her cheeks were flushed and her voice sounded suddenly sparkly, so maybe Lucy had been worrying about nothing.

'We should go inside and see if Jenna's here yet,' Hayley said.

Jenna's dad was dropping her off separately. Jenna said this was because it was on the way back from her aunt's, but Maddie said in the car it was because Jenna's dad wanted to see the youth hostel for himself. Her family was really strict, apparently. Maddie and Hayley had gossiped about it for quite a long time, saying how Jenna should stand up to them more. Claire, sitting in the front, stared out of the window and said nothing, and Lucy, in the back, squashed between Maddie and Hayley, also kept quiet, not confident enough to join in yet.

Now, standing in the courtyard with the others, she felt a wave of hope that summer camp was not going to be a disaster – that she might have finally found the group of real friends she'd longed for since they moved down here.

Just as she was thinking this, a man's voice rang out from over by the main farmhouse. 'Hiya Lucy Goosey!'

She felt her stomach muscles contract in horror at this greeting. The man walking towards them was really old – about thirty-five – but was one of those adults who thought he was still a teenager. He was wearing a *Simpsons* t-shirt and cut-off denim shorts. She didn't recognise him, but he must be Tom – her mum's friend who was running the summer camp.

'Fantastic to see you! It's been a while, but I'd recognise you anywhere. You were a chubby baby too. Such cute podgy cheeks and that great smile.' Lucy felt like she might never smile again, but Tom was ploughing on. 'Your mum and I go way back. I changed your nappy backstage at the Traverse.' When it was clear Lucy was incapable of saying anything, Tom added, enthusiasm only slightly diminished: 'And these must be your friends. Hiya guys!'

Maddie's dad, who'd been lurking at the top of the driveway, waiting for some sensible adult figure to emerge, decided against all indications to the contrary that Tom was it and shouted 'Cheerio all!' out of his window as he drove off in a cloud of dust.

Maddie barely gave him a second glance. She was already introducing herself to Tom, giving him a really big smile, and telling him how much she was looking forward to the week. Lucy's mum had said that Tom could help Maddie and Hayley get into that National Youth Theatre thing, which was apparently a great way of becoming a professional actor. Judging by the past few minutes, Lucy thought it was unlikely that Tom would be able to help you get into the back seat of a car, so she hoped her mum knew what she was talking about.

'Fantastic,' he was saying now, ticking off their names on a battered clipboard. 'Well, today's all about settling in.' He ran his hand through his hair, which was either greasy or contained too much hair gel. 'I think Lorraine's put you all in the same room, as you're friends already.' Lucy felt her heart sing at the idea of them all being friends already and some of her earlier optimism returned. 'It's actually more of an apartment. In the cottage over there. You've even got a little kitchen area to hang out in. No actual cooking required though!'

Maddie laughed as though Tom had made the funniest joke ever. They had started to follow him towards the cottage, when the roar of a motorbike made them all stop and turn. A leather-clad biker appeared around the corner of the drive, going too fast.

'Who's that?' Hayley asked. 'Is he part of the summer camp?'

The motorbike skidded to a halt in front of them. The biker turned off the ignition and removed his helmet. He looked a bit like Leonardo DiCaprio – dark blond floppy hair, bushy eyebrows and pouty lips. He ignored Lucy entirely, and she watched as his eyes slid over Claire, then remained for a while on Hayley, before moving on to Maddie.

'Sam here is our technician. What can I do for you, Sam?' Tom asked. He sounded a bit impatient. Maybe he'd also noticed Sam's gaze.

'I managed to get hold of my mate with the van. He's free this evening so I can drop the lights off then. I thought I'd clear a space in the side room.'

'Okay, I'll come and help you. I just need to get these guys settled. And I'll have to keep an ear out for any new arrivals. Lorraine's taken the car to the station to pick up another group.'

'Oh shit!' said Maddie, suddenly, and Lucy turned and saw a black shape bounding across the gravel towards them from the direction of the main farmhouse. Her heart skipped a beat. She already knew that Maddie, who was scared of almost nothing, was freaked out by dogs – especially ones that jumped up at her. A few weeks ago, on the walk back from school, she'd made them all cross the road to avoid a woman with a big grey dog that Maddie said was out of control. Lucy tried to stop this one before it could get to Maddie, but it darted out of her way, barking at her. She saw the others' worried faces. Claire and Sam tried to grab it too, but the dog just thought it was part of the game and bounded off, making a beeline for the one person who was terrified of it. To Lucy's surprise, it was Tom who finally grabbed the dog's collar, averting disaster. She hadn't realised he was capable of anything so effective.

'Don't worry. His bark is worse than his bite,' Tom said. And then seeing Maddie's face, 'Hey, I'm sorry. Are you really scared?'

'I just don't like dogs that much,' Maddie said, attempting to sound casual.

'I'll make sure he doesn't bother you again. He belongs to one of the ladies who works on reception, but he's not normally allowed to wander round. Sam, can you take him back to the office and make sure the door's shut.'

Sam, eyes on Maddie again, reluctantly took the dog from Tom and led it back towards the main building.

'Come with me then guys, and we'll get you settled,' Tom said, shepherding them towards the nearest of the cottages.

'Lorraine's in the cottage next door so if you have any problems in the night you can just knock. I'm in the main farmhouse with the others. I'll leave you guys to unpack and sort out your stuff and then we've got our first briefing in the barn at two o'clock, so I'll see you all there.'

It didn't take them long to explore. There was just a small kitchen and a bathroom downstairs, and a bedroom with six bunk beds upstairs. The others claimed the top bunks, and then lay on their backs talking. Maddie seemed to have recovered from the moment outside with the dog, and was back to her usual confident self. Lucy was looking through her rucksack for her new stripy top from Tammy Girl, worried that she'd left it behind.

'Hey Lucy Goosey,' Hayley said. 'Chuck me up my ciggies, will you?'

'Leave her alone, Hayley,' Claire said easily. 'And you can't smoke in here anyway.'

Lucy wanted to hug her, but managed to carry on sorting through her things, like she hadn't even heard the exchange.

'Sorry I breathed,' Hayley said, not sounding sorry at all. 'So... do we think Tom and the mysterious Lorraine are a thing?'

'If they were,' Maddie said, 'why would she be sleeping in the cottage when he's in the main house?'

'I don't know, but it's kind of weird that he spelt out their sleeping arrangements, don't you think?' Hayley was playing with her lighter, flicking it on and off. 'Anyway, he certainly seems to like you, Maddie. He was very keen to protect you just now.'

'He was just being nice.'

'Way too nice if you ask me.'

Chapter Twelve

'Okay. Guys! Settle down now!' Tom was standing at the front of the barn, struggling to make himself heard above the excited chatter of the group of teenagers sitting on the rows of orange plastic chairs awaiting their first briefing. Lucy noticed with satisfaction that his face was going increasingly pink with the effort. 'Guys!' he tried again, ineffectually.

'Quiet please!' said a different voice from behind them. It was a deep, confident tone and it resulted in almost instant silence. Lucy, like everyone else, turned to see who had spoken. As soon as she saw Lorraine Caxton standing in the doorway it became clear how the summer camp managed to function each year and it was nothing to do with Tom. And neither was Lorraine, despite Hayley's earlier theory. There was no way they were a thing.

Lorraine was tall and even older than Tom: maybe about forty-five. She had short dark hair, streaked with grey, and red lips, and she was wearing bright blue high-waisted trousers. There was something about her that grabbed your attention – and held it. Lucy already knew from her mum that Lorraine was the real deal. She'd won some big acting prize and she'd done all the things Lucy knew that her mum longed to do, like act with the Royal

73

Shakespeare Company and perform on Broadway. But Lucy still hadn't expected to find herself quite so mesmerised when she met Lorraine in person. Judging by the way everyone was watching Lorraine's progress to the front of the barn, she wasn't the only one. It was like the group was collectively holding its breath. And Maddie, who was sitting on the plastic chair next to her, was practically squirming with excitement. Lucy felt a surge of gratitude to her mum for suggesting this idea in the first place; Maddie already seemed to be loving it and this surely meant she'd appreciate Lucy and want to be her friend.

'Welcome everyone,' Lorraine said, in her deep voice. 'I hope you're all looking forward to this week as much as I am. Now, do we have everyone here?'

'We surely do — I counted twenty keen-bean actors,' Tom said. Which just went to show that he wasn't even any good at counting, because Lucy knew for a fact that at least one person was missing. The others had thought it would be funny to change the time on Hayley's watch when she'd been having a shower earlier and she'd headed off for a quick cigarette before the briefing started without realising that she was fifteen minutes behind everyone else. Lucy thought it was a bit mean to make her late; Hayley was going to make a bad impression and, after all, she wanted to be an actress too, or she said she did. Perhaps that was the way the group worked, though, and this trick was a way of signalling that acting was Maddie's thing and Hayley should back off — or maybe Lucy was overthinking it. Anyway, she wasn't brave enough to object and Hayley was still calling her Lucy Goosey so she didn't really feel inclined to help her out. As she glanced down the row now, she saw Claire, who was sitting on the other side of Maddie, nudge her and grin.

'Let me start by telling you a bit about how the summer camp works. Here, we do something extraordinary.' Lorraine sounded every syllable in the word 'extraordinary'. 'We put on a play in just five days. And the only way we can do that is if everyone here works as part of a team.'

'Teamwork makes the dream work!' Tom added. 'And as it happens, making the dream work is what it's all about this year, because, guess what guys? Guess what this year's play is!' He beamed encouragingly at them all, but he was greeted by confused faces and the kind of silence that he'd presumably been hoping for earlier when he was telling them to settle down. 'Come on guys! I've given you the clue.'

'This year's production will be *A Midsummer Night's Dream*,' Lorraine said, putting Tom out of his misery.

Maddie's face broke into a big smile, so Lucy supposed this must also be good news. She didn't really care what play they were performing but she wanted Maddie to be happy.

'Yes indeed – and you guys, guess what, you're the ultimate Dream Team!' This time Tom's zeal was greeted by a murmur of anticipation running round the group of teenagers, although Lucy thought it had more to do with collective enthusiasm for the reality of putting on a play than his lame pun. 'And it's going to be the best fun!'

'It's also going to be a lot of work,' Lorraine said. 'So although we want you all to have a good time, we also need you to be one hundred per cent committed. And we need you to stick to the rules – there's not many of them but they're important. No alcohol, no smoking, everyone to be in their rooms by nine p.m. and absolutely no one leaves the grounds without permission. Do I make myself clear?' Collective nodding.

'I wouldn't want to leave the grounds,' Jenna whispered. 'There is the creepiest house just down the road. We drove past it on the way here.'

'Quiet please,' Lorraine said. 'Now, in a minute I'm going to hand over to Tom to run through the different parts. There should be twenty of us,' Lucy noticed her choice of words and wondered if she'd already noticed someone was missing, 'but it's a big play so there's a role for everyone. I know some of you won't want the lead roles and that's fine, you can just let us know. Over the next five days, you're all going to be involved in everything that's necessary to put on a successful play. Now, we have our lighting technician with us this afternoon in the form of Sam.' Lorraine gestured elegantly towards the back of the hall, and a series of teenage heads turned to look where she was pointing. Sam must have come in while Lorraine was talking. As they turned, he raised his hand and grinned at them all. Lorraine was talking about the sound desk now but quite a few pairs of eyes remained locked on Sam. Lucy could appreciate the fascination without sharing it. He really did look a bit like Leonardo DiCaprio, but he also looked like he knew it. Lorraine coughed and heads snapped back towards her and Tom.

'Does anyone happen to know where the *Dream* is set?' Tom asked.

Lucy practically felt the wind rush past her face as Maddie's hand shot up. She registered the different dynamic that applied here. At school, it was never a good idea to be the first person to answer a question, but in this place it obviously no longer mattered if you looked keen.

'Oh fantastic! Yes, Maddie?'

'Athens. In Ancient Greece.'

'Spot on!'

As Tom described his vision for re-creating Ancient Greece, Lucy took a moment to study the other people in the hall. She'd been so focused on Maddie, and making sure she was having a good time, that she hadn't allowed herself time to even notice the others. She knew that the summer camp was for young people aged eleven to sixteen, but looking around she guessed that she herself was probably one of the youngest there. In addition to her group, she counted nine girls and six boys, and from the slightly uneasy way in which people were occasionally exchanging glances with their neighbours, she guessed most of them didn't know each other already. She felt a ridiculous rush of pride that she was here with a group of friends – although even as she thought it, she was conscious that her position in this new group was far from secure. She suddenly found herself wanting to do something to make it clear to the other kids that she was with Maddie – whispering to her or something – but Maddie was talking again.

'You said we could let you know if we wanted a small part, but is it okay if we also let you know if we're interested in one of the bigger roles?'

It seemed they'd moved on to questions. Again the change from school was apparent. Maddie was proving that it was fine to be enthusiastic, and although Lucy could never have brought herself to ask this particular question, even supposing she'd wanted one of the main parts, from Maddie it sounded simply right.

'Of course, Maddie. It's great that you're so keen.'

'I'm interested in acting. Professionally,' she added, shyly.

'Fantastic!' Tom beamed at her.

Before they could get any further with questions, there was a disruption at the back of the hall, where someone appeared to be trying to enter but was unable to open the door. Sam went over to help. A figure with long blonde hair wearing a tie-dye skirt slipped in. Lucy noticed her exchange a glance and then a smile with Sam.

'Come in,' Lorraine said from the front of the barn. 'And you are…?'

'Hayley.'

'You're late, Hayley. We started at two.'

'I know.' Hayley, meeting Lorraine Caxton's gaze for the first time, and feeling the full force of her personality, visibly wilted. 'I'm sorry.' Lucy glanced at the others. They were all watching her. Maddie was smirking ever so slightly. Lucy wondered if Hayley would say anything about her watch. She must have realised by now what had gone wrong. 'I got a bit lost.'

'Well not to worry now. But please do try to be on time in future. We haven't got long and we have a great deal to do, so we can't afford to waste even a few minutes. Sit now please.'

Hayley nodded and scurried towards the empty seat that had been left for her at the end of the row, next to Claire. Someone else put their hand up to ask a question and as Lorraine's and everyone else's attention transferred elsewhere, Lucy saw Hayley mouth 'You bitches,' at the others, who were grinning at her. Lucy felt the collective excitement of being part of the prank, of belonging, and tried to join in the silent laughter, but the whole thing left her feeling more than a little uneasy. A world in which friends played fun tricks on one another was all very well in theory – it was the kind of thing she lapped up in books

– but she wasn't at all sure she liked it in practice. After all, it meant it could happen to you at any point. And you might not find the trick fun at all.

Chapter Thirteen

Maddie, 1999

'Have you heard the whole story?' Sam said. It was later the same evening and the six of them were sitting on the grass behind the cottage, talking as the sun went down. Sam had been there at dinner and afterwards he'd hung around when she and the others had drifted outside. 'It's really fucked up. That creepy house you saw just up the road, Jenna?' He used the name easily, like he'd known them all for years. 'It used to belong to this bloke called Edward Duval. He was this big film star. Like the Brad Pitt of his day or something. This was way back in the 1920s.'

Maddie felt her interest quicken at the mention of old movies. She loved anything to do with the golden age of Hollywood. Her grandmother, who had a massive collection of VHS tapes, had introduced her to *Bringing Up Baby* when she'd stayed with her for her tenth birthday and she'd been hooked ever since. *The Philadelphia Story* was her favourite and she could recite pretty much every one of Tracy Lord's lines. She'd never heard of Edward Duval, though.

'He had huge parties at the house,' Sam was saying. 'Sex, drink, drugs, everything.'

'What films was he in?' Maddie asked.

'I don't know. Old ones I guess. Anyway, that's not the point. One day he invited some girls from the village to come along too. They were only kids really – not much older than you.'

'Hey,' Hayley said. 'How old do you think we are?'

'She looks about twelve,' Sam said, nodding at Lucy opposite him.

'Yeah, well she's a lot younger than us okay.'

As if to emphasise her point, Hayley removed a packet of cigarettes from her army surplus shirt, and made a show of offering them round. She already seemed to have forgiven them all for the prank with the watch earlier – one of the best things about Hayley was that she never held a grudge for very long. Sam took a cigarette and she lit it for him, her face close to his. It was obvious that Hayley liked Sam, and Maddie hadn't made up her mind what to do about this yet. In a way, it was fine because Maddie already had Amari and anyway Sam wasn't really her type; he was all cheekbones and blond hair, whereas she liked dark, muscular guys. But something about the concentrated gaze Sam kept fixing on her made her think he liked her, and this gave her a rush of the adrenaline that she found herself craving more and more at the moment. She probably wasn't going to do anything about it. Hayley was welcome to him, if she could get his attention. She was interested in finding out more about Edward Duval though.

'Go on with the story, Sam,' she said.

'So one day this Duval bloke was planning this big fuck-off party and, like I said, he invited some of the girls from the village. There was one really pretty one. Gladys, her name was. Duval really liked her. He was used to all these beautiful film stars and stuff, but she was something else.'

Sam took a swig from the bottle of White Lightning they were passing round, and handed it to her, his fingers brushing against her hand. They definitely lingered a little longer than they needed to, his touch warm on her skin. She passed the bottle on to Jenna. Even the fact the others were drinking didn't bother her tonight; she wanted to hear more about Edward Duval's parties.

'Duval gave her champagne, let her swim in his pool, and she was flattered because he was this big star. Gradually all the other guests started to leave, but he wanted her to stay.' Sam turned to look at her. 'He wanted to fuck her.'

She nodded, as though she was so used to fucking it bored her. She still hadn't had sex with Amari, or in fact anyone, despite what she'd let the others think. Recently she kind of thought she might be ready, but Amari said there was no hurry and maybe they should wait until she was sixteen. A bit of her was secretly relieved, so maybe she wasn't as ready as she thought.

Sam took a long drag on his cigarette and continued. 'Anyway, she's got other ideas – Gladys. She has a boyfriend and everything. Trouble is, he's not used to girls who say no, and he accuses her of being a cock-tease. Why has she stayed behind if she doesn't want to have sex with him? She fights him off and in the struggle, he smashes her face against the edge of the pool and cracks her skull open. Then he watches as she bleeds to death, right there on the edge of the swimming pool.'

'Oh my god,' Lucy said, her round face frightened in the gathering darkness.

'It's all right, Lucy – it's just a story,' Claire said. 'And not a very nice one.'

'It's not a story,' Sam said. 'Edward Duval was a real person – look him up. It all happened just like I said, and that's not the worst of it.'

As if on cue, an owl hooted somewhere in the woods at the far side of the field. Almost all the daylight had gone now. Sam had brought a torch from his van, but he hadn't turned it on yet.

'Do you want to know the rest?' he asked.

'Tell us,' Hayley said. 'Please Sam.'

'Are you sure it's not going to freak you out? It's not a "nice" story.'

'I think we'll cope,' Claire said.

'So, this Gladys girl – she's dead, yeah? Edward Duval has killed her, and he hides her body in a place where no one will ever find it, but everyone knows he's done it because there's blood everywhere. Even the water in the pool is red.'

Maddie knew this was bullshit. Blood couldn't turn a whole pool red, but almost in spite of herself, the image floated into her mind of a rectangle of scarlet water.

'But the cops can't prove it because they haven't got the body so they have to let him go. So he goes on living in this big old house, thinking he's safe. Thinking he's got away with it. But Gladys hasn't forgotten, and she wants revenge. He took her life away and now she's going to take his. She's just waiting for the right time.

'One night, he wakes to find her standing at the foot of his bed, with her back to him. She's wearing the same party dress from that night by the pool. He calls out her name, and, slowly, she turns round to face him, and when she does, he can see that her face is missing where he smashed it against the tiles. It's just blood and bones and

83

an eye. He screams so loudly that they can hear him for miles. It's the last noise he ever makes.

'Now Gladys's ghost haunts the house at Poison Cross and if you're unlucky enough to see it, it will turn slowly towards you and then you'll realise. Where its face should be, there's just a mess of blood and bone.'

Sam suddenly flicked his torch on underneath his face, so it was all shadows and eyes. Hayley screamed and Maddie herself only just stifled a cry of surprise.

'Christ, Hayley, can you keep it down?' Claire snapped.

'He scared the shit out of me.'

Sam was laughing now, and so was Lucy, or was she crying? Hayley pushed Sam away from her and he laughed again.

'Sorry,' he said. 'I didn't know you'd do that.'

'What happened to Edward Duval?' Maddie asked.

'He died. The ghost killed him.'

'But in real life?'

'What are you all doing out here?'

Shit. Lorraine Caxton. They'd all been so focused on Sam they hadn't heard her coming round the side of the cottages. If it had been Tom instead, they'd have been fine. Maddie would have known how to get him back on side. He might even have sat down with them and had a smoke. But Lorraine was a different matter entirely.

'Well? Cat got your tongues?' she was saying now in her rich, expressive voice. Maddie still couldn't quite believe that someone as successful as Lorraine Caxton was their tutor.

'Sam, what are you still doing here?'

'Sorry.' Sam sounded subdued. 'Just thought I'd have a chat with the girls, you know?'

'Yes, Sam, I know.'

Sam scrambled awkwardly to his feet.

'I guess I'll be on my way, then.'

'At once, please. And Sam?'

'Yes?'

'The bulb in one of those Fresnels you brought isn't working. Can you replace it please?'

'Yes, no problem.'

'Thank you. And if I catch you here again after dinner, we'll find another lighting technician. Clear?'

Sam nodded and didn't wait around.

'Well? What have the rest of you got to say for yourselves? I've half a mind to send you all home now.'

Maddie felt a rush of panic. This week could be her big chance; she couldn't bear the thought it might be over before it had even begun. She needed to win Lorraine over.

'Please don't,' she said quickly, getting to her feet. 'I really want to be here. We all do.'

The others got up too, taking her lead as usual.

'We were only talking,' Jenna said, finding her voice now that Maddie had.

'So the cider and cigarettes belong to someone else?'

'We were mainly talking,' Lucy said, her slurred voice suggesting otherwise. Maddie wondered how much cider she'd drunk. She wished Lucy would shut up and let her handle this.

'Let me make this quite clear. You're children – like it or not – and you're in our care. This is a summer camp and it's meant to be fun, but you have to stick by the rules. The rules say you have to be in your bedrooms by nine o'clock, remember? And no alcohol or cigarettes.'

'We're really sorry,' Maddie said. She was pretty sure it was too dark for Lorraine to be able to see much of her face, but she tried to make her voice just the right blend of contrite and deferential.

'Really sorry,' Hayley echoed.

'I'm surprised at you, Maddie. I thought you said you wanted to be a professional actress.'

'I do.'

'Well then, do me the courtesy of taking this week seriously. You'd be fired on the spot if you behaved like this in a professional theatre.'

In the distance they could hear the roar of Sam's bike as it took off down the drive.

'Has Sam been telling you about the haunted house?'

They exchanged uneasy glances.

'Yes,' Claire said. 'He told us a story.'

'I bet he did,' Lorraine said grimly. 'Well, you're to take no notice. It's a lot of nonsense.'

'But the house did belong to Edward Duval?' Maddie couldn't resist asking.

'Right, beds. Now.'

They bent down and picked their possessions up off the damp grass. Lorraine walked them to the door of their cottage, like she didn't trust them to go by themselves. Maddie couldn't really blame her.

'One final thing. None of you are to go near the house at Poison Cross.'

'Because of the ghost?' Lucy asked.

'No, Lucy. Because it's falling down. If I find out that any of you have been in there, you'll be out of here faster than Sam on that bloody bike of his. Clear? That place is a death trap.'

Chapter Fourteen

Maddie, 1999

'It's not bad at all,' Tom said. 'But you need to take it more slowly. You're gabbling it and I'm losing some of the individual words. Try the opening again. Let the rhythm of the lines guide you.'

Maddie frowned at her script for *A Midsummer Night's Dream*, trying to work out what Tom meant about the rhythm guiding her. She needed him to think that she was a good actress. If she made the right impression, he might recommend her to the National Youth Theatre. That's why she'd asked if he'd stay behind after the rehearsal and run through her big speech. It was their first full day at the summer camp and she was determined to make the most of it. After last night's run-in with Lorraine, she needed to demonstrate how serious she was about this. She took a deep breath, and started again.

'Call you me fair? That fair again unsay.

'Demetrius loves your fair: oh happy fair!'

She thought she was doing okay, but Tom interrupted her almost straight away.

'You're still not getting the rhythm of it. You know what iambic pentameter is, yes?'

He was sitting on one of the orange plastic chairs they'd been using in the rehearsal. The others had all been stacked to one side, against the wall.

'I think so. Unstressed and then stressed.'

'Yes, right. So De-Dah De-Dah De-Dah. Call *you* me *fair*. That *fair* ag*ain* un*say*. Each line has five beats.' He sprang up and stood opposite her. 'Let's try a breathing exercise before you do it again. Put one of your hands on your chest. Here.' Tom demonstrated on himself. He wasn't actually that bad looking. Quite tall, with an oval face and a pointy chin. A bit like a Z-list Keanu Reeves. Really old of course – nearly as old as her parents – but he dressed younger. Today he was wearing Wranglers and a Guns N' Roses t-shirt. 'And the other one just below your ribcage. Now, deep breath in. And out. Can you feel your chest expanding to allow the air in?'

'A little bit.'

'I think you need to move the hand on your chest up a bit.'

He reached out. And then he hesitated. She smiled at him.

'Can you show me?'

He took a step towards her, re-positioned her hand a little further up her chest, just where her vest top finished and her skin began. Then he stepped backwards abruptly.

'Thanks Tom.'

'Okay. Now breathe in. And out. Feel it now?'

'Yes.'

'Okay good.' He went back to sit in the chair and she wondered if she'd imagined his hesitation just now. 'Keep your hands there and do the speech again. Focus on your breathing and the rhythm of the lines will start to take care of itself.'

Maddie did the whole speech.

'Better. Much better. Can you feel the difference?'

'I think so, yes. It's really kind of you to help me. I know I'm keeping you from your lunch.'

'At the briefing yesterday, you mentioned that you want to be a professional actress.'

'Do you think I could?'

She really cared what the answer was. He turned away from her to pick up the chair and stack it to one side with the others.

'I think someone as beautiful and talented as you could do anything you put your mind to, Maddie,' he said with his back to her, and she felt a surge of validation. 'But it's a competitive old world out there. You need to be willing to go the extra mile.'

'I am.'

He walked back over to her.

'Good. Because I think you have what it takes to make it.'

His words gave her a rush of pure happiness.

'Wow. Thank you.'

He was standing right in front of her, his eyes locked on hers. There was a pause.

'Do you want me to show you again where your hand goes?'

It was her turn to hesitate. Up until now she'd felt in control of the situation, but suddenly she wasn't so sure. In the end, the hesitation was enough; he didn't wait for a reply. He took her left hand, which was by her side, in his. Slowly he raised it to her chest, but this time he kept his hand over hers. His hand was cold and slightly clammy. His fingers were brushing her breastbone. He took a step closer to her. His face was so close to hers she could smell oniony crisps on his breath. The door creaked open a fraction and instantly Tom released her and stepped away.

'Is there someone out there?' he called. 'Come in! We're just finishing up.'

His manner was casual; his voice, if possible, even more cheerful than usual. When no one replied, he went over to collect his notebook from the table he'd been using during the rehearsal.

'This building really creeps me out. It's full of strange noises.' He smiled at her. 'Everything okay Maddie?'

She nodded. Picked up her rucksack from the corner of the room.

'We can do this again, you know.' Tom ran his hand through his hair. 'Work on your long speeches I mean. And maybe get to know each other a bit better. Would you like that?'

'Sure,' she heard herself say.

'You're a star.'

'I'm going to get some lunch.' Her heart was racing, but it was okay. Nothing had actually happened after all. All she had to do was keep control of this situation for another four days.

Chapter Fifteen

Lucy, Present

'Ruby! Lucy! What a lovely surprise!'

Not that much of a surprise because I'd phoned to tell her I'd be dropping by. But with my mother-in-law, whose diary is not only organised by the hour, but colour coded, two hours' notice is still a spontaneous visit.

I managed to tell the others about the second text before we left Hayley's house yesterday and Claire says she has a plan for what we should do next, but she refuses to tell me what it is yet. She says she has the day off tomorrow and hopefully we can put it into action then. She's being very mysterious, but she says she'll call me later and explain.

I'm never very good at waiting at the best of times, so I've decided to do something else she suggested and try to find out if Naomi and Robin have had any anonymous messages too. Doing something is helping me to keep a lid on the sense of panic that threatens to overwhelm me every time I think about the two texts. Doing something is keeping me sane – just about.

'High five!' Naomi says, holding up a beautifully mani-cured hand.

Ruby lifts a sticky hand to meet it. She only learnt to do this a few weeks ago and she and Naomi are both beaming with delight at her newfound talent. I shift Ruby on my hip; she's getting so much heavier now. Naomi holds out her hands to take her from me and I gratefully hand her over. Naomi looks stunning as usual. She's seventy-three – we all went out for her birthday dinner about a month ago – but you'd think she's at least a decade younger. She has smooth ivory skin, her black hair has been dyed and expertly cut into a long bob, and she dresses like a model from one of the style supplements in the Sunday papers. The kind of trauma that Naomi and Robin have suffered is supposed to leave its mark on you physically, and in Robin I think I can see it in the strain lines around his eyes and the way his face sometimes twitches for no reason at all, but no one looking at Naomi would know that she had suffered every parent's darkest nightmare.

'Do you understand now?' She'd asked me this the second time she met Ruby, and the two of us were alone in the living room with Ruby in her Moses basket while Robin and Joe were in the kitchen. 'Do you understand now what it feels like?'

I'd known what she meant, even though I pretended not to at first to give myself time to think. *Do you understand now what it feels like to lose a child?* Did I feel differently about Maddie's disappearance now I had Ruby? Did I understand its impact in some kind of heightened way, or at least its impact on Maddie's mother? I'd certainly delayed having children for years. Joe had wanted kids right from the early days of our marriage, but I'd put him off, casually at first, and then more insistently, because the idea of having children of our own was like a knot of panic in my gut. I'd seen at first-hand what could happen; the terrible things that could happen to children.

The honest answer was, I think, that I'd understood all along. I didn't need a child of my own to imagine what Naomi and Robin had gone through – and were still going through. I'd always known. So instead of answering I took her hand between mine and just held it, and the tears spilled down her powdered face and I realised that I was crying too.

Naomi might not look damaged but, as Claire once said, she's like a beautifully wrapped parcel that's smashed to smithereens inside. She organises in the same way that other people breathe – it's like she hopes that if she plans every moment of every day, and keeps every item in its place, she can eliminate any possibility of the unpredictable, because she's had a brush with the unpredictable before and she never, ever wants to give it a chance to get her again. Last time we came over for lunch, Robin had put the tomato knife in the slot in the knife block that's reserved for the onion knife and all hell broke loose. Joe and I laughed about it on the drive home, but it's a guilty, anxious kind of humour because we know we're trying to make light of something that's profoundly wrong.

Right now Ruby is clutching onto the pale pink shirt that Naomi is wearing, her hands covered in the cheese that I fed her to keep her quiet on the car journey. One of the things I love about Naomi is that she doesn't mind about this at all. The shirt is flawless and quite probably very expensive, but all she cares about is Ruby.

'Come through,' she says, stepping back. 'Don't hover on the doorstep.'

I follow her down the familiar hallway, with its warm polished parquet flooring and duck-egg blue walls, into the living room, which is like a pale gold cocoon. The coffee is all set out on the low glass table, as I knew it would be. I'd said half eleven and, although my time-keeping is usually pretty bad, I would never be late for Naomi. She wouldn't be able to cope with it.

'Tell me your news,' she says now. 'Can you plunge the cafetiere? I thought you wouldn't want a biscuit.'

Naomi always thinks I'm trying to lose weight, even though I've never given her any reason to believe I'm on a diet. I'm a size fourteen and for Naomi that is reason enough. Joe and I talked about it the other day and agreed we'd need to watch what she said about food around Ruby; I don't want her growing up obsessed with her weight. Watching the pair of them now though, it seems impossible that Naomi could ever cause Ruby any harm; she adores her so absolutely.

'Oh, look at her little teeth! Aren't you grown up, sweetheart? She's got another one coming through at the bottom. Is she still chewing on everything she can lay her hands on?'

As if in response, Ruby grabs the cameo on a chain round Naomi's neck and shoves it in her mouth.

'She was trying to eat my car keys this morning.'

I pour the coffee: black for Naomi, a glug of milk for me, and a spoonful of sugar to make up for the lack of biscuit, although I'm sure the sugar is intended to be purely decorative.

'Give it to me, my darling.' Naomi expertly extricates her jewellery. 'You might swallow it.' She turns to me. 'How's she doing with solids, Lucy?'

'She goes crazy for Ready Brek, but I'm not sure that really counts as a solid. Oh and Joe gave her a tiny bit of chicken curry last week and she loved that.'

'Goodness, you're much more adventurous than in my day.'

This is my opening surely. I need some way of talking to Naomi about Maddie – some way of finding out if she's had any messages too – and at least the reminder that Naomi is a parent too is a way in. How hard would it be to ask what Maddie and Joe liked eating? Incredibly difficult, obviously. But possible surely.

I've hesitated too long though, because now Ruby has grabbed hold of Naomi's hair and she gives a yelp of pain in spite of herself, and the moment has passed. I extricate her. 'Poor grandma.'

'I've got some rusks in the kitchen. Do you think she'd like one?'

At least somebody gets biscuits. Naomi heads out to the kitchen, still holding Ruby. I glance up at the mantelpiece and, like every time, my heart skips a beat – there are all the usual family photos, but it's as though cameras ceased to exist a quarter of a century ago. I know all of these pictures off by heart. It starts with the one of Joe as a baby, waving a sock beside his ear as if it's an early mobile phone; then Maddie aged about eighteen months, as tall as Big Ben in the model village they're visiting; she's wearing a bright red pinafore dress and smiling straight into the lens, already confident of her place in the world. Next is a group shot of the four of them, Naomi seated and wearing a pale purple paisley dress that makes her look like a Laura Ashley model, Robin in an eye-watering patterned tie, his hand on her shoulder, and the two children, Joe a head taller, sitting cross-legged on the floor; then Maddie in school uniform in her first year at St Peter's, almost recognisable as the Maddie I knew four years later. Then, the whole family on holiday in Spain two years after that, Joe a shy handsome teenager, Maddie all legs and trademark ponytail, Naomi and Robin with their arms round each other. Finally, at the very end, the only sign that it is no longer the 1990s – a photo of Ruby playing in Hayley's garden. It's one of my favourite pictures of her. Hayley took it and sent it to me later saying *Bet even you're tempted to post this one! Xxxx*

And I was. Ruby is wearing the blue dungarees that still, in this supposedly gender-neutral world, make everyone think she's a boy and a stripy top, and she's reaching out in delight for Doogie, who was just out of shot, and the sun is bathing her in light. It makes my heart swell every time I see it. How could I not have wanted children? How could I have ever imagined anything bad could come of this?

For the first time I wonder, if Maddie really were alive, would she look like Naomi in that formal group shot? As a child she never really looked much like her mother, but maybe that would have changed as she aged. It is strange to think that she'd be older now than Naomi was when that family shot was taken. Our parents got on with their lives in a way that my generation seems unwilling to do. In fact, Maddie would have been forty this year. Is this why she's suddenly got back in touch – this milestone birthday? I want to physically shake myself, like a dog shaking off water. It's not her. It's someone messing with my mind. *You must pay for what you did*. It's almost certainly not her. Naomi is asking me about work now, while Ruby sucks contentedly on an old-school rusk.

'Joe says you're writing a book about Hollywood?'

Naomi has no way of knowing how little I want to discuss this particular topic. She knows nothing of Edward Duval and the link with Maddie's disappearance.

'Yes, for this uber-successful film producer lady who puts the fear of God into me.'

'You surprise me, Lucy. I didn't think you were scared of anyone.'

Which shows that Naomi doesn't know me as well as she thinks.

'She's so sleek and perfect, she makes me feel inadequate.'

Mind you, Naomi is sleek and perfect too, so she's not going to understand this. And suddenly I wonder, if Maddie was alive, would she look like Harriet? How old is Harriet anyway? I'd been assuming mid-forties, but she could definitely be a bit younger. The thought almost literally knocks the breath out of me, but I dismiss it at once. Harriet Holland is a person. An established person. I looked her up when she first got in touch with me. She has a career in films spanning more than a decade and before that she was a producer at ITV for years. But then it hits me: Maddie's been gone for twenty-five years. If she is still alive, she'll be a person too. She could have done anything with that time; she could be anyone. Can it really be a coincidence that Harriet has appeared in my life asking about Edward Duval at exactly the same time that someone has started sending me messages about Maddie's disappearance? I'd had an irrational fear that there was some kind of supernatural connection – that Duval was somehow cursed – but maybe there is a more prosaic explanation.

'Lucy? Are you all right? You've gone as white as a sheet all of a sudden.'

'I've been getting these strange text messages,' I hear myself say.

'Strange?' There's instantly a note of tension in Naomi's voice – it's only ever just under the surface. But I don't get the sense that she's frightened because she's had strange

97

messages too; more that she's frightened in the same way that she always is, because she knows what there is in life to be frightened of. I feel almost as bad as when Joe found me in the kitchen the other night and he thought something terrible had happened. Something new and terrible. Although perhaps, I think with the rising sense of panic that keeps threatening to overwhelm me ever since the arrival of the first message, perhaps it has.

'I don't think they're meant for me,' I say, trying to sound reassuring. 'They don't really make much sense.'

'What do they say?'

'Something about where was I and why didn't I come back.'

'Why didn't you come back?' echoes Naomi, and somehow from her mouth the words seem invested with a fresh meaning that makes me squirm.

'It doesn't make any sense,' I say again. I didn't even mean to say that much. But it's too late, because now Naomi is asking:

'Do you think… it could have anything to do with—'

'Oh god no,' I say. Joe told me once that he thought his dad started to believe Maddie was dead very quickly – when she didn't come back in that first week, it was like he gave up hope, although it didn't stop him putting up posters and taking part in the media appeals to find her. For Joe himself, it took longer. During the first few years, he held onto his own hope, but as the birthdays and Christmases passed and there was never any news, that hope gradually ebbed away and eventually he realised that he no longer believed he would see his sister again. He thought about holding some kind of memorial for her – some way of saying goodbye finally. But in the end, he abandoned the idea because he knew that his mum wouldn't be able to bear it — that she didn't want to say goodbye finally, that she still couldn't bring herself to believe that Maddie was truly lost to her forever. It took Naomi decades to come to some acceptance that Maddie was probably dead – if acceptance is the right word for the precarious kind of resignation Naomi seems to feel – and now, here I am, however tentatively, holding out, if not hope, then at least more doubt.

'I think someone's just got the wrong number. It's just a bit unsettling.' Then, because I've got to ask, because this is the whole point of being here, and because ultimately my need to know who is sending those messages is greater even than my need to protect Naomi: 'Why? You haven't heard anything, have you?'

Her eyes widen. Ruby picks this moment to throw the rusk in the direction of the fireplace, but for once Naomi's attention isn't on Ruby; it's on me.

'Nothing. I've heard nothing. Lucy, do you really think these messages could have something to do with it? With—'

I really don't want Naomi to say her name. Because something awful happens to her voice when she does.

'No, no, I don't. I'm sorry. I'm so sorry.'

I've told so many lies since all this – this thing that I can't name – started up again, and although they're to try to avoid hurting people, I'm disturbed by how easily they come to me. They remind me of the lies I told before. That we all told.

'What are you sorry for?'

I shake my head because there's no answering this. Then I take a mouthful of coffee because I need something to do with my hands, and the sugary, earthy taste of it helps me steady myself.

'Do you want to show me the messages?'

This is the very last thing I want to do. *You must pay for what you did.* It's hard to see how Naomi could read that without having some questions for me. Her voice is composed again now, and she's smoothing Ruby's chestnut hair back from her face. I shake my head and try to sound equally composed.

'No, it's fine. I think I just needed to tell someone about them.'

'You've told Joe though?'

Another difficult question.

'Not exactly. I didn't want to worry him.'

'I'm sure he'd rather know if they're upsetting you, Lucy.'

Suddenly, I just can't stop myself and I ask, 'Do you ever wonder what Maddie would look like if she were alive today?'

'Oh my love, all the time,' says Naomi, her voice breaking. 'All the time.'

And then we hear the sound of a key in the lock and the front door opening and she says perfectly normally, as if she were two different people, 'We're in here, Robin.'

Robin looks terrible. He's a big man: tall and broad, but today it's like he's shrinking into himself. The flesh on his face is all jowly, and sort of mottled. And is it just me or is Naomi looking at him with unusual intensity, like she's worried he's going to say something wrong?

'Lucy and Ruby came for coffee. Isn't that lovely?'

'Splendid,' he says unconvincingly. All his usual bounce seems to have gone out of him, but he brightens a bit when Naomi stands and hands him his granddaughter.

'Robin has been playing golf,' Naomi says.

'Did you win?'

'Hmmm?'

'The golf?'

'Oh, er, no. Got to give the others a chance sometimes, you know,' he says with an attempt at his usual jokey manner. He plants a big kiss on Ruby's forehead. 'What's this little monster been up to then?'

'Would you like a coffee, darling? It's decaf.'

He shoots a glance at her, looking worried again.

'I'll get you a mug,' I say, because it's almost like they have something to say to each other; something they don't want me to hear. Maybe they had a row before he went out and I've interrupted it. I feel protective of him, of both of them. I hope their marriage isn't in trouble now, after all they've been through together.

'Oh don't worry Lucy, I'll get it.'

'It's no trouble, honestly.'

'I hope you didn't leave your clubs in the hall for Lucy to fall over.'

'I left them in the car.'

I can't eavesdrop on my in-laws. But I do walk down the hallway as slowly as I can. All I hear, though, is silence, broken by the odd gurgle from Ruby. They're not saying anything to each other at all – as though all their conversation was only for me. Somehow this is even worse. In Naomi's magazine-perfect kitchen, I open the cupboard above the kettle and take down one of the Le Creuset mugs – the pale green one with the pink inside, which is my favourite. I pause long enough to wonder what this kitchen would look like if Joe and I owned it; even before Ruby, neither of us were tidy people.

Hayley's kitchen is stylish too, but it's also lived in: there are schedules stuck to the fridge – hers, Frank's, the kids' – and on any given day you might find tea bags spilling out of a box someone has left on the worktop, a half-empty glass of juice, the odd clove of garlic, a dog lead, some elderly Quality Street that no one likes, a set of car keys – all the usual detritus of lives being lived. In this kitchen everything is in its place, from the dove-grey dinner plates on the wooden rack that runs along one wall, to the empty and gleaming drainer on the draining board. The orange bar stools are symmetrically arranged around the breakfast bar, and precisely in the middle of the work surface is a vase of… dead tulips. I nearly drop the mug, I'm so surprised. I look around again, but everything else is just as it should be. Naomi would be mortified. I can almost feel her embarrassment, so much so that I want to snatch the flowers up myself and put them in the, doubtless empty, sensor-operated Brabantia bin.

Instead, I walk in a daze back through into the hallway. Robin's jacket is hanging on the end of the banister. Suddenly I wonder: has Robin had any messages? Could that explain why he's behaving oddly? A few minutes earlier the thought of standing outside the door listening to their conversation was mortifying; now I'm considering going through my father-in-law's pockets.

If he had got a message, why wouldn't Naomi have mentioned it when we were talking about it earlier? She's clearly in on whatever it is that's troubling him. If he had got a message, what might that message have said about me? Maybe that's why they haven't told me. I put the mug down as gently as I can on the carpet of the stairs and start my search. I can't take not knowing. The first thing my hand encounters is his wallet. It's fat – he's a firm believer in cash – and the leather is buttery smooth. I feel a flush of shame. What would I say if he caught me? I try the other pocket – it's got some kind of pills in it but nothing else. He might have his phone on him, I suppose, but as soon as I reach for the inside pocket, I know it's there; I can feel the hard outline of it through the silky material of the jacket lining. I'm banking on him still not having a security code on it. Joe's forever nagging him to add one, in case he loses it. I tap the home button, my finger shaking. The screen lights up, but maybe there is a lock on it because all I can see is his screen saver – a picture of Ruby in a Christmas outfit he and Naomi bought her. That makes me feel even more guilty. But I swipe at it again and this time it opens. I click straight on the text icon and glance down the list. I see Joe's name. I see Leighton's opticians and then I see an unknown number. The jacket slides out of my hand and onto the floor. I can only see the first message. It says:

> You say you blame yourself, but what are you going to do about it?

'Is everything all right Lucy?'

Instinctively, I crouch down and shove the phone into the pocket of my hoodie.

When I look round Naomi is standing in the doorway of the living room.

'Oh. Yes. Sorry.'

'You were so long we thought you'd got lost.'

She smiles as she says this, but there's something not quite right about the smile, it seems detached from the rest of her expression. I don't move from the floor. I don't think she's seen anything, but I can't be certain.

'Sorry I was so long, I was getting myself a glass of water,' I say. 'And then I knocked Robin's jacket off as I walked past, so I was just picking it up off the floor.'

'He should have hung it up properly,' she says, walking towards me. Then she leans over me to pick the mug up off the stairs and turns to head back into the living room. I slip the phone back into the inside pocket of Robin's jacket. I badly want to see if there are any other messages from that number, but I can't risk another look. She could be back any second. She's already going to know I didn't get a glass of water. No glass. No water marks on the beautifully clean sink. That was a stupid lie.

When I go back into the living room, Robin is sitting on the floor, next to Ruby, who's trying to haul herself into a standing position using the edge of the coffee table. Naomi is hovering in front of the armchair she was sitting in before, still clutching the mug. When I walk in, she seems to relax slightly and sits down.

'So what brings you in our direction Lucy?' asks Robin. He's pulled himself together a bit now and sounds almost like his normal self.

'I needed to drop a couple of books off at the performing arts library,' I say, sitting down too, also trying to sound normal.

'You must be the only person who uses that place.'

'It's actually usually really busy.'

Ruby's hand slides on the table and Naomi gasps and says, 'Careful Robin.'

'I'm being careful!' he snaps back, his face suddenly so full of fury that I feel frightened.

'I was only worried that she might slip and hit her chin on the glass,' Naomi says. I've seen Robin lose his temper before, but this time there had been something vicious under the surface that was new to me. Ruby, too, seems to pick up on something wrong; her eyes have gone saucer-like as she looks at Robin.

'Yes, well, I've got my hands just behind her so I can catch her if she does.'

'All right, darling,' Naomi says. 'I couldn't see. There was no need to shout at me.'

Her tone is odd too, like she's warning him of something. *Not in front of Lucy and Ruby. We can finish this later.* Ruby has crawled off and is investigating the fire tongs. Robin attempts to get back up on his feet, but he's struggling a bit so I get up and help him and somehow hauling him up again breaks the strange atmosphere. He's quite difficult to pull up and I'm conscious of both the strength and frailty of him: a powerful man, who's getting old. *You say you blame yourself, but what are you going to do about it?* I need time to think over what it could mean. But I can't go just yet. I search for a safe topic of conversation.

'It was Frank's birthday yesterday.' They've met Frank a few times.

'Oh, how is he?' Naomi asks.

'Doing well. Hayley cooked roast lamb and we all went over.'

'That's lovely that you were all together,' Naomi says. We both glance at the mantelpiece. There are few safe topics of conversation in a family whose daughter disappeared twenty-five years ago.

'Claire brought her new girlfriend, Nic.'

'How exciting. What's she like?'

'Quietly confident. And into angel healing.'

Robin chokes on his coffee.

'I see!' Naomi says brightly, as if she knows exactly what I'm talking about. 'How lovely.'

'It's a sort of therapy thing. There are people who believe that we all have guardian angels who are looking after us and then there are angel healers who can talk to those angels.'

'So she's religious? Claire's girlfriend?'

'No, I don't think so. It's more a spiritual thing.' I'm not sure I'm doing justice to angel healing. 'Like you know when you get a gut feeling about something?'

Naomi nods; Robin is looking at me like I'm talking an unfamiliar foreign language.

'Well, some people think that feeling is your angels giving you a message.'

'The only kind of gut feeling I get nowadays is when I've eaten too much,' Robin says. 'Talking of which, what's Ruby eating?'

I make a dash in the direction of the fireplace and prise open my daughter's jaws, despite her vigorous protests.

'It's all right, I think it's that bit of rusk from earlier,' I say.

As I leave half an hour later, I walk past Robin's car. There are no golf clubs in it. But then I don't have any books to drop off at the performing arts library either. So we're both liars.

Chapter Sixteen

Maddie, 1999

Maddie badly wanted to talk to Amari. Not to tell him anything about what had happened with Tom Durrant just before lunch – he wouldn't understand, would totally overreact – but she wanted to hear his voice. She thought it might make her feel better. She slid the phone card into the slot in the hostel payphone and noticed that she only had one pound of credit left. Amari's sister wasted a good thirty pence of it taking forever to find him.

The payphone was in a tiny room at the end of a corridor near the stairs to the first floor of the main hostel building. The room smelt of damp and Lynx body spray. She'd been last in the queue, so she'd already had to wait about twenty minutes for her turn, but at least she had some privacy now. She read the graffiti on the wall as she waited. *LH was 4 TP.* Someone whose name had been scored out was a wanker. Every moment was full of joy. Leah was going to get laid in 1998. Luke had a tiny cock, or possibly cook – the writer hadn't taken much trouble over forming the letters.

'Hey,' said Amari's voice eventually. He sounded distinctly cool.

'Hey you,' she said, fighting her disappointment. Maybe this wasn't going to make her feel better.

'Hey,' he repeated.

'What's up?'

'Nothing much.'

'Only you sound kind of weird.'

There was a pause while Maddie listened to Amari breathing and thought about all the things she had done wrong that he might have found out about.

'Why didn't you tell me about the break-in at your place?'

'Break-in?'

'When your front door got smashed in.'

'Oh that. That was ages ago.'

Her heart started to thud against her ribcage, and she wondered if Amari could somehow feel it too, as if each beat were being transmitted down the phone line. Why was everyone so interested in the thing with the front door?

'You should have told me.'

'It wasn't a break-in. It was just some mates of Joe's, having a laugh.'

'Doesn't sound very funny. Which ones?'

'Which ones what?' she said stupidly.

'Which total knobheads smashed the glass on your front door?'

'Oh. Like I said, they're friends of Joe's.' There was another pause. She twisted the metal cord of the payphone around her index finger. 'It's no one you know.'

'So they're not from school?'

'What is this? An interrogation?'

'No, of course not. But I want to know who did it.'

She looked around her for inspiration.

'Some guy called Luke, okay?'

'Luke what?'

'Luke Cook. Happy now?'

'I don't know him.'

'Yeah I told you, you wouldn't.'

'I'm worried about you.'

'Well, there's no need to be.'

'Maddie, does this have anything to do with…' He hesitated. His voice had become warmer now, but she felt worse than when he'd been pissed off at her. She had a terrible fear of what was coming next.

'No,' she said, way too quickly. 'Definitely not.'

'Because you can talk to me about it, you know.'

'There's nothing to talk about. That afternoon was a one-off.'

'Okay.' He drew out the second syllable, reluctantly. 'If you're sure?'

'Look, it was nothing. It's over. Okay? I don't want to talk about it.'

'Okay, got it,' he said. 'Message received.'

'You haven't even asked how drama camp's going.'

'I'm just—'

'Yeah, I know.'

'How is it going then?'

'Yeah, good thanks. Great, in fact. I've got one of the main parts in the play and one of the tutors told me he thinks I've got what it takes to do this professionally.'

'Makes sense. You're always the lead in the school play.'

'But it means something more here because the tutors are both proper professional actors.' She was suddenly anxious to make him understand. 'One of them is Lorraine Caxton!'

'Who?'

'She's properly famous.'

'Yeah? What's she been in?'

'She's a stage actor mainly, but—'

'Right. That explains why I've never heard of her.'

Maddie thought about how she was expected to know about every obscure footballer he ever mentioned – not just David Beckham and Dwight Yorke and the ones everyone had heard of, but every player involved in whatever current deal or transfer he was so excited about.

'Hey, I was thinking.'

'Yeah?'

'I could cycle down there and see you.'

'What?'

'I could come down this evening on my bike. We could go for a walk or something.'

'It's miles away. It would take you ages.'

'Only about fifteen miles.'

'I told you, there's no need to worry. I'm fine.' She could hear the tightness in her own voice.

'I'm missing you, okay? I thought you might be missing me.'

'Amari, I'll be back in four days!'

'Do you not want me down there or something?' Now he sounded offended again.

'It's not that, it's—'

'Because that's what it sounds like.'

'Of course I—'

There were a series of beeps and then the line went dead. For a few seconds she thought he'd hung up on her and then she realised that her stupid phone card had run out. She replaced the phone on the hook and waited, kicking at the skirting board with the toe of her Converse. Surely he'd realise what had happened and call her back. But the seconds ticked by and nothing. Maybe he thought she'd hung up on him. It was typical of the sort of ridiculous rows they'd been having lately; he was so over-sensitive.

There was a tap at the phone booth door, making her jump, and a fair-haired figure waved at her through the glass. Lucy. She was bobbing up and down. Maddie kicked the door open.

'Hey Maddie! I've been looking for you.'

'Have you got a phone card?'

'I've got fifty pence,' said Lucy, already digging around in the pockets of her hoodie.

'Yeah well it only takes cards so that's no use.'

'Oh, sorry.' Lucy looked briefly crestfallen, but she was like one of those annoying bouncing balls that the year sevens loved that just sprang back to you, no matter how hard you tried to get rid of it. Her face brightening again, she said: 'I can't wait to show you what I've found!'

'You've got paint on your nose.'

'I've been helping with the set.' Lucy, undeterred, rubbed ineffectually at her face with a grubby sleeve and succeeded only in spreading the green paint over her chin as well. 'We've been painting the forest.' Lucy took a thin A4 volume out of her canvas rucksack. 'Look! It's a local history book.'

'So?'

'It's got a whole chapter about Edward Duval in it, and the house at Poison Cross. There's even pictures from when he lived there.'

In spite of herself, Maddie was interested.

'Where did you find it?'

'In the hostel library.'

'Have you read it?'

'Most of it, and Sam's right – Edward Duval was a huge star – back when there were silent films.'

'And the murder?'

'That's true too. There was a girl called Gladys Rudd who went missing after one of his parties.'

Maddie started leafing through the pages.

'Look, here's a picture of him.' The black and white photo showed a sideways profile of Duval, with a sweep of fair hair, a pointy nose and pale brooding eyes. He was wearing a sharp suit and a serious expression, both of which looked like they'd be shrugged off when the publicity shoot had finished.

'There's a floorplan of the house itself too – you can see the swimming pool where it happened. It was turned into a ballroom later, but he kept a secret entrance into the old changing room.'

Leaning against the side of the phone booth, Maddie began to read. Lucy waited eagerly beside her, propping the door open. Maddie was vaguely conscious of her shifting her weight from foot to foot. Suddenly she too wanted to be moving. She needed something to distract her from her argument with Amari.

'Let's go and look at the house!'

'Now?'

'We've got half an hour before the next rehearsal starts.'

'Lorraine said we weren't to go there.'

Maddie's irritation returned. 'We're not going in, you baby. Jenna says you can see it from the bottom of the drive. I want to take a look, that's all. Are you coming or not?'

Maddie was already walking away, confident that Lucy would follow her in the end – not least because she still had the book. In a few seconds, Lucy was at her side. They passed a group of the others sitting on a picnic bench, poring over their scripts. Maddie returned their shouted greeting and felt briefly guilty. She too should be learning her lines, but she knew she wouldn't be able to concentrate just now. There was too much going on in her head and she needed the excitement and glamour of Edward Duval to drive it out.

'What do you think Edward Duval's parties were like?' asked Lucy, who was practically jogging to keep up. Still, it would do her good: she was definitely too chubby. Puppy fat, her own mother called it. And the pace Maddie was setting didn't seem to stop Lucy's ability to talk, unfortunately; she was keeping up a pretty constant stream of chatter. 'I'm imagining candles everywhere. You know, like tealights. And those cocktail glasses – the old-fashioned sort they had in the 1920s. The book says there was lots of drinking,' Lucy said earnestly. 'And wild behaviour.'

'Wild behaviour?'

'Sex, I suppose,' said Lucy, whose face was now pink, although whether from embarrassment or exertion was unclear.

And then there it was. Jenna was right. Creepy as fuck. They were up on a bank, looking down at the house. It was large, but not as big as the stately homes her parents occasionally dragged her to. It was, or had been, a family home. A tall, pitched roof, with elaborately carved tiles all the way round the edge, and a round tower – like something from a fairy story – in one corner. There was ivy smothering the red bricks. At the front, there was a kind of covered walkway, a long porch that stretched the length of the building. It was painted a dull, dark green. From their vantage point, she could just see a glimpse of a flat building attached at the back. That must have been the covered pool, which was later turned into a ballroom.

The house was neglected, but not as much of a ruin as she'd been expecting. Lorraine had called it a death trap, but it just looked abandoned – not dangerous. Quite a few of the roof tiles were missing, but there was glass still in the windows as far as she could see. Suddenly, she caught her breath.

'Did you see that?'

'What?' The sight of the house had miraculously silenced Lucy and when she spoke now, her voice sounded much more uncertain.

'There was a shadow moving at the window.'

'Maddie, don't.'

'There was. Do you think I'm making it up? That one on the end there, at the bottom. Do you think it's the ghost of Gladys Rudd?'

'I don't believe in ghosts.'

'You don't sound very sure.'

The two of them stared at the window Maddie had pointed out.

'There's no one there,' Lucy said, eventually.

But Maddie didn't answer because she felt the familiar exhilaration of a plan forming. The others would love it. She'd need Lucy's help, but that wouldn't be a problem, she was so eager to please, and if it was, well, she had other ways of making Lucy do what she wanted.

'Lucy, I've had the best idea.'

Chapter Seventeen

Maddie, 1999

'Before we go to dinner, there's something I need to tell you all.'

She savoured the concentrated attention on the faces of her three friends as they turned to look at her later that evening. Lucy, standing by the dormitory door, fiddling with her pink watchstrap, looked pale and worried. But then she knew what was coming.

'Tonight, we're all going to have an adventure.'

'What are you up to?' Hayley asked, admiration already in her voice.

'We're going inside the haunted house where Edward Duval lived.'

'The one Sam told us about?' Hayley said, as though there were loads of them.

'Inside it?' Jenna said. 'I've only seen the outside and that was shit scary.'

'That's the point Jenna. It's a dare. A challenge. Unless you're too chicken?'

'No way,' Jenna said quickly, 'I'm totally up for it.'

'Now?' asked Hayley.

'Not now. Tonight. When everyone else is asleep.'

'Wicked,' Hayley said, a note of fear tingeing the admiration this time. But she'd be there; she was never going to be the difficult one to persuade. If Maddie had said she was going to strip naked, cover herself in tarantulas and breakdance through the streets of Winchester, Hayley would probably have said 'Wicked,' and done exactly the same.

'Griffiths?' Claire was sitting on the bottom bunk, tying her Dr Martens. She'd been a bit subdued all day, and Maddie had a premonition that whatever was bugging her meant she was going to be difficult.

'You don't seriously believe the place is haunted?'

Premonition confirmed.

'There's only one way to find out.'

'I don't need to find out. I know.'

'Well, okay, if you don't think it's haunted, what's to stop you coming with us?'

'I just can't be bothered to get up in the middle of the night to go and see some stupid house.'

Maddie considered her next move. She needed all of them there; it was important for the plan. Scorn worked well with Jenna, but it was never any good with Claire, who sometimes needed to be coaxed into things. Maddie went and sat on the lime-green duvet next to her.

'Please come.' She put an arm around her friend. 'It won't be the same without you, Griffiths.'

Claire's mouth twitched into an involuntary smile. Right move.

'Oh, all right, I give in. Make me part of your crazy plan.'

Maddie gave her a triumphant hug. They were all going to be so surprised when they found out what she had in store for them.

'What about you Lucy?' Hayley asked. 'Are you in too, or will it be past your bedtime?'

Lucy, still standing by the door, went, if possible, even paler, and carried on fiddling with her watchstrap, refusing to meet Hayley's eye.

'She doesn't have to come.' Claire seemed to have appointed herself Lucy's protector for some reason – maybe it was just to annoy Hayley. 'Lucy don't worry, you can stay here.'

'Of course Lucy will be there,' Maddie said quickly. 'It will be like her initiation. You understand, don't you Lucy?' She turned her own gaze on Lucy, who looked up, her eyes round and troubled. The initiation idea had come to Maddie just at that moment, but she was pleased with it and she could see it had made an impact on Lucy. 'If you want to be part of the group, you have to do what we do. Okay?'

Lucy nodded solemnly. She looked petrified, but she was so desperate to fit in, Maddie knew she wouldn't wimp out. To be honest, she was more worried about Jenna, who was always the biggest coward when it came to this kind of dare.

'Great – it's all settled then. Now, let's go and get food.'

Claire still seemed a bit quiet on the walk over to the hostel for dinner. The others were walking ahead, Hayley poking fun at something Lucy had said, so she had Claire to herself, and she suddenly remembered she had something else to tell her.

'You'll never guess what.'

'What?'

'You know Sam?'

'Sam with the weird taste in ghost stories?'

'Lucy and I were sorting through the lighting cables earlier and he asked me if I was seeing anyone.'

There was silence. Claire had her hands thrust in the pockets of her cardigan as she walked, and her dark curls were obscuring her face.

'As in, Sam came on to me, Griffiths. Not in a bad way.' Her mind briefly and uneasily went to the moment with Tom before lunch, even though he hadn't actually kissed her, and she'd sort of convinced herself she'd imagined that that was what was about to happen. 'He was really respectful about it.'

Claire's voice when she finally did say something was almost expressionless.

'I think Hayley likes him.'

'I know that. I'm not stupid. Obviously I told him that I *am* seeing someone. Although Amari's being a total dick right now. We had this stupid argument on the phone earlier because he wanted to cycle down here to see me.'

'Amari's coming here?'

'I don't know. I told him not to, but he got all offended, and then we got cut off.'

Maddie felt like she hadn't managed to make Claire understand. She tried again.

'I just like that Sam asked me, you know – that he was upfront with his feelings. I really admire that. If you like someone you should just come out and tell them, right?'

'Right.'

The atmosphere had got a bit weird suddenly. Maybe she shouldn't have said anything about Sam at all. It wasn't like Claire to be so protective of Hayley, though.

'Maddie? Can I talk to you about something?'

'What's up?'

Because it was really clear something was.

'Not now. Can we go for a walk after dinner?' Claire said. 'Just us?'

'Sure,' Maddie said, with a rising sense of misgiving. 'It's a date.'

Chapter Eighteen

Lucy, Present

On impulse, I call in at Claire's office on the drive back from Naomi and Robin's. I'm impatient to know about the plan she has for finding out who's been sending the messages. Plus, I really want to talk to someone about my visit to Naomi and Robin while it's still fresh in my head. And it's only slightly out of my way; a shiny office block just outside Guildford. I haven't been here since she got promoted. She can show me her new office, with the mini-fridge and the view over the one-way-system, and perhaps I can persuade her to go for a coffee with me – what's the point in being a partner if you can't bunk off work for half an hour? I'm pretty sure this isn't how it works, but at the very least she might make me coffee.

The receptionist looks up. He's got pale skin, lots of very red hair and looks about twelve.

'I'm here to see Claire Griffiths from Collinson and Barnes.'

He stares at Ruby like he's never seen a baby before. He's probably nearer her age than mine. He takes my name and then punches some numbers on his phone. I hear one side of a conversation, and then he replaces the receiver and says, looking embarrassed to be giving me bad news, 'I'm afraid Ms Griffiths isn't in the office this afternoon.'

'Oh. No worries. Thanks.'

I feel weirdly cheated. It's not like we'd arranged to meet or anything, but she needs to fill me in on what we're doing tomorrow. Outside, I remove my phone from my bag. Ever since yesterday's second message, I've been treating it like a hand grenade with the pin pulled out, but there's nothing more sinister on the screen than Kindle recommending that my next read should be *Secrets to a Sleeping Baby*. Claire said she'd call me and the fact she hasn't yet probably means she's busy and I should just wait until she gets in touch, but the need to talk to her is even stronger now it's been thwarted, so I give her mobile a call. There's no answer. I sit in my car in the car park, undecided what to do next.

At the back of my mind, I'm still thinking about the coincidence of Harriet asking me to write about Edward Duval the day after I got the first message, and a tiny part of me is still wondering whether Harriet could be Maddie. I pick up my mobile again and google 'Ava Holland'. Harriet's great-grandmother was a silent movie star. Surely this is a quick way of proving that Harriet Holland is a real person and not Maddie. I remember that Ava had a son, and I suppose he must be Harriet's grandfather, but I can find nothing more than passing references to him online.

Next I google 'Harriet Holland producer', but there's very little personal information up there — just film sites and the work profiles I found when she first contacted me a few months ago, showing the same glossy photo I've seen before. Even in the photo she's wearing sunglasses. If she has any social media accounts, they must be private. I study the photo for a while as if it might give me the answer I crave. She has Maddie's olive skin and the same high cheekbones, but her face is different somehow; her nose is thinner and her mouth a bit fuller. But then I think she might have had work done, so it's hard to be sure. Hayley's looking for a plastic surgeon at the moment – a fortieth birthday present to herself, she says – so I've spent a lot of time looking at pictures she's sent me and I feel like I'm becoming something of an expert at spotting when people have been under the knife.

My mobile rings, and I jolt and almost drop it. It's Claire. I give a relieved 'Hey!'

'Everything okay? Have you had another message?'

'What? No. No more since yesterday. Where are you?'

I'm still hoping we can meet for a coffee, although she sounds pretty stressed.

'Just at work.'

I twist round to look back at the office block, as though I might see her looking out of the window.

'Lucy? You still there?'

'Yes.'

'Are you phoning about the plan for tomorrow? Don't worry, I've got it all sorted.'

'Right. So what are we doing?'

'I'll explain everything tomorrow.'

'Can't you tell me now?'

'I don't really have time to talk right now. Can you pick me up from mine about ten and we can drive down there? I'll explain on the journey down.'

'I guess. Okay. Are you—'

'Great. I'll see you then.'

She hangs up. The whole conversation is a bit odd. How long would it have taken to tell me what we're doing? I've suddenly got a bad feeling about the plan for tomorrow. Where is the *there* she said we're driving down to? I wonder whether the reason she isn't telling me is because she thinks that if I know, I'll refuse to go. I'm worried that she wants us to drive down to the house at Poison Cross. And it's the very last place I feel like I can bear to go.

Chapter Nineteen

Lucy, 1999

'Who's going in first?' Maddie demanded.

'Do we have to go in by ourselves?' Jenna asked.

Lucy, winding the cord from her jacket round her stubby, paint-stained fingers, thought Jenna sounded even less certain now they were actually there than she had earlier that evening when Maddie had first explained her plan. She could understand why. Everyone had been excited on the walk from the hostel, marvelling at how easy it had been to get out without anyone noticing, but now they had reached the house, the reality of the dare was starting to sink in. There was a very faint light from a sliver of moon, and a brighter one from the torch, but all around them were pools of darkness and noises that were difficult to place – rustling, scrabbling, the odd cry. Despite the warmth of the summer's night, she shivered.

'Of course,' Maddie said, 'it's not much of a dare if we all go in together.'

There had been a warning sign on the gates telling them to keep out; they'd used it as a foothold to climb over. Lucy had tried to find this as funny as the others seemed to. She hadn't wanted to do this at all, but Maddie had made it impossible for her to refuse. Now, though, they'd come to a halt halfway up the drive, next to a huge rhododendron bush and could see the house, with its fairy-tale turret and blank windows, like sightless eyes, and everyone had become more subdued.

'It looks very dark,' Hayley said.

'It's an abandoned house. Did you think they'd have the lights on, you div?' Claire's voice, confident. The laughter kindled again and spread nervously on the night air.

'You've been very quiet, Lucy Goosey. Maybe you should go first?' Lucy knew that Hayley was just trying to deflect attention from her slip with the lights, but she felt her breath catch in her throat as she struggled to think of the right reply.

'Don't worry Lucy,' Claire said quickly. 'I don't mind going first.'

The relief of her reprieve made Lucy almost giddy. She began to feel a bit better about being there. After all, a few months ago she hadn't even met Maddie Blake and now she really was part of the gang. This proved it. She was friends with the coolest people at summer camp. And at school. At least, she would be if she made it past this initiation. She wondered if she would have the guts to go through with the dare.

'You know what you have to do?' Maddie was asking Claire.

'Yeah, it's not difficult, is it?' Claire said. 'Go into the house, take something from one of the rooms to prove I was really there and bring it back.'

'Something that belonged to Edward Duval.'

'Maddie, how the fuck am I supposed to know what might have belonged to an old man who's been dead for sixty years?'

Lucy had never heard Claire swear before. Perhaps it was a sign that she was less confident than she seemed, although she and Maddie had been a bit snappy with each other ever since they'd come back from a walk together after dinner.

'He wasn't an old man. Edward Duval was forty when he killed himself. You have to promise to find something you think belonged to him – that's the point of the dare.'

Maddie, who had the torch, shone it round the circle and the other four were spotlighted amid the drizzle – a shadowy, excited circle of faces, about to do something momentous.

'Come on, you have to swear it.'

One by one, they mumbled promises.

'Give me the torch.'

And then Claire was striding away from them, cherry red Dr Martens scrunching on the gravel of the drive, a feeble light ahead of her. They were silent for a few minutes, watching the outline of Claire become fainter until they couldn't see her or the glow of her torch at all.

'Shit! What was that?'

Lucy thought Jenna was jumpier than any of them. Somehow this made her feel better – it was comforting to have someone who was more scared than you were.

'An owl or something,' she said, trying to sound as offhand as Claire had.

'The ghost of Gladys Rudd. She's got Claire,' Hayley suggested, sounding almost wistful.

'I've found out more about the ghost,' Maddie said. 'Do you want to hear?'

'Please Maddie,' Lucy said obediently, even though she really, really didn't want to hear any more of the story. She wanted to be curled up under her duvet, reading *The Chalet Girls* by the light of her torch – the one Claire had just taken with her. But she obviously couldn't tell Maddie that.

'This bit happened years later. Hayley, what are you doing? We need to hold hands.'

'Why?' Hayley didn't sound any keener to hear the rest of the story than she did, and Lucy wondered what would happen if they all said how they really felt and told Maddie they were going back to the hostel.

'So we know we're all still here.'

Jenna instantly reached for Lucy's hand. Her palm felt dry and her grip strong. Maddie took her other hand, and squeezed it.

'Who told you this? Was it Sam?' Hayley asked.

'It doesn't matter who told me. Do you want to hear it or not?'

No one answered, which Maddie seemed to take for agreement.

'Okay. Well, a few years back there was this woman who was staying down in Poison Cross. She was walking through the fields and she saw the house through the trees, so she went to take a closer look. At that point it still had a "for sale" sign up outside so she got in touch with the estate agent. So, she's talking to this estate agent about the house and he says he's not even sure it's safe for her to go in, and she tells him she knows he's not being straight with her, because there were people in the house when she walked past. She'd seen a man standing in the window on the first floor, and a woman in an old-fashioned beaded dress standing just behind him.

'Well of course the estate agent drove out there, even though it was closing time and getting dark. He was worried about trespassers. At first the place seemed deserted – eerily quiet, he said. But then he noticed footprints in the dust, and as he started to follow them, he almost tripped over something at the bottom of the staircase. It was the body of a man, lying there, all mangled. His neck was broken. There was no sign of the woman. But as he bent over the body, he heard the crunch of steps on the gravel.'

And then there it was, unmistakably. *Crunch. Crunch.*

Jenna shrieked and Lucy felt the bones in her hand squash together.

'Claire for fuck's sake,' Hayley said.

'Sorry, it was too tempting,' Claire said, turning the torch back on.

'You were quick,' Maddie said.

'It's not like I'm going to hang out in there.'

'What did you get?'

Claire waved something.

'What is that?'

'An ashtray. I bet Duval smoked fifty a day. It's definitely his.'

'Not bad.' Maddie's voice held a grudging respect. 'Where did you—'

'Shhhh.'

'Jenna?'

'I think there's somebody in the bushes.'

'It's just a fox or something,' Maddie said.

'I could hear somebody breathing.'

'Ghosts don't breathe.'

'Who's next?' Claire asked.

'I'll go next,' Lucy said, suddenly determined to get this over with. How bad could it be? Claire had been in and come out unscathed and it felt like she'd only been gone a few minutes. It was just an old, empty house. So what if something horrible had happened there years and years ago? Edward Duval and Gladys Rudd were both dead, and they weren't coming back. In her diet of horror films, consumed at Sarah's house back in Nottingham, it was never the ghosts that terrified her – it was the films where the monster was an actual person. And there were no actual people in this house. That was the whole point. It was abandoned.

She set off up the drive, the torch illuminating the ground just in front of her and cries of 'Go Goose!' and 'Been nice knowing you!' ringing in her ears. It was strangely comforting to hear Hayley say that, even though she knew it was meant as a joke. It felt like another sign she belonged.

She tried to focus on what was immediately in the torch beam, rather than looking around her or thinking about what was coming next. The bottom of the steps leading up to the porch. Stone. Well worn. One at a time. Six in total. Steep. There was rubbish on the ground. A faded Mars wrapper, and, hang on, was that a condom? She'd only seen one twice before: one in biology on a banana and the one Sarah had stolen from her sister. Neither of them used.

As she approached the front door, she wished she'd thought to ask Claire whether the door worked or whether she'd found another way in, but as she got nearer she could see that it was already cracked slightly open, so that was a relief. She switched the torch to her other hand and pushed. It moved very slowly, like there was something the other side holding it back. Maybe Claire hadn't come in this way after all. She felt her heart start to beat faster, despite her best attempts not to panic. Think about the condom, she told herself. Whoever would want to come here to have sex?

The door wouldn't push any further but the gap was now large enough to squeeze through. Okay. She could do this. Standing in the hallway, she shone her torch around and the beam illuminated dark wood-panelled walls, a table with some kind of fabric hanging from it in tatters, a huge light fitting overhead and a sweeping staircase in front of her. She could hear the sound of scrabbling and of wings flapping, and she realised there were pigeons everywhere, their eyes glinting in the torch beam. The place stank – of damp, of dead bird, and of decades-long neglect. She remembered her mum saying that pigeon poo carried all kinds of diseases, and this was somehow reassuring – pigeon muck was a real danger; the only danger she was in.

She couldn't see anything small to pick up, let alone anything that might have belonged to Edward Duval. Besides, she'd promised Maddie she would look at the room where the swimming pool used to be. According to the floorplan in the book from the library, if she went straight ahead down the hallway it would be the last thing she came to. *So here goes*, she thought. She began to walk, tentatively at first, as though she were walking on rotten floorboards, and not what her torch revealed to be black and white marble tiles, covered in bird crap.

She picked up her pace. Shining the torch to her right, she could see a large, closed door, and, higher up, towards the ceiling, cobwebs – like it was a joke haunted house at a fairground – and now she heard a scurrying and scratching that suggested pigeons were not the only occupants. It was as much as she could do not to turn around right then and run back outside, but, clenching her fists, she made herself keep going forwards. This was her chance to be properly part of the group – probably her only chance – and if she screwed it up, she'd never be anything more to Maddie than the baby she let tag along occasionally because her mum was on TV.

Then, as the floorplan had promised, she was on the threshold of a large rectangular room at the back of the house. It had been hard to imagine anyone living here when she'd been in the hallway, but this room still looked like – well it still looked like a room. There was furniture in it for a start. Immediately opposite her was a big, ugly sofa and as she swept her torch round she saw other sofas and chairs, some covered in sheets, arranged around the edges of the room, so that there was still plenty of space for dancing. In the book, there had been a picture of the swimming pool itself, looking surprisingly small – 'the scene of the tragic incident' – but no pictures of the room after its transformation into a ballroom. She tried to superimpose the old photograph of the swimming pool over the room in front of her. To her left was where the door to the old changing room must have been. The windows along the length of the far wall were the same as the windows in the photo – floor to ceiling, with very thin frames and arched tops.

She shone her torch over the wall to her left and spotted what she was looking for. This looked like it would work for the dare. Her heart thumping, she approached the tall dresser, shining her torch on it, trying not to think what might be lurking in the shadows on either side. There was a cupboard on the bottom and shelves on the top, complete with what looked like exactly the kind of cocktail glasses she'd been imagining. She undid the catch of the cupboard, pulled open the door and spent a while inspecting what it revealed. Eventually she took not a glass but a matchbox from one of the shelves. It almost certainly had never belonged to Edward Duval – she didn't think a matchbox would last that long – but it did look old and it would go with Claire's ashtray, wherever she'd managed to find that. Suddenly she felt like she was being watched. All those pigeon eyes. They were making her paranoid.

Then she heard it. A kind of rhythmic beat, like a heartbeat. Tap, tap. Tap, tap. Tap, tap. Against the windowpane. A branch. Or someone's fingers.

Lucy turned and fled, tearing down the long hallway in a fraction of the time it had taken her only a few minutes earlier, dodging round the gap in the doorway and out down the steps, like she was being pursued by the ghost of Gladys Rudd herself.

Once outside, she felt exhilarated, triumphant. Initiation over! She wanted to laugh out loud. The others were still standing in a circle. Hayley's arm was around Jenna. They were all leaning in, discussing something in low voices.

'How was it, Lucy?' Maddie called, seeing her torch approaching.

'It was exactly like the book said.'

'What did you bring?'

'Oh, a matchbox. From the old swimming pool room, right at the back.'

'You went all the way in?' For the first time since Lucy had met her, Hayley sounded genuinely impressed.

'It's fine,' Lucy said as casually as she could manage, but even she could hear the excitement in her voice. 'There's just a lot of birds in there and maybe rats, and there was this bit when I thought someone was watching me.'

'What?'

'From outside. I thought there was someone outside looking in, but I think it was probably just a tree or something tapping against the pane.'

'Shit. Maddie, I really don't think this is a good idea,' Jenna said.

'No way are we stopping now!'

Maddie sounded as exhilarated as Lucy, even though she hadn't been in yet.

'Tell you what, I'll go next. Okay? I'm going to go to the room with the swimming pool too. I want to see where it happened. Where is it, Lucy? At the end of the hall?'

'Yes, it's just like the book shows. In the front door and follow the hallway straight ahead all the way down. You can't miss it.'

'Right. I'm going to find something way better than you. You wait!'

Maddie was off, ponytail swinging. Confident, excited, in control.

The first few minutes passed quickly. The others were full of questions. Had she sensed anything when she was in there? Had the temperature changed? Had she actually seen any rats? Had she been in any of the other rooms? Lucy bathed in the glow of their attention, hugging to herself the hope that it had worked – now that she'd done the dare, they were already starting to treat her as an equal. After a while, though, the chatter spluttered and died. In the distance, they heard the roar of an engine and a dog barking.

It was Jenna who said what they were all thinking.

'Maddie's been gone a long time. What do you think she's doing?'

'She's probably doing a full survey of the building, knowing Maddie,' Claire said, but she couldn't entirely hide the twist of worry in her voice.

'I think we should go and look for her.'

'That's just what she wants, Jenna,' Hayley said. 'She's playing a trick on us.'

'You can't know that. Come on, let's all go in together. Please. She might have had an accident or something.'

'Jenna's right – something might have fallen on her, or she might have got trapped somewhere,' Claire said. 'You remember what Lorraine said about the state of the place.'

'Oh, all right then,' Hayley said. 'But when we find her you have to back me up when I tell her I knew she was messing with us all along. After the watch thing, I'm not falling for another one of her tricks.'

It felt different climbing the steep steps, all four of them together. Maddie had the torch and they had only the flickering glow of Hayley's lighter, but, although Lucy's heart was still beating faster than usual, this time she felt invincible. That's what friends did for you; they were a team and nothing could harm them. She wasn't really worried about Maddie. She would be hiding. Hayley was right. Typical Maddie. They managed to push the door a bit further open this time and they all spilled into the pigeon-infested hallway. She could hear rather than see the others' reactions. The sharp intake of breath.

'Well, the inside matches the outside,' Jenna said.

'Maddie!'

'Babe! Where are you?'

'Where do we look first?' Jenna said.

'Let's start with the room that had the pool,' Claire said. 'That's where she said she was going.'

'Why doesn't she answer us?' Jenna said.

'Because this is a joke, like I told you,' Hayley said. 'She's probably about to jump out at us.'

'Lucy, can you take us to the swimming pool room?' Claire said.

'It's like playing a really weird game of hide and seek,' Hayley said. 'Maddie – if you're here, you're in big trouble when we find you!'

It was hard to search the pool room properly without the light of the torch, but there was enough light from the moon to see that Maddie wasn't lying injured anywhere.

'Let's check the rest of the house,' Claire said. 'You know Maddie, she'll probably have explored a bit.'

They went back out into the hallway and tried the first door.

'Doesn't look like anyone's explored in a long time,' Hayley said. 'Look at it.'

There were eight other rooms on the ground floor. They tried them one by one. Four of the doors were locked. The others were covered in dust and it was obvious no one had opened them for years, possibly decades, but they went inside anyway. Among the old furniture, they found dead pigeons in varying states of decay, some hessian sacks full of a now indistinguishable rotting substance, a pile of what looked like railway sleepers, a rake and, most weirdly of all in Lucy's mind, a copy of *Playboy*. At Jenna's insistence, they even tried to go upstairs. But this proved impossible because most of the middle section of the staircase turned out to be missing.

'Unless she's better at the high jump than she's ever let on, she's definitely not up there,' Hayley said.

In the end, they returned to the pool room, just to make sure. Lucy stood in front of the dresser where she had found the matchbox, fiddling with the catch on the cupboard door as the others searched.

'What's that?' Jenna stooped to pick something up.

'It's Maddie's scrunchie,' Claire said.

'So she *is* here!'

'Was here. She's not here now.'

'How did we miss it earlier?'

'I think it was hidden by the door.'

'So what do we do now?'

'It's part of the game,' Hayley said. 'I know Maddie. Let's leave her to it and go back. We know she's not here. She's not lying injured anywhere. She'll find us, I bet you anything.'

'We could tell Lorraine.'

'No way, Jenna,' Hayley said. 'Maddie would kill us. You know this is a joke, too. Just think about it. Remember that thing she did at my sister's birthday? When she went missing all evening and then turned up hiding under the pile of coats on my bed. She scared the shit out of me. She loves stuff like this. And she's in it for the long haul. Let's just wait it out.'

'But how did she do it? How did she just disappear?'

'There must be another way out,' Claire said.

'Where?' Jenna said. 'We haven't seen one.'

'Well maybe she just went back out the front door,' Claire said. 'Hayley's right. This is classic Maddie. She'll probably be hiding under the bunk bed when we get back to the hostel. Come on, I'm tired, let's go.'

But Maddie was not hiding under the bunk bed. And when Lucy woke the next morning, unaccountably chilly and full of snot and dread, Maddie still hadn't returned.

Chapter Twenty

Lucy, 1999

'No sign of Maddie yet?' asked Tom, appearing alongside her and Hayley as they were choosing their breakfast in the hostel dining room later that morning.

Lucy flinched. Was it just her or was there something strange about the way Tom said Maddie's name? Like he had some kind of special interest, or claim on her.

'She has a migraine,' Hayley said. 'She's staying in bed.'

The lie made Lucy's stomach cramp. It wasn't what they'd agreed. Why had Hayley said that? She'd made the whole situation so much worse. Tom's face beneath the New York Yankees baseball cap that he was unaccountably wearing for breakfast, crumpled in concern.

'Oh jeepers! Poor Maddie. My sister gets migraines and they're the worst. I've got some headache tablets back in my room if you think they would help?'

'She's fine,' Hayley said. 'She just needs to rest.'

'The Dream Team will just have to do without its star player for the morning then.'

'Why did you say that?' Lucy turned on Hayley as soon as Tom was out of the way. 'I thought we'd agreed to tell them if she's still not back once breakfast is over?'

'No, you said we should tell them.' Hayley's eyes had big dark circles under them, and yesterday's mascara still sat in clumps on her lashes. 'I said it was a crap idea and I still think that. Besides I don't like Tom sniffing around Maddie all the time. He's such a dick.'

'But what if Maddie doesn't come back?'

'Of course she'll come back,' Hayley said impatiently. 'It will be fine, you'll see. We all lost it a bit last night because we got freaked out by that house. Maddie always has a plan. One thing I do know, and you'd better listen to me about this Lucy because I'm Maddie's best friend and I know how she thinks, if you tell Lorraine and Tom that we went to the house at Poison Cross last night Maddie will never forgive you.'

'Okay,' Lucy said, feeling dangerously close to tears. 'I just think—'

'Anyway, her rucksack is missing. Like Claire said, that proves she planned this. Stop being such a baby. Get some breakfast and come and sit down.'

Lucy looked at the cereals and fruit in front of her and tried to make sense of them. She picked up a Ski yoghurt she had no intention of eating. Hayley piled her plate high with toast and grabbed four small plastic pots of Nutella. They headed over to where the others were sitting.

'Lucy wants to grass Maddie up,' Hayley announced as she sat down.

'We agreed we'd tell them,' Lucy said, her voice wobbling. She wished she was braver. She was finding it so hard to do the right thing, even though she knew exactly what it was. These people were on the verge of being her friends, and now she was going to have to spoil it all. She'd be on her own again. The school outcast.

'That was before we found her rucksack was missing,' Claire said.

'The rucksack doesn't definitely mean she's okay,' Jenna said, and Lucy felt a surge of hope that Jenna was going to back her up.

'It's a sign she planned this,' Hayley said. 'Look, the moment Lorraine hears we were down at that house in the middle of the night, we're all out of here.' She scooped out the entire contents of the small Nutella plastic pot and spread it over the burnt white toast. 'No more drama camp. No National Youth Theatre for Maddie, or me as it happens, but probably no National Youth Theatre for me anyway. No break into the world of acting. Okay, Jenna, so you think I'm wrong and that I'm being a terrible friend, but actually it's Maddie I'm thinking about.'

'I don't think you're wrong,' Jenna said. 'I think she probably is off somewhere having some kind of mad adventure – she's my friend too, remember, and I know the kind of crazy things she does – and I also think you're right that she'll kill us if we get her kicked out of drama camp.'

'Oh.' Hayley sounded slightly deflated. 'Okay. So…?'

'But what if we're all wrong? What if she really is in some kind of trouble somewhere?'

Hayley pushed her plate, with its uneaten Nutella toast, away from her.

'All right. Let's give her until lunch. Then we decide what to do.'

Somehow Lucy got through the morning's rehearsal. At lunch she sat staring straight ahead, tearing a cheese sandwich into pieces. The others made a half-hearted attempt to chat, but no one could hide their eagerness to get back to the cottage. As Jenna pushed open the front door, Lucy caught her breath. Maybe Maddie really would be there. It would all be fine, just like Hayley had said. They could laugh and joke about what happened last night, and Lucy herself wouldn't have to do the right thing, and make enemies of the people she still hoped would be her friends.

But as soon as she stepped inside, she knew she was wrong. Jenna made a show of calling Maddie's name and going upstairs to check, but they all knew she wasn't there.

'What now?' Jenna demanded. Lucy, standing with Claire and Hayley in the cottage kitchen, dropped her gaze to the linoleum floor tiles and tried to summon up her courage. But in the end she didn't need it.

'Okay, okay,' Hayley said, leaning back against the worktop. 'I agree we tell someone. I said, didn't I? I said that if she still wasn't back by now we should tell them we don't know where she is.'

'I think it's the best thing,' Claire said, reaching out and putting her hand on Hayley's arm. Lucy felt such a surge of relief it was almost as if Maddie had been found already. 'We don't even need to mention the house.'

Lucy's relief was short-lived.

'Shouldn't we tell them everything?'

'No,' Hayley said. 'We just tell Tom that we can't find her.'

'Agreed,' Claire said. 'That way if she shows up, she won't be in so much trouble. Deal, Lucy? Jenna?'

'Not Tom,' Jenna said suddenly.

'What?'

'We tell Lorraine. Not Tom.'

They found Lorraine Caxton in the office in the main youth hostel building. She was wearing reading glasses and poring over a folder of diagrams that looked like set plans for *A Midsummer Night's Dream*. It was Claire who told her that Maddie was missing. Lorraine didn't even look up from her paperwork.

'Tom says she has a migraine. Perhaps she went for a walk.'

It was curiously hard to get the adults to care. Lucy had thought that once they'd told Lorraine Caxton she would leap into action and make everything right again. Lorraine would magically produce Maddie, who would be totally okay, yell at her a bit, and then return her to rehearsals, slightly sulky and annoyed. Instead, Lorraine seemed more interested in rearranging the folder of stage management notes and finishing her coffee.

Of course, she didn't know that the last time any of them had seen Maddie had been in the middle of the night outside a derelict house. And this was surely the point when they should tell her, whatever Hayley and Claire said. Yes, Lorraine would be angry with them and yes, it would almost certainly mean that they all got kicked out of the summer camp, and it would probably mean that none of them would ever want to speak to her again, let alone be friends with her. But none of that should matter. None of that really mattered at all.

'She's been gone a really long time,' she managed. Lorraine looked up from the folder and, over the top of her glasses, focused her gaze on Lucy, who instantly felt like she wanted to step out of it. Lorraine's bright red lips twitched into a small frown.

'It's only two o'clock now. You must have seen her a couple of hours ago.'

'A bit longer ago than that,' Claire said, which wasn't exactly a lie.

'How much longer?'

Lucy opened her mouth. Her hand, in the pocket of her hoodie, closed over the matchbox she'd taken from the house that had once belonged to Edward Duval. The house in which he'd killed Gladys Rudd, and then himself. The house where Maddie had disappeared. Tell her now. Tell Lorraine. She looked from Claire to Hayley, and the words died before they reached her lips.

Chapter Twenty-One

Extract from Brits Who Shaped Hollywood *by Harriet Holland*

The moment that changed everything for Edward Duval came in the summer of 1925, just four years after his first film was released. By this time, the star was living between his luxurious modern mansion in the Los Angeles hills and a large house in the English countryside, called Thorncroft. Duval himself, and later the press, more often referred to it as 'the house at Poison Cross' after the oddly named village nearby.

Duval was at the very pinnacle of his fame. He had just starred in the hugely successful film of Sleeping Beauty, *playing the Prince alongside no less a luminary than Ava Holland herself as the sleeping Princess whom it was his bounden duty to waken with a kiss. He'd finished shooting a new film for DeMille and had a rare month's break before he was due back on set. He decided to spend it at the house at Poison Cross. It was a decision that was to change his life forever.*

The parties that Duval held at the house at Poison Cross were the stuff of legend. Actors, artists, writers, society beauties, sometimes even minor royals, would motor down from London – a journey of little more than an hour and a half – to drink and dance the night away in the reflected glory of the company of one of Hollywood's greats. Looking at the guest lists for these parties shines an interesting light on how close the links were between early movie-makers in America and the British theatrical crowd back home. The young Edward Duval partied the night away with the likes of 'Mrs Pat' – one of the most celebrated stars of Victorian theatre Mrs Patrick Campbell – and the then little-known actor John Gielgud. Noël Coward, another Brit who felt the pull of America, was a regular, and had just had his first big hit with The Vortex. His star was on the ascendant, just as Duval's was, although nobody knew it yet, on the wane.

Some of the younger residents were excited to have such famous names visit their village, but many of the locals regarded the goings on at the Big House with a mixture of trepidation and outright disapproval. On the night of the terrible event, Duval had gone to some trouble to build bridges with the local community. He had invited some of the girls from the village to join the celebrations. Among them was sixteen-year-old Gladys Rudd, the daughter of the local butcher. Only one photograph exists of Gladys – in contrast to the hundreds that display the chiselled Grecian features of Edward Duval. In it (Fig. 5, page 94), she stands with her sister and three friends from the village, all of whom were to accompany her to Duval's final, fatal party. Gladys is standing on the far right of the group, her hair bobbed in a style she might have copied from the movie magazines that were found later in the bedroom she shared with her sister. A slight figure, stiffly holding a small terrier dog, she looks up at the camera through her fringe with shy eyes, a little awkward, forever frozen in time. A pretty child, but very much still a child, and not a particularly worldly one.

To be invited to join a party full of bright young things from London and Los Angeles must have seemed like a dream come true to these five village girls. Their parents, though, were wary and Gladys's father was to say later that he initially forbade his daughters to go, but gave in when Gladys promised that they would stay together the whole time and be back home by *midnight. As it turned out, Gladys was never to come home again.*

We will never know exactly what happened at the house at Poison Cross that fateful night in July 1925 – everyone who was there is now dead too. But some things are clear. The party was a smaller one than usual and finished earlier. Those who were there remembered it coming to an end at about two o'clock in the morning, whereas Duval's parties often used to last until dawn and beyond. Duval himself was apparently taciturn and withdrawn. Those who knew him best put this down to a visit from his father earlier that afternoon. The pair had had a difficult relationship for years, and Duval seemed to both fear him and crave his approval.

The village girls went largely unnoticed by the other guests, although one, a theatrical producer from London, remembered seeing Gladys dangling her legs in Duval's state-of-the-art indoor pool, just before he left at about half one in the morning. Swimming was a Duval party tradition, and there was always someone in the water wearing little more than underwear. The producer described Gladys as looking 'perhaps a little tipsy, but perfectly happy'. It is the last time anyone remembered seeing her alive. And in some ways, it's a curiously appropriate vision – the shy village girl dipping a toe in the water of silver-screen sophistication.

The four other local girls – Gladys's sister and their three friends – told police that they left the house at Poison Cross just after midnight – only slightly later than they'd agreed with their parents. They'd been unable to find Gladys and assumed she'd already left. The four walked back to the village of Poison Cross together, taking the path through the fields as a shortcut. Gladys's father heard the front door open and what he assumed was his two daughters returning at a little after half past twelve that night. Gladys's sister was later questioned about why she didn't raise the alarm straight away. The two shared a bedroom and it must have been obvious to her at once that Gladys had not already come home. But she claimed that she had no reason to think Gladys was not enjoying herself still at the party and she didn't want to get her into trouble with their parents.

When Gladys's bed was still empty the next morning, though, her sister finally raised the alarm. The young police constable, who'd only started his job in the village six days earlier, wasted no time in going to the house at Poison Cross. His prompt action was to be a decisive factor in how events unfolded. Arriving at the apparently deserted house on his bicycle a little after nine o'clock on a serene, sunny July morning, he was greeted by a front door that stood ajar and room upon room of all the usual post-party detritus. Cocktail glasses, champagne flutes, empty bottles and overflowing ashtrays were scattered over every surface. He noted in his report that the air smelt fuggy from stale alcohol.

When he reached the pool area, the young constable found something much more sinister. At the water's edge, on the marble paving slab, was a pool of blood. At this point, the constable could have cycled back to the village and telephoned for help, but he didn't. Keen to make his mark, and hoping that Gladys might just be lying injured somewhere, he went upstairs where he found Duval passed out on his bed, 'reeking' in the constable's words, of alcohol. Most damning of all for Duval, the constable found the shirt Duval had been wearing at the party. A rudimentary attempt had been made to hide it by pushing it down the back of an old blanket chest. The shirt was damp and stained with blood.

Of Gladys Rudd there was no sign. And indeed, her body was never found, despite an extensive search of the grounds and surrounding countryside. In a blaze of publicity, Duval was arrested and when he had sobered up, questioned. He claimed that the blood by the pool and on his shirt was his own and that, once the last of his guests had left, he had been attempting to turn off the lights by the pool, when he'd stumbled and injured his hand on a wine glass. He told the officers who questioned him that the sight of all the blood, along with the amount of alcohol he had consumed, caused him to feel faint and he had gone to bed, where he'd passed out, only to be woken by the police constable some hours later. Duval's left hand did indeed bear the signs of being cut by a glass, but the police surgeon who examined him said that he doubted the injury could account for the amount of blood found by the pool and on the shirt.

The transcripts of the police interviews with Duval still exist and show that he initially denied having any contact at all with Gladys. Her sister and three friends, however, all remembered him fetching her a glass of champagne and taking her to sit beside him on a window alcove seat. Confronted with this, Duval admitted to talking to Gladys earlier in the evening, saying that he was confused because he'd spoken to so many people that night – a statement at odds with the various witness accounts of his being unusually taciturn. Pressed about why he had approached her and what they had talked about, Duval said he noticed Gladys looked 'a bit lost' and he wanted to make her feel welcome. He said they'd talked about his latest film, Sleeping Beauty, and that Gladys had asked him questions about his co-star Ava Holland, who was a favourite of hers. Duval described Gladys as 'a sweet child' but said she was 'not the sort of girl I'm interested in'. He said he'd autographed her book of matches – all four of the other girls had seen him write something down and hand it to Gladys – and left her on the window seat while he went to join the rest of his guests. He had, he said, no recollection of seeing or talking to her again.

Duval's studio initially came to his rescue, providing him with the very best of lawyers and doing what it could to keep the media coverage to a minimum. But it rapidly became clear that no star could survive this story. The evidence was circumstantial, and in the absence of a body, not enough to make a conviction likely. Duval was never charged with the murder of Gladys Rudd, but neither, disastrously for him and tragically for her family, was anyone else.

In the weeks that followed Gladys's disappearance, Duval lost almost everything, just as surely as if he had admitted his guilt. The studio continued to pay him for the eighteen months remaining on his contract, but the new DeMille picture was never released, his part in the upcoming film was recast, and indeed he was never to be seen on screen again. Even the films he'd already starred in became toxic. Sleeping Beauty garnered record box office receipts over the weekend after Duval's arrest, thanks to a ghoulish public interest in seeing the alleged murderer up close. But facing charges of profiting from tragedy, the studio withdrew the film from movie theatres a few days later, and it was to be more than sixty years before it was shown in public again – at a retrospective of silent films at the British Film Institute.

None of Duval's friends, who'd been so eager to bathe in the pool of his reflected glory when he was in the ascendant, wanted anything to do with him now. He became a virtual recluse at the house at Poison Cross. He had the swimming pool boarded over almost straight away, and the whole room was transformed into a ballroom a few weeks later – symbolically never to be used. The curtains were always drawn, and his only contact was with the daily woman he employed from the village who cooked and cleaned for him. She was to describe him later as 'a quiet, shuffling man who lived in two rooms of the Big House' and 'mumbled his thanks'. The man who had held audiences of thousands spellbound was now barely capable of exchanging a few words with his cleaning lady.

Sometime on the evening of 13 August or on the morning of 14 August 1935, just over ten years after Gladys Rudd apparently *vanished off the face of the earth, Duval hanged himself. An admission of guilt? Or the only way out for a man who could not bear to go on living, unjustly suspected of a crime he had never committed?*

Chapter Twenty-Two

Lucy, Present

Claire's plan does not, as I feared, involve driving down to the house at Poison Cross, one-time home of Hollywood legend Edward Duval. I'm so relieved that I can't really process what we are doing, which is driving to Brighton to see the retired police officer who investigated Maddie's disappearance all those years ago. Instead, as we make our way out of London, I focus on recounting the details of my visit to Robin and Naomi yesterday.

'Hang on,' Claire shifts round in the passenger seat, so that she's angled towards me, the seat belt cutting into her orange t-shirt, sunglasses on top of her curls. 'You are saying you know that something is wrong because there were some dead flowers?'

'It wasn't just the dead flowers. Plus, this is Naomi we're talking about, remember?'

'Yes, okay. That is weird, I grant you.'

It feels natural talking to her. This is the conversation we should have had yesterday. I meant to bring it up. To say, 'Oh by the way, talking of weird things, I actually called in at your office yesterday, but they said you weren't there.' But I've had time to think about it since and probably the child receptionist was just mistaken. Or Claire was working, but somewhere else. After all, plenty of people aren't tied to their physical workplace anymore and she never actually said she was at the office. I'd be better off leaving it.

'Robin was definitely in a strange mood. You should have heard the way he snapped at her.'

'He's become a bit of a grouch over the years, Luce, that's hardly new.'

'Not like this. This was something different.'

I glance in the rear-view mirror to check Ruby has fallen asleep. She loves car journeys. In the first three months, it was the only thing guaranteed to send her off. Joe or I would sometimes put her in the car and drive her round just to give the other person a break. It's always the same — five minutes of crying just after you've put her in, then blessed peace. The only thing that stopped me doing it at four in the morning was the knowledge that I wasn't in a fit state to be behind the wheel.

'So you actually asked Naomi whether she'd heard from Maddie?'

'Not in so many words. But yes, sort of, and I'm pretty sure *she* hasn't had any messages.'

I pull up at some lights. Capital Radio tells us that it's 10:30 a.m. and that after the news we'll hear Taylor Swift's 'Lavender Haze'. Claire picks up on the emphasis I hadn't even known I was putting on the pronoun.

'But you think Robin might have done?'

I hesitate. For some reason I can't fully explain, I don't want to tell Claire about going through Robin's pockets and sneaking a look at his phone. For a start, I'm not sure the message was from the same person, but I suspect mainly it's because I feel so embarrassed about it — like it was a betrayal of his trust. There are some secrets you don't share with anyone. I've learnt this, too, over the past twenty-five years.

'Maybe,' I say finally. 'He was behaving really strangely even before he snapped at Naomi.'

A red Audi sports car whizzes past us as we pull away from the junction, cutting up the motorbike that's just behind us.

'Did you see that?'

'The Audi?' Claire says. 'Yeah, nice car.'

'Did you see the driver?'

'It was going too fast. A woman I think.'

But I think I know who was driving already. Harriet Holland, whose folder full of letters is still lying at the bottom of my desk drawer, taunting me. Harriet who is supposed to be in Mexico filming right now. And who might, just possibly might, be Maddie. I think about saying something to Claire, but I have a ridiculous fear of saying it out loud and before I can make up my mind, Claire reverts to the subject we're supposed to be discussing.

'Perhaps Robin hasn't told Naomi because he doesn't want to worry her.'

'Okay,' I say, trying to focus. There must be a million red Audis in south London. Or a hundred at least. 'So do you think I should just ask him?'

Even as I say it, I'm dreading the prospect. Robin never brings Maddie into the conversation, not even obliquely in the way that Naomi sometimes does, and when someone else mentions her, you can almost feel the protective spikes emerge. He sits there, the shell of him is physically present, but you know that inside he's wary, poised for flight. There's only one time he really opened up about her and I wasn't even there. It was at a family Christmas four years ago when Joe and Robin went for a walk up on the hill behind their house, while Naomi and I stayed in and watched the *Blackadder Christmas Special*, which incredibly she had somehow never seen, and I got drunk on a bottle of Baileys they'd won in a raffle – the only alcohol they had in the house as both of them are teetotal. Even though I was in a sugary, boozy haze when they returned, I could tell that something momentous had happened from Joe's face. Robin himself looked pale and washed out and went upstairs to rest, emerging several hours later for our traditional supper of cold turkey and Branston pickle baguettes, looking more like his old self.

Joe told me about it on the drive home the next day. It had come from nowhere, he said. They'd climbed up the steep narrow path, following each other single file and then, without talking, sat down on the fallen tree at the top, looking out across the valley. Joe was worrying about getting back before dark, but he also didn't want to make Robin carry on until he'd had a chance to rest – it's a steep hill and he'd puffed his way up it.

Just as Joe was about to suggest they should make a move, Robin had suddenly asked him if he ever thought about his sister and then it had all poured out. How Robin blamed himself for not insisting that the police were called as soon as she went missing, how he should never have let her go to drama camp in the first place, how he was distracted that summer and hadn't paid her as much attention as he should. Robin had wept and Joe had cried with him, his arms around his dad, and then, unable to think what to say next, Joe had for some reason come out with: 'Mind you, I don't miss having to act in those terrible plays she wrote.' There had been a horrible moment where Robin had stopped crying and gone rigid in Joe's arms, and then, amazingly, joyously, Robin had laughed, and they'd ended up talking about all the funny and annoying things Maddie used to do. There had been little light left when they'd finally headed back down the hill, but they'd edged down the path together, conscious of something momentous achieved.

'It's like we've turned a corner and now he can talk about her,' Joe said, wonderingly, on that wet, grey journey home, with the windscreen wipers on full throttle and the usual inexplicable traffic jam on the A3. 'The worst thing was I hadn't realised how much he blames himself.'

But Robin hadn't turned a corner; he'd just gone fleetingly round it and then turned right back round again. I know that Joe has tried again since, but whatever briefly led Robin to open up has been buried again under a pretence that none of it touches him – that Maddie had been someone else's child, someone else's tragedy.

'Let's see what comes out of talking to DI Silver,' Claire says. 'If Robin's already on edge, you don't want to push him over. Can we turn up the air con a bit?'

I reach for the dial. I still can't believe that this is Claire's plan. I can picture DI Silver as clearly as if I'd last seen him yesterday, not a quarter of a century ago. A bullet-headed, barrel-chested man, courteous, with an air of suppressed energy. A man who would find Maddie if anyone could, I'd thought at the time. Only it turned out he couldn't. Of course, he'll look rather different now. He seemed old to us then, but he was probably only about forty. Our age now.

'I can't believe you've managed to find him.'

'Well, he might not still be living there remember. This was the last address they had on file for him when he retired five years ago.'

'Didn't they want to know why you were interested?'

'I just told my copper – this guy I've been working with a lot recently – that I'd worked with DI Silver on my first child abduction case and wondered what had happened to him. It's an unusual name. He even remembered him. They'd briefly overlapped at Lewes nick, just before Silver retired. I said I'd love to write to him and he dug out the address for me.'

'Easy as that,' I say, and I don't know why, but I can hear scepticism in my voice. It's as though I've transferred my suspicion about where she was yesterday to her account of how she found DI Silver.

'I wouldn't say easy,' she says, picking up on my tone and shooting a glance at me. 'Lucky, I guess.'

Claire's phone starts ringing in her bag. She retrieves it, looks at the screen and then kills the call.

'You could have taken it.'

'Oh, it was just Nic. I'll call her back later.'

'It looked like a landline.'

'She still has a landline at her place,' Claire says. I can tell by the way she says it that my tone must have been more accusatory than I intended. I make an attempt to atone. Just because I'm keeping things from her, doesn't mean she's keeping them from me.

'How are things going with the two of you? You seem really happy with her.'

'I am,' she says simply. 'I know that you all think that she's a bit *out there*,' she continues, turning to look out of the window and avoid my gaze, which should really be on the road anyway. 'But the spiritual stuff isn't a big deal for me – it's just part of Nic being who she is as a person.'

I feel bad that we've made Claire think that we don't like Nic. I struggle to think of something positive to say.

155

'She seems very open about everything,' I say, wondering what this would be like. 'Very confident.'

'Exactly. It's one of the things I love about her.'

'And she's gorgeous.'

Claire laughs.

'There is that.' She puts her sunglasses on, as if they offer some kind of protection from my scrutiny. Then she says quietly: 'I think it might actually work out this time Luce.'

'Claire, that's brilliant. I'm so happy for you.'

In spite of everything that's happening right now, I really do feel a moment of pure happiness for her, and then, almost instantly, I feel frightened. Because happiness is so fragile. Every good thing that has ever happened to me over the past twenty-five years, especially Joe and Ruby, has terrified me. I feel like what I did that summer means I don't deserve them, and that they've only been given to me so that the pain will be greater when they're taken away again. To punish me. *You must pay for what you did*.

I glance at Ruby in the back of the car. Still fast asleep. Safe. 'Hayley is going to be so smug,' I say, trying to block out the words of the message that keep scrolling across my mind.

'She'll be Instagramming the hell out of our wedding that's for sure.'

'Hashtag HeyHailzMatchmaker.'

'It's not like she personally introduced us. She just kept on at me to try online dating.'

'That won't stop her.'

The casual way Claire mentions 'our wedding' brings it home to me. She and Nic only met about six months ago, and now she's talking about getting married. How well can you really know someone in that time? Joe and I got married after three years of going out and we knew each other long before that — if you can call what we went through in the aftermath of Maddie's disappearance knowing each other. Hayley and Frank dated on and off for five years before she finally posted a picture of her, Frank, and a large diamond. Be careful, I want to say. Be careful that something terrible doesn't happen, but I don't want to take the radiant look off her face.

Capital is now playing something loud and shouty that I don't recognise. I switch to Magic and the sound of Sophie B. Hawkins singing 'Damn I Wish I Was Your Lover' fills the car. I relax slightly. Even my musical taste is stuck in the past.

'So what exactly are we going to say to DI Silver if he is still there?'

'I think we just tell him the truth.'

My head snaps towards her.

'Shit, Lucy, can you keep your eyes on the road? I don't mean the *truth* truth. We don't tell him about what happened — you know I don't think there's any point in telling anybody that now, whatever Jenna says.'

I'm both relieved and disappointed at the same time. For a moment, I imagine what it would be like to tell the truth. The sheer, glorious relief of it, after all these years of secrecy. The other day in Hayley's garden, Jenna had said, 'Surely no one would hold it against us now.' As if secrets somehow lose their power with time. But the opposite is true — the longer you keep a secret, the more potent it becomes. The harder it is to imagine ever revealing it.

'We don't even tell him about the messages.'

'So, when you say we tell him the truth…?'

'We say that we've all been talking about Maddie recently – about what happened – and we want to know what he thinks. We want to know what his theory is.'

'Isn't he going to want to know why now? Why not at any other time?'

'It's coming up for twenty-five years since she disappeared. Anniversaries are powerful things.'

'I suppose so.' I think about all the anniversaries over the years. 'Do you think that could be what this is all about?'

After the initial gut-churning horror of the two text messages, which still returns in waves that threaten to overwhelm me, I have become obsessed with the question – why now? If it really is Maddie, why has she got in touch after all these years, and if it's someone else – someone who knows that we went to the house at Poison Cross that night – why have they waited more than two decades to show their hand?

'I suppose it could be yeah. Or it might be something else has provoked it.'

'Such as?'

Claire seems reluctant to continue. 'Like I said on Sunday, maybe it's someone who's just come into contact with you again.'

'Someone I know, you mean?'

'Perhaps. Someone you've only met recently.'

I think again of Harriet, but I've decided I'm not ready to tell Claire about my theory just yet. I'm worried that saying it out loud will somehow make it more real. There's also the fear that Claire will think I'm losing the plot – and maybe I am. I glance again in the rear-view mirror; Ruby is still asleep, her head lolling slightly to one side, three curls of chestnut hair standing up on end.

'Anyway, DI Silver will understand. He was always good at understanding. We'll tell him that what happened to Maddie has affected all our lives. That nothing has ever been the same since.'

And this really is the truth.

Chapter Twenty-Three

Lucy, Present

'The curly haired one and the chubby one.'

'That's us,' Claire says.

'He told me all about the four of you, love. Not so much at the time, but later. He used to talk about *her* a lot, too. Maddie Blake. Poor kid. There was you two and then the Asian one and the hippy one.'

Mrs Silver is reaching for mugs in the cupboard and Claire and I exchange glances. I think Jenna wins on the most reductive summary front, although I'm not really thrilled about my defining feature and I can't really imagine anyone describing Hayley, who has acquired tens of thousands of followers on the strength of what an article about influencers described as 'her uber-chic but relatable lifestyle', as a hippy, but presumably fifteen-year-old Hayley, with her long blonde hair, nose stud and air of not caring must have created a rather different impression.

'The whole case affected my Andy quite badly you see, and he had a bit of a breakdown about eighteen months afterwards. It upset him that he couldn't find her, poor kid – kind of preyed on his mind, you know.'

Karen Silver is not what I would have expected. She must have been a lot younger than him for a start, because she still only looks in her mid-fifties now. She's skinny and tanned, with peroxide hair and looks somehow too exotic for solid, savvy DI Silver.

'She's a sweetheart isn't she? What age?'

'Eight months.'

Ruby, who only woke up about five minutes ago, is regarding Karen with bleary-eyed confusion. She's like this when she first wakes up at the moment; when she was younger, she used to accept where she was without question, but now she knows if she's somewhere unfamiliar and it takes her a while to adjust and return to smiles. I worry suddenly that I shouldn't have brought her with us; as if just by bringing her here I'm mixing her up in it all. Putting her at risk. But it's one of Joe's days to be at school – he's been down to three days a week since Ruby was born – and obviously I couldn't turn Claire down. Besides, what harm could possibly come to her seeing a retired police officer?

Only it turns out we won't be seeing him. Claire seems less floored by this than I am. She managed to say all the right things about being sorry for Karen's loss and not wanting to be a bother, while I was still gaping on the doorstep. I'd accepted that he might not be at the same address, but I'd never thought he might be dead. Now he'll never know, I find myself thinking stupidly. He'll never know what happened to her – as if I still retained that childish faith he would somehow solve the case.

'How old was he?' I'd asked indignantly in the awkward silence that had followed her announcement that he'd 'passed three years ago', and I'd seen from Claire's furrowed brow that it had come out wrong. This is happening to me a lot right now.

He was sixty-two. It was a heart attack. It came out of nowhere apparently. Things do. I should know that. Once she realised who we were, the look of brisk suspicion had left her face and she'd invited us in as if we were long-lost relatives. It was strange to think of her – this woman we had never met – living with Maddie's story too for all this time.

'Could I have some hot water in a bowl to heat her bottle?' I ask, because for the moment it's all I can think to ask.

'Of course you can, love.' The kettle finishes boiling. In the background, the washing machine is whirring. 'Rooibos alright is it? It's all I've got. Gavin's doing a Sainsbury's shop.'

'Gavin's your son?' Claire asks.

'Husband.' She looks at us. 'I'm no good by myself,' she says. 'Andy knew that. He wouldn't have minded. Gavin was our best man, back when we got married. Life goes on, doesn't it?'

It's weird thinking of this person called Andy, whose best man married his wife, and trying to match him up with the police officer who seemed to us almost god-like back in those numb, terror-filled days after Maddie's disappearance. I sit at the kitchen table so that I can give Ruby her bottle. There are only two chairs and although Karen suggests Claire takes the other, she remains standing, clutching her steaming mug of tea, facing Karen.

'Do you girls blame him?'

'Blame him?'

I don't think it had ever occurred to any of us to blame DI Silver; we'd been far too busy blaming ourselves.

'Well, he never found her, did he. He blamed himself all right. No matter how much I tried to talk him out of it. Round and round we'd go.'

It turns out that, for all the time Claire and I spent discussing how we would explain why we were there, Karen doesn't even ask. She's just accepted two strangers turning up on her doorstep, more than two decades after they were involved in a crime her husband investigated. I wonder whether DI Silver would have asked more questions. Probably. He was a police officer after all.

'Andy was on track to get a promotion before it all happened. But after Maddie Blake it was like he lost his self-belief somehow. He carried on all right, but it was like the energy had gone out of him, you know?'

'I remember how determined he was,' says Claire. 'How focused on finding her. Even as a child I could see that.'

Karen smiles properly for the first time, and it softens her face.

'He was determined all right, love. It was just that it didn't do him any good this time. It wasn't his first murder.' The washing machine whirrs into sudden life behind her, as I take in the implications of what she's just said. 'There'd been quite a few others. A husband who killed his wife and their little kiddie because he didn't want her to leave him. Suffocated them, he did. An old man beaten to death for his pin number. All of them horrible in their way. But Maddie Blake got under his skin more than any of the others – it was the not knowing that did it.'

'He did think she'd been murdered then?' Claire asks.

I have an idiotic desire to cover Ruby's ears. It seems such a wrong conversation for her to be hearing, and even though I know it must make as much sense to her as a conversation in Mandarin would to me, I still worry that on some level some of it is going in. That her first words are going to be about murder. That she will wake tonight, screaming from a nightmare about pensioners being tortured for their pin numbers. She vomits up some milk over my top and Karen hands me some kitchen roll while Claire hunts for the wet wipes in the ginormous blue spotty bag that has followed me everywhere since Ruby was born.

'Not at first he didn't. At first, he thought she'd run away. That's one of the reasons he blamed himself so much. She'd done it before – gone missing. Well, I suppose you both know that – you were her friends. She was a bit of a daredevil from the sounds of it.'

'Maddie was a law unto herself,' says Claire. 'She had a lot of determination too – a bit like your husband. She knew what she wanted and sometimes she'd push the boundaries to get it. Her confidence was one of the things I loved about her.'

It's a strange echo of what she said in the car about Nic, and I wonder if she realises.

'I wasn't confident at all – shit, I was pretending to be. I spent my whole time at school pretending to be confident.'

'I know what you mean, love. Me and all.'

'Maddie was fearless, though. I remember once in primary school, I had this yellow jacket that I loved and one lunch break one of the year six boys took it and threw it up in the trees. I was in pieces. I knew my mum would kill me and I loved that jacket. Maddie marched straight up to the boy who'd taken it and threw her bottle of juice over him, and while he was still rubbing the gunk out of his eyes and his friends were just standing there in shock, she climbed up the tree and got the jacket. She must have been twenty feet up. When she came down, the whole playground clapped her, and by then a teacher had turned up and she got sent to the headmaster. But she didn't care. She never did.'

I watch Claire's face glow as she tells the story, and I think: how have I never heard this before? Sometimes I forget that they all knew Maddie so much longer than me. She was my friend for just over six weeks: from the moment she said hello to me in the canteen until the moment we last saw her going into the house at Poison Cross. A friendship that lasted little more than a month has defined the entire rest of my life, so that I sometimes feel like I knew Maddie for years and years. It's strange to think that if it hadn't ended in the way it did, Maddie might be just a tiny pinprick of a memory by now. The cool girl I hung out with one summer when I was thirteen.

'She sounds special,' Karen says, reaching out to touch Claire's arm.

'She was,' Claire says, fiercely. I realise that she's trying not to cry, and struggle to think of something to say to give her a few moments, but my mind is full of Maddie, climbing up a tree to retrieve a much-loved yellow jacket. Claire's voice is still a bit wobbly but she continues: 'So, yes, it wasn't that out of character for her to disappear and yes she had done it before. A few times actually.'

'That's what Andy said. A MisPers case they call it – that's what they thought they were dealing with at the start. She was fifteen after all – not a small child – and there was no evidence she'd been taken against her will. Everyone thought she'd turn up.'

'What made Andy change his mind?' I ask. It feels wrong to call him Andy, but I can't keep talking about DI Silver as if I'm still thirteen years old.

'The fact that she didn't, love. Of course, that didn't stop him asking all the right questions. He did all the things he should have. Organised a search. Spoke to everyone who'd been in the area. And there was a sighting of her as well. That lad with the motorbike.'

'Sam?'

'Sam, that's it. He said he'd seen her getting on a train. But they couldn't find any other witnesses, even though there were quite a few people on the station. Andy became convinced he was lying – trying to get himself out of trouble. Andy arrested him, but there was never anything to tie him directly to her disappearance and in the end they had to let him go. But you know about that.'

'Did he have any other suspects?' Anyone who might now be sending me threatening text messages. Because, after all, this is why we are here. Not to reminisce about Maddie, which we could have done at any point over the past twenty-five years if she hadn't become the most taboo of subjects.

'Oh, there were plenty of people it could have been, all right. But of course they never did find the body and that made it harder.'

'Anyone in particular?'

'He had his doubts about the dad, I do remember that.'

I feel winded with the shock. 'About Robin?'

'Was that his name? I don't remember. It often is someone in the family, you know. Nothing Andy could ever prove, mind.'

I picture Robin as I saw him yesterday, distracted, worried. Angry.

'But how could her dad have anything to do with it?' Claire says. She's waving her mug so vigorously that tea sloshes over the side. 'The Blakes lived twenty miles away. Was he supposed to have driven down in the middle of the night and kidnapped her or something?'

In the middle of the night. How easy it is to slip up, I realise, now that we've started talking about it again. But Karen doesn't seem to have noticed.

'Andy thought that she might have gone home. There was a theory that she'd gone to meet her boyfriend. I can't remember his name either, something foreign-sounding.'

'Amari,' I say on autopilot.

'That was it. There was this idea that she'd gone to meet up with this boyfriend somewhere and then gone home afterwards. Of course, the boy swore blind they'd never met up, and Andy believed him in the end I think, but he said Maddie could still have gone looking for him and, when she didn't find him, gone back home.'

'But, what if she had?'

'Well, there was something not quite right about that family, love,' Karen says, raising her voice as the washing machine becomes louder, oblivious, obviously, that she is talking about my in-laws. Ruby's grandparents. 'That's what Andy said. Some secret they were keeping. Well, supposing the daughter walked in on the secret. That was one theory.'

I feel sick. All these years I've thought of the Blakes as victims, while DI Silver thought of them as suspects. It's like I'm suddenly seeing the story from a totally different perspective, and I don't like it at all. And what does Karen mean? *Something not quite right about the family*. What was not right about the Blakes? *They were perfect*, I want to shout. Okay, so they're all a bit damaged now, but who wouldn't be? Their only daughter disappeared aged fifteen; they're allowed to be a bit strange. But before that. Before that they were like the beautiful, cool family from an American TV show – the family you wanted to be part of.

'But what made him think that?' asks Claire, who looks as shocked as I feel.

'They behaved suspiciously right from the start according to Andy. The summer camp called them on the evening of the day Maddie disappeared. They spoke to the mother and she seemed distracted apparently – not that interested in her daughter's disappearance. It was that actress that spoke to her, the famous one.'

The washing machine shudders to a halt.

'They didn't turn up at the summer camp until the following morning and even then it was just the mother and the son. The father wasn't there. What kind of a father doesn't come running when the police tell him his daughter's disappeared?'

How can I not remember this? When I play the scene in my memory, the Blakes all arrive at once, spilling out on the drive in front of the youth hostel. Robin, ashen and demanding answers, Naomi, red-eyed and un-made-up, and Joe, rigid, watchful.

'He was at home that morning when his wife and son came down to the summer camp,' Karen says. 'One of the neighbours saw him. When Andy confronted him about it, he said he hadn't been feeling well so he'd stayed at home. I ask you, does that sound normal?'

I've let the bottle slide out of Ruby's mouth and she starts crying in frustration. I manoeuvre it back, automatically.

'Did any of the neighbours actually see Maddie?' Claire asks.

'No, the police questioned them all I think, but nobody saw her.' I imagine them asking my mum. She must have known that the police suspected the Blakes and yet she never told me; she never even hinted that this was a possibility. 'They searched the family home too.'

This I do remember. You could see the Blakes' house from my bedroom and I remember the police cars parked outside. At first I thought it meant Maddie had been found and, stomach lurching, I'd run down the stairs to find my mum. She'd just spoken to Naomi. No news. The police were just searching for anything that could explain where Maddie might have gone, she'd said. Now I know that they were searching for some sign that Maddie might have returned. That she might have been murdered there. That her body was buried there.

'They never found anything to prove that she'd gone back, or that she'd been killed there. Doesn't mean it didn't happen though.'

I shudder. Karen puts her hand on my shoulder and I flinch like she's struck me.

'I'm so sorry, love. I probably shouldn't have told you girls any of this. I can see I've upset you. It doesn't mean the dad did it. I'm not saying that. I only mentioned it at all because you asked me what Andy thought.' She sounds a bit reproachful now, like we haven't kept our side of some unspoken bargain. 'Probably we'll never know who did it. Sometimes you have to let the dead bury their dead. That's what I used to tell Andy.'

Supposing Maddie really had gone home? It is possible? I think of Joe saying that he never realised how much Robin blamed himself. But DI Silver had blamed himself too. Blaming yourself doesn't mean you're guilty. We blamed ourselves. With good reason. Perhaps, after all, blame does mean you're guilty; it's just a question of what you're guilty of.

I see Karen glance at the clock. She's probably regretting asking us in at all. Wondering whether we'll be gone by the time Gavin comes back with the Sainsbury's shopping. I can see her trying to find something to say to lighten the mood. Neither Claire nor I are in a place where we're able to help her.

'Look at you both,' she says finally. 'She would have been so proud of you. Maddie. All grown up and successful. And there's the little one too. New life. She'd have wanted you to move on.'

'Let the dead bury their dead,' Claire echoes. 'My mum used to say that too. It's from the bible I think.'

But she doesn't sound convinced, and I wonder if she's thinking the same thing as me – how can you let the dead bury their dead when they might not be dead at all?

Chapter Twenty-Four

DI Silver, 1999

Andy Silver studied the four girls in front of him. He wasn't very good with teenagers – not these kinds of teenagers anyway; children pretending to be grown–ups. Drug dealers and joy riders he could do. He could do kids too – proper kids. His sister had a little girl, but she was only six, and happy to prattle about My Little Pony and Sylvanian Families; he had no idea what he'd talk to her about in ten years' time. But he also knew that if anyone knew where Maddie was, it would be these four. Teenage girls told each other everything, didn't they? Even the way they were sitting reinforced this idea, huddled as a group on the low, yellow sofa in the office of the youth hostel. The one with the curly hair had her arm around the younger friend, and the other two – the tall Asian girl and the one with the piercings and the attitude, were clutching each other's hands. They all had one thing in common: they looked frightened.

He hoped that talking to them together would be less intimidating. He'd asked for a responsible adult to be there with them, even though he wasn't interviewing them formally, and the male teacher, wearing the Guns N' Roses t-shirt, had volunteered at once. Tom Durrant. 'You may have seen me on television.' Interesting way to introduce yourself to a police officer investigating the disappearance of a child in your care. And he hadn't; he didn't watch much TV. He liked films, but he got the sense Durrant hadn't been in many of those. He wondered about Tom Durrant. Awkward, and nervous because he was in an unfamiliar situation, or something more? He'd talk to him properly later, if it proved necessary, and he was hoping it wouldn't.

'I want to ask you a few questions about Maddie.' He took the seat opposite them – a low, uncomfortable office chair – and smiled, trying to make it a reassuring smile. He knew he could look threatening, with his bulk and his shaven head, and the last thing he wanted was to make them more scared. The room itself didn't help; lit by a bright overhead bulb with no shade. 'You're her friends. You're the ones who know her best, so I need your help to find her. Let's start by talking about when you last saw her.'

If possible, they all looked even more stricken. He clearly needed to work on that reassuring smile. The Asian girl, Jenna – pretty name, he remembered it because it was a bit like his niece, Jenny – looked like she might cry.

He prompted them, 'It was in the bedroom in the cottage this morning?'

'That's right, Maddie had a migraine so she decided to stay in bed.'

'If you could let the girls answer the questions, sir,' he said, glaring at Tom-you-might-have-seen-me-on-TV, who was hovering at his right shoulder.

'Sorry, sorry. Forget I'm here.'

'What kind of mood would you say Maddie was in when you last saw her?'

'She was excited,' said the youngest of the four instantly, and then clapped her hand over her mouth in an almost comic sign that she regretted she'd spoken. She was definitely still a child – in some ways more like his six-year-old niece than the other girls on the sofa and she didn't quite fit with them. He wondered how they came to be a group; maybe she was someone's kid sister. Her friends tensed up at her words and Andy knew she'd already given away something they weren't sure they were ready to reveal to him.

'Excited? Even though she had a headache?'

They looked back at him mutely. Even the young one had clammed up now. Lucy Keeble. She was only thirteen. Young Lucy might be his best hope of finding Maddie, but he needed to take it slowly, to coax the information out of her.

'Did Maddie say anything to you that could explain where she might have gone? It might be something that didn't seem important at the time.'

'She might have met up with Amari,' said the one with the curly hair. He glanced at his notebook to remind himself: Claire Griffiths. Fifteen years old. Same class at school as Maddie Blake, like the other two, but not Lucy, who was a couple of years below.

'Amari is…?'

'Her boyfriend.'

'He's at the summer camp too?'

'No, he's from back home.'

'So she talked about going home to meet him?'

'Not exactly. They had a row.'

'When was this?'

'Yesterday. It was just a silly thing. He wanted to come down and see her, and she said no, and he was pissed off with her. It wasn't anything serious.'

'Does Amari have a surname?'

He made a note of it. He'd have an officer go round to the boyfriend's house straight away. She might be there; sometimes it really was that simple.

'She wouldn't have left summer camp to go and hang out with Amari.' This was the first time the girl with the piercings had spoken. It was said as if the statement were a self-evident truth, but he thought he also detected something more in her tone; resentment perhaps. He suddenly felt sure she hadn't heard the story about the argument with the boyfriend and that she minded not knowing. It was a reminder that a group of teenage girls didn't tell each other everything after all, or at least that there might be allegiances and rivalries, and that some of the group might know more than others.

'Why do you say that...' he glanced at the notebook again, 'Hayley?'

Hayley Lorrimer was the coolest of them all, wearing a long multi-coloured skirt and a short top that exposed her stomach, and a belly-button piercing. But the smudged mascara and bitten nails made her look vulnerable.

'Camp was too important to her. She could have seen Amari any time.'

'Maddie's enjoying the summer camp?'

'Acting's a big deal for her.'

'Maddie is quite a talent, I think it's fair to say.'

He turned with irritation towards Durrant.

'I really am going to have to ask you to keep quiet, sir.' He swivelled back to look at the girls on the sofa.

'So what else might Maddie have been excited about if it wasn't meeting her boyfriend?'

Lucy Keeble shifted awkwardly, and he knew there was more to come. He was regretting now that he hadn't spoken to them separately.

'Was there someone else she might have been meeting? Someone she liked as well as Amari?' Lucy squirmed and he felt the satisfaction of knowing that his guess had been right. 'Maddie's not in any trouble here. I just want to find her and make sure she's safe.'

'There was someone who liked her.'

All three of the others were staring at Lucy. Jenna looked tense too – like she knew, or thought she knew, what her friend was going to say, and she kept darting glances at Durrant. Claire was visibly shrinking away from Hayley on her left.

'It's the man who does the lighting,' Lucy mumbled at last.

'Sam? Sam and Maddie?' Tom Durrant sounded outraged. 'That is absolutely against the rules. I'll have words with him.'

'Please leave it to us, sir. Does Sam live on the premises?'

'No, he lives in a cottage in Poison Cross.' This sounded promising. 'With his mum. She does the cleaning here.'

He took the address. He'd send an officer round right away. Because it was a good lead and the mum might be away or just not interested.

'Was Sam at work today?'

'No, he doesn't work here full time. He just helps out when he can. I haven't seen him since last night actually.'

This was also hopeful.

'How do you know Sam likes Maddie, Lucy?'

She was picking at her bottom lip. 'I was there when he told her.'

'Sam told Maddie that he liked her?'

She nodded. She looked like a frightened rabbit.

'And how did she react?'

'She told him she had a boyfriend,' Lucy said quickly. 'But she seemed kind of—'

'What?'

'Pleased,' Lucy said, flushing.

'What about the rest of you? Did she mention Sam to any of the rest of you?' he asked.

'She told me she wasn't interested in him,' Claire said, her face also flushed.

'She never mentioned him to me,' Hayley said, and this time he could tell that it was more than resentment at being left out of a secret. So, Hayley liked Sam too. If they found Maddie at his cottage, there were going to be some awkward moments between the two of them. Sweet Jesus, let it be that easy.

'I had no idea they'd even talked to each other,' said Tom, who seemed almost as indignant.

'You told Miss Caxton that Maddie's rucksack is missing.'

The four friends nodded, acting as a single organism again, differences forgotten in the face of the developing theory of where Maddie might be.

'Can I ask you to have a look through her things and tell me what she might have taken?'

'We already did that,' Claire said.

'There are some clothes missing,' Jenna said eagerly.

He also felt hopeful, although it was a long time since he'd let that show on his face. He was more and more sure that he was dealing with a voluntary disappearance here.

It was nearly ten p.m. now; Maddie Blake had been gone anywhere between ten and twelve hours. It was entirely plausible that she'd gone to meet Sam, and spent the day with him. The clothes suggested that maybe she intended to stay overnight. Probably she hadn't realised that her friends would get worried so quickly; she thought they'd cover for her for longer.

'It's weird stuff, though,' Hayley said, fingers twisting the necklace she was wearing, which had one of those little black and white pendants on it.

'In what way?'

'She took strange things. This white slip dress. A sparkly cardigan.'

He wasn't exactly sure what a slip dress was, but the items didn't sound that odd to him. They sounded like things a fifteen-year-old girl might take if she was going to stay with her new boyfriend.

'Anything else?'

'Her make-up is missing too,' Claire said.

The older three were starting to perk up. But Lucy still looked troubled, and he wondered if there was something more to come.

'Was Maddie friendly with anyone else at the summer camp? Anyone else she might have confided in?'

Their voices overlapped as they rejected this possibility.

'Okay. Well, I'm going to go and see whether Maddie's at Sam's cottage, so I think, young ladies, you should go and get ready for bed.' Ouch. He'd turned into the kind of police officer who called teenagers young ladies. 'You've been a big help. Try not to worry too much. I hope I'll have her back before long. If not,' he saw their faces fall, 'I'll need to talk to you all again in the morning.'

They got up from the sofa, unfolding awkward teenage limbs, and made their way slowly to the door, moving as a group, and seemingly reluctant to go. Tom Durrant, on the other hand, looked keen to follow them, but he stopped him.

'Who else is on the premises, sir?'

'Well, there are twenty in the Dream Team in total, including Maddie.'

'The Dream Team?'

'The young people. I call them the Dream Team because of the play. *A Midsummer Night's Dream*. By Shakespeare.'

'Right, thank you. Right now one of those young people is missing, so if you could just cut the crap and tell me what I need to know that would help me to do my job, sir.'

Durrant looked like he'd been slapped.

'Who else?' he repeated.

'There's Lorraine and me. And Sam and his mum Millie come in most days. That's about it I think.'

'You think or you're sure?'

'I'm sure. Oh and there's Lisa and Rupa, who do our cooking for us and look after reception.'

'If Maddie isn't at this Sam's house, I'll need to talk to everyone.'

'You do think she's there though? That she's with Sam?'

Durrant had gone from sounding outraged at the idea of Maddie and Sam together to sounding positively enthusiastic about it. Possibly the seriousness of his situation had just hit him. He and Lorraine Caxton were *in loco parentis* and if Maddie Blake didn't turn up soon, there would be some difficult questions for both to answer.

'At the moment it's our best hope, sir.'

'I'll let you get on with it then.'

Durrant sank onto the yellow sofa.

'I'll be back.' With Maddie, he hoped. Out in the corridor, he saw the four girls hadn't gone far. They were standing by the empty reception desk. He wondered if they'd overheard his conversation with Durrant.

'All right ladies?' He was doing it again. Was saying ladies any better than young ladies? 'Was there something else you wanted to tell me?'

His radio crackled into life. It was probably one of the two uniforms he'd brought with him, who'd been having a look round the cottage and the grounds.

'Excuse me a moment.'

He glanced back at them as he answered his radio. Now they were all holding hands, clutching onto each other tight like they would never let go.

Chapter Twenty-Five

Lucy, 1999

'Claire! Oh god it's so good to see you.'

Lucy froze in horror at the sight of Maddie's mum coming out of the youth hostel. It was the morning after they'd spoken to DI Silver, the police officer who seemed so sure he'd find Maddie, but there was still no news. She had no idea Maddie's family had arrived and, judging by Claire's expression, neither did she. Mrs Blake hurried across the courtyard towards the two of them. She looked nothing like she'd looked the previous times Lucy had met her — she was wearing leggings and an old purple jersey top and her black bob was messy and all over the place, not sleek like usual. Lucy had literally no idea what to say to her, but it turned out she didn't need to say anything, because Mrs Blake didn't seem to notice her at all. Instead, she wrapped Claire in a tight hug that seemed like it would never end.

It had been Lucy's idea to come outside. She'd told the others she was going to use the payphone to call home, but really she just wanted some time by herself to try to work out what she should do. Claire had said she'd walk over to the main building with her, as if she didn't want to let Lucy out of her sight in case she disappeared too. For a few seconds the fresh air had helped. Claire's shoulders had dropped, and Lucy had been conscious of the sun falling warm on her bare arms; then the sight of Maddie's mum brought the reality of the situation crashing back.

Now, finally, Mrs Blake released Claire from the hug, and, looking at her with fierce intensity, asked, 'She's going to be all right isn't she?'

Lucy watched dumbly, fiddling with the hem of her t-shirt, as Claire found the words. 'Of course. Of course she is. She'll be fine.'

It was like Claire was the adult and Mrs Blake the child, but at the same time Mrs Blake looked much older than last time Lucy had seen her. Was it just because she wasn't wearing any make-up? There were long lines running from either side of her nose to her chin that Lucy didn't remember being there before.

'They thought she was with this new boyfriend. This Sam.'

Mrs Blake was clutching Claire's arms now. Lucy could see her fingernails digging into the flesh.

'I don't think he's her boyfriend,' Claire said.

'But when they went down there to check he said he hadn't seen her,' continued Mrs Blake as if she hadn't heard her. 'They searched his house, that's what the Inspector said, and there wasn't any sign of her. But supposing he's already done something with her?'

'She's going to be all right,' Claire said. Lucy could tell she didn't know what else to say. It felt wrong that Mrs Blake had no one else with her. There should be another adult to look after her.

'Where's Mr Blake?' Claire asked, as if the same thought had occurred to her.

Mrs Blake dropped Claire's arms and took a step backwards.

'Robin's on a business trip. He'll be here as soon as he can.'

Suddenly Mrs Blake's eyes alighted on Lucy, as if seeing her for the first time.

'Lucy! Do you know him? This Sam? Do you think Maddie would have gone to see him?'

'I... I don't know,' Lucy stammered, and Mrs Blake, already dismissing her, turned her gaze back to Claire, asking with fresh urgency, 'What about Amari? Do you think she could have gone to see him? The Inspector said they'd had an argument. Do you think she went to make it up with him?'

Lucy didn't know what to do. It was surprisingly hard, after all, to tell the truth. The question the adults should have been asking was, 'When did you really last see Maddie?'

Yet, again and again, they failed to do so, and every minute that passed the lie they'd told became harder and harder to unpick. Lucy knew that it still wasn't too late. She could interrupt Mrs Blake now. She could say it. *We're really sorry, there is something we should have told you that we didn't. We left Maddie in the middle of the night in a haunted house.* The trouble was she didn't know how. She could find the words in her head, but she couldn't get them to come out of her mouth. Not without a pause, a hesitation, a question. It was strange, because the previous times she'd met Maddie's mum she'd felt a bit like she could look inside her head – in the words of the Peter Sarstedt song that Lucy's dad loved so much. Yet just at the moment when looking inside Lucy's head was the most useful thing Mrs Blake could have done, she seemed to have lost the knack entirely.

'Of course, she's run off before,' Mrs Blake was saying. 'The police keep asking me about that. I told them it's different this time. It was a protest before. The kind of thing that teenage girls do to their mothers all the time. You agree, don't you, Claire, that it feels different this time?'

Claire nodded, although Lucy knew that she still clung to the hope that this was exactly what had happened. They'd been talking about it in the bedroom of the cottage with Hayley and Jenna just before they came outside. All three of them were competing to convince each other that Maddie had a plan and was off having a good time, or at least an adventure, somewhere. When she got back, she would be angry and embarrassed that the police had been called, but she'd eventually tell them all about it. Lucy wanted to believe this too, but she found it harder than the others, and maybe they didn't really believe it either, because now Claire was making a whimpering sort of noise, which Mrs Blake didn't even seem to notice.

She swept on. 'Before, it was like she was punishing me. But she's never been gone for this long. She wouldn't do that to me. She's never stayed away overnight, not the whole night. And she doesn't know this place. It's not like home. Where would she go?'

Lucy had heard some of the stories of times when Maddie had gone missing before; the others had traded them earlier that morning, like talismans that would somehow make everything turn out all right this time too. The weird thing was how little any of them – Maddie's best friends – seemed to know about where she'd actually *been*. And sometimes, what she told them wasn't true. One Saturday night when she'd supposed to be going with them to see *Sliding Doors*, and hadn't shown up, she told them afterwards that she'd been with Amari. But Jenna had overheard a year nine saying that he'd seen Maddie walking on the metal girders underneath the railway bridge, high above the river. He was telling a group of other year nines about it. Maddie was fearless. That was what they all said. The trouble with fearless people, Lucy thought, was that they sometimes did very dangerous things.

'The police think it's part of a pattern,' Mrs Blake said. 'Do you think they're really looking for her? Do you think they're taking it seriously?'

There were now two police jeeps parked on the drive to the youth hostel, in addition to DI Silver's car. Lucy thought the police were taking it seriously. Then, as if from a long distance, she heard Mrs Blake say, 'This Sam told the police he saw Maddie getting on a train.'

Lucy's heart lurched. 'A train?' she said.

'When?' Claire asked at the same time.

'Yesterday afternoon. He told the police he saw her walking into the station. Why aren't the police at the station? Why aren't they asking if anybody saw her? Do you think she really was there?'

Time seemed to slow down as Lucy tried to take the words in, to check she'd understood them correctly. Sam saw Maddie yesterday afternoon. After they'd last seen her. So did that mean they weren't to blame? Maybe it was going to be okay after all. It didn't matter where they saw her last because he'd seen her since. Part of the burden she'd been carrying since the night in the haunted house shifted slightly. Please God, she prayed to the deity she'd told her mum she was sure didn't exist, let it be all right. Please God let Sam have seen her. Let it not be my fault. Let Maddie be all right.

Chapter Twenty-Six

'Hi.'

The voice made Lucy jump. Maddie's brother Joe was sitting on a bench, beside the edge of the path, his face ashen, his hair rumpled. It was strange but she didn't feel the same frozen horror she'd felt when she saw Maddie's mum earlier that day. She still didn't know what to say though.

'Oh. Hello. Sorry.'

'Why are you sorry?'

'Well you probably want to be by yourself.'

'Actually, that's the last thing I want.'

'I'm Lucy by the way.'

He smiled. A small smile that escaped him involuntarily and was almost instantly gone again.

'I know who you are.'

'I wasn't sure if you'd remember.'

She hovered awkwardly beside him. She didn't have long. But something about the way he'd said he didn't want to be alone made it impossible to leave him. He looked at her properly then. Brown eyes with big dark circles under them.

'Lucy Keeble. Year Eight. Likes Agatha Christie and Thom Yorke. Famous mum. How am I doing?'

She pulled a face.

'Put me right, Lucy Keeble.'

She sat down beside him on the bench. The wood scratched her thighs where her denim shorts ended.

'I don't like Thom Yorke. I just said I did. And my mum's not really famous.'

'No?'

'She's just on TV sometimes.'

'Blame my sister. She's the source of all my information.'

Now that he'd mentioned Maddie, she obviously had to say something too, but although talking to Joe was much easier than talking to Maddie's mum, she still didn't know what to say. The closest comparison was back in Nottingham when her friend Sarah's grandma had died and she'd avoided her all day at school because she hadn't known what to do. When she'd confessed that evening her mum had told her that all that mattered was that she said something – something simple and straightforward. Not that Maddie had died. It felt wrong even to connect her with death in her head, as if thinking it might make it happen. She stopped peeling the paint off the arm of the bench with her fingernail, and glanced sideways at Joe. She took a deep breath. 'I'm so sorry about, you know, about this.'

'Thanks.'

The conversation faltered and she worried she'd said the wrong thing after all. That it hadn't been simple or straightforward enough. But just as she was about to launch into another version, he said, 'Three-quarters of missing people are found in the first twenty-four hours, you know.'

She had not known.

'It's been more than that already.'

'That still leaves a quarter,' she said. It sounded idiotic even to her own ears.

'It does.' To her surprise, he smiled at her again. 'It does, doesn't it? You know what, I'm normally a really positive person, but I'm finding it tough right now. It's horrible watching my mum and dad like this. They're in pieces. I feel like I've got to be the strong one, you know. The one who keeps telling them it's going to be fine. But I don't really believe it. Deep down I'm not sure it's going to be fine at all. Supposing someone's taken her, Lucy.'

His eyes were wet with unshed tears.

'Some of those quarter must get found,' she said, sticking to the thing that seemed to have helped.

'Yes, they must.' But he sounded less convinced this time.

'Do you know what the police are doing?'

'Not really. They haven't told us much. I think they're talking to the lighting guy Sam again. He's the last one who saw her. But if he saw her get on a train yesterday afternoon, I don't understand why they're still here. Why aren't they trying to find where she went?'

'Maybe there are other police doing that.'

'When the people from the summer camp called yesterday, I was out with some mates having a drink. You know, just a normal night out. A couple of beers in the park.'

Lucy nodded, as though she were always having a couple of beers in the park. She didn't want to risk too many words, because she still wasn't sure how to find the right ones. She remembered something else her mum said. Maybe it wasn't about her talking at all. Maybe it was about listening to Joe. 'As soon as I opened the front door

I knew something was wrong. Mum practically threw herself at me. I've never seen her like that. She can't stop crying. Dad's even worse.' Something strange flitted across his face, like he wanted to say more. 'I just don't know what to do, you know?'

Again she nodded.

'I'm sorry, I shouldn't be bothering you with all this, but you're easy to talk to, Lucy Keeble. I can see why Maddie chose you as a friend.'

In spite of everything, she felt a stab of happiness. At the idea that she was Maddie's friend. That she had been chosen. That she fitted in. Even that Maddie's brother thought she was easy to talk to. She felt her face grow hot with shame. What a ridiculous thing to think right now. Joe was looking at her.

'Won't they be wondering where you are? Back at the hostel.'

'I said I was going outside to look for my mum. She's coming to pick me up.'

She glanced at her neon pink Swatch watch – the one that had been a birthday present the last birthday before her parents split up. Her mum said she'd be there at four. She had just under twenty minutes. She was sure Claire and the others would cover for her, even though she hadn't told them her plan.

'You should head back. You don't want to miss her.'

'I think all the parents are coming. Tom and Lorraine phoned them. They said that the camp can't go on now and I think they just want everyone out of here.'

'Yeah, well I guess they can't put a play on now.'

'Of course not,' she said, mortified that he might think she thought they could. 'You're right, I should get back.'

He didn't smile again, but he said, 'Thank you for listening, Lucy Keeble,' and she thought he meant it.

She left him, sitting hunched over on the bench. If he wondered why she was heading away from the hostel rather than towards it, he didn't say. Perhaps he didn't know the place well enough to realise. She glanced at her watch again. Fifteen minutes. She still had just about enough time to go down to the house at Poison Cross. She couldn't tell anyone about that night, she knew that – of course she did – but she could go to the house herself. Now that Sam said he'd seen Maddie, she hoped it wouldn't matter. But, still, one final check before it was impossible. One final chance to be sure that her silence really wasn't going to make a difference. She could get there if she ran.

Chapter Twenty-Seven

Lucy, Present

When I get home after driving down to see Karen Silver, Joe and I have a row. We hardly ever argue because Joe would do almost anything to avoid conflict. I sometimes wonder if this is a reaction to Maddie's disappearance, but I try to resist the urge to psychoanalyse all his personality traits in the light of this one event, as though it's the only thing that could have shaped him as a person. And god knows he'd have enough material to go on if he ever returned the favour. In the early days, we argued a few times about having kids – big, draining arguments that went nowhere and were zinging with subtext, because I could never bring myself to say exactly why I didn't want them and Joe, although I'm sure he thought he knew, was too scared or too kind to spell it out.

'Did you and Claire have a good day out?' he says, as he washes some of Ruby's bottles.

'It was fine.' I'm busy attempting to clear clutter off the kitchen table ahead of dinner. He turns round to look at me, his hands dropping suds on the floor.

'What did you do?'

'We went for a drive,' I say. The art of the half-truth.

'A drive?' he says, sounding understandably incredulous. I don't think going for a drive has counted as a day out since the 1930s. 'Where to?'

'Oh, just out into the country.'

'Is something wrong, Lucy?'

'No, of course not. Why?'

'You've been behaving a bit strangely these past few days.'

'Are you still going on about that run?'

'Well, you have to admit it's not like you to go for an early morning run.'

He's right to be suspicious. The run is just an excuse for the four of us to meet up tomorrow morning and discuss what to do next – at least I hope it is. I avoid exercise with the same dedication that Joe avoids conflict.

'Just because I didn't want to go running with you and Jenna doesn't mean I'm not into running okay?' When Ruby was a tiny baby, Joe had gone on quite a few long post-baby runs with Jenna – the mere idea of which had left me clinging to the sofa for dear life. 'I'd literally just given birth – it wasn't a great time to go running.'

'I get that. I'm sorry.'

'Besides, I already told you. Tomorrow is something Hayley suggested. It's probably for an Insta story or something. It's one morning, all right? If you can't look after Ruby, I'll take her with me.'

'You know it's not about that. I'm happy to look after Ruby. But I'm worried about you.'

'Because I'm taking some exercise?'

'Because you're not yourself.'

'You're using the wrong brush,' I say. 'You need to use the pale green brush for her bottles.'

'I know. I dropped the old brush on the floor last night, so I bought a new one,' he says. 'So?'

'So what?'

'You've been really distracted and, I don't know, on edge ever since you got that text the other night,' he says doggedly.

'It was an upsetting message, okay? Sorry if I got upset about it.'

I don't sound sorry at all; I sound defensive.

'It's more than that. What about on Sunday at Hayley and Frank's? It's like you were physically present but your mind was somewhere else entirely.'

'Well, hello? I drank too much wine. Blame Frank.'

'No, it wasn't that. I've been married to you for ten years – I know what you're like when you're pissed. Sunday was different.'

'You're not scrubbing it enough. It needs to be really clean. If there's any milk residue the bacteria will grow.'

'For fuck's sake, Lucy, I know that!' He throws the bottle and brush into the sink and water splashes up over his t-shirt and onto the kitchen floor. 'I'm not a moron. I've been washing Ruby's bottles since day one.'

'Okay, whatever. Excuse me for being concerned about our daughter's health.'

'Why do you always do this?'

'What?'

'Deflect. Why won't you tell me what you're really thinking? I know something's bothering you. Why won't you tell me what it is?'

The strange thing is that, although at various moments over the past few days I've longed to tell Joe about the messages – I've imagined the relief of it, the sharing of the burden; I've imagined him wrapping me in his arms – at this precise moment, when he is literally begging me to tell him, I don't feel tempted at all. Quite the reverse. I feel terrified that he's somehow going to guess. Because, apart from the moments when I think they might be from Maddie herself, what I fear most about the messages is not the public shame of having our secret revealed, but the thought of Joe knowing what we did. Maybe he would understand. Maybe he would react the way I sometimes imagine and would forgive me, comfort me. But maybe isn't enough. I can't risk everything on a maybe.

'I've just been worried about you and Ruby,' I say.

'Why, what's wrong with Ruby?' he says quickly.

'Nothing. Nothing's wrong with her. I can't explain. I know I've been in a bit of a funny mood, but sometimes I get scared that I don't deserve you both.'

He studies me.

'Why would you think that?'

'I don't know. I guess I've never quite grown out of my inferiority complex.'

I try to work out what he's thinking. Probably that I'm deflecting again.

'You know that you can talk to me about anything.'

'I do know that. Thank you.' But I only meet his gaze briefly. 'I'm going to check on Ruby.'

'I'll put the pasta on,' he says sadly.

Chapter Twenty-Eight

Lucy, Present

I'm walking to the Tesco Metro at the end of the street, because I really need some chocolate. If I had a dog I could pretend I was taking it for a walk. But I tell Joe the truth for once.

'Don't go now, Luce. It's gone ten.'

As a substitute, Joe – contrite about the earlier argument, even though it was mostly my fault – offers Pringles, and, hilariously for a man who has been married to me for ten years, almonds. He even offers to go for me, but I turn him down. I suddenly want to get away from the sofa where I have been sitting all evening, not-watching Netflix with Joe, trying to make sense of what Karen Silver told us.

Chocolate is not the only reason I want to get out of the house though. I need to check my phone. I daren't keep it on in front of Joe, let alone look at it. Claire sent a bare-bones summary of our visit to Karen Silver to the Fab Four WhatsApp group in the car on the way home – promising more details at our debrief tomorrow morning. As soon as I'm round the corner of our road, I stop under a streetlamp and take out my phone. The Apple symbol appears and, frustratingly slowly, the phone comes back to life. My hand not entirely steady, I tap the text icon to double check I have no new messages. Nothing. Supposing that's it? Supposing I never get another message from that number. Only it already feels too late to go back; I can't just forget what Karen Silver told us.

I notice there's a missed call from Harriet Holland, but the last thing I want to do right now is talk to her. I have eighty-seven new WhatsApp messages. The Fab Four group has clearly been exploding with messages all evening and no wonder because, under pressure from an impatient Hayley, Claire has revealed that DI Silver thought there was something wrong about the Blakes.

> WTF???????

Is Hayley's eloquent response. But it's Jenna's next message, a few minutes later, that stops me scrolling.

> Okay, I know you maybe don't want to hear this, so don't shoot me down, but there was something wrong wasn't there? Why did she keep running away? What about that time when someone tried to smash down their front door? Maybe it was something to do with her dad. There's no way I think any of them had anything to do with it – I'm not saying that. But there was some kind of family secret – something she was keeping hidden from us.

Some kind of family secret. I get to the end of the street, playing these words in my head and wander round the near-deserted aisles of Tesco in a daze. If there really was

195

a family secret, surely Joe would know what it was? I try to think of a way of asking him, without having to reveal any of the whole shameful saga to him. But why should he tell me his secrets, when I have kept mine hidden from him for so long? I pay for my chocolate and leave.

'Can you spare any change?'

The question makes me jump. I've seen the woman who emerges from the shadows at the side of Tesco a couple of times before, nearly always in the evening. She looks terrible – a haunted, hollow face under the hood of a parka. The arms that stick out from the sleeves of her jacket are so thin they look as though they would snap at the slightest pressure.

Joe has a policy of never giving money to people who are begging, balanced by a policy of always buying the *Big Issue* if he passes someone who's selling it, even if he's already bought one. Often we have four copies of the same magazine.

My attitude to people who beg on the streets is more mercurial. I don't have a blanket policy; I don't think the world can be divided into people who sell the *Big Issue* and are deserving and people who ask for money on street corners and aren't. But I've never given this woman anything. There's something about her that makes me feel ashamed. Usually I scurry on and pretend I haven't heard her.

Tonight, because my mind is somewhere else entirely, I've not noticed her in time to avoid her. Now she's standing so close to me that I could reach out and touch her and I think about how I must look to her, prosperous, well fed – very well fed and clutching a giant bar of Galaxy – and content. I fumble in my bag for change and that's when I find it. My fingers close on the thin, glossy surface and the strange thing is that although my bag is full of crap I know instantly this is an alien object. I just don't know exactly what it's going to be until I pull it out, but even as I'm handing the woman a couple of pound coins, and she's thanking me, her face too close to mine, her breath on my skin, I'm imagining the worst. I want to know though and it has to be now. I can't stand waiting until I get home, and I can't risk Joe seeing it. I already know it's going to be that kind of find. So I take it out and examine it under the streetlamp. It's an old photograph.

Innocuous enough in itself. But I feel sick as soon as I see it. It's the five of us. In Maddie's garden, on her sun-scorched lawn, rope swing in the background, in the summer of 1999. Our arms around each other. Maddie at the centre, shining. The person marked out for something different. Something special. We just none of us realised what. I shove the photo back in my bag and I can taste the fear in my mouth, sour on my tongue. It's not what it is – although that's bad enough – it's how it got there. My mind races with questions. Who put it there, and when? And why?

I long to be home, but I can't go back to Joe in this state. I stand under the distorted orange glow of the street-light, outside the Tesco Metro, trying to pull myself back from succumbing to the panic that threatens to swallow me up.

I try to think about it logically. The photo could have been there for ages. It's a big sack of a bag, with layer upon layer of detritus. I don't often reach right for the bottom – it was because I was looking for the pound coins that I know sometimes lurk there that I did tonight. Perhaps one of the others put the photo there. Perhaps Joe did. Or Naomi. Perhaps it was intended to be a nice thing

– a reminder of a happy moment before the tragedy. But although I'm desperate to find a reassuring explanation for its presence, I can't really believe that any of them would think a surprise photo of Maddie would be anything other than a huge shock. I know the photo has something to do with the messages.

I take the photo out again and scrutinise Maddie's face hungrily, as if it holds all the answers. Seeing a new photo of her is like a fresh perspective; so she looked like that, I find myself thinking, as well as like all the other Maddies frozen in time on Naomi and Robin's mantelpiece. She looks impossibly young, in her cut-off denim shorts and pink vest top. That was how old we were when it all happened. How young. I can't look at myself in the photo. Somewhere in the shadows down the side of the shop something shifts and I realise the homeless woman is probably watching me, wondering what the hell I'm doing. When I think this, I realise I'm ready to start walking home.

I'm conscious of footsteps behind me. Well, that's not so unusual. There are quite often people around at this time of night, taking their dogs round the block or coming back from the station after an evening out in central London. The footsteps seem to be keeping pace with me, though. I feel like they could go faster if they wanted. Still, this is familiar territory. My street. I've done this walk a thousand times before. It's not even that late. There are families gathered in living rooms, TVs flickering, light seeping out through the curtains, but there are also hedges, parked cars and patches of darkness.

Still I hear the soft tread of footsteps behind me. Maybe it's the homeless woman. I turn round. There's no one there; no one that I can see. And the footsteps have stopped. I pick up my pace, somewhere between a walk and a jog. I think about darting up one of the driveways, and hammering on the door. But I can almost see my own driveway up ahead, I just need to turn this corner. I think I can hear the footsteps again, but it's hard to tell because my head is full of my heart beating and my own breathing.

The message said it. *You will pay for what you did.* Until now, I'd imagined that it meant a public shaming – the final revelation of the secret I'd kept all these years. But maybe if it really is Maddie, she wants to make me pay more directly. Maybe I only just found the photo in my bag because someone only just put it there. When I see Joe silhouetted in our front doorway, dressed in his old running shorts and faded black t-shirt that I love, which smells of laundry powder and him, I want to cry with relief. Then we're hugging, holding each other tight, the argument earlier, and the awkwardness that followed it, forgotten for the time being at least.

Sex has been rare since Ruby – we're both too tired at the end of the day to do anything other than fall into an uneasy sleep – but tonight is different, and for a while it really does help. For a while, it's the only thing I'm thinking about. But the feeling doesn't last. As we lie in bed afterwards, my thoughts return to the photograph almost at once. Joe's arms are around me, hugging me from behind, but it makes me feel trapped, rather than safe. I'm too hot and I need a drink of water. Joe is gently snoring. I don't want to wake him, so I lie wide-eyed in the darkness until I can bear it no longer. I pull away from him, and he gives a couple of louder grunts, rolls onto his back and resumes his rhythmic snoring. I'm free and I know exactly what I'm going to do next.

I sit on my own in the locked bathroom, staring at the photograph from my bag, wondering who put it there. And that's when I notice what it says on the back.

It's time

I think it could be Maddie's handwriting.

Chapter Twenty-Nine

Lucy, Present

'Not like you to be up so early.'

Frank looks irritatingly perfect, dark hair still wet from the shower, trademark crisp white shirt – like he's just been taking part in a photoshoot for Hayley's Insta feed, and maybe he has. Even though it's still only 7:30 a.m.

'Frank, this is a lie-in. Since we had Ruby, anything after five in the morning is luxurious.'

I'm very jumpy this morning. I sat in the bathroom into the small hours and beyond staring at the photo of the five of us, willing it to tell me something else – something that will confirm the identity of the sender – wondering what the words on the back mean. *It's time.* Whatever it's time for, I'm sure it's nothing good. When I finally crawled back to bed beside a still-snoring Joe and fell asleep, I dreamt Karen Silver told me Maddie's body was buried in our front garden and as I bent over the wall to look, Maddie's arms reached out for me. I woke to a wailing that was part Maddie's, part Ruby's and wholly unnerving. Driving over to Hayley's for our 'run', I kept glancing in my rear-view mirror, although what I expected to see I don't know. On the south circular in rush hour, everyone is following you.

'I'm glad those days are behind us. Not that Benji's a great sleeper now. He seems to wake about six every day and sneak into our bed.' I've interrupted Frank making breakfast; while @heyhayley is big on overnight oats, Frank is reassuringly helping himself to two thick slices of processed white bread. 'Can I get you anything?'

'Just a coffee please.'

I feel so jittery that even the thought of buttery toast isn't tempting. In his basket, Doogie raises a bleary head and gives his tail a few half-hearted wags.

'Hailz will be down in a minute, she's just getting ready.'

I glance down at my old black joggers and the t-shirt that was a freebie from our local burger place. I worry briefly that we are actually going for an early-morning run.

'Americano all right?'

Frank puts a glass beaker under the posh coffee machine – the sort that I always break when Joe and I come across them in hotels – and then opens a new packet of coffee pods.

'Hailz says the four of you have been talking about Maddie.'

I feel a cold knot of dread in the pit of my stomach. I haven't even heard him say her name before and now he brings her up casually, as if she were a mutual friend we haven't heard from in a while. How much does Frank know? I've never really thought of Hayley and Frank as the kind of couple who tell each other everything. I know for a fact that he didn't tell her that his new mountain bike cost nearly £10,000 – Joe, whose financial instincts are puritanical, was so shocked that it was the first thing he told me when we were back in the car after a night at the pub with Hayley and Frank last year – and she certainly hasn't told him about the hot guy from Insta who's been direct messaging her off and on for the past few months like a modern-day version of *You've Got Mail*. He's called @vagabond_guy and he's currently touring Cuba on his motorbike. Vinales is stunning, but not as stunning as Hayley apparently.

'I think that it's good you've been discussing it.' Frank hands me the coffee from the machine. 'It was a terrible thing that happened to you all, but it can't help keeping it buried. Are you okay, Lucy? I'm sorry. I shouldn't have brought it up without warning like that. I guess all I'm saying is, it's natural that you wonder what happened to her.'

'It was all a long time ago.' It's all I can manage, even as I take in the fact that she doesn't seem to have told him very much at all. Not about the messages, and that means definitely not about what really happened.

'Do you and Joe ever talk about it?'

'Not much.' I take a mouthful of coffee, but it's too hot and I can feel it burning the roof of my mouth. 'It's… it's difficult, you know.' Understatement of the century.

'Of course. For Joe, more than anyone. It must help having you, though. At least you understand.'

The doorbell goes. Doogie stirs himself from his basket again and trots off, muttering to himself under his breath.

'That'll be Jenna or Claire,' I say.

'Don't worry,' he says, toast in hand. 'I'll get it. You finish your coffee.'

I take a long breath in and then out again, focusing on Hayley's shelf of cookery books, which are pristine and called things like *Simplicity* and *Plenty*, rather than *Ten-Minute Meals* like in our house.

'Morning, Lucy,' says Claire. 'Wow, you look awful.'

'Thanks.'

'No, sorry. I meant, you haven't had another—'

'No, nothing else.' Why don't I want to tell her about the photograph? I think it's because it feels way more personal than the messages. The photograph was put there by someone close to me. Someone who got close to me. But that someone is surely not Claire. That would be ridiculous. I open my mouth to tell her, but instead I hear myself say, 'Where did Frank go?'

'There was some kind of commotion out in the street. He went to take a look. Where are the others? I haven't got long. My first meeting is at nine-thirty.'

Oh god, I should do some work too – I haven't finished the Edward Duval chapter, and the letters Harriet gave me are still buried deep in one of my desk drawers, as if hiding them under a pile of bank statements and other crap will somehow rob Duval of his potency. But I know I can't face the letters today. I glance out of the kitchen window. On the gravel, I see Jenna, standing by her bike. Standing next to her, really close, with his arm around her, is Frank. Suddenly it hits me – the person Jenna really likes, the person she's known a long time and doesn't know if he likes her too, could that person be Frank? She'd said that the situation was messy. That would certainly be messy.

'I hate mornings.' Hayley's voice. I spin round, terrified she's going to look out of the window and see them too, but she's still coming down the stairs.

'I thought mornings were when you were enthusiastic about meditating and starting the day in a positive head-space,' Claire says.

'I hate it when people quote me at me,' Hayley says, without rancour. 'Hi babe.' She grabs my arms above the elbows and kisses me on the cheek. She opens a cupboard and reaches for a glass. She looks stunning. Her leggings and crop top match and they show off her flat stomach.

'Sorry I'm late down. I had to get Tallulah and Benji dressed too.'

'I've not got long,' Claire says impatiently.

'Well Jenna's not here yet either.'

Hayley is fiddling with their posh tap that dispenses sparkling water and I risk another glance out of the window. They've gone. Thank God. The front door shuts, and moments later Jenna and Frank are standing next to each other in the kitchen doorway. Still pretty close, it has to be said, to my newly opened eyes.

'Someone's just knocked Jenna off her bike.'

Chapter Thirty

'It's probably just a coincidence,' Jenna says.

We jog our way down the street, but once we reach Wandsworth Park, to my relief, we slow to a walk. Contrary to what Joe thinks, I can run if I have to, but I like to go at my own pace, and my pace definitely isn't Jenna's. Frank hadn't wanted Jenna to come at all, but she'd insisted. 'I'm not hurt.'

She doesn't look hurt. Her clothing isn't dirty or damaged. There are no marks on her hands. She might never have been knocked off her bike at all. I wonder if they saw me looking and made the whole thing up as an excuse. But all at once this seems absurd. What am I basing this on? Frank was comforting Jenna after an accident. Jenna's complicated relationship with someone she's liked for ages could refer to any number of people. Besides, Jenna is serially truthful. Or at least this is how I think of her; after all, there's a limit to how serially truthful you can be when you've lied about your friend's disappearance for twenty-five years.

'The driver glanced my back wheel and luckily I was slowing down to pull into the drive anyway so I just kind of toppled off.'

'Did you get the registration number?' Claire, as always, keen to pin down the details.

Jenna shrugs. 'It was just a big red car. But it wasn't the car's fault. Some idiot on a motorbike pulled out of the road opposite at about fifty miles an hour and the car had to swerve sideways to avoid it. It's no big deal – just some dumb guy. It gave me a shock, that's all.'

Maybe it's a bigger deal than she thinks. I explain how I thought I was being followed last night. For some reason, this is easier to share than the photograph.

'Shit, babe, are you sure?' Hayley says.

'Okay, now we should go to the police,' Jenna says. 'Someone is stalking Lucy. Surely that's enough. We don't have to tell them about the messages.'

'Did you get a look at them?' Claire says. 'Male? Female?'

I shake my head.

'Height?'

'I don't know.'

'So what did you actually see?' Claire asks and I can tell she's wondering if the whole thing is just my over-active imagination. In the sun-dappled park, with the river shimmering alongside us and an early-morning rowing crew gliding by, I almost wonder the same thing.

'I had a sense it was a woman, but that could just have been because of the woman outside Tesco. She was begging, she asked me for money when I came out.'

'Could it have been her following you, babe?' Hayley asks.

'I mean maybe. I've seen her a few times before and she usually just stays around the shop. I've never seen her on our street.'

'You've seen her before?' Jenna says sharply.

'A few times.'

'Is there any way she could be—' Jenna doesn't finish, but she doesn't need to, because I'm already cutting her off.

'No way,' I say. 'You can't fake how she looks. She's so skinny she looks like she'd break if you touched her – she's emaciated, and her eyes are sunken into her eye sockets. She's clearly on drugs.'

For a few seconds, there's silence between us and the park noises – shouts, barking, the faint throb of someone's music, the louder throb of traffic – fill the gap.

'How old is she though?' Jenna says quietly. It hits me as if she'd punched me – if Maddie could be the glamorous and successful film producer Harriet Holland, she could equally be the homeless woman outside Tesco.

'It's not her. Oh god. I don't think it's her.'

'Okay,' Hayley says, and I catch her shooting a glance at Jenna. 'Okay, I'm sure you're right.'

'DI Silver thought Maddie was dead,' Claire says.

'You didn't hear that from him, though, did you?' Jenna says. 'You're only going by what his wife told you.'

'Anyway he thought Robin killed her and that's crazy,' Hayley says.

'She didn't actually say that,' Claire says. 'She said he thought the Blakes were hiding something, and Jenna, you agreed with that.'

'I think they were keeping something secret,' Jenna says. 'That's all. It might have nothing to do with what happened to Maddie.' I notice she's stopped talking about going to the police again.

We're on our second loop of Wandsworth Park, which is pretty busy even at this time in the morning – military fitness, yoga and a few purposeful dog walkers. It feels a safe place to talk, though; everyone is intent on their own business and no one is listening to us. It's been a while since the four of us have spent any time together without at least one set of kids – usually one or both of Hayley's, and more recently Ruby too. We wouldn't be doing this if it wasn't for Maddie, but then we wouldn't still be friends at all if it wasn't for her. She's what we have in common.

'I was looking online last night,' Hayley says, 'and I found a story about this guy who was missing for five years. Another guy was even charged with his murder and then the police found him living in a tent in the middle of this forest.'

'Maddie's not living in a forest, Hayley,' Claire says.

'If you're suddenly so sure she's dead,' Jenna says, 'who do you think killed her? Not Robin?'

Claire shakes her head.

'I don't know who. We all told the police everything we knew at the time. Okay, okay,' she says, reacting to our expressions, 'everything except *that*, I mean.'

'There wasn't anything you held back?' Jenna says. And suddenly I know – I can tell from the way she says it – that there's something my serially truthful friend hasn't told us.

Chapter Thirty-One

Later that morning, I'm pushing Ruby along the Thames path, when my phone rings. My phone is freaking me out right now and this is a mobile number I don't have in my contacts. I slide to answer it, and then hold it cautiously at a distance from my ear, as if this is somehow going to help diffuse whatever is on the other end.

'Hi Lucy?'

'Who is this?'

It's not The Number, as I now think of it – the one the texts come from. I'd recognise that all right. I've stared at the digits so often I know them off by heart – as if they're some kind of code that could reveal the identity of the sender. I even spent several hours in the middle of the night googling how to trace an unknown mobile number. It turns out there are all kinds of people who want to do this and companies that offer to do it for you 'for your safety and comfort' and my heart briefly thudded with the relief of being able to find out. But more reading revealed it's not that simple. That some numbers can never be traced – that you can never truly be safe and comfortable.

'It's Harriet. Harriet Holland.'

The words 'the person who's paying you to write a book for her' hover unspoken in the ether.

'Oh hi Harriet!' I say, trying to make up for my failure to recognise her voice with a display of enthusiasm so extreme that she's probably holding the phone at a distance from her ear now too. A middle-aged man who's walking past me as I wheel Ruby one-handed along the path, scowls at me.

'Are you okay?'

'Yes, fine. Sorry, I just didn't recognise your number.'

I weave the pushchair out of the way of an enthusiastic dog the size of a small pony, which, thinking I'm playing, instantly bounds back towards me. Its owner hurries over, apologising. I mouth my forgiveness.

'I'm calling you on my work phone.'

'Ah right. Are you still in Guadalajara?'

Now I sound suspicious again. I don't think she is in Guadalajara. The line sounds really clear, not that slightly fuzzy line you sometimes get with mobile calls from another country. And what time would it be in Mexico? The middle of the night surely.

'No, I didn't go in the end. The start of the shoot's been delayed by a few weeks. It's a giant pain in the backside actually.'

'Oh that explains it.'

'What do you mean?'

Now that I'm talking to her again, it seems almost impossible that Harriet could be Maddie. I try to imagine fifteen-year-old Maddie drawling: 'It's a giant pain in the backside actually'. But then I can't imagine fifteen-year-old Hayley saying that I can create my ultimate wellness baseline with a few simple breathing exercises, as she did the other day. People do not stay fifteen forever.

'Lucy?'

'What?'

'What does it explain?'

'I thought I saw your car the other day. On the way down to Brighton.'

'I don't think so. Driving to Twickenham and back is it for me at the moment. Now, Lucy, listen, I've been thinking. Have you had a chance to read Edward Duval's letters yet?'

I mumble something vague about not having had time to have more than a quick look. I obviously can't tell her that I have been avoiding the letters with a superstitious dread. Already the thoughts are chasing round in my head again. Edward Duval cannot possibly have anything do with Maddie's disappearance. The rational part of my brain knows this. But – and there's no escaping this thought as it comes crashing back again – Duval was the reason why we went to the house at Poison Cross in the first place. If it had just been a boring old ruin of a house, without any attendant movie-star glamour, Maddie might not have got so excited about it and she might not have come up with the idea for the dare in the first place. And if she hadn't insisted that we each went into Duval's house alone, in the middle of the night, then today… well today she might still be here. And the coincidence of the two of them – Maddie and Duval – both bursting back into my life at the same time is more than I can deal with. The very last thing I want to do at the moment is read those letters.

'I've written some more of the chapter about Duval himself though,' I say, hoping to appease her and save myself from having to read Duval's own words in Duval's own handwriting. I think again about the handwriting on the photo. I have nothing Maddie wrote to compare it with. But Naomi and Robin would have. 'I can email you what I've got so far.'

I don't know if it's just talking about Duval, but I've suddenly got this weird feeling there's somebody just behind me, following me down the path. But when I glance round I can't pick out anyone in particular – just the usual river path crowd.

'I was hoping we could meet up.'

'Again?' I say without thinking.

'There's something I want to show you.'

'Sure.' I try to make my voice breezy and confident. 'Do you want to drop by? Or I can come to you?'

'Let's meet in Highgate. There's a little coffee shop I know. I'll send you the address. Can you make Saturday afternoon?'

'Yes, okay. Joe's playing football so I'll have to bring Ruby.'

'Who?'

'My daughter.'

'Shall we say two?'

'Fine. Harriet, sorry I've got to go.'

Because suddenly Claire's girlfriend Nic is standing in front of me on the Thames path.

Chapter Thirty-Two

Extract from Brits Who Shaped Hollywood *by Harriet Holland*

Did Edward Duval murder Gladys Rudd in the small hours of the morning of 24 July 1925 and conceal her body somewhere it has never been found? We cannot know for certain. He is by no means the only suspect. Gladys had been 'walking out', as her mother put it, with the blacksmith's son. The pair had quarrelled on the day of Gladys's disappearance and several witnesses heard him threatening to end their relationship if she insisted on going to the party at the house at Poison Cross. Did he go further and end her life? He was certainly known to have a nasty temper, but there were no witnesses, and no physical evidence to place him at the scene.

Perhaps because her body was never found, there continued to be sightings of Gladys Rudd for years after her disappearance. The credibility of these tales varies, as it always does in cases like these, but Gladys's own mother is among those who claimed to have seen her in the years following her disappearance. This could well be grief-stricken wishful thinking, but, in the absence of a body, it is at least possible that Gladys ran away that night for reasons of her own.

Inevitably, over time, these sightings of Gladys turned into village legend, and she became the star of her very own ghost story; the innocent victim of Hollywood's worst excesses, destined to haunt the house at Poison Cross, seeking vengeance for the wrongs done to her. After Duval's death in 1935, the house at Poison Cross stood empty for several years, but eventually, just before the start of the Second World War, it was sold to a school. Some attempt was made to clear the house of Duval's remaining furniture and possessions, but the new owner was killed in a bombing raid before much progress had been made. The story in the village was that Gladys's ghost had been seen on the night the bombs fell. The house has lain empty ever since — an abandoned, haunted ruin of a once glorious mansion. And Duval himself — whether a killer or a victim — is now almost entirely forgotten.

Chapter Thirty-Three

'This is really nice,' Nic says.

'I know. I think it's the peanut butter they put in them. Best brownies ever.'

'No, I mean this. Getting a chance to talk to you properly.'

'Yeah, I know,' I say. 'It was a joke.'

Nic smiles, but more as a reflex than anything else. She's wearing a tiered smock dress that would make me look like a walking lampshade, but which suits her, and her hair is twisted into a neat bun on her head.

'The brownies *are* good.'

'This place is famous for them.'

Nic takes a mouthful of peppermint tea and then says in a rush, 'I was worried that you didn't like me.'

I'd have been happier if the conversation had stayed on baked goods for a while longer, but Nic clearly thinks the small talk is out of the way. I remember how much Claire said she liked Nic and manage to infuse my reply with the requisite amazement. 'Seriously?' I ask. 'That's crazy.'

Her face relaxes. The truth is I don't dislike Nic; I just don't often think about her. And that's even worse. She and Claire have been going out since November – nearly six months – and although I know some things about her, I still don't feel even vaguely close to knowing what she's like as a person, despite having just spent a whole afternoon with her for Frank's birthday. She designs gardens and she's into angel healing, but I feel like we exhausted both those topics on Sunday.

'You're so important to Claire, the three of you. I wish I had a group of friends like that.'

I get my usual buzz from hearing her say this; I'm at some arrested stage of development where having cool friends still defines me. Nic's next words, uttered as I lift the muslin covering the pushchair to check Ruby is still asleep, set alarm bells ringing though. 'I'm sure it's partly because you all went through such a lot together.'

'Well, we've known each other a very long time. Since we were at school.'

But Nic is not to be deflected.

'I meant when your friend disappeared. Maggie.'

'Maddie. Claire told you about that?'

She nods and leans forward over the rickety table we've found ourselves at, outside the riverside cafe.

'It sounds like a place with bad energy.'

'What does?'

I'm still trying to process the fact that Claire has told her about Maddie. First Hayley with Frank and now Claire with Nic.

'The place where it happened, where she went missing.'

'I'm not very used to talking about it.' I hope that she will take the gargantuan hint and move on, but instead, hazel eyes boring into me, she continues.

'I mean, there was the murder that took place there before.'

I crumble my remaining bit of brownie between my fingers. Oh god, not Edward Duval again.

'The village girl who was killed at the party in the house nearby. Gladys Rudd.'

She'd said Maggie instead of Maddie, but she had no trouble recalling the name of a girl who'd gone missing in 1925.

'Did you ever go there when you were at the summer camp? To the house?'

'No.'

Way too quickly and emphatically.

'What was she like? Maddie,' she says her name slowly and carefully, like she's pronouncing a word in an unfamiliar foreign language. 'She clearly meant a great deal to Claire.'

'Look, Nic, I'm really not—'

'The thing is, I think there's something Claire's not telling me about what happened.'

Oh god, I hope so.

'It's like she feels guilty about something that happened back then. Like she blames herself. That's not healthy, Lucy. I really want her to see a therapist. To talk about it. What do you think?'

I pick up my cappuccino, but my hand is shaking and I put it straight back down again.

'I think it's something Claire needs to decide for herself.'

There's a silence. I busy myself with removing the muslin from the pushchair, while I try to think how I could have stopped the conversation getting to this point.

'Were Claire and Maddie having a relationship?'

My head snaps back in her direction.

'A relationship? What do you mean?'

'Were they a couple?'

'What? No. What makes you think that?'

'The way she talks about her. I think she loved her.'

'We all loved her.'

Ruby, the bright sunlight now shining in her face, wakes and starts to cry.

'You know that's not what I mean.'

I start unstrapping Ruby from the pushchair. I wonder whether it was a coincidence that Nic and I bumped into each other on the Thames path, or whether the person I sensed following me was Nic all along. Ruby is rubbing at her eyes with her tiny fists – a sure sign that she's still tired and has been woken from her nap too soon. My fault, like so many things. But at least she's providing me with an excuse not to look at Nic.

As I take her in my arms and start bouncing her up and down on my lap, I'm trying to take in the implications of what Nic just asked. Were Claire and Maddie a couple? If they were, I didn't know anything about it. The trouble is, my memory of that summer is so heightened that I think I can remember everything that happened, but there must be so much I've forgotten too. So much I never even noticed. And maybe one of those things explains what happened to Maddie. Maybe I need to be braver about asking questions of the people who might remember. But I can't start with Claire. I will start with Jenna: I need to know whatever it is she didn't tell us all those years ago.

'Look, I'm sorry Nic, I need to get Ruby home.'

Chapter Thirty-Four

Lucy, Present

It feels like a big deal phoning Jenna. It's not like we talk on the phone that often. Hardly ever, in fact. We see each other most weeks, so why would we need to? Messages fly backwards and forwards all the time – mainly on the Fab Four WhatsApp group, sometimes between the two of us – but the days when we'd have long, relaxed chats analysing in minute detail a date, or a party, which used to happen quite a lot in our early twenties, are long gone. Hayley tells me no one calls each other nowadays anyway – for Generation Z phone calls always signal disaster apparently. And although we decrepit Millennials haven't quite entered that territory yet, calls have certainly become increasingly unusual.

My calls are nearly all business now – like the one I had with Harriet earlier today. I remember Harriet's disquieting insistence that I meet her in Highgate and I wonder what she has in mind for me, because I'm not sure I can take anything else right now.

Then I think about the letters waiting for me in the drawer of my desk in the living room. Instead of calling Jenna, I could read them. Joe isn't back from work yet and Ruby is happy in her bouncer. It's the perfect opportunity. Instead, I sit at our kitchen table and take out my phone. It rings out for so long that I start to think Jenna isn't going to pick up at all.

'Hey Lucy?'

My hand closes around the mug of tea in front of me. Jenna sounds wary but then every time she's seen me in recent days I've thrown an unexploded bomb into her carefully ordered life, so who can blame her?

'Hey,' I say, trying to sound reassuring and clearly failing because her next words are sharp with anxiety.

'You okay?'

'Yes. Yeah, I'm fine. I just fancied a chat.'

'Oh. Okay.'

Now she just sounds a bit confused.

'Is now an okay time?'

'I'm out running.' I picture her pounding along, listening to a podcast – she loves *American Scandal* – getting interrupted by the phone ringing and then seeing it's me. Slowing to a walk and deciding to answer. 'But I could do with a breather, so yeah, it's good.' She doesn't sound even remotely out of breath and she can run for hours so I know this is pure niceness, or concern.

I wonder if maybe I should have done this in person – suggested we meet up for a coffee before work tomorrow or something – but then I dismiss the thought. I know I need to do it now, before I lose my nerve. I tighten my grip on the mug of tea, feeling the heat against my fingers, and look across at where Ruby is playing with the smiley-faced cloud attached to her baby bouncer. I'm worried she's getting too old for the bouncer now, but she seems so happy in it, I haven't got the heart to take it to the charity shop yet. I take a deep breath. If I'm going to do this, I should just go for it. I'm going to try the truth for once.

'Actually, it's a bit more than just a chat. There was something I really wanted to ask you about.'

There's silence on the other end of the line. I wonder for a moment if she's hung up.

'You still there?'

'Yes.' Her voice is flat and expressionless.

'It's about something you said earlier.'

'Right. What did I say?' She sounds almost relieved, as if there was something else she thought I was going to ask her about. I wonder again whether I'm right about Jenna and Frank, and she knows that I clocked them when I was looking out of the window and whether she's scared I might tell Hayley. And I wonder if I would, or if it would be just one more thing I'd keep secret.

'It was when we were in the park.' I can only deal with one secret at a time, and for the moment I have to be focused on Maddie. 'You asked us if there was anything we held back. At the time. Anything we didn't tell the police.'

'Oh that.' Now she sounds wary again. It would be so much better if I could see her face; all I've got to go on at the moment is her voice, and all I've got to convince her is my own. 'I was just curious, you know,' she says, trying way too hard to sound offhand. 'I didn't mean to spook you.'

'It sounded like you were thinking of something specific.'

'Honestly Lucy I didn't mean anything by it. It was just a stupid comment.'

'You know what you said the other day, about how nobody could hold it against us now? What we did when we were children?'

There's silence again.

'Jenna?'

'Yes. I remember.'

'The point is if there was something you didn't tell the police at the time, no one would blame you now.' I'm far from sure about this, but I need to know what she's holding back. I try to keep my voice reassuring and steady. 'But it could be useful. It could help us to work out what's going on now – because something is.'

At some point, I've abandoned my grip on the mug of tea and picked up Ruby's muslin, which I'm twisting between my fingers. 'And I'm scared.' My voice is not so steady now, I notice. 'I want to get to the bottom of it. And if you know something, I really, really think you should tell us what it is.'

I can hear her breathing.

'Please Jenna. I know there's something.'

'Okay.' Silence. I have literally no idea what she's going to tell me. I start to wonder whether this was such a good idea after all, and now it's me who's tempted to hang up, but then Jenna starts again: 'It's just weird talking about it after all this time.'

'Whatever you did, it's done now.'

'It wasn't something I did. It was something I saw.'

'At the house?'

'No. Before. Earlier in the day.'

'Earlier the day Maddie disappeared?'

'Yes, just before lunch. I wasn't spying on them or anything. I'd lost my script, and I was stressing about it. I thought I might have left it in the rehearsal room and I was already freaking out about learning all those lines, so I decided to go back and look for it.'

'Who? Who weren't you spying on?'

'Maddie and Tom,' she whispers.

'Tom as in actor Tom? My mum's friend Tom?'

I haven't thought about Tom in years. Of course, he was at the summer camp, but in my memories of that summer he's very much a background player. An authority figure utterly lacking in authority whose stupid summer camp screwed up all our young lives. But now, as I sit at my kitchen table, his image comes back to me as clearly as if I'd seen him a few weeks ago – an oval face with a pointy chin, and shorts that were always too short.

'Yes,' Jenna says impatiently. 'Who else?'

'Okay. So what about them? Why shouldn't they be in the rehearsal room? Maybe they were rehearsing – she had a big part in the play didn't she?'

'Lucy, will you let me tell it now you've dragged it out of me?'

'Yes. Sorry. Go on.'

'The door was slightly ajar and for some reason I didn't go straight in. It was like there was some instinct telling me not to. I could see them both through the gap in the door, though.'

'Right?'

She's lost me.

'He was about to kiss her, Lucy.'

'No way!' My reaction is instant. 'Yuck! That can't be true.'

'I'm telling you what I saw. They were standing very close to each other. One of his hands was sort of on her chest and his other arm was round her waist. She looked trapped.' I can tell that Jenna's seeing the image again as she describes it. 'And then he leant in and his lips were almost touching hers, and I must have taken a step backwards or something because the floor creaked, and then they just sprang apart.'

'Oh god. That's horrible. Poor Maddie. Why didn't she say anything?'

'I don't know. Maybe she didn't know how to, or she felt too embarrassed or something. I did wonder whether I should ask her about it – tell her I'd seen them – but I didn't want her to think I'd been spying on her. I didn't know what to do.'

'And you never mentioned anything about Tom to the police?'

I try to make my voice as non-accusatory as possible. After all, given my own silences, I'd be the biggest hypocrite ever if I blamed her for hers.

'There never seemed to be the right moment somehow.'

I think about how much I'd wanted to tell someone about the haunted house and how the adults never asked the right questions, and I think I know what she means.

'I should have told them though, shouldn't I?'

'The important thing is you've told me now.' I put the muslin down on the table and glance over at Ruby in her baby bouncer. She's gurgling contentedly. 'Do you know what? I think we should go and talk to Tom.'

'Why?' She sounds appalled.

'Because he might be the person sending me the messages – if he was somehow involved with Maddie.' Even saying that makes me feel revolted.

'I'm not sure it's a good idea. How would we even find him?'

'My mum might know. Jenna, seriously, we need to find out what he knows.'

It takes me a few more minutes to persuade her, but when she does agree she sounds suddenly certain.

'Okay. Let's do it. I'm in. I'm even off work tomorrow if you can find him before then.'

'I'll call my mum. Thanks Jenna.'

'No need to thank me. I've waited a long time to ask him about this.'

I try to keep the conversation going a while longer, but Jenna is suddenly very keen to get back to her run, as if she is frightened about what else she might tell me, now that I've persuaded her to tell this much.

Chapter Thirty-Five

Lucy, Present

Tom Durrant is an old man. As I watch him stoop over orange geraniums in the front garden of his bungalow, I try to conflate the shrunken figure in front of us with the scene Jenna described yesterday evening. He straightens up as we approach and asks politely whether he can help us. I'm doing rapid mental arithmetic. He can't have been more than thirty-five at the most when we last saw him at the summer camp, which must mean he's no more than sixty now. Younger than Naomi and Robin. But he looks like he belongs to a much older generation. His skin is mottled with age spots.

'I'm forever doing battle with the weeds.'

He looks delighted to have someone to talk to. Maybe he thinks we want gardening tips. I don't know how to start a conversation with this mild-mannered pensioner, but then I remember what Jenna told me about Tom and Maddie last night, and my heart hardens.

'We need to talk to you.'

'Everything all right, Dad?'

The real Tom emerges from the side of the bungalow and I'm so pleased to see him I break into an involuntary smile of relief. There had been something terrifying about thinking that the passing of so many years had apparently rendered perpetual teenager Tom into a frail grandfather figure. Yes, this Tom looks older, but he's so obviously still Tom. The floppy hair has long gone – he's almost bald. But he's wearing a faded *Ghostbusters* t-shirt and shorts that would have been too short for him in 1999, let alone now.

'Can I help you?'

'Hello, Tom,' Jenna says. Her voice sounds tauter than usual and I wonder whether coming here with her was such a good idea after all. Like she said, she's been waiting a long time for this and it's as if she's stored up her disgust over a quarter of a century. I can tell from the way Tom's face freezes that he's recognised us, too. Or maybe my mum has told him we're coming, even though she promised not to. She'd been reluctant to give me his contact details at all and of course she'd wanted to know why, and I'd been forced to stammer out some more half-truths about closure to try to explain our sudden interest in talking to him again.

'He might not want to talk about it at all – you have to bear that in mind too,' she said when she'd eventually agreed. 'Something like that touches everyone involved. The Blakes and the four of you, yes, but it affected so many other people too. Tom was never quite the same afterwards. He never really acted again either.'

'Hello you two.' Tom's voice sounds extra-jovial, even though his eyes are wary. I half-expect him to call me Lucy Goosey. 'It's all right, Dad,' he tells the older Tom. 'These two are old friends of mine.'

The old man beams at us.

'Actors are you?' he asks.

'Used to be,' I say. There's no point in troubling him with the real reason for our visit, and Jenna and I did used to be actors once, briefly, many summers ago.

'Ah. The most common type of actor, the used-to-be actor,' he says chuckling at his own joke.

'Do you two want to come round the back?' Tom says quickly. 'We can sit on the patio. I'd invite you both in,' he glances apologetically towards the bungalow, 'but Ma's asleep.'

Despite what my mum said, it seems like Tom does want to talk to us, or maybe he just wants to get us out of earshot of his father. We follow him down the flagstone path at the side of the bungalow, exchanging polite smiles with the old man, who looks at us wistfully, but knows better than to follow.

'You're here to talk about her? About beautiful Maddie.'

Creepy. Perhaps Tom was always creepy and I just never realised because I was too busy being embarrassed by him. Jenna is behind me on the path, but I can imagine her face.

'Did my mum tell you we were coming?' I ask and instantly feel wrong-footed. I shouldn't have mentioned my mum; it's like I'm thirteen years old again.

'Sonia?' He actually stops in his tracks and turns to look at me. 'I haven't spoken to Sonia in nearly twenty years. How is she?'

'Doing well,' I say tersely, and then, because something else seems called for, 'Still in the business. She's in a show at the moment actually.'

'I'm pleased for her,' he says. He sounds anything but pleased, but at least he starts walking again. We find ourselves in a surprisingly big back garden; the bungalow has been built on a large plot. It's a vast rectangular lawn, mowed in symmetrical lines, with beds around the edges filled with bright marigolds and busy lizzies: it's a very 1980s plant collection. There's a patio, covered in the same weedless grey flagstones as the path, with a wooden table and four chairs. Tom pulls one out and flings himself into it.

'I knew you'd find me one day.'

Actors never stop self-dramatising, it seems, even when they stop being actors.

'Sonia managed to track you down,' I say, taking a seat opposite. Jenna sits down next to me, so that we're facing him across the table. It's hot out on the patio and there is no sunshade. Tom reaches for the pair of mirrored sunglasses on the table and puts them on.

'I moved in with my folks a few years back when Ma had her first stroke. I'm surprised any of the old crowd would know where to find me.' His voice is bitter. 'It's a long time since I heard from them.'

'Well thanks for agreeing to talk to us,' I say briskly, because I sense that if I don't interrupt him, this could turn into a monologue on the subject of friends past.

'Why now?'

'It's been nearly twenty-five years.' I'm already learning that, for most people, this anniversary is enough to explain things. It worked with my mum – at least I think it did; I can never really tell whether she believes my lies, or just wants to. 'We've been talking about Maddie again. The four of us.'

'You're all still in touch then?' he asks. 'That's nice.'

The word hangs on the air for a few seconds.

'We're still trying to make some sense out of what happened,' I say.

'You were there,' Jenna says. It's the first thing she's said since we sat down, and it definitely doesn't sound friendly. 'You were part of it.'

Is it my imagination or does he flinch?

'We thought talking to you might help,' I add. Definitely good cop, to Jenna's bad.

'That summer ruined my life.'

Welcome to my world, I want to say. Jenna, though, is unfazed. I needn't have worried just now: she's very much in control of this situation. She even looks cool, dressed in a navy A-line sleeveless dress, her hair tied back in a high ponytail. I'm all sweaty and I know without looking in Tom's mirrored sunglasses that my face is beetroot.

'In what way?' Jenna asks.

He laughs mirthlessly.

'I couldn't work for a long time afterwards. I was broken up with worrying about it all, and nobody can be expected to act when they're in that kind of state. But when I came out the other side, when I was feeling up to working again, did anyone want to employ me? Did they fuck. My agent said I'd become unemployable, just because I'd been there.'

'I suppose it's inevitable.'

'You think? It didn't happen to Lorraine fucking Caxton though, did it? Want to know what I do now? I'm a driving instructor. A fucking driving instructor, with two divorces behind him, who's living with his parents.'

Without missing a beat Jenna asks, 'Did you tell the police at the time about you and Maddie?'

I'm expecting him to deny it – or at least, to hesitate, to look frightened. But he does none of these things. There's actually a smile on his face, a furtive sort of smirk that makes me feel sick.

'Did Maddie tell you?'

'Not exactly.'

'I thought she might have done. We had something special – Maddie and me.'

I can see Jenna and me, our outraged faces reflected in his shades. He chooses this moment to remove them and put them back on the table. As though he wants to be particularly frank, and they're getting in the way.

'They were different times,' he says squinting across the table at us. 'I know what you're thinking, but you can't judge by today's standards.'

'She was fifteen,' Jenna says. 'You were her teacher.'

'Maddie was very mature for her age.'

'The point is she was a child – a child in your care.'

'Yes, well, I wouldn't expect you to understand. You're from the "Me Too" generation. It's all changed now. Maddie was special. She was different.'

'We're from the same generation as Maddie,' Jenna says. 'I was fifteen too.'

'Maddie wanted me.' He has a dreamy expression that is making me want to vomit, or shove him so hard in the chest that he goes flying across the patio into the net-curtained glass doors. 'I could tell.'

'I think what she wanted,' I say, 'was a place at the National Youth Theatre.' And I feel pleased when the dreamy expression is replaced with a scowl. I wonder how much of this fantasy about Maddie he actually believes.

'Did you tell the police?' Jenna asks again, her voice resolutely unemotional.

'Lorraine said not to,' he says sulkily, replacing the sunglasses. I feel Jenna shift beside me. 'She said that the police wouldn't believe me, that they would think that I had something to do with her disappearance.'

'Did you?' I ask, my role as good cop forgotten.

'Of course not. I loved Maddie.'

'You knew her for two days.'

'It was long enough to know that we had feelings for each other.'

I only knew Maddie for six weeks and, in my head, she is one of the best friends I ever had. Maybe I'm just as mad as Tom.

He's rambling on, 'She had tremendous talent too – a real gift. We could have acted together. If someone hadn't snatched her away, we could have had a future together.'

'What do you think happened to Maddie?' I ask. He looks annoyed to be interrupted.

'Nobody knows.'

'You must have a theory,' Jenna snaps. 'You must have wondered.'

'For what it's worth, I thought at the time it might be the boyfriend.'

'Amari?'

'I've always wondered if she met him to tell him about us, and he killed her because he was jealous.'

I am pretty sure that of all the things that might have happened to Maddie, this is not it.

'The police never proved she met Amari after she left for summer camp.'

'Yes, well, the police proved diddly squat, didn't they? Doesn't mean she didn't meet him. If it wasn't Amari, there were plenty of other men sniffing after her. Sam, for one. Do you remember him? Our lighting technician? Couldn't take his eyes off her. I told the Inspector. DI Silver. I told him. Sam wanted a bit of her, I could tell.'

'What happened to Sam?' I ask.

'How should I know?'

'You didn't keep in touch?'

'He was a lad in the village who we employed to do our lighting. He wasn't a mate. Not that I had many of those, as it turned out.'

As much to stem the self-pity as anything, I choose this moment to say, 'Have you ever wondered if Maddie might still be alive?'

He looks genuinely astonished at this and, unless he's a better actor than I'm prepared to give him credit for, I'm fairly sure the possibility of Maddie as a living, breathing woman of nearly forty, as opposed to a fantasy teenager who's passionately in love with him, has never entered his head for a moment.

'Surely that's impossible.'

His voice quavers slightly, as if he's actually quite frightened by the idea. But then I'm pretty much freaked out by it myself. It's disturbing how much Tom and I seem to have in common.

'Unlikely but not impossible,' Jenna says calmly. 'When did you last see her?'

'I've never seen her,' he says, sounding properly scared now.

'I meant at the time.'

'Oh. Right.'

'Don't you remember?'

'Of course I remember.'

'So?'

'It was the evening of the day before she disappeared,' he says slowly and I guess that this time, he is remembering something that actually happened. The real Maddie, not the version he's constructed in his head over the past two decades. 'I went for a cigarette after dinner. I was just wandering through the grounds, not heading in any particular direction, you know, and then I saw her. She was wearing this little yellow sundress and talking to that other girl. The one with the curly hair.'

'Claire?' I ask, my mind racing. I'd forgotten Claire and Maddie had gone for a walk after dinner that night.

'If you say so. They were having some kind of squabble so I left them to it.'

'Squabble?' I say. 'What were they saying?'

'It was twenty-five years ago. How do you expect me to remember that?'

'It was the last time you saw Maddie. If she really was so important to you, I think you'd remember.'

'All right then,' Tom says. 'Something about how their friendship wouldn't be the same now. The usual teenage girl stuff. I'd have taken Maddie away from all that kind of nonsense. We would have been so good together. It wasn't all about the physical side of it.' His voice has become wistful again. 'Yes, there was a strong attraction there, I'm not denying that, but it was a meeting of minds. Maddie had a tremendous appetite for learning.'

I'm not sure how much more of this bullshit I can take and even Jenna is starting to twitch a bit, as if what she'd really enjoy is punching Tom in the face.

'What exactly happened between you and Maddie?' I demand.

He flashes me a sly, calculating glance, as if trying to weigh up the risks of the different possible answers.

'I said. It wasn't physical.'

'I saw you try to kiss her,' Jenna says. 'I was outside the door.'

Tom flushes. 'If you already know, why are you asking me?'

'What else?'

He hesitates. 'We never got the chance for anything else.'

It sounds plausible, but then he used to be an actor.

Chapter Thirty-Six

Lucy, Present

Jenna and I don't talk much when we first get back in the car. We didn't talk much on the way here either. It's been a while since I spent much time with her without Hayley and Claire there too – she's been busy with work and training for a marathon, I've been busy with Ruby – and it's almost like we've lost the knack of how to be relaxed with each other. Maybe it's partly also the aftermath of our phone call last night. After all, I practically forced her to tell me what she was keeping secret and I wonder how she feels about that, and whether she's grateful to have shared her own secret at last, or she resents me for dragging it out of her. We stop at a service station to use the toilets and then sit in the car draining the icy cans of Diet Coke we bought.

'So,' I say, determined to break the weird silence, 'interesting things about our meeting with Tom?'

'Our parents basically sent us to a summer camp run by a creepy fantasist.'

I choke and Diet Coke starts spurting out of my nose. Jenna hands me a wet wipe from the pack I leave in the car for Ruby-related emergencies and offers to thump me on the back to stop me choking. We're both briefly gulping with laughter and, for a while, it feels like things are back to normal.

'What was my mum thinking?' I say, dabbing at myself. 'Tom was her friend.'

'Yeah but how well did she really know him, Lucy?'

'I think they knew each other at drama school and then they stayed in touch afterwards, but it's not like Tom ever came over to our house or anything. I must have seen him when I was a kid I guess, but summer camp was the first time I remember meeting him.'

'Will you tell her what he's like?'

'She hasn't seen him in decades, I don't think she's going to care now.'

I discard the wet wipe with the rest of the detritus in the back of the car and ask as casually as I can, 'What about the thing about Claire?'

'What about it?'

'Well, what do you think they were talking about?' I choose the word 'talking' carefully. Not arguing.

'I don't see how it can matter now,' Jenna says. I hear Nic saying, *I think she loved her*, and I wonder if that's what Claire tried to tell Maddie that night. I move onto safer ground. 'Do we think Tom is the person sending me the messages? That's why we went after all.'

Jenna screws up her face.

'Well, he's obsessed with Maddie, or some version of Maddie that exists only in his head, so I wouldn't rule it out entirely, but I don't think so. You?'

I'm mid swig and I shake my head.

'He didn't seem worried to see us – it was almost like he was pleased, in fact. Also Lucy, I keep wondering—' She trails off, but I think I know what she's going to say next.

'You think it really is Maddie sending the messages, don't you?' I say.

'I don't know. But I've always wondered if the thing with Tom was what made her run away. Maybe it got too heavy for her and she wanted to get away from him. I should have told the police at the time.'

'You told Lorraine, Jenna. She should have told the police.'

'That's the thing. I didn't. I didn't even know she knew.'

'I wonder how she found out, and why she never said anything.'

'Well we can't ask her now.'

Lorraine Caxton died of cancer five years ago. Her obituary described her as one of the country's leading stage actresses and made no mention of the still unsolved disappearance of a schoolgirl at a summer camp she ran two decades earlier. Tom was right about that – she certainly didn't become unemployable. Fat drops of rain start falling on the windscreen. I turn the key in the ignition. Time to start heading back.

'Lucy, there's something else I should have told the police.'

I slam on the brakes and a guy on a motorbike just behind us narrowly avoids catapulting into the back of us, swerving out of the way.

'I didn't tell Lorraine, but I told Amari. I told Amari about Tom and Maddie.'

Chapter Thirty-Seven

Lucy, Present

'Hi there!'

Amari spots Hayley and me first and gets to his feet. He has a big smile that reaches his eyes and he seems really pleased to see us. He was in Joe's year at school so he must be forty-one or forty-two, but he's aged well. His dark skin is unlined and his pale blue shirt tucked into a pair of skinny, sand-coloured chinos reveals no signs of a middle-aged spread.

On the drive back from the meeting with Tom, Jenna used the Fab Four group to fill the others in, and messages of surprise, revulsion and anger eventually gave way to ideas for what we could do next. It was Hayley who suggested contacting Amari, and who managed to find him half an hour later on Instagram – that simple. She set up a meeting for the following evening and insisted on coming with me – the others agreed to keep it to just us two, in case four people was a bit overwhelming.

'Grab a seat,' he says, hugs over. The hug took me by surprise. I don't really feel like I ever knew Amari. I mean I knew of him, in the way I knew of all the popular kids, but I don't think I ever exchanged a single word with him. It's different for Hayley; she *was* one of the popular kids. I still find it strange that at some point none of this matters

– Amari is pleased to see me because I went to the same school and it doesn't matter that he would no more have acknowledged me there than he would have snogged Miss Matthews, the Maths teacher with bad BO. It's all different now and I'm the weird one for being conscious of it at all.

'I hope you're okay here? It's a bit cramped.'

He's found us a little round table in the corner of the BFI bar. It was his choice of venue; I hardly ever go out in central London anymore, so the Southbank feels impossibly exotic. I'm wearing what I think of as my 'Going Out' top – a black t-shirty thing from Ted Baker, with a sequined heart on it – but looking round at the other tables, I decide I look simultaneously like I've made too much and not enough effort. Hanging out with the cool kids still makes me feel on edge.

I make brief eye contact with a tall, awkward man standing at the bar, who is the only other person who looks like he doesn't belong here. He's wearing beaten-up jeans – the kind he might actually have worn to work rather than bought in an expensive vintage shop – and an old sweatshirt and is clutching a bottle of Peroni like it's his only link to a more familiar world.

'Here's great,' Hayley says, sitting down on one of the little round bar stools. As usual, she looks just right in a belted denim dress and Birkenstocks.

'What can I get you to drink?' Amari asks, indicating his own half-full glass of white wine. We decide on a bottle of Viognier and he goes to the bar to get it.

'So what do you think?' Hayley demands, as soon, or possibly before, he's out of earshot. 'He seems lovely doesn't he? And he's still really hot. Did you notice if he had a wedding ring?'

'No, but you do.'

'I wasn't thinking of me, babe. One bit on the side is enough for me.'

'What?'

'Vagabond Guy.' Hayley's Instagram crush.

'You're still messaging each other?'

'There's no need to sound so disapproving. It's just a fun thing, you know. We tell each other stuff about our days – you know how sometimes it's easier to share stuff with someone you've never met? Anyway, back to Amari. I was thinking about Jenna. Now her mystery guy seems to be out of the picture again, I was thinking she might be ready to meet someone else.'

It's clearly never occurred to Hayley that the mystery guy could be Frank, but then why would it? For all her talk of bits on the side, I'm pretty sure she would never cheat on him – it's no accident that Vagabond Guy is safely in Cuba – and it would certainly never occur to her that he might look at anyone else.

'Okay but it would be weird if that someone was Amari,' I say.

An uneasy silence falls between us as we both remember why we're there. When Amari comes back with the wine, we jump back into sociable mode and ask all the questions you ask when you haven't seen someone in more than two decades – the how do you spend your days and who do you spend them with questions – but it's not awkward and the conversation jumps backwards and forwards as we exchange news.

Amari already knows that I married Joe – the school grapevine must still be working pretty effectively – and asks me to say hi from him. Which I obviously can't do because Joe has no idea I'm meeting Amari and hopefully will never find out. Amari's face glows with enthusiasm when he talks about his own family and his job at, of all places, the Bank of England, where he turns out to be a senior analyst, whatever that might be. Another thing I can never get over is when people I went to school with turn out to have high-powered jobs. It's terrifying, for instance, to think of Ricky Hooper – who famously tried to dissect a frog in biology using his fake ID card rather than the scalpel provided – practising as a GP somewhere. Unhappily for Hayley's matchmaking, but happily for him, Amari turns out to be married.

'With two little girls – and another on the way. Holy terrors, both of them,' he says, smiling. He shows us a picture on his phone. 'That's Chiara, my wife, she's Italian, and these two are Belle and Maya. Belle is seven and Maya here is five.'

Chiara is petite, with lots of curly black hair and huge eyes; she doesn't look anything like Maddie, which shouldn't surprise me because it's not like people go round looking for photofits of their childhood loves. Although now I wonder if that's exactly what Claire's done. I think again about Nic's question, and about the photograph I've still got in my handbag, and about how much Nic resembles that long-ago snap of Maddie.

'Aw, they're super-cute,' Hayley says, handing back the phone.

'You wouldn't say that if you'd seen them trying to persuade me and their mum to buy them a McDonalds last weekend. Maya was lying flat out on the kitchen floor, pounding her fists on the tiles.'

'Oh, Tallulah has tantrums like that too. Frank says I should just ignore her, but he's not the one standing next to her in the biscuit aisle in Waitrose.'

I join in the laughter. I'm starting to feel almost relaxed now – in fact, more relaxed than I have in days – Amari is good company and the buzz in the bar is making me feel strangely safe, as if I'm cocooned in a world of film-loving thirty-something drinkers. I wish that this was just a reunion with an old friend – I'm even thinking of Amari as a friend now, when only an hour ago I was conscious that we'd never been friends – and that we could carry on chatting about our jobs and our kids and our grown-up lives. In the end it's Amari who brings up the subject, when Hayley comes back from the bar with a second bottle.

'So what is it that's made you both think about Maddie again?' I notice that he's twisting the wedding ring that Hayley and I failed to notice earlier round on his finger. 'I mean, why now in particular?'

'Lucy's been getting these strange messages,' Hayley says.

I'm a little taken aback at her directness. When we discussed how to approach this evening, we agreed to start by using the twenty-fifth anniversary as the reason and then sound Amari out and see whether he had any reason to think Maddie was still alive. But I can understand why she's gone straight for it – Amari's so easy to talk to.

'Yeah? What kind of messages?'

Hayley fills up our glasses.

'Well,' I say. I might as well go for it: 'It's like they're from Maddie.'

Amari puts his glass back down without drinking from it.

'As in signed by her?'

'They're not actually signed by her, but they're written as if they're from her and it's stuff that she would have known about. Stuff from back then.'

'Yeah? That is weird. Have you still got them?'

'Uh-huh,' I say, ignoring the unspoken request. I like what I've seen of Amari, but there's no way I'm showing him the actual messages.

'What are these messages? Emails?'

'They're texts.'

'I'm guessing you've tried calling the number they're from.'

'No one ever answers.'

'That's really horrible, Lucy.' He reaches out and squeezes my hand. His palm is dry, the skin a little bit rough. 'I'm so sorry. Someone must be hoaxing you. What a really evil thing to do.'

'Yeah.'

Suddenly his brown eyes are fixed on mine.

'You're not thinking they're actually from her, are you?'

'It's hard not to wonder,' Hayley says.

Amari's glance transfers to her briefly and then he takes a large swig of wine.

'That's exactly what this person, whoever they are, wants you to do. They're clearly trying to frighten you. It's probably some nut-job who's read about the case and gets their kicks out of spooking people.'

'The thing is,' I say, gripping my own wine glass tightly, 'Maddie could still be alive. She could be sitting in this bar now.'

I glance round uneasily, as though the bar is suddenly going to be populated with fifteen-year-old Maddies. Hayley follows my gaze, but Amari shakes his head.

'No way,' he says, and there's no doubt in his voice. 'She's dead. She died at the time. This is just some sick person who's trying to make you believe otherwise.'

'What makes you so sure?' Hayley asks.

'I just know,' Amari says. 'I knew at the time she was dead. From the moment the police called round at our house that evening, I knew.'

'I never asked you about that,' Hayley says. 'It must have been awful for you.'

'Yeah, well, none of us ever really talked about it did we? It was the way back then. Now we'd probably get counselling or something. I certainly would for my kids if, god forbid, they were ever mixed up in anything as horrible as that.'

I do remember sitting on the upstairs landing and listening through the banisters as my mum talked to my dad on the phone about whether I needed to see someone, but when she raised the idea with me a few days later I was emphatic that I didn't want to. I wonder if I'd be in such a mess now if I'd talked to a professional at the time.

'Shit yes, me too,' Hayley says. 'At the time my mum was so focused on my little sister, it was just when her anorexia was really bad. I think she just assumed I was dealing with it all, but I cried myself to sleep for about a year afterwards. I used to lie there in the dark with the tears running down my face, trying to cry quietly so I didn't wake anyone up.'

I would wake screaming in the night – the same nightmare every time. I'd killed Maddie. In my dream, it was never clear how; I just knew I'd done it and now I was going to have to explain to everyone, and nothing would ever be the same.

'We were all grieving,' Amari says, 'and at the same time we had to deal with all these questions and all this speculation about Maddie. It wasn't just the kids, the adults were as bad – like what happened to her was some kind of TV crime show or something, and they were trying to guess the ending.'

'Oh my god yes. I'll never forget going back to school after that summer,' Hayley says. 'Huddles of people talking in corridors, and they'd go all quiet when they saw you and you knew they'd been talking about Maddie.'

'You know some of the kids thought I did it,' Amari says, and I can hear the pain in his voice even now. 'I was her boyfriend, so, you know, obviously I was a suspect and it got out that the police had been round my house.'

'Oh babe,' Hayley murmurs, reaching out to touch his arm.

'That must have been horrible.'

I need to ask Amari about what Jenna said. Now that he's sitting here in front of me it seems almost impossible that he could have had anything to do with what happened, but I still need to see how he reacts to the idea of Maddie and Tom. I take a deep breath. Now is as good a moment as I'm going to get.

'I think the police had lots of suspects. Apparently, Jenna saw the guy who was running the summer camp make a move on Maddie.'

He nods.

'You knew about that?'

'Jenna phoned me to tell me what she'd seen,' he says. 'I thought she was just making trouble between us – even though she said she was trying to help. The last time I spoke to Maddie, we had this stupid argument. It was

247

partly because of what Jenna told me I guess. I didn't believe it, but it lodged in my mind, you know.'

'What did she say when you asked her about it?'

'That's the stupid thing. We didn't talk about it at all. We were rowing about that crazy time with the front door – you know when her dad smashed it in.'

'Wait, what?' Hayley says.

'You must remember. It happened the same summer – before she went to the camp.'

'That wasn't her dad,' I say.

'I don't know exactly what happened, because she wouldn't tell me, but it was obviously something to do with him. Just like when she used to run away. It was because of her dad.'

Hayley and I lock eyes.

'What about her dad?' I manage. At the same time, I can feel the panic welling up inside me. The family secret – could this be it? Perhaps DI Silver had been right after all.

'Oh, nothing like that. Nothing bad. I mean it was bad, but it's not what you're thinking. Sorry, I thought you knew. I thought she'd have told you.'

'Told us what though?' Hayley demands.

'Her dad was an alcoholic, right?'

'Robin was?' Hayley says.

'Yeah. Did you really not know?'

'Nope. She never said. Shit. Shit, shit, shit.'

'He used to go on these binges. He'd be sober for weeks and then something would set him off and he'd drink until he could barely stand. That's when Maddie used to clear out. She couldn't bear to be around him, she said. And she hated how her mum reacted. She was always on at Maddie, criticising her, and so on, but when Maddie tried to get her to do something about her dad, her mum would deny that there was even a problem. She used to pretend it wasn't happening. It drove Maddie mad.'

'I don't understand why she didn't tell us,' Hayley says, and, after all these years, she still sounds hurt. I can understand this; I feel indignant too, with much less reason. Hayley was Maddie's best friend, or one of them. At times like this, I have to remind myself that, however much she has dominated my life since, I was never Maddie's best friend, or perhaps even much of a friend at all. I was a hanger-on she adopted for a summer. She was hardly going to tell me her father was an alcoholic. My husband, on the other hand… but I have no right to resent Joe for the things he hasn't told me, when lying just underneath the surface there's always been this thing I've never told him.

'I think she felt ashamed,' Amari says. He looks worried that he's upset us. 'She only told me because I was over there one day when he came back from work smashed out of his skull. She practically dragged me out of the house and then she was so angry it all just came pouring out.'

'Right,' Hayley says, sounding unconvinced.

'Crap. Lucy, I've just thought. Maddie's dad is your—'

'Father-in-law. Yes.'

'Sorry. For a moment there I wasn't thinking. I wasn't connecting it up.'

'Don't worry. It doesn't matter.'

'I take he isn't still… he doesn't still—'

'No, I don't think so.'

Because I'd know, wouldn't I? I've been married to Joe for ten years. I'd know if his dad was still an alcoholic.

'He and Naomi don't drink,' I add. But I think about Robin's strange behaviour last time I was at their house and I wonder.

'Well, that's something at least. I'm glad,' Amari says, on safer ground now. 'It's a tough thing to beat. I'm sure if Maddie was here she'd be so proud of him.'

I like the way he can talk about her straightforwardly, as if he doesn't have any baggage associated with her and with what happened to her. None of us has ever been able to do that.

I excuse myself and go to the toilets. Once there, I sink back against the concrete wall and google 'Selincro' – the name of the pills I found in Robin's pocket when I was looking for his phone. I'd assumed they were for blood pressure or something, but a quick glance at the search results tells me it's the brand name of a medicine that's used to treat alcohol addiction. So Robin is drinking again – and it says something about my state of mind that what I mainly feel, as this realisation sinks in to the sound of hand driers and running taps, is relief that what was making him behave so out of character the other day was not something worse. That the secret isn't a more terrible secret. I also think I know where Robin was the morning after Maddie's disappearance and why he didn't come down to Poison Cross. He was drunk. Too drunk to search for his own daughter.

It's only as I walk back to Hayley and Amari, nearly cannoning into the tall guy with the beaten-up jeans who's still here and heading down the stairs just as I'm coming up them, that it occurs to me to wonder what has made Robin start drinking again. Hayley and Amari are still talking about Maddie.

'The worst thing,' Amari is saying, 'the thing that made me really sad – was that for a long time, I couldn't really remember Maddie herself at all. When I thought about her I just remembered that dark time after she disappeared and all the suspicion and fear. But, you know what I discovered? Time really does help and, this isn't to diminish what happened to Maddie at all, it did become easier, and then one day, I was thinking about her and I realised I was actually thinking about *her*, you know – Maddie. Not Maddie who disappeared, but Maddie my girlfriend at school. I could remember her again, and it was such a relief.'

His eyes fill with tears. I think Amari has done okay, even without the help of a counsellor. He has somehow processed this horrible thing that happened when he was little more than a child and managed not to let it ruin his entire life, and after Naomi and Robin, and DI Silver, and Tom Durrant – not to mention me, and Joe, and Hayley, Claire and Jenna – it's something of a relief to me to discover that it is possible to do this. That what happened to Maddie, or the uncertainty about what happened to Maddie, hasn't destroyed everyone who was touched by it.

'Oh babe, it's so lovely that you remember her without the sadness,' Hayley says.

'I remember how beautiful she was, and how brave. And confident.' He smiles his big, open smile again. 'I want my daughters to grow up like that,' he says, and he looks so sure that I don't say what I'm thinking. That it might have been her confidence that led to whatever happened to her. I want Ruby to grow up careful. Careful does it. I want Ruby to grow up. I drink about a third of my new glass of Viognier in one go and then help myself to a big handful of sweet chilli crisps from the packet that Hayley's split open on the table. The bar has emptied out a bit now – presumably at least some of the people drinking here have come to see a film. The buzz of conversation has dropped a bit and it's possible to make out that 'Wonderwall' is playing – even the music seems determined to take us back to the Nineties.

'To Maddie,' Amari says and raises his glass.

Hayley and I raise our glasses too. Mine is smeary with fingerprints and bits of crisp.

'To Maddie,' Hayley and I mumble, not meeting each other's eyes. It's as if we're frightened we might summon her up.

Chapter Thirty-Eight

Lucy, Present

'You never asked,' Joe says warily, clutching the screw-driver like he might need to use it as a weapon. 'Look, I need to finish fixing the patio door before I go to football. Can we talk about this later?'

Joe was asleep when Hayley and I got back last night and I've waited until now to confront him.

'I'm not going to ask you if your dad's an alcoholic, am I? There are some things you tell people even if they don't ask the question.'

Even as the words leave my mouth I realise they're not true. I've spent most of my life not telling something because nobody has ever asked the right question. Besides, I don't want another argument with Joe. I think again about how we're not an arguing kind of couple. I'm frightened about what it would mean for us – for the existence of an us – if we suddenly became one.

'It was a long time before I met you – before we got together,' he corrects himself. 'It was ancient history. Not worth talking about.'

'The thing is,' I say, forcing myself to sound less accusatory, 'I think he might be drinking again.'

Joe looks, if possible, even more uncomfortable.

'It's okay. He has it under control.'

'You knew?'

'Mum told me. She's worried about him.'

'Of course she is.'

'But it's okay now. It was a few weeks. Nothing more. And he's gone back to AA meetings. He has a sponsor.'

Why didn't you tell me? I want to scream. But I know that I, of all people, have no right to ask that particular question. Sometimes I think I'm just going to do it. I imagine what a relief it would be to tell Joe the truth. *I left Maddie to die. We left her in that haunted house. And we never told anyone.* I imagine him gathering me up in his arms. *It's all right, I know. I've known all along. I forgive you. I still love you.* But I can't be sure this is what's going to happen, so instead I say, 'Can I ask you about something that happened a long time ago?'

'You know you can.' He puts the screwdriver down on the coffee table, next to the cold remains of a cup of tea.

'Okay. Do you remember that night when the glass on your front door got smashed? Was that Robin?'

He reddens, and then nods.

'He got hammered at some work event and then when he got home he hadn't got his key, or he was too drunk to find it more likely, and for some reason he thought the easiest way to get into the house was to break the door down. Maddie came down and found him.'

'I can't believe she never said.' So much for being non-accusatory. I'm not sure it's any better to accuse Maddie, who isn't here and can't answer back, than Joe who is and can. 'I mean, we were there in the house when it happened.'

'Maddie would have rather died than have anyone find out,' Joe says, and we both wince as the expression hits us.

'What made him stop drinking?' I ask quietly.

'Depends what you mean.' He picks up the dregs of the cup of tea and nurses it. I wait. 'Maddie's disappearance made him stop drinking. You'd think it was the kind of thing that would drive you *to* drink, right?'

I manage a half-smile to match his.

'But he was so ashamed about being drunk the night we got the phone call about Maddie, I think it shocked him into wanting to stop. He thought that if he'd been sober that night, he could have done something to change what happened. It's nonsense probably; nothing he could have done would have made a difference, but the point is, that's how he felt. But if you mean what actually helped him to stop, it was his sponsor. He had this great woman he used to talk to for ages on the phone. She was always there for him. He said without her he never could have done it. That's why I think he's going to be okay this time. Mum says he's got another great sponsor. A guy this time. Younger. Keeps messaging him. Won't take any bullshit. Makes Dad take responsibility for his own actions.'

'That's good.'

I remember the text I saw on Robin's phone: *You say you blame yourself, but what are you going to do about it?* That could certainly be a message from Robin's sponsor. It's such a relief to have an explanation for what's troubling Robin that I momentarily forget none of this explains who's targeting me.

'How did you find out?' Joe asks.

'What?'

I suppose I should have seen this question coming, but it totally floors me. I really don't want to have to tell him about meeting Amari, because that will lead to so many other questions that I can't answer.

'How did you find out about Dad's drinking?'

'I saw some pills. At their house, the other day. I didn't think anything of it at the time, but later I was curious and I googled them. It's a medication used to treat alcoholism.' This has the advantage of being part of the truth at least, but Joe doesn't look convinced.

'That's it?'

'What else could there be?' I hedge. His forehead furrows into a frown.

'You can tell me if there is something. I'd rather know.'

But I've no intention of telling him anything else. And besides, there's something nagging at me. Something important.

'What do you think made him start drinking again this time?'

'Does it have to be a single thing?'

'No, of course not. I just wondered if you had any idea.'

'It could be anything Lucy,' Joe says, and drains the remains of the cold cup of tea as if that's a perfectly normal thing to do. And I know then that I'm not the only person in this relationship who's not telling the truth.

Chapter Thirty-Nine

Lucy, Present

Later, as I negotiate the Northern line with Ruby in her sling and a bagful of baby equipment, my worry over why Joe won't tell me what made Robin start drinking again alternates with my paranoia that someone is following me. I'm also cursing myself for agreeing to meet Harriet Holland on the other side of London. It's a nerve-shredding journey to Highgate. I've had no more messages, no more photos, but I can feel eyes on me wherever I go. Whoever it is had got close enough to put something in my bag. I feel sick every time I think about that photo.

By the time I finally see Harriet standing outside the coffee shop she mentioned, I'm a mess.

'You look hot,' Harriet says, her eyes running critically over me and leaving me in no doubt about the sense in which she is using the adjective.

'Actually I am a bit,' I say as politely as I can manage. Harriet is wearing a pale grey jumpsuit that fits her perfectly, emphasising her slim waist and long legs. She's wearing sunglasses again – this time a pair of Aviators – and she looks as cool as a cucumber that has just been removed from a very expensive Smeg fridge.

'I got you a flat white.'

'Oh. Thanks. Aren't we going in?'

I can't believe Harriet has dragged me across London to go to a coffee shop that she picked and now we're not even going inside. Besides, I could really do with taking this baby sling off for a while – an eight-month-old baby is surprisingly heavy when she's strapped to your chest for an hour.

'No. I suggested this as a meeting place because it's easy to find. It's not why I brought you here.'

'Oh.' My uneasiness increases. Why has she 'brought me here', as she puts it? 'So where are we going?'

'I've got a surprise for you.'

'Right. I'm not that into surprises actually.'

She laughs and hands me the coffee.

'Follow me, Lucy.'

We set off up the hill. She doesn't offer to help me carry Ruby's bag, even though all she's carrying is a little leather bag the size of an envelope. Once again she has failed to acknowledge Ruby's existence and although part of me admires her resolute lack of baby interest, it does strike me as a little weird, not to say rude, not even to say hello to Ruby.

As we walk, she tells me about why her Guadalajara film shoot was postponed – something to do with a fire at the main location they wanted to use and a star who's being difficult about completing a Broadway commitment on time. Normally, this is the sort of gossip I love, but I've missed the star's name entirely and I'm having trouble concentrating on the rest of the story too.

Now that I'm with her again, I'm trying to think of some way of establishing once and for all that Harriet Holland really is Harriet Holland and not Maddie Blake. I could ask her something about her family and where she grew up and went to school, but I don't see how it will get me any further forward. If she really is Maddie and she doesn't want me to know it, she's hardly going to tell me the truth. I still haven't told the others about my idea that Harriet could be Maddie. None of them has ever met her, but at the very least I could show them the photo of her I found online and see what they think. But I can't get rid of this fear that by articulating the possibility I will make it more likely to be true, and so I've kept it to myself.

We come to a stop outside a pair of tall, black wrought-iron gates.

'Here we are.'

'You've brought me to a cemetery?'

'Surprised?'

I certainly am, although I suppose it's the one thing Highgate should have suggested to me. I know the cemetery is a tourist attraction in its own right; it's got all kinds of famous people buried in it. I've never been before because a cemetery, however illustrious the inhabitants, isn't my idea of a good day out. Too many ghosts, and I've never been keen on those. I wonder if this is where Harriet's great-grandmother is buried. I think Ava Holland died in London, in the early 1960s, all but forgotten by then. The man in the ticket booth offers Harriet a map but she says she doesn't need it and, once we're inside, she sets off confidently.

In spite of everything, I'm fascinated. The graves, monuments and mausoleums aren't arranged in regular rows – they're scattered about all over the place and there are trees, bushes and little paths everywhere.

'Did you know George Eliot is buried here?' Harriet says. I turn to look where she's pointing. Beneath the headstone is a selection of tributes people have left: a jar of fresh violets, a bunch of pink roses – dying now – a notebook, a pot of pencils.

'*Here lies the body of George Eliot,*' reads the inscription and then underneath, '*Mary Ann Cross*'.

'It must be strange not to be known by your real name,' Harriet says.

I stare at her, wondering if I should be reading more into this.

'Even Cross is her married name. She was Mary Ann Evans. Is Blake Joe's name?' she asks.

'Yes.'

'So what were you originally?'

'Keeble. I was Lucy Keeble.'

'I prefer Blake. Keeble makes me think Feeble.'

I feel another stab of apprehension. It's a strange thing to say, but not entirely out of character – she's always been a bit abrupt, bordering on rude. I was looking right at her when I said my maiden name and her face didn't change, but then why would it. If she's Maddie, she already knows who I am.

'Yeah well, some of the kids at school actually used to call me that.'

Although never Maddie herself, who probably wasn't even aware of my existence until her mum told her about me.

'We need to go up here.' She indicates a path between a sea of elaborate stone crosses. I hesitate. If there's even a small possibility that she's Maddie, should I be following her to god knows what remote spot she has in mind? She's ahead of me now, not even looking back, confident of being followed. And follow her I do, because part of me just wants to know. It's the not knowing that I can't bear. If she's Maddie I want to know.

After a few moments, she takes a narrower path to the right. The path stretches ahead of us, long and basically straight. It looks like an ordinary footpath through a forest, except that, if you look again, you can see that the forest is full of old gravestones, sinking sideways into the soil as if someone has come along and shoved them all over. This is not a popular part of the cemetery. I doubt it gets many visitors. There are no flowers or gifts on the graves here, just a carpet of soil and leaves. Some of the graves have low, rusted railings around them. The stones themselves are covered in ivy and many of the inscriptions are difficult to read, although there's not much time to linger anyway; Harriet is walking purposefully and we seem to be going deeper and deeper into the wood. Perhaps I should be leaving a trail of rusks. She comes to a halt in a clearing between the trees, where the sunlight is breaking through and illuminating her auburn hair and a marble headstone, taller and slightly more recent-looking than the stones around it. I stand by her side, fighting the urge to turn and run.

Edward Duval

Actor

1895 to 1935

'You are not lost, but merely sleeping.

When the time is right you will return to us'

Harriet is looking at me like she's expecting me to say something and when I don't, she turns back towards the headstone and says, 'Ava arranged it all.'

'The inscription is a bit creepy,' I manage.

'It's a quote from *Sleeping Beauty*. The last film he and Ava made.'

'Of course.'

'Are you all right Lucy?'

'I thought he'd be buried in Poison Cross.'

'The villagers didn't want him. I had a look in the graveyard when I went down there. It was the verger who told me he was buried in Highgate, and I came to have a look for him the other day. The cemetery people were really helpful – they even have Ava's original letters arranging the details. I thought this might make Duval more real for you,' she says. But the very last thing I want is Duval to be more real. 'You could begin the section on Duval by talking about this hidden corner of a crowded cemetery – contrast the obscurity of his resting place with the glamour of his lifestyle in Hollywood.'

'Maybe.' Writing about Duval is bad enough; I'm certainly not going to begin with his grave. If Harriet is so full of ideas, she can write it herself.

'Ava originally had a different idea for the dedication; something about him being more sinned against than sinning.'

'She really did think he was innocent then?'

'Haven't you read the letters yet?'

'I've glanced at them.' Or more accurately, at the manila folder that contains them, before I buried it at the bottom of the desk drawer.

'Look at them properly, Lucy, and see what you think. Apparently, Ava used to come and visit the grave when she was in London – she would tidy it, pull back the brambles and so on.'

Harriet is standing very close to me, her impeccably made-up face inches away from mine, and as she's talking I stare back, mesmerised, trying to see Maddie's features from those long-ago photos in her adult face. She has the same high cheekbones, but her nose is wrong, too thin – at least I think it is. And her eyes are hidden behind sunglasses as usual. Over her shoulder, in the corner of my vision, something moves in the spindly trees that surround the clearing we're standing in. My stomach clenches and my arms go round Ruby in her baby sling. My eyes are now fixed on the woods. All I saw was the impression of a shape. There must be animals in those woods. But somehow, I know it was the shape of a person.

'Let's go,' I say, and Harriet responds to the urgency in my voice.

'What's wrong?'

'I need to feed Ruby,' I say over my shoulder, and she starts to follow. I feel eyes on me as I retreat, almost jogging down the narrow, uneven path. I don't know exactly what, or who, I'm frightened of right now – the person who might be following me, the ghost of Gladys Rudd, Maddie, or Duval himself, 'not lost but merely sleeping'. Or just shadows.

Back in the light and bustle of the main drag of the cemetery, I take a couple of big gulps of air and start to feel better. A group of students is taking selfies in front of Karl Marx's monument and a coachload of tourists is just coming in the main entrance, clutching maps. Ruby wakes and promptly starts to cry. Harriet says she knows another cafe just around the corner, but we don't make it that far. We sit down on a bench and I get the formula out of the baby bag and tip it into the bottle, struggling with the screw top as Ruby bawls – you'd think I'd be used to juggling baby, formula and bottle by now.

Harriet's talking about the chapter I emailed her the other day, but I'm finding it difficult to concentrate on what she's saying, what with Ruby and the memory of the shadow moving between the trees. There are trees behind the bench we're sitting on now. Is there still someone out there? Watching me and Ruby?

Turning to look behind me, I miss the moment when Ruby decides she will try to stand up, but I feel her wriggle and twist in my grip and topple sideways.

Harriet grabs her.

'I'll take her while you do that.'

'Thank you.'

I'm watching her, and the way she's looking at my daughter as she sits on her knee, no longer crying now that she has the novelty of a new face to take in, and suddenly I'm not so sure that Harriet is indifferent to Ruby. She has taken her sunglasses off and she's looking at Ruby with something very like adoration. As I watch, tears start to spill down her face.

'Maddie?' I whisper.

'What?' she says, looking at me, and her expression gives me certainty of a kind. She looks merely confused.

'Sorry. I don't know why I said that. You reminded me of someone I once knew. Are you okay? I mean, you're obviously not okay. What's wrong, Harriet?'

'I had a miscarriage,' she says flatly. 'Just over a year ago. My baby would have been Ruby's age.'

Chapter Forty

Lucy, Present

It's Joe's turn for a night out; drinks with some of his teacher mates. It's been on the shared calendar for weeks. When I was pregnant with Ruby, we agreed we'd take it in turns – one week I'd get a night out, next week Joe would. We wouldn't turn into one of those couples who become hermits as soon as they have kids, or who can only socialise during the day, baby in tow. We'd still do fun stuff in the evenings; we'd be the ones who bucked the trend.

Of course, it hasn't worked out quite like that. I spent my first designated night out curled up in a ball on our bed, trying desperately to catch up on some sleep; the idea of leaving the bedroom, let alone the house, was laughable. But gradually we've improved. I've managed a couple of nights out at the cinema and one in a wine bar with a group of the other mums from our NCT class. And as Ruby has become a slightly better sleeper, I've even started enjoying the nights when it's Joe's turn to head out. I usually watch a movie on Netflix that I know he'd hate and eat my way through a tub of Ben & Jerry's Cookie Dough ice cream.

Tonight, though, I've got too much work to catch up on. Much as I'd like to forget all about Edward Duval,

Harriet Holland is my sole source of income at the moment. Besides I feel both bad and relieved about her – bad for mixing her private tragedy up with my own fears, and relieved that she is not, after all, Maddie. Of course, I can't be totally sure and the logical part of my brain knows this. I suppose the miscarriage could even have been the thing that made her decide to come back into our lives after all these years. But I don't think anyone could have acted the confusion I saw on her face when I called her Maddie; I'm as certain as I can be that she had no idea what I was talking about. Harriet and I are never going to be friends, but I do feel closer to her after she opened up to me about her miscarriage, and I think yet again what a powerful thing it is to tell somebody a secret. How it can bring you closer, or drive you apart. And how you can't necessarily tell which it's going to be.

I've opened a bottle of Sauvignon and ordered myself a Deliveroo. While I wait for it to arrive, I open the Word file on my Mac and re-read what I've written on Edward Duval so far. The baby monitor is sitting on the desk and every now and then I glance at it and I can see the blurry shape of Ruby, sleeping on her back, her arms thrown out to the sides. It's one of those nights when looking at her makes me feel anchored and secure, rather than panicked. She's so peaceful; so dependent on me.

I would never have thought it but visiting Duval's grave earlier today has helped; maybe Harriet knew what she was doing after all. Over the years, Duval has acquired the status of a mythical bogeyman in my head; the reason that everything went wrong all those years ago. But seeing his grave has somehow brought me perspective. Edward Duval was just a person and, whatever else he might have been, he is long dead. He's not sleeping and he's not coming back. He can't hurt me. For once, I really believe this.

I open the A4 manila folder that contains his letters to Ava Holland. There are five of them and I spread them out on the table in front of me. The paper is thick and only slightly discoloured with age. Each sheet has a letterhead: *Thorncroft House, Poison Cross, Hampshire*. But even seeing this doesn't make me panic.

Duval's handwriting is flamboyant and difficult to read at first but gradually making out the words gets easier. The letters are dated with the day and the month but not the year, but judging from the content, I think they must have been written a year after Gladys Rudd's death and Duval's spectacular fall from grace and I'm pleased when I find a passage that confirms this:

> *A great tragedy about Rudy Valentino. They say 100,000 people lined the streets of Manhattan for his funeral. I wonder how many people would line the streets for mine, although perhaps I am feeling maudlin without reason, my darling. My fans still adore me, it is the studios who want nothing to do with me. I have written a dozen or more times to June Mathis who, as you know, promised me a part in one of her pictures when the fuss had died down. The bitch hasn't even had the good manners to write back. If you should run into her, Ava darling, please do put in a good word for your little Eddie. I feel I only need one decent break for my luck to change.*

This paragraph dates the letter firmly to 1926 – Valentino died in August – and is fairly typical of the overall tone of Duval's writing; a mixture of saccharine, venom and injured vanity. Strangely, it reminds me a bit of Tom and his indignation about how swiftly he was dropped by his industry friends. Harriet said that the letters made her think that Duval might not be guilty of Gladys Rudd's murder, but so far I haven't come across anything that makes me think the same. He hasn't referred to Gladys at all and the closest he's come to mentioning her disappearance is the reference to 'the fuss', which has to rank among the more oblique ways of describing being arrested for murder.

I'm interested in the reference to June Mathis; she was one of the first female executives in Hollywood. There must be a book in June Mathis, but it is not, unfortunately, the book I am being paid to write. I pour myself some more Sauvignon and start to type, the words tripping easily from brain to screen. At this rate, the Duval section is going to turn out to be one of the easiest to write in the whole book.

I hear the sound of a motorbike and get up to go to the front door, hoping to head off my lamb madras before the delivery guy rings the doorbell and wakes Ruby. I see a headlight go off, but nobody appears. I'm just about to shut the door again, when a skinny youth in a fluorescent yellow cycling helmet hurries up the drive towards the open door. He hands me a brown bag, saying, 'Have a nice evening,' – accompanying it with a smile that brings it to life – and then he's gone. In the kitchen I unpack my curry. I notice absently that they've forgotten the garlic naan, but I have a great pile of pilau rice so I'm not going to go hungry. My head is full of Duval and I'm keen to get back to writing.

I make room for the plate on my desk, and forking curry and rice into my mouth with one hand, I scroll through what I've just written with the other. Not my finest prose, but it does the job. When I've finished, I pick up the letters and start reading them through again, looking for quotes I can use – after all, the letters are a unique primary source. A unique primary source that is about to be covered in the sauce left over from lamb madras if I'm not more careful. I push the baby monitor back a bit to make more space, noticing that Ruby has shifted position slightly but is still fast asleep. Then I find a passage I haven't read before:

> *Ava, my darling, you will never guess who your little Eddie saw at Brighton railway station this morning. It was only the girl from the party! The Miss Rudd whose disappearance caused all that bother last year. Naturally she looked a little different; she has had her hair waved and her face was powdered and rouged. Nonetheless, I am absolutely certain it was her. She had the same snub nose and rather protuberant eyes, but I am forgetting that you never met her for you were fated not to be at the party that night. She was buying a magazine at the newspaper stand on the platform opposite and when she had finished, she turned and looked straight at me. It gave me quite a turn. I immediately made for the stairs with the idea that I would change platforms to reach her, but by some misfortune a train was pulling in at the time, and she must have boarded it or left the station, because by the time I reached the platform, she had gone altogether. I questioned the porter,*

but the dolt of a man said he had not noticed
her go. He admitted he had seen her buying the
magazine, but he could not recollect whether he
had ever seen her on the platform before. There
was something almost uncanny about her vanishing
quite so suddenly, but you do see, my darling Ava,
what this means? Miss Rudd has been alive all this
time and the indignities I have been forced to suffer
have had no basis in fact. This changes everything
and the studios must be made to see it.

I see what Harriet is thinking; if Edward Duval really
had murdered Gladys Rudd, he would hardly be spotting
her on railway stations a year later. Of course, Harriet
is overlooking the fact that he could have made up the
whole story in order to get Ava to pull strings with the
studio bosses, but there's something about the encounter
that rings true to me and if he was making it up, surely he
could have come up with a better story; something more
definite than this fleeting glimpse across a railway station
platform.

I wonder if the original source of the Gladys Rudd
ghost story could possibly be Duval himself. Did he share
his tale with anyone in Poison Cross and did it gradually
change over time into a story of a supernatural encounter,
to be embellished and expanded over the years with tales
of other brief sightings of Gladys, the ghostly lady in the
sparkling dress, out to get her revenge?

The baby monitor whimpers into life and I switch my
gaze from the letter to Ruby. Sometimes she wakes briefly,
cries for a few seconds and then settles herself again, so
Joe and I have learnt to wait a few minutes before going
in to comfort her. This time she gives a couple more tiny

gulps and then her breathing evens out again and she's back asleep. I turn back to the letter and as I do so, I see a shadow move past the living room window. I freeze. It was probably a branch moving on the cherry tree or a bird. Or maybe it's the Deliveroo guy with my missing naan – stranger things have happened. I haven't pulled the curtains because it's got properly dark almost without me noticing it. If there is somebody out there, they must be able to see right in.

Suddenly all my lovely feeling of being in control has gone. I take a deep breath. I know I should go and look. I stand to one side of the window. I take in the car, the garden wall, the magnolia bush, the cherry tree. It all looks familiar and unthreatening. And then, as I watch, the trunk of the cherry tree moves fractionally. I think that what is moving might be an arm and, just as I'm thinking and trying to reject this, I make out the edge of a motorcycle helmet.

My mouth is dry, my heart racing, and the message is back looping round and round in my head: *You must pay for what you did*. Could it possibly be Maddie? I'm wasting time; there is someone in a motorbike helmet creeping around my front garden. I need to do something. Phone the police. Where the fuck is my mobile? Did I even put the latch on the front door after the Deliveroo guy left? I would normally when at home by myself, especially since the messages started, but I was distracted thinking about my chapter on Duval. I move away from the window and quickly back out into the hallway, which is in semi-darkness – in my absorption it seems I've forgotten to turn any lights on anywhere else in the house too. I make it to the front door and feel a rush of relief as my fingers find the latch. It's already across – thank god. I add the deadlock for good measure. Then I lean with my back pressed up against it, as though I'm safe. My phone rings, sending my heart catapulting into my mouth, but at least I know where it is now, somewhere in the kitchen. I'm back down the hall and searching for it under the takeaway packaging. It stops ringing, but I carry on searching and eventually find it under the tea towel I've discarded on the work surface. I see a missed call from Joe on the screen and, phone shaking in my grip, I unlock it. Immediately it starts ringing again.

'Hi Lucy, I was only—'

'There's someone in the front garden.'

'Lucy? What's going on? Are you okay?'

'There's someone prowling around our front garden right now.'

'Have you called the police?'

'I couldn't find my phone.'

'Are the doors locked?'

'I just checked the front door.'

'What about the patio doors?'

'I haven't been out there.'

'I can't remember whether I put the bolt across when I was fixing them.'

'I'm going now.' I head back towards the living room, where there are French doors leading out to our tiny back garden. Which can be reached from the front garden because we never bothered to get a latch on the gate. Heart thumping, I push the bolt into place.

'Okay, patio doors are locked too.'

'Good. Can you still see him?'

I walk towards the front window again and then I notice it – there's a leaf on the carpet, just beside my desk.

A leaf that I'm pretty sure wasn't there when I left the room. A leaf that must have fallen off someone's shoe.

'Shit, shit, shit.'

'What is it? What's wrong?'

'I think there's someone in here. What do I do?'

'Just get out of there. I'll call the police.'

'Joe, I'm scared.'

'Get Ruby, get in the car and get out of there. Go!'

He hangs up. Miraculously, I can see the car keys in the bowl on the bookshelf, where they live but are hardly ever to be found. I snatch them up. There's a cry and instinctively my eyes go to the baby monitor, and then my heart stops.

Chapter Forty-One

I can't see Ruby anymore because there's something obstructing the view on the baby monitor. It's hard to work out what, but I think it might be the elbow of a leather jacket. I go into the kitchen and take a knife from the cutlery drawer, and I don't even hesitate – I'm terrified, but my course of action is never in doubt. Someone has crept into my house and is upstairs with my baby. I have to go to her, no matter what; I need to save her and I don't care what happens to me.

I force myself to go slowly up the stairs, trying not to think about what might be happening to Ruby, praying that an element of surprise might help me. I'm gripping the handle of the knife so tightly that I can feel my nails digging into my palms. Outside the nursery door, I pause again and listen. All I can hear is Ruby crying. I change my grip on the knife so that I could plunge downwards with it, take a deep breath and fling open the door.

Any hope that I might have imagined the whole thing vanishes. There is a figure in black motorbike gear standing behind Ruby's cot, amid the packs of nappies, wet wipes and baby toys that we never quite manage to clear away entirely. Whoever it is, it's not Maddie. I'm pretty sure it's a man and it's someone a good foot taller than Maddie. You can change lots of things in twenty-five years, but not your height. I don't know whether to be relieved or disappointed. I never really thought it was her – I knew it couldn't be – and yet… He is not doing anything, just standing there. Ruby herself is standing up, holding onto the bars of the cot, crying hot tears. Fear tips over into rage.

'What the fuck are you doing with my baby?'

I move forward to pick her up and he moves forward too.

'Get back!' I yell, but as I reach down towards her, I feel him seize my wrist, and twist. I give a cry of pain and drop the knife onto the cot mattress. Then we both make a grab for the things that matter most to us. I pick up Ruby and hold her tight, but he's moved between me and the door and now he's got a weapon.

'I only want to talk to you.'

His voice is slightly muffled by the helmet but I don't recognise it. I retreat behind the cot, putting it between me and him.

'Who are you?'

One-handed, he removes the helmet. The man standing in front of me is in his forties or early fifties, with fair hair, thinning on top, a slight snub nose and little ratty eyes that are darting from my face to the rest of the room. He looks vaguely familiar, but nothing more.

'Come on Lucy, how hard can it be to talk?' I never thought hearing my own name could make me feel so afraid. He knows who I am all right. 'I wasn't going to hurt the baby. I wanted to see her. I wanted to know if she looked like Maddie. I haven't seen her for twenty-five years but I have this image of her – it's like it's locked in my head and I can't get rid of it. I thought the baby might be like Maddie living on.' It's a disconcerting echo of what Naomi said about Ruby when we first brought her back from hospital. 'You still don't know who I am, do you?'

My inability to recognise him is making him angry and that's the very last thing I want right now; I need to keep him talking until the police get here. Maybe I should lie and pretend I know who he is? He's someone who knows – who knew – Maddie. Someone who was so obsessed with her that he needs to know if her niece resembles her. Maybe one of the kids I've forgotten from school. Most of my mind is intent on getting out of that room, but at the same time I'm feeling a strange adrenaline rush of relief. I haven't been going mad. This has been happening to me and there is an explanation for it. It isn't the explanation that's been haunting my days and my nights for the past week – Maddie isn't alive and seeking her revenge for the wrongs we did her as school children. Instead, it's some deranged man who is fixated on Maddie and has transferred that fixation to me for some reason. Ruby is wriggling in my arms, still crying. I'm holding her too tight, bouncing her up and down like her life and mine depend on it. I remember what he said about not wanting to hurt the baby – maybe I should try to build on this.

'Please just let us go. I won't say anything. I just need to calm my baby down. Please. You can see she's upset.'

'It's Sam. You must remember me.' He's pacing up and down in front of the doorway, but he never moves far enough for me to risk making a run for it. 'I can't believe you screwed up my entire life and you don't even remember me.'

'Sam?'

Then it hits me. This tall middle-aged man is the hot biker guy who first told us the story of Edward Duval and Gladys Rudd. Sam who did the lights. Sam who saw Maddie getting on a train at a railway station, just as Edward Duval claimed to have seen Gladys Rudd.

'Now she gets it!' His voice is full of fury. He's stopped his pacing and is facing me over the cot. 'I lost everything because of you.'

'I don't understand.'

'No, you've got no fucking idea. You don't know what it's like to be arrested for murder. Everyone in that place turned against me. Everywhere I went people were talking about me. And there was no escape. Nothing I said made any difference.'

I don't know if it's the way he says it, like he's trying to puzzle something out, or the idea that he, like Edward Duval, might have described what he wanted to see, but I suddenly know one thing for sure.

'You never saw her, did you?'

'What are you talking about?'

'You never saw Maddie getting on that train – like you told the police you did.'

'I had to tell them something,' he says, sounding almost reasonable now. 'It was the first thing that came into my head, a way of getting them out of my hair. I needed time to breathe, to work out what to do.'

'You lied to the police,' I say, without thinking.

'You can talk,' he spits at me.

So he does know that we lied about where we last saw Maddie. I feel a coldness inside.

'I still don't understand.' My own voice comes out all croaky, barely audible above Ruby's crying. 'If you knew, why didn't you tell anyone at the time? Why did you wait all these years?'

'I told them again and again.' He's waving both helmet and knife around and although I think at this moment he's almost forgotten he has the knife at all, this doesn't make me feel any less afraid. Right now, he's just as likely to catch Ruby by accident as stab either of us deliberately. 'They didn't believe me because you'd already told them I was having a relationship with her. Christ, I probably only spoke to her about three times. Maddie Blake. Three conversations and the rest of my life I'm a murderer.'

I try to take all of this in, over Ruby's increasingly impassioned wails. Did I hear him right? Did Sam just confess to killing Maddie? But why does he blame me for it? Did Sam find her in the house where we left her? Am I still somehow responsible?

'What did you do with her body?'

'Christ! You really think I did it?'

'I thought you said—'

'I've lived with the suspicion all my adult life because you lied to the police about me and her.'

'I lied to the police about you?' I echo dumbly.

'Why did you do it?'

I don't remember telling the police anything about Sam, but I know that if I say this it will push him over the edge that he's just about still teetering on.

'We only told the police what Maddie told us.'

'Maddie told you that we were together?'

And then I do remember.

'I just told them you liked her,' I say quickly. 'Nothing else.'

'Why would you tell them that?'

'I was there,' I say, sure about this at least. 'I was there when you asked her if she was seeing anyone.'

'That was it? That was the conversation that ruined my entire life? My life is over because I asked some pretty girl if she had a boyfriend?'

'How did you find me?'

'Through Hayley.'

'You know Hayley?'

'I found her online. I wasn't looking for her or anything – I'm not some weirdo.' I manage a nod. 'She was mentioned in this article I was reading. She has a website and it has her maiden name in the biography section. It even has her address. And then I saw she had an Instagram account. I followed her for a while, and then I started direct messaging her. To start with, it was just a way of making contact, of finding out what you were all doing. I wasn't even sure it was her for a while, although she looked like I thought she would in the photos. We got really friendly, her and me. She told me all kinds of stuff.'

Oh shit.

'You're Vagabond Guy.'

'It's a good name, don't you think?' He genuinely seems to want my approval. Again, I nod – a quick movement of my chin, all I can manage. 'I found it online too. It means fugitive. That's what I am, a fugitive from everyday life. That's what you made me.'

'You were in the bar last night. At the Southbank. You were standing by yourself drinking Peroni. You were following me.'

'I'm not going to hurt you. I wanted to talk to you. I wasn't going to do anything, I swear. To start with, I just wanted to know where you were, what you were doing. But then Hayley started messaging me saying that you had started looking for Maddie again and I couldn't stand it. I couldn't bear for it to start again. I can't go through that again. You understand? That's why I started following you. I thought if I could talk to you, I could make you stop.'

'Did get my number from Hayley too?'

If I have a plan at all, it's to keep him talking. Because maybe if I can somehow befriend him, he'll let me and Ruby go. After all, he keeps telling me that he doesn't want to hurt us. But every time he says it, I can feel my throat constrict a bit more, and it's getting harder and harder to breathe normally. I still can't quite believe that this man holding me and Ruby hostage is Sam. The Sam who told us spooky stories, gave us cider, and fancied Maddie.

'Number?'

His eyes, which have been roaming round the nursery, sliding over my daughter's toys – her wooden Paddington Bear skittles, the furry avocado with legs that Claire gave her, the annoying plastic trumpet that plays nursery rhymes – fix on mine.

'My mobile number.' My voice comes out squeaky, despite my best attempts to sound like we're just two old friends, having a chat. 'To send the messages.'

'I didn't send you any messages.'

His eyes are still locked onto mine, waiting for me to say something back. Daring me to disagree.

'Oh,' I manage. 'Okay.'

'You don't believe me?'

Ruby twists suddenly in my arms, her hot little body determined to escape my grip, and I almost drop her. When I look at him again, he's holding the knife up in front of him and I feel my stomach muscles contract. I need to say the right thing – the thing to make him like me. But it's gradually dawning on me that it's much too late for that. The knife is one that Joe and I bought as part of a special set in John Lewis – it's got a wide blade with little notches in it. It tapers to a very thin point. It's the meat knife. It cuts through flesh.

'Why did you tell the police, Lucy?' he asks again.

This time his voice is almost pleading. He lurches towards me, the knife held aloft. He smells of leather and sweat. I twist out of his way, keeping my body between him and Ruby, and feel a sharp pain in my right arm, just below the shoulder. He moves in for a second attempt, and I watch him, as if it's all happening in slow motion and there's nothing I can do to prevent it now. Ruby is wailing and I cradle her body in mine, protecting her from what's about to happen. I see him raise his arm again. I notice the tear in the elbow of his biker jacket, his bitten nails on the handle of the knife. See him step forward. Then, suddenly, he stumbles on the plastic trumpet and goes flying backwards.

I dodge round him towards the door, but I feel strong fingers on my ankle. I kick at him with my free leg. He writhes out of the way, and pulls harder. Ruby is unbalancing me and I'm terrified we're both going to end up on the floor with him. I can see his fingers stretching to reach for the knife he dropped as he fell.

Then, over the top of Ruby's wails and the trumpet playing 'If you're happy and you know it, clap your hands', the front doorbell rings.

The grip on my ankle loosens and I tip forwards towards the floor, and just break my fall by reaching out with one hand for the door jamb. Sam scrambles to his feet, out onto the landing and I hear him half-stumble, half-jump down the stairs. I sink to the floor, Ruby still clutched tightly to me, my back against the nursery wall, my socked feet making an imprint in the thick pile of the nursery carpet. Ruby's stopped crying by the time the police officers find us, but I'm weeping enough for both of us.

Chapter Forty-Two

Lucy, Present

'Tell us again what he said.'

It's the next morning and I'm lying on our sofa, bruised ankle resting on a cushion, mug of steaming tea within easy reach of my non-injured arm. Claire is perched on the other end of the sofa, Jenna is curled up in the armchair and Hayley is sitting on the floor, playing with Ruby and heading her off every time she attempts to crawl out of the room. The sun is streaming in the window, bathing Hayley and Ruby in light and warmth.

Joe has gone out to pick up a prescription for painkillers for my ankle. It's hurting worse than the knife wound just below my shoulder, which didn't even need stitches. More of a graze than a wound. Joe hasn't left my side since he turned up last night in an Uber to find me sitting in a police car on our drive, and police officers swarming into our house, but he was finally persuaded to go when the others arrived en masse and insisted they would look after me and Ruby.

To start with, Joe and I weren't sure whether they would allow us back in the house at all. It was a crime scene, after all, and there was talk of finding us a hotel room, but eventually the forensics people said they were finished and we could go back if we avoided the nursery

– something I was more than happy to do. We ended up putting Ruby to bed in the travel cot in the corner of our bedroom.

The ever-so-slightly too enthusiastic victim liaison officer the police sent round this morning talked about flashbacks – the trauma can be particularly acute, she said, gooseberry-green eyes flashing, when the incident takes place in the victim's own space. I'm guessing that your child's nursery is about as much your own space as you can get. When I told her that I feel fine – that I've had no flashbacks and slept better last night than I have done for weeks – she said that the shock might not have kicked in yet. Joe listened intently as she outlined the symptoms we should look out for – even making notes on his phone – but I felt like she was talking about someone else. I don't feel traumatised; for the first time since I got the messages, I feel safe. I feel like I have my old life back.

More than anything, I feel relief. Knowing it was Sam who was following me all along and it must have been Sam who sent the messages too, even though he won't admit it. The atmosphere in the living room suggests the others feel the same way. There's an air of suppressed excitement and everybody is behaving more like their usual selves than they have for days. Claire brought round a big box of cupcakes and even Jenna has eaten one, and I've eaten three.

'He said he came across your name in an article he was reading, Hayley, and then found your website.'

'I can't believe you put your address on your website, Hayley,' Claire says.

'It's my business address, all right? Sometimes I get sent products to endorse.'

'But it's also where you live.'

'I'm aware of that, thanks, Claire.'

'You made it so easy for him to find you.'

'Yeah, well, I didn't know Lucy was going to have some crazy stalker trying to track her down,' Hayley snaps. Then she turns and puts her hand on mine. 'I'm really sorry, babe. I just can't believe Vagabond Guy was Sam. I keep trying to take it in.'

'He certainly doesn't look anything like his photo,' I say from my prone position on the sofa, hoping to move the conversation on, although even Hayley and Claire sniping is somehow soothing in its normality.

'Yeah and he turns out not to be exploring Cuba on his motorbike.'

'Man on social media making stuff up shock!' Claire says.

'Yeah, well, it's easy to be wise after the event.'

'He doesn't even look like the old Sam,' I say. In my mind, the Sam of 1999 had the looks of a Leonardo DiCaprio of about the same vintage – all fair hair and cheekbones. 'He does still have the motorbike, though. The weird thing is I even heard him pull up last night. I just thought it was the Deliveroo driver, although I should have realised the Deliveroo driver was cycling because he was wearing a cycle helmet – isn't it strange how your brain doesn't join things up at the time?'

I'm rambling. I try to remember if that was one of the signs of delayed shock that the enthusiastic victim liaison officer mentioned; Joe would know. Jenna suddenly swings her legs down from the armchair.

'Oh jeez, I've just thought, do you think he was the idiot on the motorbike who pulled away from Hayley's house and sent that car swerving into me?'

'I bet it was him. He's been following me around all week. He told the police he followed me and Joe back from lunch at yours Hailz – you know, on Frank's birthday. And then he probably followed me and Claire down to see Karen Silver and he's admitted he followed me down the street that evening when I was coming back from Tesco's. There have been half a dozen times since then when I had the sense someone was there. I definitely think he must have been there in the graveyard with me and Harriet yesterday – I was sure I saw a movement out of the corner of my eye, like a shadow flitting between the trees.'

'Shit, babe, what were you doing in a graveyard?'

'Oh, Harriet wanted to show me something,' I say vaguely. I'm back to feeling superstitious about mentioning Edward Duval's name, as if that could start it all up again. I know it's ridiculous, but it's even occurred to me that I was reading Duval's letters when Sam broke into the house and perhaps the letters somehow summoned him up. Perhaps Duval really is cursed. I'm never going to get over this stupid, childish fear of him, no matter how confident I felt last night that I'd cracked it. Fortunately, Jenna jumps in before Hayley can ask anything else.

'All this is because he blamed you for telling the police about his relationship with Maddie?'

'His point is that he wasn't having a relationship with Maddie.'

'You were only trying to help,' Hayley says. 'You were a kid. You told the police what you saw. Ruby, come back here!' My daughter is making another bid for freedom. If she's traumatised by the events of yesterday, she isn't showing it either. Last night, she'd been examined by the police doctor 'just to make sure that she didn't come to any harm while she was alone with him for those few minutes'. Waiting for the doctor's verdict was easily the worst ten minutes I've had in my adult life. Joe and I held hands and said nothing. But she got the all clear. Sam had said he didn't want to harm her and strangely I believed him about that.

'If he's had a grudge about it all these years,' Jenna says, 'doesn't that sound like he might actually have done it?'

Jenna doesn't need to specify what *it* is. Now we are all firmly sure again that Maddie is dead, the question of who is responsible hovers in the background, as it always has.

'I don't know.' For a few seconds last night I'd thought that Sam had killed Maddie and for those brief moments I'd felt some kind of closure, but now I wasn't so sure. He'd seemed genuinely horrified when it became clear I thought he'd killed her. I don't think he was putting that on.

'The innocent can hold grudges just as much as the guilty in my experience,' Claire says. 'More so sometimes.'

'He broke into your house with a knife,' Jenna says. 'So he's obviously capable of violence – a violent offender with a link to Maddie. Surely that's just too much of a coincidence.'

'He didn't break in with it,' I say. 'I was the one with the knife. To start with, anyway. He grabbed it from me.'

'Okay,' Hayley says, 'but Jenna's right, he's clearly unstable.'

I don't point out that Hayley has been messaging him for two months without spotting his clear instability. Besides, she's right – no one in their right mind follows someone for days and then breaks into their house to try to talk to them.

'Why did you tell him about Maddie?'

Hayley goes red. 'I didn't tell him, I told Vagabond Guy – stupid name.'

'Okay, but why?'

'I don't know exactly, Lucy. I'm really sorry, lovely. When you got that first message, I was really scared. I didn't want to let you girls see how scared. I needed to talk to someone and of course I knew I couldn't tell Frank. Vagabond Guy was always easy to talk to. Telling him felt safe. He wasn't someone any of us knew, or I thought he wasn't. He was a million miles away, travelling round another country on a motorbike. I honestly didn't think it could do any harm. Even then I didn't tell him everything. I promise I didn't tell him about that night. Just that a friend who we all thought was dead seemed to have come back to life and that you were trying to find out if it really could be her.'

'And that's what made him start following Lucy?' Jenna asks, picking up Ruby, who's crawled over to her chair and sitting her on her knee. Ruby immediately starts pulling on Jenna's ponytail.

'But if he didn't want us to start digging into Maddie's disappearance,' Claire says, 'why did he send Lucy the messages in the first place?'

'He claimed he didn't send them.' I've deliberately not been thinking about this. I'm assuming he was lying; I'm just not sure why.

'It must have been him,' Jenna says quickly.

'Of course it was him,' Claire says. 'I'm just saying that his story doesn't hold together. He told Luce that he was following her because she'd started talking to people about Maddie's disappearance, but he must have been obsessed with her long before that. Obsessed enough to catfish Hayley anyway.'

'I think he'd spent twenty-five years feeling bitter about what happened to him and then he came across Hayley's name and it was some kind of trigger that pushed him over the edge,' I say.

'I still think that suggests he did it,' Jenna says. 'Why would coming across Hayley's name have pushed him over the edge if he hadn't? I don't see how being arrested for murder can really have ruined his whole life. They let him go, after all.'

'Poison Cross was a little village, Jenna,' Claire says. 'People would have talked.'

'But there's a whole world out there, he didn't have to stay in Poison Cross.'

'That kind of suspicion has a way of following you around. He was the only person ever arrested for her death. His name was in the press at the time and he's been mentioned in every article that's ever been written about the case since then.'

'The police said his mother died,' I say, unwillingly. I've been trying not to think about this too. Another life destroyed.

'As in, she killed herself?' Hayley asks, wide-eyed.

'She wrapped her car around a tree, apparently. Two years after Maddie disappeared.' About the same time my dad died, as it happens. Sam and I both lost parents at the same time. 'It could have been an accident, the police said, and that's how it was treated at the time, but there were no cars involved, the weather was fine – there was no reason why she should have crashed.'

'Oh my god, that's so awful,' Hayley says.

'I know.'

'That would certainly give him reason for a grudge,' Claire says.

289

'After his mum died, he left the village.' My liaison officer had been very forthcoming. She seemed to think I would want to know all the details, although actually, to my own surprise, I discovered that I really didn't; I'd have been happy hearing nothing more about Sam ever again. I just wanted to know that it was over. I tell the others what else the liaison officer told me. 'He lived in Sheffield for a while – he had a brother there I think they said – and then he spent twenty years drifting round the country, and other countries – he may well have been to Cuba at one time Hailz, even if he wasn't there anymore – doing jobs here and there, still working as an electrician, never staying in any one place very long, never putting down roots.'

'Poor Sam,' Hayley says.

'Let's not forget he stalked Lucy, trapped her in her own home and attacked her with a knife,' Claire says.

'And may still turn out to be responsible for murdering our best friend,' adds Jenna.

'Yes okay,' Hayley says. 'You know I didn't mean it like that.'

'You always did like him,' Claire says.

'I fancied him a bit twenty-five years ago – I don't think you can hold that against me.'

'It will all be raked up again for the trial, won't it?' Jenna asks. She sounds suddenly scared – a reminder that the fear hasn't entirely gone away. 'The original case, I mean – Maddie's disappearance.'

'There won't be a trial if he pleads guilty,' Claire says. 'And even if there is, I doubt they'll go into it much. It's not like trials on TV. They won't spend ages going over his motive. The fact that he was caught in your house with a knife by a patrol car full of police officers will be more persuasive.'

'What have they actually charged him with?'

I know this too, thanks to all the victim liaising. I take a mouthful of tea.

'Actual bodily harm. The knife wound wasn't serious enough for anything more apparently. My liaison officer thinks they might get him on a stalking charge too.'

'He'll go to prison, though?' Hayley asks.

'Yes,' Claire says. 'For a few years.'

'And if he had a grudge before, he'll definitely have a grudge when he comes out,' Jenna says quietly. Ruby has fallen asleep on her lap. She looks so peaceful, tufts of hair standing up, mouth slightly open. She's wearing my favourite babygrow – the one with the little rainbows that she's almost too big for now. 'Look at her,' the liaison officer had said this morning. 'The picture of innocence.' *We were all babies once*, I wanted to say. Everyone who ever did a terrible thing was a baby once. At what point do you stop being the picture of innocence, and why?

'I don't want to think about it now,' I say. 'What matters is that he's been caught.'

'Of course, babe,' Hayley says, reaching out for me again. All three of them are looking at me with worried expressions. But what's troubling me right now, really isn't the thought of Sam being released from prison, it's the thought of what I might have done to Sam – a thought I've been trying to avoid all day. *You must pay for what you did.* Was I, however inadvertently, responsible also for the death of Sam's mum? Not because I told the police about him and Maddie. For a start, Hayley's right: I just told them what I saw. But am I responsible because of what I *didn't* say? Because that meant Maddie was never found, and Sam will forever be the man who might have killed her, and his mum drove herself into a tree rather than live with that.

Chapter Forty-Three

Lucy, Present

'How are you feeling?' Joe asks.

'Fine.'

'You're sure?'

'Honestly, I'm totally fine.'

I know it's unreasonable, but Joe's concern is making me feel claustrophobic. When he's not checking up on how I'm feeling, he's gazing at me with anxious eyes. What I'd really like is to just go for a walk by myself, feeling confident that I'm not being followed, knowing that the ghosts of the past are firmly back in their closets, or wherever it is ghosts go. But I've got a busted ankle and a husband who, ever since last night, seems to have been stitched to my side.

We've put Ruby to bed in the nursery again – the crime scene people came back a couple of hours ago and now it's 'all ours' apparently. Joe and I cleaned and vacuumed it while Ruby was strapped into her baby bouncer on the landing; a deranged stalker is basically what it takes to get us to do housework. I was determined to go back in there straight away, despite Joe's insistence that I didn't need to. I'm not going to let Sam stop me going in my daughter's nursery.

Now, I'm back on the sofa, trying to read the latest Marian Keyes on my Kindle, although it's difficult to get more than five minutes without interruption. Joe, sitting on the floor in front of me, is supposedly watching a repeat of *Celebrity MasterChef*, but it doesn't seem to be holding his attention.

'Can you see okay?'

'Yeah, I'm fine, thanks.'

'Would you like the table lamp on?'

'No, I'm fine.'

I return to my book and manage another half a page.

'We haven't got much food in. Shall I order us a takeaway?'

The memory of the Deliveroo guy from yesterday is there instantly, and then the sight of Sam's elbow on the baby monitor and the feeling of his hand on my ankle. Something in my face must give me away because Joe is instantly even more solicitous. 'What is it? Luce? What did I say?'

'No, it's fine. I just don't fancy a takeaway.'

'Shit, sorry, I didn't think.'

'No, honestly, it's fine.'

'I think there's some eggs, I can make us omelettes.'

'Perfect.'

'Or I could do scrambled eggs. Would you prefer scrambled eggs?'

'Fine.'

'Tell me which you prefer.'

'I don't mind.'

'Just say.'

'Either.'

'Be honest.'

'I couldn't fucking care less!'

Joe's handsome face crumples and he turns away. Instantly I feel bad. I sit up properly and lean forward to put my hand on his shoulder, my own shoulder where the knife grazed the skin aching a bit as I do so. His old grey t-shirt is soft to my touch.

'I'm sorry. I'm being a giant bitch.'

I squeeze his shoulder and he reaches his hand up and puts it over mine, but he doesn't look round.

'Why do you never talk to me, Lucy?'

I loosen my grip but don't remove my hand.

'What do you mean?'

'You're pretending everything's fine and it obviously isn't.'

'It kind of is fine,' I say, trying to make him understand. 'Mainly I'm just so relieved that they caught Sam. It makes me feel safe again.'

He twists round to look at me.

'But that's just what I mean. You never told me that you felt unsafe before.'

'Okay,' I say, carefully. 'So I suppose that sometimes I'm not very good at communicating how I'm feeling, but that's not because I don't want to tell you. It's because if I say my fears out loud I'm worried that it somehow makes them more real.'

'I can understand that, truly I can.' With his free hand, Joe reaches for the remote and mutes John Torode who is in rhapsodies about a lamb shank and some pomegranate. 'But you can tell me, Lucy, I'm your husband. We're supposed to share everything.'

'It's not like you tell me everything,' I say, stalling.

'I'm always telling you stuff, Luce.'

'Surface stuff. What's worrying you at school, who said what to who in the staff room, whether you can get a football team together for Saturday. Not your deepest, darkest fears.'

'That's not true. I mainly tell you.'

I note the mainly. Interesting. I pull my hand away from his shoulder and sit back.

'You never told me that you were worried your dad had started drinking again.'

'I would have done. I was just waiting for the right moment.'

'And you're still not telling me why he started again.'

'I told you. I don't know. There's not necessarily a reason.'

'There was a reason why he stopped.'

'Yes, I said: he blamed himself for being too drunk to travel down to Poison Cross when we first got the news that Maddie was missing. He was so ashamed – not that he ever said as much to me, but he didn't need to because I could tell. I think he thought that if he'd been there from the start he could have made a difference, not that there's any logic to that.'

'Maybe he could have done.'

'What do you mean?'

I don't even know why I said it. I look away, focusing on the screen instead. I can see Gregg Wallace spooning something involving whipped cream into his mouth and grinning with super-human enthusiasm.

'I guess I just mean who knows what would have made a difference – there are a million tiny things that could have changed whatever happened, we'll just never know what they are.'

'Yeah, I suppose you're right. I know there are things I wish I'd done differently.'

I look back at him. 'Are there?'

'I should have listened to her more,' he says. I can hear his voice breaking and watch as he makes an effort to control himself. It makes me want to take him in my arms and hold him as tight as I held Ruby last night, but as I shift forward on the sofa, he starts talking again: 'She was just my kid sister and I never really paid her that much attention, and when the police were asking me all these questions about who she might be with and where she might have gone, I realised I didn't know that much about her life at all. I wasn't sure whether she'd fallen out with Amari, or if she liked anyone else. I couldn't help them because I didn't really know.'

'That's what older brothers are like, Joe. Most kids that age don't know much about their little sisters.'

'What about you?'

'What about me?'

'Are there things you wonder about? Things that might have made a difference to finding Maddie?'

If I'm ever going to tell him, this is the moment.

'Of course there are.'

'Like what?'

I think about the one thing that might truly have made a difference. 'We had this silly argument about a bracelet. I wish we'd never had that.'

He frowns. 'How could that have made a difference?'

'My point is that it's impossible to know what would have made a difference.'

He turns away and hugs his knees. I can't see his face. But something about the slump of his shoulders tells me he's disappointed and I wonder whether it's possible that he really has known about the lie we told all along.

'I'm sorry I didn't tell you about the messages. I didn't want to worry you.'

He gets to his feet without looking at me. 'I'm going to make those omelettes.'

And for a man who has been inseparable from me for the past twenty-four hours, he suddenly seems very anxious to be out of my sight.

Chapter Forty-Four

Lucy, Present

'I don't know,' I say. 'Do you think that's a good idea?'

'What do you mean?' Joe asks. 'Ruby, no.'

It's early the next morning and Ruby, swathed in the giant bib that's like a reverse plastic mac, has just thrown a piece of banana on to the floor. I retrieve it and pull a face at her. Ruby giggles with delight and throws another piece down after it. 'You know, with your dad and everything?'

'He's fine, Lucy.'

'Have you actually spoken to him?'

'I spoke to Mum, and she says he's doing okay. He's going to meetings. He's phoning his sponsor. He's doing all the right things. He's got this.'

'Let's hope so.'

'It would do them good to have Ruby. It would be a distraction.'

'Well, okay, I suppose I could use a day to myself to get on with Harriet's book.'

'Why don't you do something for you?'

Joe is wiping Ruby's banana-smeared face and fingers with a wet wipe. He seems more normal today; still concerned about me, but less tense and he seems to have forgiven me about the messages. He can sometimes hold a grudge but he seems to have made up his mind to move on. It's important to me that I meet him halfway.

'Well, I guess I could finally go clothes shopping.' I've been talking vaguely about a post-pregnancy shopping trip for months now, but somehow I've never actually got round to going.

'Yes, great idea. That's exactly the kind of thing I was thinking. Is your ankle okay to drive?'

'It'll be fine,' I say quickly. 'It was just bruised.'

'You could message Hayley and see whether she's around to come with you. You could go to Westfield or Oxford Street or something.'

I know Hayley has a photoshoot scheduled for this morning, but Claire mentioned she had the day off, so I give her a call instead. But when she picks up she sounds weirdly awkward about her plans. I'm about to ring off when she says, 'Actually Lucy, there's something I need to tell you.'

My stomach contracts. I don't know what I'm expecting, but it isn't what comes next.

'Nic and I have decided to try for a baby. That's where we're going this morning, to the clinic. Nic's going to have IVF. So if I've been a bit, well, mysterious recently, that's probably why. We didn't want anyone to know. Not until, you know, we had some good news to tell you all. But I feel like the time for secrets is over.'

'Wow,' I say. 'Claire, that's brilliant news.' And I really mean it. It turns out there are good secrets too. It seems suddenly absurd that there was a moment when I wondered whether Nic could be Maddie.

'I know it might seem a bit soon to the rest of you. We've only known each other six months and everything. But I just know, Luce. I know she's the person I want to spend the rest of my life with. And having kids is something we both want, and well, we're neither of us getting any younger blah blah, so we just decided, you know, why wait?'

'That makes total sense,' I say. 'It's not too soon when you're sure.'

'That's exactly how I feel. And we're looking for a place together too – for all three of us, hopefully. Obviously, it's very early days at the moment.'

Now that Claire has decided to tell, the information comes pouring out of her. 'We've been reading all this stuff online about how IVF is this emotional roller coaster and we've told ourselves that we're going to try not to get too hung up on it, but it's going to be hard to stop it taking over our life. And it's going to be tough for Nic, with the injections and everything. She's got this thing about needles, so I'm going to do the injections for her.'

When I come off the phone, I feel a wave of happiness for Claire, and, for once, it's not accompanied by my usual feeling that the happiness is fragile. I message Hayley. I want to tell her Claire's news, but I know Claire will want to do that, so instead I say:

> Off on a shopping trip – just for me! X

She replies instantly:

> Yaay! Send pics xxxxx

I drop Ruby off at Naomi and Robin's at about ten. Joe has promised he'll pick her up after school, so I have the whole day to myself. The first time this has happened since Ruby was born. Naomi invites me in for coffee but I turn her down, suddenly worried that if I don't manage to strike out on my own I never will and the whole precious day will be spent at my in-laws, picking over what happened with Sam and being bathed in well-meaning but stifling sympathy.

Of course, I don't manage to extract myself without mention of Sam altogether. It's the first time Naomi's seen me since it happened and naturally she has questions. I restrict myself to answering them in the hallway, with Ruby on Naomi's hip, the bag of baby stuff at my feet and the gentle hum of Radio Four in the background. Joe told me he gave his parents a watered-down version of what happened because he didn't want to worry them, 'especially now'. It's an impossible task, though. Naomi is worried. She's always worried and now there really is something to worry about. I do my best to reassure her.

'So you think this man,' she says, refusing to use his name, 'was the one sending you the messages you mentioned the other day?'

I wonder if she told Joe she knew about the messages and that was why he was so upset last night, because I'd talked to his mum and not him.

'Yes, I guess I should have been more worried about them at the time.' I'm certainly not going to tell Naomi that it would have been impossible to be more worried about them. 'The important thing is that the police have arrested him now.'

'But he came to your house, Lucy,' and I can see the anguish in her eyes. 'Anything could have happened.'

'But it didn't. He was more sad than threatening.' This is also a lie. Sam *was* sad and I did even feel sorry for him, although this is obviously impossible to say to Naomi, but he managed to be both sad and threatening with no difficulty at all. You can find someone pathetic and still be terrified of them, it turns out. I try to block out the memory of Sam's hand around my ankle.

'How did he know where you live?'

'Oh, the internet, I think,' I say vaguely. I don't want to bring Hayley into this. 'I didn't even recognise him.'

'People can change a lot in twenty-five years, Lucy. I have to ask you this, you don't think this man could have—'

'I honestly don't,' I say. I don't want her to have to say it. And I am sure now – sure, I think – that Sam did not kill Maddie. It's something about the way he reacted when I thought he'd confessed. 'I think one of the things that's made him a bit, well, a bit strange, is having to live with the suspicion all these years.'

Her mouth opens to say something, but she closes it again and I wonder what it might have been. Instead, she nods tightly. I want to change the subject, but the only other topic I can think of is difficult as well. I don't feel like I can leave without at least asking after Robin, though.

'He's doing okay, thank you for asking. It's a relief to have you know about it, if I'm honest. I've been fretting about it for about a month now.'

At this point, Ruby getting restless sitting on Naomi's hip, suddenly interrupts with a cry that sounds like 'Nana'.

'What did you say, sweetheart?' Naomi asks. 'Did you say Nana? Aren't you a clever girl! Did you hear that, Lucy?'

After this morning's breakfast, I think it's just as likely that she's trying to say banana, but Naomi is so excited I haven't the heart to tell her. Instead, I plant a big kiss on my daughter's forehead.

'You're a star, Ruby.'

'Isn't she just! Such a clever girl.'

'Thanks for taking her, Naomi.'

'A day with my clever little granddaughter is my idea of heaven.'

'There's formula and some snacks in the bag. Watch her with the yoghurt – she gets it everywhere. She had a sleep in the car but don't forget she'll need another one about midday. Oh, and she's got a bit of nappy rash so I've put the cream in there.'

There suddenly seems an awful lot I need to remind Naomi about.

'Don't you worry about a thing,' she says, and I remember how good she is at this.

'Joe will be round to pick her up early afternoon.'

'There's no rush. We'll be fine. Won't we, Ruby? You go off and enjoy yourself.' Naomi shifts Ruby to her other hip. 'Some me time, isn't that what it's called? You certainly deserve it.'

'Thanks. You're a star too,' I say, and suddenly, impulsively, I lean in and kiss her on the cheek. Her skin is papery and cool.

'I'll take good care of her.' It doesn't sound casual – the way most people would say it. It's said with fervour.

They stand at the doorway and wave at me as I get in the car. I can hear Naomi saying: 'Nana. Say, Nana, Ruby. Nana.' And again, there's something beyond the ordinary grandmotherly excitement in the way she says it, a kind of intensity that's disturbing. I try to put this out of my head and focus on the morning ahead of me. When I get to the main road I hesitate, still not entirely sure where I'm going for my shopping trip. Oxford Street suddenly seems way too ambitious, but I think I can manage Kingston and I can drive there – I don't even need to get the train.

I park in the John Lewis car park. Half an hour later, my phone pings with a message while I'm still in the store. The message is from Hayley:

> Hows it going? Bought anything yet? xxxx

I send her a photo of a highchair.

> Noooooooo! Go to Zara. Now!!!!!!

It turns out to be surprisingly hard to shop for myself. But once I'm in Zara I suddenly get into it, trying on an armful of things and even buying a couple of tops. I send Hayley photos and get a smiley face emoji back and a series of thumbs up. I get a coffee and brownie in Café Nero to celebrate and then start exploring the shops in the market square. By the time the church clock strikes one, I've got several more carrier bags, and I'm feeling more relaxed than I have in weeks. I notice that Coast has a sale and wonder if I might find a summer jacket there. They have two I like and as I follow the assistant to the changing room, I find a beautiful floral summer dress, in a pale blue fabric. In the changing room, I can't decide whether it shows too much cleavage, so I take a photo in the mirror and send it to Hayley for a second opinion. I try the jackets over the top of it and as I'm twirling about in the second one, my phone pings. I reach in my bag. Hayley. No, not Hayley. Another number.

> I have Ruby.

It must be Naomi. Or Joe. But why don't I recognise the number? And then I do recognise it. It's *the* number. I'm still staring at the message when my phone pings again.

> Don't call the police.

Oh dear god, no.

> She's safe with me.

And instantly another message:

> After all, I am family.

My brain can't make sense of the words. Suddenly my phone starts ringing. I stare at it. Oh god. It's her. It's her and she's got my daughter. The phone keeps ringing. *Joe Mobile* says the screen. My hand is shaking so much that I can't make it swipe the screen to answer and I almost smash the phone on the floor in frustration. Instead, I force my finger towards the screen and hit Joe's name to call him back. He picks up at once.

'Lucy?' His voice sounds funny. 'I just went to pick Ruby up and she's not there.'

'Maddie's got her.'

'What?'

'I've just had a message. Maddie's got her. We've got to find her. We've got to…'

'How can Maddie have her? You're not making any sense.'

'I got this message. It says she's family.'

'Who's family? What are you talking about?' Joe's voice is quivering with frustration and fear.

'Everything all right in there?' calls the shop assistant through the changing room door. 'Can I get you any other sizes?'

'We've got to find her, Joe. We've got to—'

'I'm calling the police.'

'No! The message said not to.'

'I don't care what the message said. What choice do we have?'

'How could your parents let this happen? Where did they leave her?'

'It's not their fault. My dad thought she was asleep in the travel cot in their room, but when I got there and we went to look she was gone.'

'How can she be gone? Are you still there?'

'I'm outside on the drive. I thought there was a chance that you might have—'

'What? Sneaked in and picked her up without saying anything to Naomi? Are you mad?'

'Stop yelling at me. I'm as worried as you. I'm going to call the police.'

'Please don't. I think I know where she is. I mean, I think I know who Maddie is. I'll call you back. Joe, please let me do this.'

'Lucy, what is it you're not telling—'

I hang up and instantly my phone starts ringing again, but it's Joe and I shove it in my bag. I rip the jacket and dress off. I literally hear the dress tear, but I don't care. I scrabble into my maternity jeans and shirt and burst out of the changing room. There are three shop assistants huddled outside, all in their early twenties, all looking at me with round eyes and concerned faces, but I'm already on my way towards the door, as one of them calls, 'Madam, are you all right?'

As I jog down the street towards the car park I pull out my phone again. My mind's racing. First, I call the number the texts come from. Just in case. But no one picks up. I never really thought they would but it was worth a try. Next, I click on Nic's name in my contacts – she gave me her number when we were having coffee – but it just rings out. I'm at the multi-storey now and pounding up the stairs because I'm too impatient to wait for the lift. Nic's voicemail kicks in and I open my mouth to leave a message but I have no idea what to say. *Are you my long-dead school friend and have you kidnapped my daughter?* As soon as I hang up, I see Joe is calling me again, but I can't talk to him now. I wait for it to stop ringing and then I try Nic again.

The phone is balanced between my ear and my shoulder because I'm rooting through my bag, looking for my car keys. I pray that I didn't put them in one of my carrier bags, because I've left those behind somewhere. They must still be in the Coast changing room. It seems incredible that there was a world in which I cared about buying new t-shirts. Nic still doesn't answer. I find the keys, but where am I going?

Only hours ago, it seemed absurd to me that I'd ever thought Nic could be Maddie, but that was when I thought Maddie was dead; now I know she's alive, and I feel certain it's somebody I know, or somebody I've met at least. Claire said Nic wanted a baby – perhaps that was some kind of coded threat and the baby she wanted was mine all along. Nic really does look very like Maddie – more than Harriet ever did. Plus, Maddie was scared of dogs, and Nic doesn't like Doogie. It all adds up. Half of me sees everything with crystal clarity; half of me suspects I'm losing it entirely.

More than anything, I need to make sense of what's happening, and quickly. My mind races over the other possibilities. Supposing Maddie really is the homeless woman outside Tesco. How am I ever going to find her? Then it occurs to me that I do know where Nic lives. She pointed out the block of flats when we were walking back from the river that day. It's not even that far away. I turn the key in the ignition. Now at least I have a destination.

I wonder if Joe is calling the police, but how could they find Ruby? How could I possibly explain all this to them? The car jerks forward then comes to a shuddering halt as I slam on the brake pedal. The guy I've almost driven into shakes his head at me and I want to scream back. *My daughter is missing, you sanctimonious twat. Get the fuck out of my way.* I force myself to breathe. I need to get to Nic's in one piece, for Ruby's sake. How could Naomi and Robin let this happen? How could they, of all people, let my daughter out of their sight? They've already lost one kid, for Christ's sake. How could they let it happen again? I beat my hands against the steering wheel in fury.

I spend the journey to Nic's making the kind of bargains you make with God when you suddenly decide that believing in him is the only way this could possibly turn out okay. *If Ruby's there, I'll the truth about everything. If she's there, I'll never tell another lie. I promise, God.* And underneath it all is a feeling of inevitability. I always knew something terrible would happen if I had a child. I just never thought it would be this.

The building Nic pointed out is an art-deco style apartment block, painted a white that's turned grey over the years. I don't know which flat she lives in. I try her number again. Then I start stabbing all the buzzers. Twelve in total. One after the other. Even if she has Ruby, she might not be here. No one else seems to be in. I try Claire's number. She'll know. Still no answer. Where the fuck is everyone? I work my way down the buzzers again and this time a bleary male voice – I've no idea which flat he belongs to – tells me to try flat nine for Nic. I hold the buzzer down on flat nine. Suddenly it crackles to life.

'Who is it?'

And miraculously I recognise the voice. Claire.

'Why aren't you answering? Have you got her?'

'Lucy?'

'Is she there?'

'Lucy, I'm coming down.'

She must have run, because it feels like only a few seconds later the front door to the block of flats opens and there she is, standing on the pavement in front of me.

'Shit, Goose. What's wrong? What's the matter?'

She envelops me in a hug and for a few seconds I feel safe. She smells of the deodorant she always uses.

'Ruby's missing,' I say and suddenly the tears are streaming down my face.

'Oh Goose! What do you mean missing? What happened?'

'I think Nic's got her.'

'Why would Nic have her?' says Claire, sounding puzzled but patient.

'I think Nic might be Maddie,' I whisper.

Claire's arms drop and she takes a step backwards.

'What did you just say?'

'She looks just like her, Claire.'

'You think Nic is Maddie? That's mad. Plenty of people look like that.'

'You just don't want to see it.'

'Don't you think I'd know if she was Maddie?'

'No. It was twenty-five years ago. I don't think you would know.'

'But you do?'

'She asked me all these really intense questions about that summer. About what happened at Poison Cross. I think it's her. She's got my daughter.'

'Ruby really is missing?'

'Of course she's missing!'

'Okay, okay. Don't worry,' she says, idiotically, 'I'm going to help you. Have you called the police?'

'Why weren't you answering your phones? I called you both.'

'I told you. We were at the clinic. We had our phones on silent. We've only just got back.'

'Why wouldn't you let me in?'

'You really do think Nic has her.'

I nod. I'm itching to get past her.

'Lucy, I promise you she doesn't, but if that's not enough for you, you can come up and look.'

Our eyes meet and I know what I say next is going to make or break our friendship, but I can't help it. 'Let me in.'

She wheels round and presses the buzzer for flat nine.

'Nic, it's me, can you buzz me in?'

As she pushes open the door, she says over her shoulder, not looking at me, 'In case you're wondering, that wasn't a signal. I just didn't come down with any keys.'

We walk up two flights of stairs in silence. There seems nothing left to say. I think I know Ruby's not there, even though I've just blown a quarter of a century of friendship by refusing to let go of the possibility that she might be.

The door to flat nine is ajar, and as Claire pushes it open, Nic's voice calls out. 'Is everything okay? Did you bring Lucy up with you?'

'Everything is not okay, no,' says Claire, in a strange, toneless voice I've not heard her use before. 'Ruby has gone missing and Lucy thinks we've taken her.'

Nic appears in the doorway to the living room, hair pulled up onto her head in a bun. 'Ruby's missing?' she asks, eyes wide. 'Have you called the police?'

'I need to know if she's here,' I say doggedly.

'Why would she be here?' Nic says, sounding genuinely puzzled.

'Just let me look.'

'Go ahead and search, Lucy,' Claire says. 'Make sure. It's a small flat. It won't take long.'

And I do, even though I know I'm not going to find anything, because Claire's right – I have to be sure. I go into the galley kitchen, where something that makes me want to heave and involves bones is simmering on the hob and then through to the living room, which is tiny and features a gong, a purple macramé wall hanging, and a shelf of spider plants, but no baby.

I can hear the pair of them talking in low voices back in the hall. Claire must be explaining. Lucy has gone mad. She thinks you're our dead school friend. Except Maddie clearly isn't dead. She's alive and she has Ruby and if she

312

isn't Nic, she must be somebody else. But who? I have to work it out.

As I emerge into the hallway, Claire theatrically opens a door and says, 'The bathroom. Good luck fitting a baby in there.' It's tiny – basically a wet room with a toilet and basin. There's mould growing on the ceiling and it smells of old towels. 'And the bedroom is the next door down. I think you'll find that's baby-free too.' Her voice is heavy with sarcasm and I realise just how angry she is. Nic, though, looks merely worried, as though she is witnessing someone having a breakdown in front of her, and maybe she is. I look in the bedroom too, mainly to delay the moment when I have to decide what to do next. It's also small – the double bed, covered in an old-fashioned patchwork quilt, takes up most of the space. There are more spider plants on the windowsill. I stare at them, as if somehow they are going to offer me the answer. In my bag, I feel my phone start to vibrate and then ring out. Joe again. I can't talk to him now.

'Lucy?' Nic is standing in the doorway. She reaches out tentatively and touches my arm. I jump like she's punched me and she starts too and moves back a few steps. 'We want to help you.' Behind her in the hallway, I hear Claire exhale. 'But you have to tell us exactly what happened.'

'Maddie took Ruby.' My voice comes out as a hoarse whisper.

'Okay,' Nic says, and I can hear in her voice that she's humouring me. 'When did you last see Ruby?'

'I was shopping,' I say. 'Why did I go shopping?'

'You lost her when you were shopping?'

I shake my head. 'Maddie took her. From Naomi and Robin's.'

Claire pushes past Nic and grabs me by the arms, just above the elbow.

'Lucy. Look at me. I know you've been through a tough few weeks. But it's not Maddie. It can't be Maddie. That was Sam freaking you out – we know that now. We need to call the police and – what are you doing?'

I'm wriggling in her grip. I need to get my phone out of my pocket. It's just beeped with an incoming text. And I know it's going to be from her.

> If you want to see Ruby again come to the house at Poison Cross

I shove the phone at Claire and watch what happens to her face as she reads it. It kind of collapses in on itself and then she sinks onto the bed, still holding the phone. 'Oh Jesus,' she mutters.

Nic takes the phone from her and reads the message. 'Isn't that where…?' She doesn't finish. She can probably tell by looking at us.

Claire looks up at me from the bed. 'Goose, is your car outside?'

I nod.

'Let's go.'

I feel an immense rush of love for her.

'Whoah,' Nic says, as Claire brushes past her out into the hallway. 'What are you doing? You're not just going to do what it says, are you? You should call the police.'

'No!' I say fiercely. 'She said not to. I need to go and get Ruby. This is between me and her.'

'But it could be dangerous.'

'Lucy, come on, we're wasting time,' Claire says, as if Nic hadn't even spoken. The bedroom suddenly feels way too small for Nic and me. I stumble into the hallway.

'Claire,' Nic tries one more time. 'Listen to me.'

'Please, Nic. I know what I'm doing. Stay here. I'll call you when we find her.'

'But—'

With her hand on the front door latch, Claire turns back to look at Nic. 'I promise.'

'Okay. Call me. I love you.'

Claire is already out the door and halfway down the first flight of stairs. I snatch my phone back from Nic and follow behind.

Chapter Forty-Five

Lucy, Present

'Are you okay to drive?'

I nod. Now that Claire is back on my side and I know for certain where Ruby is, I feel strangely calm. Almost in control. Claire types *Poison Cross* into Google maps on her phone, as if this is any old journey, and the magic of sat nav directs me towards my kidnapped daughter and back-from-the-dead school friend.

As we navigate towards the A3, Claire uses my phone to call Hayley. I wonder if I should call Joe, or ask Claire to. Or at least send him a message. He must be beside himself with worry about me as well as Ruby. But I want her back – I want her in my arms – before I call him. I want to be able to say, *our daughter is safe. I'm sorry. I messed up. But she's safe now. I saved her.*

I hear Claire succinctly outline what's happened, her voice carefully modulated, but with vibrations of something else – something fundamental: fear, adrenaline, even excitement. I can hear Hayley's cries on the other end, eventually calming to a barely distinguishable murmur.

'She's coming too,' Claire says, as she hangs up. 'She's going to call Jenna and pick her up and then drive down there.'

'Do you think it's all right?' I ask stupidly. 'That we all go?'

I pull out into a lane of traffic and the blast of a lorry's horn sears across my consciousness. I'm probably not quite as okay to drive as I thought.

'Wanker!' Claire yells. Then: 'This is about all of us, isn't it? We're all mixed up in it. We're not leaving you now.'

'Thank you,' I say. I've never been so grateful for my friends. We really are all in this together, and with them, I think there's a chance I can get out the other side. I feel guilty that I ever thought of them as a burden, tying me to the past. I know now that they're the only way I can ever banish it.

'I'm sorry. You know, for what I said about Nic, and for doubting you. I just couldn't think straight.'

It starts to rain. Big splodges falling on the windscreen. I turn the wipers on.

'You're going through hell right now, Goose.'

'I still shouldn't have doubted you.'

The wipers swipe up, Ruby's okay. The wipers swipe down, Ruby's hurt. Ruby's dead. Up, down, okay, dead, okay, dead, okay, dead.

'Lucy! Jesus. You're way too close to that car.'

'Sorry. I'm sorry.'

'Are you sure you don't want me to drive? We can pull over at the next layby.'

'No. It will waste time. I'm fine. Honestly, I'll concentrate, I swear.'

We drive for a while without talking, the only noises the splash of the tyres on wet tarmac and the squeak of the windscreen wipers.

In half a mile, take the exit, says the Google Maps lady.

'Can you check my phone? She might have sent another message.'

Claire reaches into my bag and retrieves it. 'Nothing,' she says.

'Not even from Joe?'

'Nothing from him either.'

'Is there a signal?'

'Yup. You have a zillion messages from Hayley and Jenna. They're about half an hour behind us from the sounds of it.'

Take the exit.

Why has Joe gone quiet? I'm sure he must have called the police by now but they'll never know where we're going so it's all right. Again, I can feel the hysteria welling up. All right. Did I seriously just think that?

Now take the exit.

'Can you bear to tell me what happened this morning?'

As I drive too fast down twisty, rain-soaked country lanes, I fill her in on everything I know, which isn't much.

'Goose, do you think it really is Maddie?'

'Who else could it be?'

'Is Sam still in police custody?'

'It's not Sam,' I snap, slamming on the brakes as we meet a car coming in the opposite direction. 'The messages were never Sam.'

'But why would Maddie take Ruby?'

We pass the sign for the village: Poison Cross. There are two large square wooden planters either side of it, overflowing with bright pink and red blooms.

'Revenge.'

'Because we never told?'

I leave Claire's question unanswered.

'She'd have to be crazy.'

We drive through the village, and I have to slow down because there are parked cars lining the street on either side of the road, reducing it to single file and necessitating a very British performance of ducking into a gap and allowing other drivers through. If it had been up to me I'd have ploughed through at fifty miles an hour and left the other drivers to dive for cover, but the car in front of me has other ideas. We pass a coffee shop and Poison Cross Co-op. It's all so ordinary. The hairdresser is called *Curl Up and Dye*. And I wish that Maddie had, or that I could.

You have reached your destination.

'Oh shit. I just put in the village. Not the house itself.'

'Well, where's the house?' I can hear the panic in my voice.

The village doesn't seem familiar at all, but perhaps we never even came here. Perhaps we approached the youth hostel from the other direction.

'Hang on, I'm looking at the map. The youth hostel is still there.'

'We don't need the youth hostel.'

'I know, but it will help us find the house. Okay, here it is I think.'

'You think?'

'Keep following the road out of the village, we'll go up a hill and then it's on the left-hand side,' Claire says levelly. 'Hailz and Jenna have just taken the turning off the motorway. Hailz says to wait for them.'

'No way.'

'It might make sense. Safety in numbers.'

We're climbing the hill out of the village now.

'No way am I waiting.'

I don't ask her what she thinks we need protecting from. Strangely, given all that's happened, I'm not scared of Maddie at this moment. She's crossed a line in taking Ruby and what I'm mainly feeling now is fury. I've slowed down so that I don't miss the turning, but we see the house before we reach it: its fairy-tale tower looming over the treetops. We turn a sharp bend in the road and the driveway is on our left. There is a big red board: *William Hobday and Sons: Considerate Construction*. So someone has finally bought it. I swing into the drive and the car jerks downwards as we encounter a giant pothole. I force myself to drive more slowly. In the passenger seat, Claire turns her whole body towards me and looks at me, with frightened eyes.

'What are we going to say to her?'

The age-old problem of a reunion with an old friend.

'We're going to tell her to get her fucking hands off my baby.'

Chapter Forty-Six

Lucy, Present

It's nearly four o'clock on a May afternoon, but it's as grey as a winter's day and the rain keeps on falling. I skid to a halt on the scrubby grass that must once have been the centrepiece of the driveway. There are no other cars in sight.

'Do you remember on the night? There were gates. We climbed over them. Do you remember, Goose?'

Claire has chosen a really weird time to start reminiscing.

'And then Maddie asked who was going to go in first.'

How can she think about the stupid dare, when all I can think about is Ruby? Has Maddie been feeding her? How would she know what to give her? Does she know anything about babies? Has she got her own? If she's not Harriet, or Nic, who the fuck is she? Because I'm sure I'm going to recognise her.

'And I volunteered to go first. Only, here's the thing, I didn't actually go in. I only pretended to go.'

This barely registers.

'Yeah well, who cares? How could it matter now?'

'Supposing there was someone in there waiting,' continues Claire, doggedly. 'If I'd actually gone in, it might have been me instead of Maddie. Except you did go in, didn't you, Luce?'

'How are we going to get in?'

'You did go in. Didn't you, Luce?'

I nod, but without looking in her direction. I'm utterly uninterested in who went in then; all I care about is how we're going to get in now. There is blue hoarding up all around the building and the place seems deserted. Supposing this was a hoax. Supposing Maddie never intended to bring Ruby here. She's run off with her and I will never see her again. The world spins and I feel Claire's hand on my arm.

'Steady. We'll find a way in. Come on.'

We follow the hoarding, past an architect's drawing of the apartment block they're planning to build here, peopled with attractive inhabitants and their cute dogs, as if they'll be supplied along with the plate-glass balconies and manicured courtyard garden.

'Here we go!' Claire says. There's a doorway cut in one of the pieces of hoarding. The sign on it reads:

DANGER! CONSTRUCTION SITE.

'There was a danger sign that night too,' Claire says. 'On the gates.'

The door has one of those metal bars that you can pull across to open it up, but also a chain and a padlock. Claire holds up the end of the chain. Someone's cut through it. I feel a surge of hope again. So Maddie is here. I wonder how she broke through the chain. Did she come prepared? With tools. Then I hear something that makes me stop dead. Faintly, ever so faintly, I can hear a baby crying. I can hear Ruby.

'Oh god.' I start to run towards the steps up to the front door.

'Slow down, Goose. Wait for me. You don't know what you're going to find in there!'

In spite of myself, I do slow down. Claire's right. I know Ruby's here. I know she's alive. Both these things are so wondrous, I can't afford to fuck this up. I wait for Claire to catch up with me, and we climb the remaining steps together. The front door is ajar, but as I try to push it open further, it catches on the flagstones in the hallway and won't budge. I force myself through the gap and Claire follows.

I can hear music. 'Baa, Baa, Black Sheep' playing eerily in the gloom and the crying again, louder this time. Both are coming from the back of the house and I remember walking down the hallway that night all those years ago, looking for that particular room. Because it turns out it's hard to stop remembering, even if you'd much rather not. The flagstones are covered in the dirt and pigeon crap of decades of neglect, but our footsteps still echo as we walk on them. Maddie must know we're coming. She must be able to hear us.

The door at the end of the corridor is pulled over but not quite closed and daylight is escaping from the slim gap between the door and the doorframe. The crying has stopped, but the music is still playing.

Yes, sir, yes, sir, three bags full.

Claire and I stop outside the door and look at each other. Her face is so familiar and yet alien at the same time; I feel I know her totally and also not at all. Her expression is a mixture of fear and almost incredulity, as though she can't believe we're back here. She opens her mouth to ask me something. I push the door open.

The first thing I see is Ruby, in her travel cot – directly in our line of sight on the far side of the room. She's had a change of outfit, and now she's wearing her navy babygrow with the tiny yellow stars. How did Maddie get the babygrow, I wonder, as if this could possibly matter. Her brown eyes are open and the tuft of hair that will never smooth down is at its usual jaunty angle. She looks fine. She's fine. I feel a rush of love and relief. I don't need to see anything else. Without thinking, I'm moving across the room towards her. The music has stopped.

'Don't touch her!'

It's a woman's voice. And I do recognise it. I turn in surprise. She's in the far right-hand corner, sitting on the wide window ledge that runs along the side of the room.

'Naomi!'

How did she get here before us? Did Maddie message her too?

'Thank god. How did you find her? Where's Maddie?'

But Naomi just stares at me. Maybe she's in shock.

'Has she gone?'

I look round, worried that Maddie might still be there.

'Goose.' Claire's voice now. It's warning me of something.

'Where's Maddie?' I repeat. Claire's hand is on my arm now, restraining me, but I don't know from what. I just want to pick up Ruby.

'There's no Maddie,' Naomi says, and her voice as she says it sounds unutterably bleak, but also, disturbingly, as though she's about to laugh. She gets quickly to her feet and moves soundlessly over to the travel cot; she scoops Ruby up and holds her tight against her. 'There's been no Maddie all these years.'

'Then who took Ruby? Who brought her here? Have you called the police?'

Naomi's eyes, over the top of Ruby's head, are fixed on me and suddenly I feel scared. I remember thinking a long time ago, when we were children, that sometimes Naomi could see inside my head. That's exactly how I feel now.

'I wanted you to know what it felt like,' she says meditatively. 'Just for a while, of course. It's not the same thing at all. But it felt like a fitting punishment. To lose a daughter.'

'A punishment?' I echo.

I feel rather than see the door open behind me. Then Hayley's voice says, 'Oh my god, guys! I'm so relieved you're all right!'

'Hello Hayley,' Naomi says. Her voice sounds almost normal again – a bit maternal, like we're kids and we've all come for a sleepover. 'And Jenna too. I'm glad you're all here.'

'Oh Naomi! I'm so happy you're okay!' Hayley says, going to hug her, but then Naomi's lip curls back in an involuntary snarl and Hayley stops in her tracks, suddenly conscious that Naomi is not okay at all. Very much not okay. And finally, I get it. I stumble backwards.

'You. It was you.'

'I sent you the messages, if that's what you mean, yes,' Naomi says.

'But why? Why would you do that?'

'I wanted you to tell Joe what you did. That's all.'

The blood freezes in my veins.

'This was the last place you saw Maddie alive. You lied about that. All four of you. To everyone. You lied about it to me. *You*,' and she practically spits the word at me, 'lied about it to Joe.'

'How did you find out?'

'Joe told me.'

'Joe knows?'

'He found out recently. Ask Jenna if you want to know how.'

The three of us turn on her. 'I told him,' she says quickly, wrapping her arms around herself as though this is going to protect her. 'I'm sorry. I honestly didn't think it mattered that much, anymore.'

'How could it not matter?' Claire says. 'We've never told anyone. We promised each other. All these years.'

'Why?' Hayley says. 'Why would you go behind Lucy's back like that?'

'Tell them the whole story, Jenna,' Naomi says, and again it's like we're children and she's unpicking some ridiculous playground squabble. Jenna is staring at Naomi, her eyes wide with fear. She turns back towards me. She seems to realise she has no choice; either she tells me, or Naomi will.

'I, well, I was trying to make Joe think badly of you. I'm sorry, Lucy. I'm so, so sorry. I was drunk, and I felt so humiliated. I wasn't thinking straight.'

I stare at her, confused. 'Why would you want to make Joe think badly of me?'

'Because she wanted Joe to leave you,' Naomi says. 'Jenna had it in her head that he liked her.' I remember Joe and Jenna going for those post-baby runs together. And how abruptly they'd stopped. 'That they had a future together. But he loved *you*,' she says this with real venom. 'He turned her down. And then she told him what you'd done. What was it you said, Jenna?'

But Jenna is mute with shame.

'*Lucy isn't as perfect as you think.* I believe that's what you said.'

I watch as Jenna, standing beside me, covers her face with her hands. I notice as if from a great distance that the shellac on her nails is a pretty burgundy colour and she's wearing the ring that we all clubbed together and bought for her thirtieth – a moonstone on a double band of rose gold.

'*Joe* was your mystery guy?' Hayley says.

'This isn't about Jenna and Joe,' Naomi snaps, and suddenly all eyes are on her again. Her and Ruby. She's holding Ruby tightly – too tightly? I don't think she'd deliberately harm her, but right now I don't think she's in any position to know clearly what she's doing. I need to get Ruby back.

'The point is that Jenna just left him to deal with this – this huge thing Lucy had never told him. I knew as soon as I saw him that afternoon that something was terribly wrong. I'm his mother. Of course I knew. He didn't want to tell me at first, but I got it out of him. We talked about it – the three of us. Robin, Joe and me. Robin said we should let it go. You were children, he said. *Let it go.* I pretended to agree with them. But I couldn't let it go. That's why I sent you the messages. Did you find the photo I put in your bag?'

She says this almost conversationally, and I find myself nodding.

'I thought seeing Maddie would help you do the right thing. And you read my message?' she says more urgently. '*It's time.* I needed you to tell us. I needed you to tell Joe. He was so hurt, Lucy – you have no idea. I needed you to own up to what you did.'

Throughout this speech, Ruby has remained silent. I have a sudden horrible fear that she might have stopped breathing. I take a step towards Naomi, and she swiftly moves across the room, keeping the distance between us, like she's circling me. But as she moves I see Ruby turn her head to look at me, and I know she's okay. I just have to think how to get Naomi to give her back to me.

'I wanted to tell Joe. So many times. I really did. I wanted to tell you. But I was scared.'

'Naomi, we're sorry,' Claire says. 'Honestly, we're so sorry we didn't tell you.'

'We were children,' Hayley says.

'You were children then. You've been adults for a very long time now and you've never told. You could have saved Maddie's life. My daughter – my precious daughter – could have been here all along.'

'She wasn't here. We looked. I promise we looked,' Claire says.

'It wasn't for you to decide!' screams Naomi, with a ferocity that sends all of us scuttling closer to each other for cover. She lets out a great sob from somewhere deep inside her and then she begins to cry – her eyes screwed up, her body heaving. Ruby joins in with loud baby tears. In all these years, I've never seen Naomi cry like that. I move towards them both; the need to comfort them is almost instinctive. But Naomi doesn't want to be comforted, at least not by me, and as soon as she sees me move, she starts running towards the door, wrenching it open.

'Naomi! Stop!' I shout after her. We all follow as she flees down the hallway and then, suddenly, miraculously, Joe is there and she is running into his arms and he is holding both of them. He's wearing his old pink shirt with the frayed cuffs. He looks so familiar. I meet his eyes over the top of the hug in which he has enveloped Naomi and Ruby and I see something in them that I have half-seen and not properly registered for weeks: judgement. I retaliate before he can even start.

'Did you know what she'd done?' I yell at him.

Incredibly, he manages an answer that sounds almost reasonable. 'Not at first. I really did think Ruby was missing. But then I found the note Mum left me – saying where she'd gone with Ruby.'

'I'm sorry, darling,' Naomi says, her voice thick with tears. 'I'm so sorry that I made you suffer. I thought you'd find the note straight away. I never intended to punish you. Just Lucy. I would never have hurt Ruby, you know that, don't you?'

'Of course I know it, Mum.' His tenderness towards her is breaking my heart. 'It's all going to be all right.'

'Did you know it was her sending me the messages?'

'I didn't know there were any messages until after Sam broke into our house. You didn't tell me. If you had, perhaps I might have guessed. I could have talked to Mum.'

I can't bear his calm.

'I suppose you hate me now!' I say, childishly.

'I don't hate you, Lucy,' he says, with such sadness in his voice. 'You were a little girl. I just wish you could have found it in you to tell me.'

Chapter Forty-Seven

Lucy, Present

We've all six of us trailed back into the ballroom – raw, ashamed, exhausted – to retrieve Ruby's things. As Joe picks up Ruby's toys and Hayley comforts a shrunken Naomi, I move to stand beside the dresser, feeling for the catch with the fingers of my left hand, and that's when Jenna remembers.

'What are you doing?'

I am incapable of saying anything.

'You did that that night too. You stood in front of the dresser and played with the catch.'

She looks round wildly, waiting for someone else to remember. I move away quickly, back into the centre of the room. Claire and Hayley are looking at her with contempt. Less than half an hour ago she publicly admitted she tried to steal my husband. They're not her biggest fans right now. Naomi, who's now hunched over in the corner, as Hayley stands with her arm around her, doesn't even look up. Neither does Joe, who's putting on Ruby's cardigan, and has been avoiding even glancing in Jenna's direction ever since he arrived. But it's no good, because now Jenna's worked it out. Or part of it.

'It's a hidden door,' Jenna says. 'The dresser is a door. Look at this.'

She starts tugging. Claire goes over to her and together they pull the door back.

'Shit. She's right. Look. I think there's a secret room. Did you know, Lucy?'

Suddenly, Hayley is beside them too. I'm relieved that neither Naomi nor Joe has moved. That Ruby is nowhere near the opened door. I don't go back over; I don't need, or want, to. I can guess what they're going to find inside the secret room. Who they're going to find. Because I locked her in there twenty-five years ago.

Chapter Forty-Eight

Lucy, 1999

'Honestly, Maddie, I don't want to.'

'Don't be such a baby.'

They were walking side by side across the field leading back to the hostel.

'It could be dangerous. We don't even know if the hidden door is still there. That book I found in the library is really old.'

Now that Lucy had heard the rest of the plan she was even more sure it was a bad idea. Okay, she wouldn't be the person hiding in the secret room that led to the old swimming pool, but this house sounded like it was on the edge of collapsing. What was it Lorraine had said? A death trap. Just going inside was dangerous, and if something happened, she was sure she'd get the blame. Tom would tell her mum and her mum would sit her down on the sofa, perching on the edge, like she didn't want to be there at all, her face sagging with disappointment again. She wished she'd never even shown Maddie the stupid book.

'Of course it's still there. Why wouldn't it be?' Maddie asked, with the confidence of someone for whom life always worked out exactly as she intended. She was walking so quickly that Lucy almost had to run to catch up.

'Look, it's not that complicated. You go into the house before me and check the hidden door is where the book said it is. Then when I go in, I'll hide in the secret room. After a while, everyone will wonder why I haven't come out and you'll come in and look for me, but of course you won't find me. You'll know where the door is, so you can make sure they don't come near it. Then, when they've looked for me for a bit, you have to make them all go home. I'll let myself out, put on my Gladys Rudd costume – I've got the perfect sparkly cardigan from Topshop and this slip thing that will work as a dress – and come and stand at the end of your beds. It will freak them all out big time! You'll see. The most important thing you have to do is remember to leave the door to the cottage open so that I can get back in. It's not difficult. I don't know why you're making such a fuss about it. We do this kind of thing all the time. If you want to hang out with us, you're going to have to grow up.' And then, perhaps remembering that charm might work better than scorn, Maddie added: 'Please, Lucy. It'll be funny. You'll see.'

Lucy, almost breathless with the effort of keeping pace with Maddie, whispered, 'I really don't want to.'

Maddie stopped walking, turned impatiently towards her and snapped, 'You might want to rethink that.'

Even as Lucy registered the change in tone, she thought how effortlessly cool Maddie looked, in her Ray-Bans, her hair pulled back from her face and her sea-blue t-shirt just tight enough to show off her slim figure.

'What do you mean?'

'I know things about you, Lucy Keeble.' Lucy's stomach constricted at the words. 'Things you'd rather no one else found out. I wasn't going to mention it, because I thought you were my friend, but now—'

Maddie let the word hang.

'What? What do you know?'

'I went up to your room, remember. Your mum sent me up there to get the leaflet thing. About summer camp. Well, guess what I saw?'

'I didn't take it, I found it,' Lucy said quickly.

'Oh yeah. Then why didn't you give it back to Becky Rogers? Why is it sitting in your jewellery box?'

Lucy felt a rush of indignation. 'Why were you even looking in my jewellery box?'

Maddie laughed, hand on hip. 'I really don't think you're in a position to accuse me of anything. I bet you took the other things that have gone missing too, didn't you? You know what that makes you? A thief. Is that why you had to leave your other school?'

'No,' Lucy felt her eyes fill with tears and turned her head away in a doomed attempt to prevent Maddie from seeing them. It was all coming to an end, after all. She would never be in Maddie's gang, or anybody else's either. She would never have any friends again. She knew it had been too good to be true. It was her own stupid fault for taking the bracelet. She didn't even know why she'd done it; she'd promised her mum she wouldn't. That was one of the reasons they'd moved: a fresh start, her mum had said.

Becky's locker door had been half open and Lucy had been curious to see what kind of things Becky had in there, that's all. The bracelet was a pretty thing. A tiny pretty thing. Becky Rogers always seemed to have so many pretty things, Lucy hadn't thought she'd miss one of them.

'Imagine what the others will say when I tell them. I don't think they're going to want to be friends with

334

you anymore, do you? I don't think anyone in the whole school is going to want to be your friend after what you've done.'

The idea of being alone again terrified her. 'Please don't tell, Maddie. I'll put it back. I promise. I'm sorry.'

Maddie shoved her hands into the back pockets of her jeans and stood contemplating Lucy.

'I might not tell. I haven't made my mind up yet. I don't like Becky anyway – she's way too full of herself. But you have to stop taking things, and you have to do what I tell you, okay? You have to help me with the Gladys Rudd plan. Okay Lucy?'

Chapter Forty-Nine

Lucy, Present

I'm sitting in the back of a police car. I haven't been arrested. You can't charge someone with murder on the basis of a hazy memory of her pushing a catch across on a door a quarter of a century ago. They're being very nice to me actually, the police. I think it's because I've got Ruby. People make judgements like that. If you've got a baby they assume you're a nice person. Joe hadn't wanted to hand her over, but she kept wailing and my presence was the only thing that made her stop. One of the officers, a short lad with curly brown hair who looks barely older than we were when Maddie went missing and talks like he's my kindly uncle, even retrieved Ruby's bag for me. Naomi had brought it with her – ever-organised.

'Here you go.' The back door of the police car is open and he passes the bag into me. 'You just let us know if you need anything else. Have you got nappies, and so on, in there?'

'Yes, thanks,' I say meekly.

He shuts the door and talks to me through the open window.

'We're sorry to keep you hanging around. It's just my boss is going to want to have a chat with you all when she gets here. But I think she's going to want to see the scene first. It's easier to keep you all here for a bit longer if you don't mind the wait. You can go and sit with your friends if you prefer?'

I shake my head. He looks at me curiously. He'll be even more surprised when he learns that one of those friends is in fact my husband.

'I hear you all think you might know whose body it is.'

'We think it's our friend Maddie Blake,' I say, bouncing my legs up and down so that Ruby, who has gone through this momentous day entirely unscathed, gurgles with happiness. 'She disappeared a long time ago.'

'Is that right?' says the police officer, his manner still avuncular. The name doesn't seem to mean anything to him. He probably wasn't even born when she disappeared. 'Well, I'm sorry to hear that.' He bends down a little, leaning towards the window, his young, eager face suddenly much nearer mine. 'It's too soon to be sure of course.'

It's not too soon for me to be sure. I've waited decades for certainty. I honestly wasn't sure Maddie was dead until they found her body in the secret room. She could have got out somehow. Maybe someone came along later and heard her shouting and let her out. Maybe there was another way out from the secret room. Maybe there were dozens of ways out. Maybe she got out and somebody else found her and killed her. Maybe she got out and ran away. Maybe, maybe, maybe. My whole life has been consumed with maybes.

I really did think those messages might be from her. It was almost a relief in the end to discover that it was Naomi. It's not hard to understand why I might not be keen to meet Maddie again after all these years. Everyone has secrets. And, like most people's, mine started out as a little secret. I did a bad thing. I stole Becky Rogers' bracelet. And that led to the next thing, and then the next, and that's how the really terrible things happen. They're an accumulation of little things.

I didn't mean to kill Maddie. It wasn't planned or anything. I mean, she knew I took Becky's bracelet and the other things and if she'd told my life at school would have been hell, but it was only when the four of us were in the ballroom looking for her that I had the idea of sliding the catch across. Even then I only meant to scare her. She was so sure of herself. So confident in her power. I meant to go back, to let her out. It was a silly, childish impulse. I was thirteen years old, for Christ's sake, and without even really thinking much about it, I did something that changed my world, and the worlds of dozens of other people, irretrievably, forever.

The stupid thing is that, today, I only played with the catch to make sure it was unlocked when they found her. Because if her body was there, they'd almost certainly have found it once they started developing the site. If I hadn't touched the catch though, Jenna would never have remembered.

'Sorry it's taking so long.' The constable is replacing his radio and bending down to talk to me through the back window again. 'There's been a bit of a complication.'

'A complication? What complication?'

Because what more could there be? How could this get any more complicated?

He looks uncomfortable.

'I can't tell you that, I'm afraid, madam.' The *madam* makes me feel impossibly old, and it's strange that I can feel this at the same time as I feel a fresh frisson of hope – hope that there could still be some other explanation.

That I do not after all bear all the guilt for what happened to Maddie, and for everything that has happened since – for all that human misery. 'My boss will be over shortly. She'll fill you in.'

The hope is short-lived.

DCI Laurence is a tall, elegant black woman, wearing navy trousers and a dove-grey blazer. She doesn't waste any time.

'Mrs Blake. We've found a second body. Any idea whose it could be?'

I stare at her dumbly. Maybe neither of the bodies is Maddie and what we have stumbled on here is something else entirely. She's waiting for me to say something, her expression inscrutable. And then it hits me.

'Actually, yes,' I say.

Her eyebrows flicker. 'Who?'

'Is the second body older?'

This time she can't hide her interest. 'It's too soon to say, but yes, the second body seems to have been there much longer than the body you found. Perhaps decades longer.'

'I think her name is Gladys Rudd.'

Chapter Fifty

Lucy, Present

For a while I feel certainty; Edward Duval was a killer after all, and that letter he wrote to Ava Holland, Harriet's great-grandmother, about seeing Gladys on the railway station platform – well, that can only have been lies: a last desperate attempt to recover what remained of his tattered acting career. But the certainty doesn't last. Later – much later – DCI Laurence confirms that the body they found when they opened the trapdoor in the hidden room was indeed that of Gladys Rudd. That fact, at least, they could establish beyond doubt.

It seems that you can recover DNA even from a body that's a hundred years old and that's exactly what the police do and then they compare it with the DNA of Gladys's relatives: her great-niece, to be precise. They also know beyond doubt what killed her. A blow to the front of the head so savage that it shattered her skull. What they don't know, and can now never know for certain, was how that blow was inflicted. The likelihood is that someone struck her with a heavy object. The likelihood is that someone was Edward Duval – the man at whose party she was last seen alive and whose blood-stained shirt was found hidden the next morning. The man in whose house her body was found nearly a century later. The newspapers waste no time in turning this likelihood into a certainty – after all, you can't libel the dead – and Duval's Grecian good looks stare out from their pages under headlines like *Movie star murderer* and *Monster of the silent screen*. They're almost certainly right – Duval struck Gladys because she refused to have sex with him, or maybe he raped her and killed her to stop her telling her story. But maybe she simply fell and smashed her head against the side of the pool – she'd been drinking, it was dark, the pool area might have been wet and slippery – and Duval, fearful of what it would mean for him if he was found with the body of a woman who'd met a violent end, with whom he'd been flirting earlier in the evening, hid that body – temporarily at first and then more permanently when he had the swimming pool converted into a ballroom.

Even if that isn't what happened, maybe Duval convinced himself it was. The point is, no one will ever know for sure; everyone involved is long since dead and Duval didn't leave an explanation – just a series of wounded and confusing letters. Case closed, as far as the police are concerned. Harriet has called me numerous times, no doubt keen to give me her take on it and to find out how the book is progressing, but I haven't answered.

But what of Maddie Blake? The people involved in that case are very much alive. The police asked me about the catch on the door. What made me push it open? How did I know it was there? Did I remember touching it before? Of course, I don't tell them the truth – I don't know how anymore. They seem satisfied with our story of the dare – of how we visited the haunted house all those years ago. I can tell they think it was a horrible accident, and that they feel sorry for me because I could have saved Maddie's life if we'd revealed to the police at the time where we last saw her.

I'm free to go.

And this is the worst thing of all. Because I have nowhere and no one to go to. I'll never give Ruby up, but I don't know how I'm going to face my husband again. He knows I locked Maddie in there. All of them know: Joe, Hayley, Jenna and Claire. And even Naomi must know on some level, although I don't think she can bring herself to take it in. So now everyone knows. Once I'd imagined this might be a relief – a lifting of a burden I've carried with me for two thirds of my life – but it's not a relief at all; it's a nightmare.

I'm alone now. The thing that terrifies me. And somehow I've known all along that this is how it was going to end. Every time a good thing happened to me, I knew I didn't deserve it. The fear of being alone is pretty much why I did it, I think: my sheer horror at the idea that Maddie knew my secret and might reveal it to the whole school, making me an outcast. She had so much power and I wanted her to have a taste of her own medicine. So it's a fitting punishment, as Naomi would say, that I've ended up alone after all.

Ruby, at least, is too young to know. And, the more I think about it, the more I don't think they'll ever tell her. What could they say? How could they possibly explain? It will be a new secret, and I pray that this one doesn't damage Ruby as much as all the other secrets damaged us. Ruby is the only thing that's keeping me going at this point. Which is strange, when I think about how long I argued with Joe about not wanting a child. Thinking about that time, though, takes me to an even darker place.

When we had those arguments, Joe always thought I didn't want children because I was scared of losing them, as he and his family lost Maddie. But it wasn't that at all. I didn't want children because I know what children are capable of.

The thing is, I did go back.

Epilogue

Lucy had to stop to catch her breath after she'd run up the hill. She bent over, her hands on her thighs and took in big mouthfuls of air. Then she glanced again at her neon pink Swatch watch. Her mum would be there at four. She shouldn't have spent so much time talking to Joe, but he was so upset. She liked Maddie's brother. That had been their first proper conversation. She liked how he obviously wanted to be the strong one for his parents, but that he also clearly adored his sister too.

She started walking again in the direction of the house, and after a few minutes, she saw it laid out below her. There weren't any police around but why would there be? They had no idea Maddie had even been to the house. As far as they knew, she'd gone missing from her room in the youth hostel. If the others had told the truth about when they last saw her, if they hadn't made Lucy lie too, Maddie would probably have been found by now.

The police had never been part of the plan either. Not that there had been a plan. Lucy had imagined slipping back the next morning to let Maddie out, and the pair of them, friends again, laughing over the trick Lucy had played. 'I totally freaked out!' Maddie would say. 'I didn't think you would dare!' She'd be annoyed of course, but mainly admiring and respectful – she'd recognise that she'd been wrong to threaten Lucy. And she'd be grateful to be free.

But somehow the next morning it hadn't been that easy to get away, and she began to think it might be better if the adults went down to the house and found Maddie there and it seemed like she'd got locked in by accident. But when they'd told Lorraine she was missing, they still hadn't mentioned the house. And then suddenly it seemed a much bigger deal to sneak down and let her go. But of course, she still had to do it. Then the police had arrived. Big, solid DI Silver, with eyes that looked right into you, and she was sure he'd just guess. But he hadn't, and so here she was. Her last chance, because she was about to be picked up to go home. They all were. She just had to hope it wasn't too late. It had been more than thirty-six hours since she'd shut Maddie in there, but people could survive longer than that without food and water. She knew because her mum had told her about a girl who got lost walking in the mountains in Canada and she'd survived in a cave for five days without water. Maddie would be so relieved to see her, although she'd have to swear her to secrecy. Lucy would have to pretend that she hadn't meant to lock her in. That it really had been an accident.

Rather than go down to the drive and climb over the front gate, Lucy decided to clamber down the steep grass slope and over the wall to get to the back of the house that way. It would be quicker. As she slid down the bank, the reality of what she was about to do confronted her, and the doubts began. Would Maddie be quite as pleased to see her as she was imagining? Would she be willing to believe she just got stuck in there, by accident? She steeled herself. None of this really mattered. What mattered was that she had to bring this to an end. Yes, she would be in big trouble if Maddie tried to claim Lucy had shut her in there. But they'd understand it had just been a joke, wouldn't they?

The wall at the back of the house was crumbling so that in places you could step over. Lucy did this and approached cautiously, as if the house itself might attack her. It didn't look nearly as bad in daylight as it did at night, but it still had an unhappy feel to it, like it was a place where bad things had happened. The ballroom jutted out from the main body of the house, a line of seven arched windows facing the garden, one of them partially open.

Lucy stopped outside the open window. She could hear shouting – faint but audible. She felt relief course through her. Maddie was fine. She was making a noise. Lucy hurried round to the front of the house and in through the front door. The hallway looked even dirtier in daylight than she had imagined in the dark and she could see shapes scuttling into corners and hear the pigeons cooing. Maddie would be so grateful to be free. Of course she would be. Lucy should have brought water and food with her. She pushed open the door to the ballroom, hearing the creak, feeling the smooth wood against her fingertips. She walked towards the big mahogany dresser. She reached out her hand for the catch. The shouting had stopped. She imagined their conversation:

'*We've been looking for you everywhere. I suddenly wondered if you were still in here!*'

'*Lucy! I'm so pleased to see you.*'

'*What happened?*'

'*I couldn't get out. I was stuck in there.*'

'*Oh no, that's so horrible. You poor thing.*'

'*Why didn't you come and find me sooner?*'

Lucy's hand fell to her side. There would be so many questions. And it would be so much easier, after all, not to have to answer them.

She stood for a few more minutes, listening. Then, she turned away, and walked out of the room, out of the house and back down the hill to her lift home.

A Letter from Joanna

Dear Reader,

I want to start by saying a big thank you for reading *The Summer Dare*. For me, one of the most exciting things about writing is the idea of the characters and story I've created coming to life in someone else's head, so it's brilliant to have this novel out in the world!

Ever since I was about ten and my mum read me Agatha Christie's *The Man in the Brown Suit*, I've been addicted to crime fiction. I love a good twist – one that I didn't see coming but makes total sense when I look back. I discovered psychological thrillers quite late on in my life of crime, but I was instantly hooked by the way they make you wonder what you would do if you were in the same situation as the characters.

The inspiration for *The Summer Dare* is my enduring fascination with crimes that take place a long time ago and are never solved, and the impact that has on all the people involved – both the guilty and the innocent. I'm a big fan of the TV series *Unforgotten*, which I think does this brilliantly. I also wanted to explore how the decisions we take as children shape our adult lives.

I had the idea of a group of old school friends, who are now adults and are bound together by something that happened to them twenty-five years ago that they can no longer even talk about. Then one of my friends told a really spooky ghost story on a weekend away, and I started to play with the idea of a dare involving a supposedly haunted house and a sudden disappearance with an all too human explanation.

The Summer Dare involves three different timelines: the present, when my characters' lives are starting to unravel in frightening ways; 1999, when they were school friends and took part in a dare that changed all their lives forever; and the 1920s, when a legendary star of the silent screen is accused of murder after a glitzy showbiz party. I'm interested in the tricks memory plays and the difficulty of definitively establishing what happened many years earlier. There's something intriguing about the stories we tell each other – and ourselves – about what happened in the past. If you'd done a bad thing years ago, would you think you'd got away with it? Can you escape the truth forever, and eventually, do you start to forget what the truth actually was?

I hope you've enjoyed reading about the lives of Lucy, Maddie, Jenna, Hayley and Claire as much as I've enjoyed writing about them. If you have, it would be great if you would consider sharing a review and telling your friends. Thank you very much!

X/Twitter: @jkdwriter
Instagram: @jkd_writer

Acknowledgements

There are lots of people I need to thank for bringing *The Summer Dare* to life, starting with my amazing agent, Lisa Moylett, and Zoe Apostolides and Elena Langtry, at Coombs Moylett Maclean. Lisa and Zoe – your early feedback was really helpful, and I can't thank you enough for loving and believing in the book. Elena – thank you for all the updates and help.

I'd also like to thank the team at Hera for being fantastic to work with: right from the start I felt excited by your passion for this book, and the following months confirmed my feeling that *The Summer Dare* had found its perfect home. Thank you in particular to Keshini Naidoo for championing the book and to my brilliant editor, Jennie Ayres. Jennie – all of your feedback has been so in tune with what I've been thinking. It's been a dream working with you. Thank you also to Lisa Brewster for the cover: I was so excited when I saw it.

One of the absolute best things about my journey to publication has been discovering how generous other writers are with their time and support. There are two in particular I want to mention, because without them I don't think I'd be writing this right now. To Lauren North, many thanks for offering to read an early draft of *The Summer Dare* and providing such useful feedback. Your encouragement kept me going and gave me hope just when I needed it. To Simon Brett, thank you so much for reading the finished draft and for enjoying it and telling Lisa about it. I've been a fan of your books for a long time, so having your support means a lot.

Last, and by no means least, a huge thank you to my fabulous family and friends for supporting me through the highs and lows of writing life. Mum and Dad – thank you for bringing me up on a diet of *Murder She Wrote* and Agatha Christie, and for always being there for me, no matter what. Thank you to David and Claire, who both read drafts of this book and whose insights and enthusiasm were invaluable, to Liz for all the writing weekends and conversations, Jax for the writers' group, Steph for the conversation about a fitting ending, Anne for advice on crime, and Veronica for making me think about ghosts. To all my friends – when some of you heard I was writing about a toxic friendship group that had lasted decades, you joked that it was clearly based on real life. You're as far from toxic as it's possible to get and I'm grateful to have such lovely people in my life. So, thank you for all the lunches, drinks, parkruns, Edinburgh Fringe trips, plays, and nights out down through the years. May they long continue.